NEW WOR LDS

NEW WORLDS

Edited by NICK GEVERS & PETER CROWTHER

NEW WORLDS ISSUE #1

EDITED BY
Nick Gevers & Peter Crowther
Copyright © 2022

COVER ART
Front cover illustration by Bob Wilkin
originally published in *New Worlds* #1, 1946

ISBN 978-1-786367-22-8

10 8 6 4 2 1 3 5 7 9

Design & Layout by Michael Smith
Printed in England by T. J. Books

PS Publishing Ltd
Grosvenor House
1 New Road, Hornsea
East Yorkshire, HU18 1PG
England

e-mail: editor@pspublishing.co.uk
website: www.pspublishing.co.uk

CONTENTS

INTRODUCTION

SCIENCE FICTION'S PHOENIX — THE MANY LIVES OF *NEW WORLDS*

MIKE ASHLEY

IT MIGHT BE STRETCHING credulity to link *New Worlds* magazine with the Antarctic expedition of Captain Scott, but it's a more exciting starting point than the Nuneaton Chapter of the Science Fiction League.

But Nuneaton it has to be, the Long Shoot road to be precise, where Dennis Jacques lived. In June 1935, Jacques, along with fellow fan Maurice K. Hanson, who then lived in Leicester, had been granted their own chapter of Hugo Gernsback's Science Fiction League. They began to organize meetings and, in March 1936, produced the first issue of Britain's first science-fiction fanzine, *Novae Terrae*. Hence the loose connection with Scott of the Antarctic. His ship, the *Terra Nova*, meaning 'New Land', was known to all school children in Britain—Hanson was seventeen and Jacques eighteen. They don't mention Scott or the ship anywhere in their magazine, but they didn't need to. The image of Scott and his heroic team and the ship that had taken them to a remote and alien continent was symbolic of all science fiction. They pluralized the name as *Novae Terrae* and translated that in the first issue as *New Worlds*. From the second issue *New Worlds* ran alongside *Novae Terrae* on the title page so, regardless of its Latin name, *New Worlds* was born.

Jacques and Hanson managed to publish a number almost every month, cranking it out on an old duplicator, producing twenty-nine issues by January 1939. They ran the occasional 'storyette' but it was not known for its fiction but for its news, opinion and occasional humour. Many of the fans who would later establish a writing career appeared here, including John F. Burke, Arthur C. Clarke, David McIlwain (better known as Charles Eric Maine), William F. Temple, Sam Youd (better known as John Christopher) and, not least, E.J. Carnell (known as Ted or John), who for a while served as an associate editor. The magazine became the official organ of the newly formed Science Fiction Association and played a large part in the organization of the first British Science Fiction Conference in Leeds in January 1937.

During the summer of 1937 Maurice Hanson moved from Leicester to London and took *Novae Terrae* with him. He was soon in league with Arthur C. Clarke and William F. Temple, at the notorious 'Flat' in Gray's Inn Road and between them they produced *Novae Terrae*. By 1939, though, the work had become onerous for Hanson but rather than fold the magazine, Ted Carnell took it over and renamed it *New Worlds* from March 1939, reverting to Number 1. This was its second incarnation.

1939 was not the most encouraging year for attempting new ventures. After three monthly issues and some rivalry between *New Worlds* and John Burke's *The Satellite* for their roles with the Science Fiction Association, *New Worlds* paused before issuing a bumper fourth issue dated Autumn 1939. These four issues were lively because of the involvement of Clarke and Temple, and the magazine even ran material by Ray Bradbury, Sam Moskowitz,

Robert Lowndes and Donald A. Wollheim, so it was more than a British affair.

With war declared on September 3rd many fans were called up over the next few months and there were other priorities than publishing a fanzine—paper would soon be in short supply. *New Worlds* thus entered its first dormancy—though not without a glimmer of hope.

In January 1940 the writer William J. Passingham alerted Carnell to the possibility that the firm The World Says might be interested in publishing a science-fiction magazine. There were meetings, plans, possibilities, and almost a mock first issue before it was revealed the company was fraudulent and it was forced into liquidation. Other publishers showed interest but with paper rationing restricting the launch of new publications the first professional *New Worlds* was still-born.

After the War, thanks to Frank Edward Arnold, who had also appeared in *Novae Terrae*, Carnell was introduced to another writer, Stephen Frances—the original Hank Janson—who ran Pendulum Publications. Thanks to Frances, *New Worlds* at last appeared as a professional magazine in July 1946—its third incarnation. Unfortunately it lasted only three issues before Pendulum went bankrupt. Those issues are not ones to shout about though they did run fiction by Arthur C. Clarke, John Beynon Harris (John Wyndham) and John Aiken—brother of Joan and son of Conrad Aiken. The first issue sold poorly but sales for the second issue improved. Carnell suspected it was the cover, which depicted a spaceship, whereas the first had shown a nuclear explosion. The first issue was rebound with the second cover and apparently sold out. Perhaps we can call that a semi-reincarnation, but after a much delayed third issue in October 1947 New Worlds entered its second dormancy.

In the heroic spirit of Captain Scott, Carnell, along with several writers and fans, took matters into their own hands. Carnell was convinced that *New Worlds* would sell and believed he could publish it with a new company. He had the support of Walter Gillings, Ken Chapman and Eric Williams, and with Vince Clarke acting as catalyst, help from Frank Cooper, who had invested his war-service gratuity into a bookshop. Cooper drew up a company prospectus and was soon floating shares. Nova Publications started business in early 1949 with John Beynon Harris as President. *New Worlds* reappeared with its fourth issue (and fourth incarnation) in June 1949. There were a few hesitant quarterly issues before it became bi-monthly in 1952. These years showed a steady progression as British writers clustered around a regular market. It was here that the original version of Arthur C. Clarke's 'Guardian Angel' appeared (Winter 1950), the seed for *Childhood's End*, along with the debuts of E. C. Tubb and James White, and UK appearances by A. Bertram Chandler, John Christopher and J. T. McIntosh. It also acquired a companion magazine, *Science Fantasy*.

Not all was plain sailing. In 1953 Carnell tried a new printer to reduce costs but the result was a disaster. The May issue was a mess and had to be reprinted appearing, instead, in June. The next issue, #22, was even worse and although planned to be released in January 1954 it never appeared. By then, Carnell had been approached by the publisher Maclaren who were expanding their business. They agreed to take over Nova Publications as a subsidiary. Carnell prepared a new issue #22 which was published by Maclaren in April 1954 and put *New Worlds* on a firm monthly schedule. This was its fifth incarnation. Incidentally all but Carnell's copy of that original unpublished issue #22 were pulped. The fate of that copy is unknown. It was believed to have been bought by British fan Brian Burgess after Carnell's death in 1972 and destroyed after Burgess's death in 1997, but maybe it's still out there.

New Worlds now entered its Golden Age which lasted until at least 1961 but was fading by 1962 prompting Harry Harrison to ask in a guest editorial, 'What is Wrong with British Science Fiction?' (July 1962). But those years from 1954 to 1961 saw the emergence of Brian Aldiss, J. G. Ballard, John Brunner and Michael Moorcock, plus Kenneth Bulmer, Colin Kapp, Philip E. High, Donald Malcolm, John Rackham and many others I shall be accused of forgetting. I have not forgotten the many American contributors of new material including Robert Silverberg and Joseph Green, the South African Clifford C. Reed and the Australian writers Lee Harding, David Rome and one of the few women contributors at that time, the British-born Norma Hemming.

But all Golden Ages come to an end, and by 1963, with sales dwindling, Carnell believed that the future was in paperbacks, not magazines. At a meeting of directors in September 1963 it was agreed that both *New Worlds* and *Science Fantasy* would cease with the April 1964 issues. The printer of the magazines, looking for work to fill the gap, contacted David Warburton of Roberts & Vinter who showed interest in taking on both magazines. When Michael Moorcock learned that *New Worlds* was folding he wrote an impassioned letter to Carnell. He had already bemoaned the state of British sf in a guest editorial in the April 1963 issue where he argued that mainstream writers were capable of taking over science fiction themselves and remove the genre label. He named specifically Angus Wilson and Anthony Burgess, but there were many others such as Naomi Mitchison and J. B. Priestley. Moorcock explored the possibility of a new magazine with Ballard and even produced a dummy issue, which was similar to how the magazine later became.

Carnell recommended Moorcock to Roberts & Vinter and within weeks Moorcock became editor of *New Worlds* whilst Kyril Bonfiglioli took over *Science Fantasy*. When the first new issue of *New Worlds* appeared dated May/June 1964 it was as a standard paperback. It had entered its sixth incarnation.

And what a transformation. This was when the 'new wave' hit science fiction. Moorcock jettisoned most of Carnell's stable of writers unless they could deliver what he wanted—Arthur Sellings adapted well to the new requirements, so did Barrington Bayley, John Brunner, Brian Aldiss and, of course, J. G. Ballard who was, to some degree, the magazine's figurehead. Carnell took his other writers with him to his anthology series *New Writings in SF*, whilst Moorcock searched for new writers who could deliver a modern, non-formulaic form of speculative fiction. The phrase 'science fiction' no longer seemed appropriate. Stepping up to the mark came Langdon Jones, Charles Platt, Richard Gordon, David Masson, Daphne Castell, David Redd, Michael Butterworth, and notably Hilary Bailey whose Hitler-wins story, 'The Fall of Frenchy Steiner' in the second issue, proved memorable. Moorcock's own 'Behold the Man' (September 1966) won the SFWA Nebula Award. American writers took notice, especially Roger Zelazny, Thomas M. Disch and Jack Vance, whilst Vernor Vinge made his first sale with 'Apartness' (June 1965).

But another change was looming. The magazine's distributor, Thorpe & Porter, went into receivership in July 1966 owing Roberts & Vinter a considerable sum. The publisher decided to concentrate on its more profitable girlie magazines whilst both *New Worlds* and *Impulse* (the new name for *Science Fantasy*) were borderline. Thanks to Brian Aldiss an Arts Council grant was secured but the writing was clearly on the wall.

Moorcock decided to publish the magazine himself with help from David Warburton, and with Charles Platt as designer. Now he could produce the magazine he wanted, A4-size on coated stock with scope for illustrated features. Entering its seventh incarnation, *New Worlds* went for broke. American writers in particular took *New Worlds* to their heart. Along with Roger Zelazny came John Sladek, James Sallis, Pamela Zoline and in particular Thomas M. Disch whose 'Camp Concentration' was the new magazine's first serial.

Unfortunately, sales proved poor, David Warburton withdrew and the November 1967 issue could have been its last but it was rescued by Silvester Stein of Stonehart Publications. *New Worlds* missed a month and then continued as before, with its blockbuster serial, 'Bug Jack Barron' by Norman Spinrad. This caused ructions, because of vividly descriptive sexual episodes. Both W.H. Smith's and John Menzies refused to stock the magazine and questions were asked in the House of Commons as to why the Arts Council was 'sponsoring filth'. Stein withdrew his support leaving Moorcock to go it alone from the April 1969 issue.

The period from late 1968 to early 1970 might be seen as *New Worlds*'s Dark Age yet it was also when it published some of its most memorable stories and encouraged new writers. Robert Holdstock, M. John Harrison and Ian Watson all appeared during this period, and the award-winning stories 'Time Considered as a Helix of Semi-Precious Stones' by Samuel Delany and Harlan Ellison's 'A Boy and His Dog'. It still published much that was experimental and self-indulgent to the extent that by August 1969 Charles Platt declared *New Worlds* was 'not a science-fiction magazine.' Platt was handling most of the editorial duties because Moorcock had almost written himself into the ground producing books to help subsidise the magazine. In the end both Platt and Moorcock exhausted themselves, the money ran out, and it seemed the end of the road. The last magazine issue was #201 for March 1971, the Arts Council grant was cancelled. Moorcock took the Carnell escape route and contracted with Sphere Books for a pocketbook anthology series, *New Worlds Quarterly*—the eighth incarnation.

As a paperback anthology *New Worlds* lost some of its rebellious bite. Although it included interior art, notably by Mal Dean and Mervyn Peake, the opportunity provided by the larger format had gone. Despite publishing some renegade material, it felt as if *New Worlds* was confined. If any one author shone through it was Keith Roberts, whose reputation had grown in *Science Fantasy* under Bonfiglioli but with its successor *Impulse* having ceased he needed a new market. The series continued to attract new authors, notably Geoff Ryman who debuted in the final, tenth volume.

Moorcock edited the first six volumes, though it had ceased to be a quarterly after the first four. Hilary Bailey edited the final four to which Moorcock was able to contribute several of his Dancers at the End of Time novellas. But sales dwindled, and Sphere dropped it after eight volumes, and Corgi published the last two.

Between them, Moorcock and Platt had exhausted themselves and started to doubt their achievements. It is only through hindsight that we can see how much their work had accomplished in both Britain and the United States though it would not be until the cyberpunk era of the 1980s that it would be appreciated.

The tenth volume appeared in August 1976 and with that *New Worlds* entered its third dormancy. But not for long. Its ninth incarnation was upon us. Moorcock resurrected it as an amateur magazine with issue #212 dated Spring 1978. It took on the form of a tabloid newspaper reporting the news in an alternate timeline. This first issue was crudely photocopied from items previously published in the magazine *Frendz* but for the next issue Moorcock had the help of the printing facilities of Charles Partington and Harry Nadler in Manchester. Now looking like a true 'alternative' magazine, *New Worlds* ran through five of these issues, with Moorcock clearly having fun, and assisted by Jill Riches, Michael Butterworth, David Britton and Charles Platt amongst others. These issues reflect the true spirit of *New Worlds*. They may not have had much influence on the wider world, but they showed that at its heart *New Worlds* could still subvert reality and reinvent the world.

With the last of those issues, #216 in September 1979, it looked like *New Worlds* had finally given up the ghost. But as Captain Oates remarked when he left Scott and the others in the Antarctic, 'I'm just going outside and may be some time.' In the case of *New Worlds* it was twelve years—a rather long dormancy—but, unlike Oates, it did return, for its tenth incarnation.

In one sense it entered a nomadic stage—as if it hadn't been nomadic enough since the mid-sixties. First, in 1991, under contract to Gollancz, David Garnett, with Moorcock's approval, edited four annual volumes as anthologies, and though numbered one to four on the cover, internally they were recognised as issues 217 to 220. By now a new generation of writers, proven to push or at least tweak boundaries, became contributors—Ian McDonald, Storm Constantine, Paul Di Filippo, Simon Ings, Charles Stross, Kim Newman, plus diehards Brian Aldiss and Ian Watson. *New Worlds* was now the grand-old-magazine of British science fiction, fast approaching its sixtieth birthday, but it had a reputation for originality, boldness, and defying convention. Garnett did a good job presenting a fresh face of science fiction within a non-renegade format.

However, poor sales saw the series cancelled and while Garnett sought a new publisher, Moorcock put out a fiftieth anniversary issue (based on the 1946 rebirth) in magazine format in 1996, as issue #221. It thus flashed through an eleventh incarnation before Garnett produced his fifth volume as #222 in 1997 before it entered its fourth dormancy.

To many that was the last they saw of New Worlds because, unknown to most, they did not witness its twelfth incarnation, online, in 2012. Now called Michael Moorcock's New Worlds, it was produced by a team calling themselves Dave's Dream Company. The website was full of a variety of news and commentary as well as fiction, and though less anarchic than the rebellious New-Wave New Worlds, the underlying thread of subversion remained as shown by the title of 'Follow Me Through Anarchy' by Jetse de Vries in the first issue, about an individual's uncontrollable life. The stories were unusual and provocative and almost completely overlooked. This version relied on subscriptions, and only a few items at the website could be read for free. New Worlds soon stumbled, and after a second issue in May 2013 it faded into its fifth dormancy.

So here we are, eighty-five years on from when the Nuneaton Science Fiction League produced Britain's first sf fanzine, which would survive years of trouble, strife and slumber, and through twelve incarnations, refusing to die. And let's hope it never will. The spirit of New Worlds is the British spirit of 'we will never surrender' and of doing things our way. New Worlds more or less created the nature of British science fiction and even though it had to sacrifice itself many times in the process, it gave us the works of hundreds of writers who developed and promoted the field so that it grew and prospered. Many of the contributors in this new volume have been beneficiaries of what New Worlds achieved.

Hail the new incarnation.

NEW WORLDS

THE IMPROBABLY COMPLEX HIGH-ENERGY STATE

ALAN MOORE

I T WAS THE BEST OF TIMES; it was the first of times. In that initial femto-second of it all—and if a femto-second lasted for a second then a second would last sixty-something years—in that bolt-upright quantum startle, with the whole idea of past still in the future, everything was perfect.

Clattering out of blank nothing there eventuated an exquisitely contrived arrangement of what might have been translucent lacquer tiles. Lacking a medium to carry sound the clattering was purely visual. Without scale, the toppling tiles were unimaginably massive or infinitesimal. Impossible, of course, to speak of shape or colour in the blank and empty run-up to those qualities, but the emergent form had something like the perfume of geometry, within its spin a premonition, more a taste, of clear cold pink in mixed-state oscillation with the rich blue of a peacock's shoulder. By its very nature, it was beautiful beyond compare. This incomparability was also true for the duration of the subatomic instant these preliminary phenomena occurred in: having yet to reach the smallest measure of chronology, it felt like it went on forever.

The event, arresting and unprecedented, not yet even on the brink of substance, had instead for its material what could be called an eidolon of light, an optimistic diagram for energy and matter. Having thus spontaneously generated a precursor to solidity and with it a primordial object, the insensate mathematic force that had unwittingly precipitated ontological eruption seemed compelled to run through every plausible contingency of structure, as the cascade of increasingly elaborate surfaces crashed silent into being. In a fabulous kaleidoscope dilation there were steam pavilions, tessellated runways, grand Alhambras, spectral lidos, avenues, concourses, corridors of an incalculable stature, opening and closing and unfolding like a schoolchild's paper oracle. Spontaneously germinating kiosks blossomed into Futurist cathedrals, ripened into unimaginable cities that were iterated to the limits of the gradually swelling moment. Abstract architectural logic shimmered, radiant with manifest contingency. Although an arithmetical inferno beyond definition or description, this quickly evolving situation was as close to heavenly as anything would ever get.

Characteristically, the aforesaid initial object, exponentially accumulated and incessantly self-complicating, implied and indeed necessitated an initial subject. From the fizzing symmetry, as multiplying stadia unpacked themselves from empty vacuum everywhere about, a rumour of sub-microscopic particles converged with highly ordered randomness upon a striking new configuration, a fortuitous stylistic breakthrough with a shocking absence of straight lines. Back then, of course, in the euphoric algebra of that first femto-blink, improbability was not yet even possible. As choreographed accident, untrammelled by unlikelihood, the scrum of proto-atoms and incipient molecules collided into a foreshadowing of organism. Now, and there was only now, suspended at the centre of a stately void whose inner eggshell surface was embroidered with basilicas, there coalesced a self-possessed ellipsoid of uncertain size. Lit by the same inflection of pink/blue as its progressively elaborate surroundings, glistening and crenelated with a fractal tracery of creases, this primary entity was what would be eventually referred to as a Boltzmann brain.

The Boltzmann brain, sentient life extemporaneously formed from subatomic happenstance, inevitable consequence of a non-finite universe as per the thought-experiment of nineteenth-century physicist and theoretician Ludwig Boltzmann was, in that fast-breeding and surprisingly well-regimented paradise before statistics, no less probable than any other outcome. Nonetheless, from the brain's own barely congealed perspective, its existence was an unbelievable surprise.

Born into a condition of black silence that, lacking the notions of both sound and whiteness, was not even understood as such, the disconcerted prototype of consciousness became at first uneasily aware that it existed, then aware of that awareness, and with these initial principles in place thus was philosophy invented, as was solipsism. Relatively quickly, if it's possible to speak of quickness in that femto-splinter of beginning, the emergent locus of cognition, slippery and blind, developed a hypothesis as to what might be going on, an opening stab at what in later eras would be called reality.

Blithely originating reason the brain reasoned that if it existed, as appeared to be the case, it seemed conceivable that there might be some broader pasture of existence; somewhere for it to do its existing in. Further to this, while incidentally creating the activity of noticing things, the brain noticed that its speculations with regard to a potentially wider field of being must have necessarily arrived at some point following its earlier feat of noticing; the moment it had noticed it existed. Through this inference of a sequential nature to events and its conjectures on the possibility of a location, the detached cerebrum, still in the traumatic processes of being born, construed both time and space. It was, clearly, on something of a roll.

Giddy with genesis, the Boltzmann curiosity next posited that its just-recently deduced continuum might not be the black, solitary emptiness it seemed. In the brain's own hastily crystallised opinion, an alternative hypothesis could point to an existence in which there were various other points of information signalling their nature, but that lacking any means of registering these imagined signals, the blue/pink electrified blancmange remained oblivious to everything. If only the almost-material form it sensed that it possessed could be augmented by some kind of apparatus sensitive enough to note the least perturbance, the most subtle fluctuation in whatever medium this preliminary business was all taking place.

Although without scale in its own terms, by the standards of the present day the entire rapidly developing continuum inhabited by the cerebral fluke of probability was smaller than the most elusive quanta, and was thus susceptible to quantum principles. For instance, the observer effect that with time would be hypothesised by Werner Heisenberg was, in an infinitely tiny nascent universe with only one observer, more dramatic and immediate by several factors, and no sooner had the singular observer made its observation than the blurry fog of almost-particles surrounding it began to congeal into visibility and form by way of a protuberant new structure on the brain's anterior upper bulges. This new shape, ghostly at first but rapidly accruing definition, was essentially a conical construction not dissimilar to a witch's bonnet of soft felt, the point pushed down inside the pointed crown to form a deep concavity. The novel ornament was thus at once both penile and vaginal in its contours, slumping forward to depend from the brain's 'brow' much like the luminous appendages that would one day be worn by lantern-fish.

From the sensory deprivation tank perspective of the Boltzmann thought-experiment itself, this vaporous growth-process was experienced initially as a vague, non-specific tingling sensation. This was still, however, a sensation; something which had not existed previously and was therefore to be marvelled at. The brain was thus already lost in wonderment before the organ sprouting from its frontal lobe developed a lush carpeting of hairs or filaments on its exterior and interior surfaces, millions of individual cilia suddenly quivering with information as the freshly minted nightmare of perception thundered unannounced into the black and solitary silence of creation's first inhabitant. Which, we may freely speculate, was quite a thing.

A militant chrysanthemum of mosques and locomotives swelled out from a centrally located nowhere, filling almost instantly the floating brain's newfound field of awareness, even as more recent contradictory wonderlands expanded up from the arrangement's previously hidden interstices to replace it: sword lagoons, wedding-cake icebergs, stilt panopticons, and so endlessly forth.

And talk about loud. The furry cone that drooped from the front upper surface of the Boltzmann brain like a damp hat had simultaneously allowed the advent of the earliest spectator and the earliest listener, which meant that the vibrations flooding the emergent femto-cosmos could be meaningfully described as sound. Though in the main this could be typified as oceanic and inchoate white noise, there in that initial flicker of untrammelled probability the hiss and crackle would occasionally resolve itself into brief snatches of contingent symphony or accidental aria. The whole incessant and hallucinatory eruption into being was accompanied by possibilities of music; by the jingles, hymns, and heavy metal of a billion yet-to-happen worlds. Randomly permutated voices likewise trilled and soared between the budding marvels of that flickering blue-pink Creation, outcries of innumerable speculated physiologies or vocal apparatuses, with somewhere in amongst the happenstantial glossolalia and trickling cadence a precursory idea of language.

Hung stunned in the billowing extravagance and struggling to assimilate its first experience of an experience, the floating brain came, not unreasonably, to associate these random sonic outbursts with whatever visual aspect of the spectacle its bristling and indented fore-sprout happened to be pointed at. By these means, purely as a way to inwardly both classify and categorise the incoming information, a cacophonous vocabulary was achieved. To offer an example, a brief trumpet fanfare in C major was associated with what looked like a pincushion of conjoined chess-pieces, although only pawns and bishops. Meanwhile, a colossal fountain that produced a spray of stylised duo-decapods was represented by the sharp-edged tinkle of a shattering bottle. Mostly nouns to start with, then, though soon acquiring noisy verbs and even a few adjectival screams, bleats, or explosions.

Utilising its own improvised syntax and grammar, it determined that the type of sonic cluster representing discrete entities could be referred to as a noun—something like the word *minimal* pronounced through a harmonica—while each distinct activity engaged in by these entities, all of the manifesting, toppling, and whizzing, could be called a verb—a sound-effect resembling a large quadrupedal mammal falling down a flight of stairs. Accompanying this latter coinage was the brain's dismaying realisation that it was itself a noun that had no verb attached: in all the seething metamorphic panorama spread before its newfound scrutiny, it was the only thing not visibly involved in an activity; the only object not engaged in manifesting, toppling, or whizzing.

Observing that, with its manifestation already accomplished, most other verb-activities apparently involved some form of movement, it attempted to imagine an appendage useful to that end. Once more exploiting Heisenbergian indeterminacy, as with its flaccid sensory apparatus, it was able to produce from the surrounding soup of proto-particles a vaporous posterior plume that rapidly congealed to a whiplike flagellum with articulated vertebrae, some twenty-five times longer than the brain itself and coloured a pale gentian.

Instinctively attempting an experimental shimmy of its splendid new extension, the brain found itself propelled some distance forward from its prior position, which had been the only place that it had ever previously known; had been its birthing-point. The Boltzmann speculation gloomily concluded that the probability of again occupying this precise spatial location must be vanishingly small, and in this way provided the initial rough sketch for nostalgia before once more flexing its new tail and rocketing away into the overboiling foam of form, a sapient spermatozoon. With a rapid rotary action swiftly proving to be most efficient, the trial spinal streamer functioned rather like an egg-whisk, stirring up an effervescent contrail of minuscule bubbles from the fluid medium through which it travelled, the clear albumen of space-time.

Over melting terraces and recombinant palisades, through glassy tunnels like the bore of some tremendous wave, between the scything ocean-liner blades of an immense electric fan the brain torpedoed, with its wake of froth, into the strobing pink and blue of everywhere. It soared exhilarant above metallic ornamental gardens that had threatening bladed topiary, and oh the cryptic miracles it witnessed, the orchestral havoc that it heard. Many were its adventures during this, its headstrong youth: the laughing chandelier affair; the incident of the self-referential obstacle; that sobering episode with the winged maisonettes; a rhombus-avalanche; and the quickly obsessional advent of numbering, to name but five. It planed alone down avenues gone exponential and reflected, for the first and last time, that this would be possible without self-consciousness or irony, that in all of its explorations it had made significant discoveries about itself.

The brain had learned, for instance, that it had a tendency to waver between recklessness and trepid over-caution. It had haltingly deduced a periodic table of its own responses, with preliminary elements like paranoia and bewilderment already set in place, leaving suggestive gaps for as-yet-undiscovered substances such as ennui or lechery. Having met the absurd futility of what appeared to be a massive self-dismantling roundabout with an obscure forerunner of amusement, it had postulated the conceivable existence of a sense of humour somewhere in the swelling cosmos but at length accepted, with some disappointment, that it didn't have one.

On a more pragmatic and less self-absorbed front, Boltzmann's thought experiment had learned that it could skilfully vibrate the follicles which coated the whole surface-area of the sensor-cone worn on its prow like a ship's figurehead and, in the way that modern microphones can also serve as speakers, could rebroadcast audial and visual impressions by precisely reproducing the vibrations which accompanied said content's first reception. Acoustically this sounded like an early synthesiser, while the visual transmissions were delivered as a hologram-style bubble that contained the expressed scene in miniature, much like a pictographic cartoon speech-balloon, albeit realised in three dimensions.

Following this innovation, the preliminary creature's passage through the burgeoning geometries that flared and flickered all about it was accompanied by glittering snow-globe utterances, suspended in its frothy wake at irregular intervals; jewel-like vignettes, each wrapped in its accompanying soundtrack; eerie trailers advertising a forthcoming animated feature. With its bridal train of purpling surf bedizened by these drifting image-opals the augmented Boltzmann brain continued its exploratory cruise into the stupefying formal overgrowth, the ghastly premonition of a tourist lost in that unfathomable Eden.

Wriggling down algebraic arcades for shelter during a brief but intense monsoon of flutes, the brain used this involuntary period of inactivity to invent indoor play. Experimenting with the willed vibration of its sensory filaments it realised that it was not merely forced to reproduce the sights and sounds that it had actually experienced, but that it could create new visions and disaster-symphonies from its own rapidly developing imagination, non-existent noises made by things that hadn't happened. Thus, with the cessation of the woodwind downpour, it once more set forth across the pastures of amok manifestation, but now with a necklace string of lies and artworks at its back amid the nearly violet spume. Eternity's first monster splashed and frolicked, glorying in its singularity and its unique abilities.

Finding the second brain, then, was a dreadful shock.

It happened during the initial entity's traverse of several huge typewriter-like constructions that were fused, ingeniously, to comprise a marvellous emporium of pecking, plunging characters, and punctuation. Hanging roughly at the central point of this arrangement was what the by-now-experienced voyager at first took for a fault with its own sensory equipment: a blurred area of its visual field shaped like an egg and made, apparently, from fog. Suspecting that its optical protrusion was becoming cataracted in some way, the Boltzmann daydream stopped dead in its fizzy tracks in order to examine this ghostly anomaly at closer quarters.

On inspection, the new thing proved to be a phenomenon in its own right, rather than the anticipated optic flaw. It was a vaporous ellipse, a tendrilled smoulder gathering shape and slippery texture as it curdled towards substance. Noting a resemblance between the object's misty composition and the similar particle-fog that it had witnessed while materialising its own bone-chain of a tail, the brain haltingly comprehended that this must be how it had appeared, when it first coalesced into awareness from the riotous quantum broth. Rapidly adding free-floating unease and existential dread to its evolving periodic table of responses, the brain realised with a start that it was looking at the birthing process of another individual like itself. Confirming this unsettling apprehension, the inchoate cloud shook off the last vestiges of its former fuzziness and twinkled into pin-sharp focus with a sticky glister on its lobes, its crenellated folds. It was, beyond all doubt, another brain. Lacking for audiovisual organs or a method of propulsion, the perplexing new arrival hovered there in the ongoing rush of architectural generation, insensate and motionless. It didn't even know it was a noun.

The universe's former sole inhabitant here twitched its trailing length of spine in a display of agitation or, to use the brain's own terminology, element eighty-three. This worrying turn of events, it knew, necessitated some wrenching adjustments to its formative vocabulary and worldview, all arising from this unannounced intrusion on a previously sublime solitude—which, having up to then not even been perceived as solitude, provided a perfect example. Foremost among the great many philosophical anxieties that this occurrence represented was the hitherto unknown and therefore unexamined question of identity, a thing which until that point, as the former lone inhabitant of anything, it hadn't really felt a need to contemplate.

This upset would require additions to the brain's internal language system, certainly some sort of pronoun to describe itself as separate from any other brain that happened to drop by, and possibly a different pronoun to refer to this unwelcome upstart that, to its unpractised sensor-hump, seemed smaller, less attractive, and less charismatic than itself. Admittedly, its concept of 'attractive' was not very much advanced from 'non-repulsive', while charisma was seen only as a lack of dismal unimportance, but nevertheless the Boltzmann horror was increasingly persuaded to its own scornful appraisal of this relatively dull and ugly interloper. It seemed possible that more than pronouns would be needed to distinguish between the original brain and this dreary dwarf successor.

Perhaps some kind of identifying label process could be implemented, something that went beyond simply 'Boltzmann brain' and managed to convey a sentient being's status and significance; its unique personality? This process, it conceived, should be named naming. Warming to the idea, it contrived to fashion from its memory of sounds and syllables an appellation wonderful enough to represent itself, and while it felt that the sound-sequence 'Panperule' held all of the requisite awe and grave magnificence, there was still something missing. In a flash of inspiration, it inaugurated the definite article—a soft implosion—as the indicator of a given thing's uniqueness and pre-eminence. The Panperule. It had a ring to it. There could be any number of intruding brains, but none of them could ever be The Panperule.

Feeling much better for its acquisition of an impromptu identity, The Panperule turned its attentions once more to the other brain that bobbed before it, blissfully oblivious. So, what was to be done about it, this anonymous blob that was nowhere near as large or interesting as The Panperule? Unnoticed, great brick chimneystacks assembled themselves into an immense industrial sea-urchin somewhere overhead while the first Boltzmann brain assessed its various options, racked with indecisiveness (element nine). The course requiring the least effort on The Panperule's part would be simply to ignore the new arrival and continue on its foaming violet way, though it conceded this might lead to greater difficulties later on. What if the new brain in its turn evolved a way of sensing its environment, of moving through it, acting on it? What if it should come to the absurd conclusion that this self-inventing funfair of existence was in some way the new brain's domain, not realising that it was instead for the convenience of The Panperule? Might that not lay the ground for future conflict?

After some deliberation, a more elegant alternative became apparent. Since the new brain was not presently observing anything, the Heisenbergian loophole could still be exploited. Theoretically, this would allow The Panperule to alter the latecomer's proto-substance as it had its own, with sensory awareness and mobility within its gift. Much better that the gate-crasher be taught this bursting universe according to The Panperule than formulate a rival worldview of its own, and better yet to have the new brain feel indebtedness (element thirty) from the outset, rather than element eighty-seven, animosity, or forty-two, resentment. As an afterthought, the senior brain decided that it would at first bestow only the wilting quiff of sensory equipment, leaving the bone tail, and thus the chance to swim away, until after The Panperule felt that its introductory lessons had been properly absorbed.

With that resolved, it concentrated on the smeared potential smouldering about the junior entity, quantum scintilla hesitating over what to be. This focussed observation by The Panperule began instantly to collapse the wave of probability into a thin spray of the actual, and the more-developed brain looked on with interest as an indistinct smog of hypothesis reduced to one specific form. Seen from the modern point of view, this process most resembled slowed-down footage of an aspirin dissolving in a glass of water, but played in reverse. Superpositioned particles in powdery suspension gathered frothing substance as they streamed towards a point immediately above the younger brain, where a faint stippled outline of the slumping and indented forehead bonnet was teased into view then gradually coloured in with semblance and solidity. It was perhaps a little smaller than The Panperule's own hunch-brain mound of sound and vision, just because this seemed most natural and appropriate. Unfinished, naked, functionally useless without its follicular embellishments, the newly fashioned sensory tumour came with rolling blue/pink highlights in its snakeskin sheen before these were obscured by spreading blotches of quivering filament, sensitive suede upholstery that swathed the neurologic polyp's inner and external surfaces in carnival sensation. Once again, this coat of individually vibrating hairs could possibly be seen as less luxuriant than the glossy coiffure that The Panperule had lavished on itself but, in that sparsely populated femto-moment, seen by whom?

As riptides of perception, luminous and howling, crashed into the black and solitary silence of the second brain's awareness all its fibres stood on end, much like those on the backbone of a threatened cat. Some several thousand of the delicate erectile spines shrilled and vibrated, one upon another, and The Panperule was startled by the high-pitched and protracted signal, plainly of distress, with which the foundling greeted its first glimpse of glorious existence: it was screaming, and this was by definition primal. Puzzled by the vehemence of this reaction when its own attainment of sensation had elicited only mute awe (element one) and stunned bewilderment (element two), The Panperule did not consider that the newcomer's initial vision of reality contained The Panperule itself—a disembodied brain crowned with a shivering beehive hairstyle, skeleton propeller dangling beneath it like the downstroke of a horrifying question-mark—as a predominating foreground feature. It could only conclude that this second Boltzmann fluke was rather highly strung, and inwardly congratulated itself on its earlier decision not to furnish the new brain with means of locomotion or escape.

Waiting until the fledgling had exhausted its paroxysm of terror, with the frightened ululations at last dwindled to an apprehensive hush, The Panperule commenced its tutelage. This was accomplished by the generation of ellipsoid information-beads, speech bubbles, glass egg utterances that contained both image and identifying sound, so that the captive/pupil could be taught the rudiments of language, although as the only such existing then, that language would of course be Panperule. As if to illustrate the egocentric nature of this process, the first glinting word-globule emitted was a heavily idealised portrait of the senior brain, a huge

Halloween tadpole, with attached to it the sampled thighbone-trumpet fanfare that was, onomatopoeically, the sound-group 'Panperule'. After the hundred or so repetitions of this image-bauble thought sufficient to embed it in the understudy's memory, the lesson moved on to the many other monumental nouns, the restless verbs, the decorative face-powder adjectives, the somehow accusatory pronouns and inflection-shifting punctuation. This took quite a while. From the perspective of the non-consenting student, born from nothingness into a secondary-education language class, it took eternity.

Once the indoctrination was complete and the now-educated secondary brain was relatively fluent in Panperule, there followed a short session for questions and answers. While translation from a mode of speech composed of moving pictures and accompanying random noises can be only inexact, the femto-verse's opening conversation is approximately reproduced hereunder:

'What is all this highly structured stuff that's going on? I'm terrified (element ninety-five)!'

'Why, my young disciple, this is simply what existence looks like when it all comes pouring out of nowhere. When you've lived as long as I, it will seem commonplace and even disappointing.'

'I'm still terrified, but now I'm also intellectually intimidated (forty-four) and envious (thirteen). Although I'll almost certainly recall your oft-reiterated name forever, I must ask, who are you, and how did you come to be?'

'The Panperule, The Panperule, I am the Panperule! I am a marvellous collision of unlikely pseudomolecules that happened into being with the advent of this thundering and tumbling cosmos, and before me, nothing was. The Panperule!'

'I remain ninety-five-stricken, but this is now tinged with (one) awe, and (three) paranoia. Am I to deduce from your previous speech-trinket that you are, by implication, the self-made creator of this existential torrent; this suspiciously well-organised exploding whirligig?'

'It would be false if I did not deny that that was not the case. The Panperule!'

'Are you then my creator also? Please forgive my incredulity—it is but that your semblance is, to a trifling degree, somewhat unsettling (seventy-one).'

'As I have clearly said, it is hardly erroneous to refute that I am not this posited almighty being. I am, with great certainty, The Panperule, adorned by the most cataclysmic adjectives, and in my own exquisite image have I made you!'

This last crystalline pronouncement, which contained The Panperule's first use of the term *you* in reference to the newly hatched brain, was accompanied by an unflattering representation of the younger Boltzmann organism, which until that moment had not had the least idea of what it looked like. What it looked like was a crumpled lump of offal that was entering puberty, and though it did not go on for as long, the screaming this time was perhaps more plaintive and despairing (sixty-four). When the lament at last subsided to a hyphenated trail of tinkling pearls that were equivalent to hiccups or else snuffles, the apprentice entity, afflicted now by a tremendous loss of self-esteem (eleven), haltingly resumed brainkind's first awkward and uncomfortable attempt at dialogue.

'I'm sorry. It was just rather a shock to see myself in that condition ... but I notice that I am not wholly in your image, lacking as I do one of those flexible nether extensions that appear to help with moving, gesturing, and other verb-activities. Could you provide for me an osseous flail of my own, in your capacity as manufacturer of all things that exist?'

'We'll see. For am I not The Panperule?'

'That is the firm impression that I am incessantly receiving. May I ask if, in addition to the hoped-for train of knucklebones, I am to have an aural label of my own, a name by which you might informally refer to me?'

The Panperule weighed up this proposition as a murmuration of titanic windmills, vanes a spinning blur like aeroplane propellers, droned across the panoramic spread of miracles behind it. In the end, the elder apparition grudgingly selected a one-syllable cross-section from a harp glissando, unaware of its coincidental similarity to the much later terrestrial English boys' forename.

'You shall from this moment forth be known as Glynne.'

'I am The Glynne, then?'

'No. No, you're just Glynne.'

A short while after this exchange, the swarm of windmills now replaced by crackling foil chrysanthemums of equal size, The Panperule relented and rewarded Glynne with the requested knobbly tail, strenuously observed into demi-material existence and only a little more discoloured, spindly, and feeble than its maker's own. While this intentional disparity was largely motivated by no more than boundless vanity (fourteen), it was also a practical consideration born out of The Panperule's concern that Glynne might view the gift of motion as an opportunity to wriggle off and hide: with the new body-part consisting of, essentially, a length of knotted string that trailed from Glynne's hindquarters in the style of goldfish excrement, The Panperule was confident that any such absconding could be hunted down successfully within a body-length or two. In the event, however, this precaution proved unnecessary, Glynne being intimidated by the whole incarnated existence thing and anxious to remain in the proximity of blue/pink spacetime's self-proclaimed creator.

Thus was the impending universe's first relationship commenced; its first romantic fable, its first drama, and its first long con. The exploits of The Panperule and Glynne—which in their glassy speech-balloon recounting by the former were a predecessor to the broadside ballad—would be sung exultantly throughout the furthest reaches of the bustling cosmos, by The Panperule and Glynne, although chiefly The Panperule. There were hair-raising anecdotes of how The Panperule's heroics had saved Glynne from, chronologically, a life without the benefit of education, a stampede of maddened octahedrons, brick moths, what was possibly a violent gang-war between libraries and boutiques, a candlestick tornado, and a dangerous clockslide.

Obviously, it wasn't all adventure. There were memorable frolics, gambols, idylls, romps, and games of chase in glades of monumental corkscrew. There were epic conversations—or, more accurately, interrupted monologues that literally twinkled with The

Panperule's paperweight epigrams. There were companionable silences, as when they both observed the spectacular setting of an intricately folded origami sun, and for a moment the spine-tips of the two brains would coil about each other hesitatingly, as though by accident. During the time they'd spent together, amid all the frisking and the fun, The Panperule had slowly come to see Glynne in a different light. The smaller stature of the younger creature now seemed less stunted inferiority than it seemed slender or agreeably petite. Sometimes The Panperule would notice how appealing Glynne's perceptual pompadour looked now it had grown out a little, or would gaze transfixed at the accelerated sinuous wriggle that Glynne had acquired to compensate for having a considerably shorter tail. Why had it never noted previously the aesthetically beguiling contours of Glynne's plump occipital lobes, as seen from the rear? How had it overlooked the adolescent brain's endearing speech impediment, the way that Glynne extruded audiovisual crystals that were less ellipsoid than they were cylindrical? The Panperule, both intrigued and alarmed by these unprecedented feelings, teetered unaware upon the brink of lechery (seventy-eight), or even love (one hundred and eleven).

The inevitable consummation happened in the deep, mauve-shadowed valleys of a king-size ornamental ladies' fan, where the hallucinatory couple drifted recreationally. The Panperule gently directed their discussion to a philosophical consideration of the sensory experience itself, moving by increments to a debate on methods by which this experience might be pleasurably enhanced. Without directly saying so, The Panperule strongly insinuated that, as supreme being, it was generously offering Glynne initiation into the most sacred mystery of all creation. Glynne—coquettishly, as it seemed to The Panperule—affected to be unsure what exactly was being proposed, practically begging the more knowledgeable brain to employ bottled film-clip language that was more explicit and direct, even more crude, the little tease. Above the great fan's stiffly folded ridges floated laundry cloudbanks, lavender light dappling on crease and wrinkle, on unravelled cirrus threads.

'It can be shown, empirically, that conscious and perceptive beings such as we are space-time's prime phenomenon, and therefore fully realising our perceptual potential is a holy duty and an existential obligation, wouldn't you agree? Oh, Glynne, the gelatinous lustre on your come-hither parietal flank drives me crazy! We know that the vibration of our sensor-filaments permits both sight and hearing, while when these aforesaid hairs vibrate on one another, this allows our fishbowl phraseology and pictographic discourse. Glynne, I'll bet you've got the tightest little hippo-campus. By extrapolation from our metabiological design we may deduce, then, that the ultimate perceptual experience is that induced by one sentient individual vibrating their sensory follicles against those of another. Baby, let's get freaky, you and me. As for the practicalities of this exchange, it would appear most natural for the younger party to float upside down, above and facing their more venerable co-participant. Glynne, you're so hot, I'm worried that I'll prematurely shower you with shiny beads of moving light and music! It would seem mechanically expedient at this juncture for the inverted junior brain to tense its sensory protrusion and next introduce it to the open and relaxed concavity in the detector-wimple of its more mature and worldly colleague. Oh, Glynne, stick your ear-stalk in my hairy eyehole and I shall not lose respect for you! The Panperule!'

While not without misgivings, Glynne was, relatively speaking, a newcomer to existence, with no reason to suppose that what space-time's self-styled creator had suggested was not something commonplace and wholly normal. Carefully perusing what amounted to a three-dimensional instruction manual in The Panperule's suspended dialogue-bubbles, Glynne rose to the recommended elevation and obligingly proceeded to turn upside down. In doing so the Boltzmann ingénue observed that the surrounding cosmos, full of endlessly reiterated symmetries, looked much the same whichever way up one happened to be. Having attained the correct orientation, Glynne attempted to tense their perceptual forelock as The Panperule had stipulated, finding that the subsequent compression made the organ denser, slightly narrower, and possibly a little longer. After glancing to confirm

that the presumably experienced older brain was in the right
position just below, with its sensory toupee suitably dilated and
unclenched, Glynne apprehensively inched forward to accomplish
the required insertion, all the while expecting only darkness and
abrupt curtailment of sensation. On that issue, Glynne could not
have been more wrong.

The Panperule, for its part, had developed a cerise cast to its
colouration and was trembling excitedly at frequencies that
generated a distinct subsonic hum. Receptor-cowlick gaping and
relaxed, the universe's firstborn shivered, several hundred thousand
smart-hairs bristling in anticipation as they measured the approach
of Glynne's fibrous and sensitive baguette. Unable to restrain itself
The Panperule lunged forward for a sort of skull-free headbutt,
hairstyle yawning like a dislocated python as it swallowed that of
the inverted youngster, almost to the gleaming pseudo-scalp
provided by Glynne's frontal lobe, and then—

And then a firework-show involving beetle carapace and nebula;
involving squeal, bleat, and full orchestration as both individuals'
neural filaments fired randomly, shrilling against each other, back
and forth, a strenuously bowed crescendo on a pre-organic violin
of sparks and voices. Gasping cryptic arthouse movie clips with
inappropriate scores, the shuddering abominations squashed their
coifs together furiously in a fugue of mutual, mixed-media
sensation. Lubricated by a sweat of light and music, they
exhilarated in the strobing slideshow rush of tessellated goldfish,
blancmange demolitions, and a landslide of soundbite non-
sequiturs, the bursts of imagery and noise occurring rhythmically,
with an accelerating tempo. Growing more accomplished in this
very satisfying new activity, the pair experimented daringly: Glynne
was the first to shyly wonder just what it might feel like to rotate
his signal-monitoring mohawk rather than just move it in and out,
commencing with a single brain-roll that gave the cerebral
adolescent's hirsute growth a solitary turn inside that of The
startled-but-appreciative Panperule, like a repulsive pencil in a
histrionic sharpener. So moved by the manoeuvre was the senior
Boltzmann cheese-dream, it insisted Glynne continue this delicious

clockwise circling motion while The Panperule commenced a complementary rotation in the opposite direction. They quickly discovered that the faster this was done, the more delirious and titillating the resultant riptide of berserk perception. Soon the two were spinning in the manner of a Catherine Wheel, bony flagella flung out by the centrifugal force and whipping up a radiating halo of aerated pink-blue micro-bubbles to surround their loud and dazzling consummation, their ridiculous debauch.

Beginners luck permitted them to simultaneously attain to a climactic and convulsive state of rapture, a point where the chaos of input overwhelmed the duo's capacity to process further data. There was an obliterating flash of something that they didn't know was white, a double thundercrack as whirling spine-tips snapped through the prelude to a sound barrier, and then a falling away from each other, enervated and both panting murmur-diamonds. There ensued a period of recovery. When dignity and the preceding air of scholarly composure were sufficiently restored, The Panperule vibrated up a lengthy glass-egg monologue describing the communion with Glynne in luridly embellished terms, originating both the lovers' sonnet and pornography.

Now there began a golden era, or at least an era of a richer pink, a deeper blue. The liberating intimacy of their recent shared experience effected profound changes in The Panperule's view of existence; shifts in how it saw itself and, as importantly, how it saw Glynne. The senior intelligence now understood that prior to finding and accessorising its young protégé, life had been incomplete. It realised that the entire fast-breeding expanse of creation could have only been contrived as perfect backdrop scenery for the erotic passions of The Panperule and Glynne, an arbour of incessantly erupting form from where to conduct their legendary trysts and amatory gyrations, their salacious meeting of the minds. It was as if the whole continuum, born to perfection, was contriving to improve on that already flawless state by first providing a svelte younger playmate for The Panperule, and then a means by which this tousled youth could drive the more full-bodied and mature brain past the brink of ecstasy (seventy-seven).

The immaculate world, multiplying in its bounty all around them, was made truly Paradise by the advent of Glynne and the unending entertainment that Glynne represented. The unprecedented feelings that this thought engendered in The Panperule could be viewed as a loose equivalent of horniness, or free-floating arousal (ninety-one).

All in all, the situation showed a marked improvement that would reinforce The Panperule's slowly congealing philosophical position. In an as-yet unimagined nutshell, this revolved around the notion that existence—being a phenomenon entirely engineered for the convenience of The Panperule—had an inbuilt direction, which was that things would, of physical necessity, get better, better yet, continually better, a perfection with no top to it, perfection escalated without end. The Panperule privately named this principle Thermo-never-die-namics, the idea that energy was like a party that might start out quiet and reserved but would warm up as it progressed. This satisfying—or at least self-satisfying—teleology would come eventually to have pivotal significance, but for the moment it served to provide The Panperule's increasingly lascivious advances to the maybe-underage brain with a justifying philosophic gloss. The sky, it seemed, was barely the beginnings of the limit.

The initial femto-second of existence was at this point roughly halfway through, and in that blissful afternoon The Panperule and Glynne excursed with libertine abandon. Through Arcadian meadows of car-aerial that swayed and whispered in a Brownian breeze the pair disported themselves, shameless in the endlessly expanding pleasure-garden that was theirs alone. At every opportunity, the couple would put into practice the delightful new sport they'd invented, turning coital cartwheels above hybrid structures caught at an implausible halfway-point between boxing-glove and jukebox. They would roll together, sticky with found footage and industrial noise, and in their gooey pillow-talk they would refer to this enthrallingly indecent pastime by the pet name [STACK OF CROCKERY DROPPED IN AN ECHO-CHAMBER], a verb, best transliterated as 'clattersmashtinkling'.

The Panperule clattersmashtinkled Glynne without surcease, both vertically and horizontally, from a libidinous variety of angles. If the mood was right, The Panperule would sometimes start on top and be the partner doing all of the compressing and inserting. In their meta-rut, they rattled the inflating aerodromes and stained the ever-dropping fire escapes of Heaven with their documentary ejaculate. Unsupervised they gloried in their wanton freedom, though Glynne not so much, and scarce an instant passed but that The Panperule exulted in this unimprovably licentious universe, seemingly made for just the two of them.

It was around then that they happened on the other brains, one and a quarter hundred of them.

Blind and mute without their hairpiece augmentations they hung in a cube formation, five by five by five, a school; a squadron; a flotilla; glinting like fresh mackerel. None of them knew the other ones were there, suspended in their ordered rows, oblivious as commuters. They were situated, tailless and thus motionless, in a void area between gargantuan duelling gyroscopes. However, owing to The Panperule and Glynne's then-ongoing preoccupation with a bout of heavy petting and their oblique angle of approach, the floating block of newly formed brains didn't really register until the shrieking and tonsorially entangled couple were on top of them. There was a moment of stunned silence that went on for far too long before The Panperule remembered that it was supposed to have created everything. Not keen to be diminished in Glynne's sensor-follicles, The Panperule went for a rather unconvincing save along the lines of, 'See, Glynne, the incredible surprise gift I have fashioned for you on our anniversary! The Panperule!' Which anniversary, of course, remained unspecified.

From this point on The Panperule was improvising frantically, though careful to sustain its aura of omniscient calm. When Glynne enquired what it was meant to do with all these brains, the senior organism haltingly explained that the new creatures were meant as a peer group for the young apprentice, friends of Glynne's own age, that kind of thing. In an extemporaneous afterthought, The Panperule announced that it would generously allow Glynne to modify these new companions, and endow them with the sensate wigs required for them to learn the rudiments of spoken Panperule. It hinted that Glynne should regard this time-consuming task as a promotion, given that the youngster would be blessed with the extraordinary power to bring things into manifested form with only forceful observation. That Glynne had in fact owned this ability right from the outset was not mentioned.

Luckily, thanks to the careful grooming of The Panperule, naivety was Glynne's foremost defining quality. After a fairly slapdash lesson in applied manifestation from its lover and immediate superior, Glynne set industriously to work, imagining perceptive haircuts into being on the hovering platoon of inductees. Following The Panperule's instructions, Glynne at first provided the insensible recruits with only bare protuberances, thus far unadorned by their plush of receptive cilia. In this way, the whole one hundred and twenty-five of them could simultaneously receive their rug of quivering antennae, and so get all the preliminary wailing over with at once.

Predictably, when Glynne came to this part of the procedure, the effect was deafening. More unexpectedly, the vocal mass hysteria was also oddly moving. Floating there in front of the assembled screaming brains as though a medalled tyrant overlooking a parade, The Panperule found itself stirred by all those frightened voices lifting in a unison of terror; the appalled diapason of that trauma-choir. Although initially annoyed by this intrusion on the hanky-panky it had so enjoyed with Glynne, The Panperule could see how having many Glynnes as subjects—an extended fanbase, if you will—might be to its considerable benefit. As a significant improvement on conditions that seemed optimal already, this accorded nicely with the doctrines of Thermo-never-die-namics and The Panperule's own personal philosophy, regarding its ongoing incremental betterness. When the sheer pandemonium of some ten dozen new-born minds in horrible distress at last subsided into intermittent sobs and sniffles, space-time's first self-satisfied panjandrum glided forward eerily to make its presentation. As was customary, this commenced with getting on a thousand repetitions of the blown-glass glyph and hunting-horn acoustic that identified The Panperule. The second word in the vocabulary, 'Glynne', by contrast, had reiterations that were barely into double figures.

The tutorial on this occasion went on for much longer than it had done during Glynne's indoctrination, with there having been so many new experiences and therefore new bubble-words coined in the intervening time. Another reason that the lesson overran would be The Panperule's decision to include additional material after the language course was over, almost in the way of bonus extras. First, the captive audience were treated to a recitation that reprised 'The Ballad of The Panperule and Glynne' in all its many, many stanzas. Next there came what might be termed a blooper reel, wherein the sparkling speech-ellipsoids captured moments when Glynne had done something wrong, or had come close to injury in an amusing way. The final and most controversial feature was a perhaps over-vivid explanation of the term 'clatter-smashtinkling', illustrated by a crystal-ball recording of that special first time for The Panperule and its considerably younger brainfriend, single quotes or commas in attempted soixante-neuf. This test-run for a sex tape was, by virtue of The Panperule's prescient grasp of media, viewed by everybody in the universe. The trapped spectators, to be fair, had no idea what they were looking at. A stag film broadcast to a crèche, a pink/blue movie, it elicited only confusion (eighty-seven), nausea (twelve), and fear (nineteen).

The following question-and-answer session was a lively one, even with Glynne's outstanding stint as moderator. The major conundrums of existence—how did it come into being; does it have a purpose; why is there sentient life; what's that thing over there, somewhere between a dead snake and a Teddy Boy?—were all cleared up quite early on in the exchange, their single answer being several further repetitions of 'The Panperule'. This wasn't even monotheism, as that term would imply some manner of imaginable alternative. The fleet of student brains seemed to accept their subordinate roles as readily as Glynne had done, reasoning that this setup must just be the way existence was and having nothing at hand to compare it to. The Panperule's supremacy established, the discussion moved on to a clamorous demand for tails, and also a surprising number of requests for supplementary information on clattersmashtinkling.

With this out of the way, when work conditions and some basic standards of behaviour had been established, Glynne commenced the allocation of the spinal flails. Even with five of these materialised at once, a column at a time, this was a lengthy process that was highly reminiscent of a Ford assembly line, and thus of fascism. Once outfitted with tailbones, each successive quintet of new converts was encouraged to assemble a short distance off, still in their vertical formation, and in this way reconstruct the group's original cubic assemblage as Glynne's ministrations deconstructed it. This was because The Panperule had taken quite a shine to the impressive discipline of the arrangement, which had something of the marching band about it, albeit realised in three dimensions and with Boltzmann brains that did not march but only wriggled. It may have been this military aspect, or at least some premonition of that bearing, which inspired The Panperule's management-style once Glynne had done the necessary work and the entire platoon was mobilised.

Chattering and excited, the freshly augmented pups were understandably keen to try out their new flagella, though The Panperule insisted that this be enacted in an orderly and even stately manner. To this end, the one hundred and twenty-seven extra-cranial grotesques embarked upon a long theatrical tour of the endlessly expanding provinces. While maintaining their relative positions in the cube, the congregation of sapient hamburgers squirmed forth across mutating pastures with The Panperule up at the front of the procession, followed by the royal consort: Glynne had been pressed into service as a combination of drum majorette and orchestral conductor, bone tail swishing metronomically, leading the box-shaped brain armada through 'The Ballad of The Panperule and Glynne' in an ambitious polyphonic remix.

The resultant sound—an oceanic swell of anguish—was forerunner to the later choral compositions of György Ligeti,

although more apocalyptic. Like a receding tide before a great
tsunami of despair (one hundred and four), it rang out through
the cascading ironing boards and humming-tops of space-time as
the terrifying choir continued with its outing. Naturally, the
expelled speech-lozenges from such a vocalising multitude were
quickly in the hundred-thousands and soon after that the millions,
a polluting backwash of spent karaoke ornaments yet still the
hideous fleet sailed on. The Panperule was, as expected, having the
most perfectly amazing time, and if left to its own devices would
have seen this Bedlam pageant carried on for the remainder of
eternity. Glynne, being more attuned to rumblings of dissatisfaction
in the ranks, eventually suggested that they'd best soon call a halt,
preferably at some meaningful destination that might justify the
whole dispiriting ordeal.

Creasing its frontal lobe into a frown, The Panperule belatedly
accepted that a destination would have been a good idea, but also
understood that now was not the best time to admit this. A
confession of that kind would surely undermine the aura of
omniscience, the air of deity on which its pantomimed imperium
depended. Improvising furiously, it confided in its deputy that, by
a marvellous coincidence, the nondescript terrain that they were
then approaching was indeed their journey's end. Here Glynne
responded, in a furtive whisper of miniature language-globules,
that the area ahead seemed to be no more than a levitating
wilderness of cyclopean doughnuts. Making it up on the spot, The
Panperule declared that the apparently dull neighbourhood was
actually the precise centre of existence, well aware that this
pronouncement would be near impossible to verify. Since Glynne
did not immediately ridicule this claim, The Panperule went further
and explained that the unprepossessing but historically important
site would make an excellent location for a novel institute of
learning, the concept for which had lately crossed the older
creature's naked mind. In literally floating the idea to Glynne, The
Panperule strongly implied that their continuum could not be
thought of as a proper universe without a reputable university.

At once intrigued and taken in by this, Glynne brought the

marching minds to a dead stop, though tactfully allowing them to finish the verse of the ballad they were halfway through. Surprisingly, the rumbles Glynne had taken for dissatisfaction did not end with the parade, suggesting that they were instead a product of the background ambience. When this was brought to the attention of The Panperule, it was declared that these reverberations were most likely aftershocks resulting from The Panperule's original act of creation. This caused Glynne to point out that the rumblings were not gradually fading as might be expected but, if anything, were growing subtly stronger. Issuing a sharply pointed speech-ellipsoid which implied a tone of mounting irritation with the younger brain, The Panperule retorted that according to the well-established principles of Thermo-never-die-namics, everything just went on getting even better, even bigger, all the time, and that included aftershocks. It added, rather waspishly, that Glynne's apparent ignorance of basic science only demonstrated the necessity for educational establishments, such as the hub of academic excellence lately put forward by The Panperule. The implication, clearly evident, was that the sooner Glynne and the new workforce built their required campus, then the sooner they'd be liberated from the need for idiotic questions.

Glynne, it's fair to say, was not best pleased by this high-handed attitude, but wasn't going to risk a confrontation with the thing that had allegedly created space-time. Thus was born passive aggression: taking on instinctively the role of union representative, Glynne stipulated that their new brain-army should be given individual names before they set to work constructing this legacy project of The Panperule's. When these demands were met with an ellipsoid splutter of affronted indignation from the universe's unelected management, Glynne countered with additional conditions such as clauses guaranteeing rest and recreation periods for the newly formulated proletariat, insinuating that there would be no clattersmashtinkling of any kind until these issues were resolved.

Following this robust exchange of views, The Panperule grandly announced to the still-hovering cube of pressganged cerebellums that they were to be rewarded with both names and holidays for their forthcoming labours on a fabulous academy, to be known as The Panperuleum.

The naming ceremony was brisk and efficient, bordering, in Glynne's opinion, on perfunctory. All one hundred and twenty-five names were a monosyllable, fractional samplings of much longer sounds, and all of them commenced with the same phoneme, which was 'gl'. So there were Glack, and Glod, and Glimp, and Glert, and also many whose names were coincidental homophones for later English words, like Glue, Glow, Glove, Glide, Gloat, Glum, and at least three Glares, though all with different spellings. Glynn suspected that The Panperule associated short names that began with 'gl'—names like Glynne's own—with pitiful inferiority. That said, the newly christened lower ranks seemed more than happy to be given even rudimentary identities. With names, they at last had a self to inflate, be infatuated with, deceive, or justify. A name, being almost a quality, was something to be proud of; something one could think superior to other names and which thus made all sorts of satisfying prejudices possible. For instance, later, once the brains had been released from their cubic formation, Glynne would note their tendency to congregate only with brains whose names had the same vowel-sound as their own. Glynne also observed, while in conversation with Glytte, Glig, and Glimp, that brains whose names contained an *oo*, like Gloot and company, were generally indolent, untrustworthy, and avaricious. This was a purely aesthetic judgement, but also the only form of racism that was then readily available. Although, in Glynne's defence, it was a very different time.

After the glut of appellations had been handed out, including one for Glut themselves, The Panperule once more ran through its vacuous charade of granting the amassed Boltzmann militia an ability to manifest through observation, which they already unwittingly possessed. The brains were then permitted to relax their hexahedron, which allowed an opportunity to fraternise and chatter while The Panperule and Glynne designed the proposed universal university, though frankly it was mostly Glynne. The rookies revelled in their shore-leave while the higher ranks were in discussion, with the entry-level entities jiggling everywhere and eagerly attempting glassy, bulbous conversation when there really wasn't much as yet to talk about. The limited number of topics dominating these first stabs at dialogue were, in descending order, a debate on what that rumbling was and how come it was getting louder, some deliberation as to Glynne's degree of perceived hotness, and a general agreement that all brains who had a different vowel-sound in their names were fat and ugly. These initial discourses were typically concluded when the subject of clattersmashtinkling came up, it being soon discovered that to talk about the practice led, almost inevitably, to the practice of the practice. Space-time, all too quickly, rang from end to end with a prolonged concerto of dropped crockery.

No matter how quaint or appealing such a seething orgy of aroused flagellant brains might sound upon first hearing, for The Panperule and Glynne it was a gruesome inconvenience. While they were trying to concentrate upon their architectural intentions—or at least while Glynne was—everywhere about them was the thrust and squelch of copulating combovers. Mathematically, the horde of virginal participants had signally increased the number of erotic permutations possible, with more scope for perversion. Polyamorous arrangements seemed particularly popular, with many of the rockabilly seats-of-consciousness convening three-somes, whirling in a horrid Manx triskelion of untrammelled lust. There were also some foursomes, although these configurations bore unfortunate resemblance to self-molesting swastikas. The all-encompassing debauch looked dreadful, countless plugs of hair circling unseen bathtub plugholes, and it sounded like a raunchy landslide. Nothing in this was conducive to municipal design.

The Panperule's initial blue-sky visualisation for the mooted place of learning had been hugely disappointing, even to The Panperule: a number of that region's monstrous floating doughnuts piled up like a stack of tyres or lumpy oil-drum, it would have lent an already-barren zone the aura of a city-limits junkyard. When Glynne tactfully suggested making some minor improvements to the elder thing's original design, The Panperule was more than happy to sit back and watch the unrestrained brain-on-brain action that continued all around. Arcing ejaculations of speech-droplets went off here and there amongst the heaving proto-bodies, like timed fountains. Though most congress tended to be homophonic, between those whose names shared vowel-sounds, there quickly emerged a heterophonic subculture that found a frisson in what *oos* and *ees* and *aas* could do for one another. This became immediately fashionable, although there remained a general consensus that clattersmashtinkling with anyone called Glup, Glum, Glug, Gluph, Glut, Glud, or the like was tantamount to bestiality—which doesn't mean it wasn't going on.

Observing this erogenous phantasmagoria transacted in the flickering pink and blue, The Panperule found that it was becoming unendurably aroused. Sensing that Glynne was currently immersed in planning and would not appreciate advances of that sort, The Panperule experimented with alternatives. It soon discovered that if the indented tip of its fun-fur proboscis were turned outside-in, so that the sensory cone was curled up into its own cavity, The Panperule was quite good at clattersmashtinkling itself. Admittedly, the act seemed somewhat dull and repetitious without the sensory input of a partner, but was an improvement over not clattersmashtinkling at all. At least, this was The Panperule's opinion. Glynne, attempting to design space-time's first school despite the continuing brain-debauch and The Panperule having invented masturbation, saw things differently. For one thing, what The Panperule was doing was supremely unattractive to an onlooker, much like a woolly mastodon somehow inhaling its own hairy trunk. Rotating its perceptual cilia in a despairing eye-roll, Glynne returned to work amidst the hovering ellipsoid diagrams.

The rumbling continued, but by this point everyone was used to it.

Eventually, in the faintly sordid and wholly exhausted aftermath, when everybody in the start-up universe apart from Glynne was drifting limp and spent amongst a trillion rose-and-cornflower bubbles and used speech balloons, the urban planning was completed. Waiting for the six-score disembodied libertines and their autoerotic generalissimo to rouse from their disreputable torpors, Glynne expelled a polite cat's-eye marble cough to attract the post-coital crowd's attention, then explained the technical specifications of their new academy.

The outer structure would be made from three of the tremendous floating doughnuts. Two of these, vertically oriented, would be fused together at right angles to each other, with the third hoop, horizontal in orientation, looped around them like a waistband. Skeletally spherical, this basic outline would then be adorned by the mass-observed materialisations of the wriggling freshers. Crucially, the sphere's hollow interior was to be fitted with a cube of six amphitheatres, turned inward and facing one another to create a global lecture space without an up or down. There would be tunnel entrances at top and bottom, with four more at the cardinal points of the horizontal ring, where it intersected with the pair of upright circles. All in all, in both its beauty and utility, it was a bold and very modern statement that possessed great dignity.

The Panperule described this triumph of design as 'doughnuts stuck together', thus implying that the idea was entirely of its own devising. It went on to suggest minor tweaks, including a slight flattening of the proposed sphere, plus the addition of an observation-sculpted tail and sensory kiss-curl so that the academy would, in effect, be a gigantic statue of The Panperule. Nobody liked this concept save The Panperule, but as is frequently the way, this was the version that was pink-and-blue-lit and immediately implemented.

Twenty six-brain work-gangs laboured on the edifice, relentlessly observing it into existence, supervised by Glynne and five appointed foremen, one from each of the main vowel sounds. This took quite a long while. Much like any building-site, the undertaking also turned out to be loud and messy. In their swooping, staring squadrons, each one half-a-dozen strong, the muscular young Boltzmann beefcake strived and sweated sound-effects through rolling clouds of quantum dust that crusted mauve on sticky lobes. From the remove of an unused free-floating toroid, an unsightly pharaoh checking progress on a deformed sphinx, The Panperule surveyed this vista of cerebrospinal toil that was pre-reminiscent of the great Russian constructivists, clatters-mashtinkling itself to near-unconsciousness while doing so.

The uproar of construction, for a time, drowned out The Panperule's glass gasps of self-inflicted ecstasy and even masked the gradually increasing background rumble. Meanwhile, space-time elsewhere carried on as normal: getting bigger; ticking through its femto-lifespan; vomiting its careless, ceaseless prodigies and permutations. Brobdingnagian harps, trilobites, cooling-towers, and anchor-bouquets were amongst the only nameable components of this ongoing eruption into form, at least from a modern perspective. It need not be said that all of these spontaneously generated shapes were much more interesting and magnificent than the distressing effigy that the brain workforce was then in the process of erecting—a sideshow exhibit in a jar, displayed in company with masterpieces.

Finally, The Panperuleum was finished, to the satisfaction of The Panperule alone. So pleased was the eponymous dictator/deity by the dimensions of this loathsome idol that it failed to notice how the quiff-tip of the graven image was turned inwards, pleasuring itself. This subtle touch—The Panperule forever wanking at the alleged centre of the universe—had been devised by an increasingly resentful Glynne, and executed by the deputy director's phonetically sympathetic cohort Glytte, Glig, Glimp, and Glock, that last of which chose to identify as an entirely different vowel-sound. As the proto-university's first term commenced, Glynne's clique looked on with carefully supressed amusement as the influx of collegiate brains filed solemnly into the multi-oriented auditorium beneath a semblance of their demiurge, captured eternally in flagrant self-abuse.

This palaeo-academic era, while it lasted, was largely congenial, aggressively erudite, and crushingly monotonous. This was because The Panperuleum employed only one lecturer and taught only one subject, that being Thermo-never-die-namics. Worse, the single lecturer appeared not to have fully thought this self-invented theory through, and offered only a few heavily opinionated anecdotes in its support. Chief amongst these was the oft-repeated notion that the rumbling—by now loud enough to render many of the lectures unintelligible—was merely an aftershock being all that it could be, in a universe of everlasting self-improvement. Typically, The Panperule would make a rambling presentation of these same ideas, over and over, followed by the customary session of questions and answers, before calling for a recess. These break-periods, during which socialising and, inevitably, much clattersmashtinkling were allowed, were demarcation points as critical as dawn or dusk in that unvarying bluish-pink continuum. They were also the only thing that made the academic life remotely bearable; all that prevented more of the assembled students from becoming restless and politically radical than there already were.

Glynne could not help but notice that the frequent calls for recess offered ample opportunity for the sole lecturer's philandering amongst the student body, many of whom seemed inordinately flattered by their creepy principal's advances. There would regularly be a dozen or so scholars that competed for The Panperule's attention, always floating in those spaces closest to the lectern, teasing up their sensory extensions into ever more outrageous styles and flirting openly in the question-and-answer intervals. They made Glynne sick, with their pretended under-standing of and interest in Thermo-never-die-namics, their sycophantic tittering each time The Panperule attempted an ellipsoid joke. Apparently, it only knew the one, this being a display of something stupid, actual or invented, that Glynne was reputed to have done. In fact, 'the Glynne joke' in its many variations had become so widespread that a number of the students had suggested glassy dissertations on the subject, their preposterous sound-library voices ringing in The Panperuleum's deranged acoustics.

During recess periods The Panperule would make itself available for one-on-one tuition with whichever simpering cerebellum had been fluttering their cilia most invitingly, these episodes invariably taking place off-campus, usually in the vicinity of the leftover levitating doughnuts. On one such occasion, Glynne suggested that the eager-to-please Glock should follow lecturer and student to establish the validity of these extracurricular excursions. Unsurprisingly, when the culturally appropriative hanger-on reported back to what it called its 'vowelies'—Glynne, Glytte, Glig, Glimp, and company would shudder visibly whenever Glock used this expression—it regurgitated a long-lens ellipsoid image of The Panperule lewdly frolicking with glee, and, coincidentally, with Glee: off on the so-called dark side of the nearest hovering toroidal lump, master and pupil made 'the beast with two brains'. Endlessly repeated in Glock's paparazzi loop, The Panperule and Glee entwined their spinal tails as an obscene caduceus; mashing their hairy fascinators one against the other in delirious abandon. With a hardening hippocampus Glynne gazed coldly at this pitiful and grubby assignation, the unsightly older brain making a fool of itself with the squeaking juvenile. Glynne didn't excrete so much as a single cut-glass word, but all of its companions, even Glock, knew that the second-in-command was both resentful and humiliated (forty-two and fifty). Glynne was literally bristling.

It was a story old as time, which was to say less than a femto-second.

The inevitable confrontation happened at the start of summer term, although in accordance with the principles of Thermo-never-die-namics they were all summer terms. The rumbling sound was so pronounced by this point that the bulbous declarations of The Panperule were necessarily the size of glass dirigibles, in order to be heard above the thunderous reverberations. The bore of The Panperuleum's entrance-tunnels had been widened so that these spent conversation-globules could more easily be swept into the outer void by students made to serve as Boltzmann janitors, yet still the garrulous detritus tended to accumulate in corners of the multi-planar auditorium, shimmering and jingling unappealingly.

The Panperule had just concluded a meandering account of how Thermo-never-die-namics implied that the classic Glynne joke would just keep on getting funnier and funnier the more it was repeated, then called for a session of questions-and-answers with its furry sensor lecherously pointed at the giggling front-row students. It was here that Glynne and a tail-picked team of phonetic cronies made their entrance, shimmying into position between lecturer and audience with cerise suds everywhere. In the immediate apprehensive silence, while The Panperule contracted its receptor-cone into a perplexed squint, Glynne volunteered a carefully considered question.

'For whom can this perpetually improving universe be said to be improving?'

The Panperule, taken aback by Glynne's enquiry, blustered a long stream of floating ornaments to the effect that space-time was continually getting better from its own perspective, and that surely this must be the same for everyone and everything. Aware that this could be seen as a flimsy argument, The Panperule fell back on the increasingly loud rumble as supporting evidence, then ended with a flourish of arch rhetoric by asking if Glynne had a more convincing theory. Glee, Glam, Gloop, and all the other fawning teacher's pets were tittering already at their tutor's classic putdown, were agreeing that this ill-planned intervention took the whole Glynne joke to the next level, when the deputy brain dipped its velvet prong in an affirming nod.

'Yes, I believe I have. It seems to me that this existence, far from constantly improving on perfection, is in no small measure getting worse. As evidence, I too would cite the mounting volume of the rumbling noise that makes our discourse pointless and inaudible; that forces us to cough up speeches like translucent zeppelins. How does this, in any sense, improve our situation?'

Reeling from this heresy, its sense-aperture hanging slack with disbelief, The Panperule here accidentally loaned weight to Glynne's proposal by exclaiming, 'What?'

In audiovisual bubbles now inflected with a heavily ironic tone, Glynne condescendingly reprised those opening remarks, then went on to make matters worse by calling into doubt the customary explanation for the worsening grumble of eternity.

'I put it to you that, rather than high-spirited aftershocks, it is more likely that these sounds are instead the fore-rumble of some cataclysm yet to come.'

Spluttering incoherent image-beads, The Panperule loudly insisted that this absurd notion contradicted the established tenets of Thermo-never-die-namics, and at this Glynne merely nodded.

'I contend that it is well past time for Thermo-never-die-namics to be superseded by a more substantial theory of my own devising. I contend that our improbably well-organised continuum is in fact degenerating, with the advent of self-aware creatures actively contributing to that decline: putting a bunch of brains in charge of space-time is, quite evidently, a disastrous idea.'

The omnipresent rumbling was briefly challenged by the incredulous murmur of the students as they tried to comprehend Glynne's radical new train of thought. The Panperule anxiously noted that Glee, Glam, Gloop, Glow, and Gleam—its fan-club/harem—were all gazing gooey-haired at Glynne, using the tips of their spine-tails to toy coquettishly with their luxuriant forelocks. From The Panperule's perspective, none of this was going well. As space-time's self-described creator dithered over how best to subdue the insurrection, Glynne calmly continued its incendiary monologue.

'My theory states that our unlikely universe will shift to a condition of continual collapse, perhaps commenced by whatever catastrophe is presaged by these current rumbles. This slow disintegration will eventually end when our continuum is stripped of all complexity; of life, and form, and energy; unburdened of the many tropes that comprise its existence. This untropic state, inevitable, unavoidable, I have named Untropy.

'Further to this, I can predict with confidence that in whatever eras of the cosmos follow, signs of Untropy will be so common-place they will establish my conjecture as a universal fact. Indeed, these later ages will be so immersed in Untropy, in all existence running down to frigid, black disorder, that our world will only be imaginable by assuming that the universe began in a high-energy state of near infinite complexity, as a logical opposite of its eventual end in cold, and dark, and utter disarray: in Untropy. And other than this meaning that The Panperule will no longer be tangling tonsures with cheap floozies up on the leftover doughnuts, I'm afraid I really can't see frozen nothingness as an improvement.'

Though the by-now sensor-splitting rumble drowned the odd word here and there, everyone caught the gist. Some of the more highly strung brains fainted, floating quiff-down and unconscious in amongst their gaping colleagues. Glee and Gloop applauded by slapping their undersides together. It may have been this final indignity that drove The Panperule to its unfortunate reaction.

Howling, 'Glynne! The Panperule! That's quite enough! The Panperule!' in a speech-glob big as a double-decker *Hindenburg*, The Panperule lifted its skeletal flagellum up above the shivering hairpiece in the manner of a not-yet-extant scorpion. Before it had the time to fully understand what it was doing, the infuriated elder lashed out with a bone whip in the general direction of its smirking deputy. The crack as the tail's flexible tip broke a prototype sound-barrier was like an atom bomb, audible even through the all-consuming seismic background noise.

Intended as a reprimanding slap, the narrow tail-end caught Glynn squarely on the frontal lobe and smashed the younger brain to pseudo-molecules. Glynne's twitching tail, no longer anchored to a central cortex, fell unhurriedly into the depths or heights of the stunned auditorium.

The Panperule was as surprised as anybody. Having only just invented homicide, it had been previously unaware of the brain-form's alarming vulnerability. With this in mind, it was already starting to materialise a hard, protective carapace around its softer parts, an armour-plating in metallic blue that left only the hairpiece and the tail exposed. The student brains, still numb with shock and watching Glynne's remains tumble away from them into The Panperuleum's immense concavity, did not immediately notice what The Panperule was doing. When they did, they quickly realised there was nothing stopping them from modifying their own forms in the same way.

It was immediately a quasi-biologic arms race. Now adorned with frightful morningstars that turned each thrashing tail into a mace and chain, both Glytte and Glig launched themselves at The Panperule in a consuming lust for vengeance (one hundred and fifteen). Fortunately for the startled tyrant, a still-loyal squad of *ee*-named brains that had evolved a sort of belly-mounted crossbow intervened between The Panperule and his Glynnist attackers. Bolts of bone fizzed through the fluid atmosphere on bubbling trajectories, blasting a fatal hole through Glig but giving Glytte the instants needed to evolve a more robust defensive shell, a metal-plated galleon with two rows of cannon poking through its gun-ports on each side.

The femto-second was within a hair's breadth of its end; the rumbling a hair's breadth of its crescendo. Wriggling away from the engagement's epicentre to a safer vantage point, The Panperule was disconcerted by how rapidly the incident was escalating, how this in its turn drove the advance of military technology into a murderous fast-forward blur. Elsewhere in the university-turned-battlefield the homophonic triplets Glare, Glheir, and Glhey're had modified themselves with buzz-saws before slaughtering a gang of diphthongs that had only managed catapults. The much-maligned brains with an *uh* sound in their names meanwhile extruded petrol engines, biplane fins and submachineguns, settling scores with the more privileged vowels that denigrated them as brutish and promiscuous. The Panperuleum's vast interior became now a Hieronymus Bosch firefight, scarred by arcs of funeral-black smoke as Glup or Glug went down in flames. It was a Boltzmann blitz, and everywhere the steel-jacketed combatants streaked through a hail of cannonballs and cluster-bombs, performing haphazard lobotomies on one another as they went.

The rumbling was now visible, and everything was shaking. Ugly cracks began to race across the concave inner surface of The Panperuleum, just as Glytte sprouted guided missiles and attained a nuclear capability. You couldn't see for bits of brain.

'Clattersmashtinkle', thought The Panperule, approximately and belatedly.

Somewhere hydrogen was happening, and it was all downhill from there.

THE WAITING PLACE

LAVIE TIDHAR

T HE ROOM WAS VERY BRIGHT and the child frail. He was frail in a sort of doll-like way, like one of those anatomical models where you could see the bones drawn onto the skin surface. The boy's eyes were large and a guileless blue. It was the blue of waterfalls and deep clear skies in the late afternoon. How his eyes got their colour the man never knew. His own eyes were green. But he never stopped marvelling at this child, not just from the moment that this tiny bundle first emerged into the air outside the womb, when the man, for all that he was petrified, was given the scissors to cut the umbilical cord, for all that he tried to protest; but earlier, as the boy grew bone by bone and limb by limb in its mother's womb, when he could feel it moving there, inside. The boy hiccupped a lot in the womb. And the man talked to him, through that thin membrane of skin, and sang to him, too: he did that a lot, back then.

But he never stopped marvelling at this, his boy, and those eyes which he had secretly always thought would fade away to grey once the boy passed his first year; but they never did.

Now the boy lay, patiently, on the sliding table of the machine. He didn't speak and the man held his hand but said nothing either. He had run out of words long before. The doctors moved about the room like white ghosts. They were brisk and efficient and gave nothing away. The room was kept very cold. A motor hummed and the tray that the boy lay on slowly slid towards the belly of the machine. The machine kicked into life and the boy disappeared inside and the man and the woman waited. They had been waiting a long time and were destined to wait for a long time more.

A cloud of butterflies engulfed the broken train in the night. The train crawled along the tracks, a wounded, dying beast, and the butterflies kept hitting the broken windows and burst inside and fluttered along the corridors, where blood-soaked carpets lay ruined. The Kid and the Stranger were holed up in the engineer's cabin and the engineer kept muttering and twiddling his instrument panel and in the boiler the ghosts kept fluttering half-heartedly. It was possible that the butterflies were drawn to the ghosts, for it was said that butterflies, on the Escapement, were merely the vessels of departed spirits from that other place, and who was to say whether it was true or not?

The butterflies eventually vanished as silently as they had come. The ghosts in the boiler faded away to nothing and the engineer stopped muttering and his hands were still, and the train came to an ungainly halt at the nearest stop: an outpost of the Thickening in the middle of a great empty plain. A solitary wooden sign, planted in the hard ground, gave the name of the terminal: *Lugar de Espera*.

As soon as the train stopped, the engineer collapsed to the floor and remained there. He was fast asleep. The Kid and the Stranger disembarked. The Kid was covered in ghostly substance and the Stranger in blood. They stood there, in the pale light of dawn, and looked on the terminal.

It was not really a town, merely a waiting station on a branch line, and it was miles still from any habitation. Nothing around.

The sky spread over the grey empty plain like a mirror which only served to enhance the place's isolation. There is nowhere to go, it seemed to suggest. There is nowhere to run. Not from here.

There was a long terminal building built with wooden walls and a sloping tin roof, and a garage, which was shut, and a convenience store, which was also shut. The Stranger looked to the distance and he thought he hadn't looked properly before. Somewhere out there on the plain, a group of people, ill-discerned, were digging. But what was there to dig?

There were a few isolated buildings dotted around here and there in what passed for a town, homes or sheds it was impossible to say. The only other large building was made of bricks and looked like a factory though there were no workers he could see, nor smoke coming out of the chimneys. Attached to the factory building there was a clock tower and its clock kept beating, and the sound of the seconds reverberated through the town and into the ground and into the Stranger's soul.

He did not like this place. It was hard to look straight at the clock. The hour hand was stuck on twelve and the minute hand on five to twelve and the hand that counted the seconds was the only one moving, but it was trapped against the minute hand and only kept beating out its signal against the same neverending time, moving in place like a captured moth trying to break free. He looked at the Kid and the Kid shrugged.

'I need breakfast,' the Kid said. He stretched and yawned. 'Think anyone's serving in this dump?'

'Horses first,' the Stranger said. The Kid just shrugged again.

The Kid and the Stranger fetched their horses. They were creatures of the Escapement, with no ties to that other place and little regard for the affairs of Colossi or pupae. The Stranger's horse nuzzled his face and the Stranger stroked the horse's long neck. They had travelled together for some time and were destined to ride together for a time longer. As they came back towards the front of the train, the Stranger saw a solitary figure approach them.

He was a tall thin man in the uniform of a conductor, with a head too large for his body, and entirely bald, so that he appeared like a marionette whose head would not quite stay on properly. 'What happened here? Who are you? Where is the engineer?'

'We came under attack over the Chagrin,' the Stranger said. 'The engineer is in his cabin. He got us this far. There are wounded on the train, as well as the dead.'

'Dead passengers? But this is most irregular!' the conductor said. He looked at a pocket watch and shook his head mournfully. 'This is terrible, the timetables will be all out of tune!'

The Stranger noticed that the pocket watch seemed to bear no hours or minutes and that all its hands were missing, but he kept his thoughts private. The conductor muttered to himself, ignoring them.

'You must arrange for the other passengers,' the Stranger said. 'We did all we could but—'

'Yes, yes,' the conductor said. 'It is taken care of.'

The Stranger looked back and he saw that the conductor was right. A group of figures in grey, shapeless clothes, perhaps the workers he had seen earlier, digging out there on plains, were now moving lethargically but with purpose across the cars. They brought down the dead and the wounded, but what they did with them and where they took them he couldn't tell. He felt disinclined to ask. They were in the Thickening now and this was a job for the railway company. He followed the Kid towards the long cabin and saw that the sign indeed said *Waiting Room* on the door. They went in.

The floor was clear if unswept. Long benches lined the walls and he saw with some surprise that there were many people waiting there. They sat with their backs to the walls, the men in worn suits and hats, the women as drab as the men, and all looking down at the ground with dull and listless eyes. They looked as though they had been waiting a long time, and were ready to wait for a long while more. The Stranger himself felt bone-tired and robbed of vitality. He wanted nothing more now than to sit down on those self-same benches and wait. He wondered how long they'd been waiting. Surely the train came past here often enough?

At the end of the long hall there was a small kiosk. They made towards it. No one looked up at them or observed their passing. He heard no chatting or rustling of pages, nothing but a dull silence. He was somewhat surprised to discover, upon arrival, that the kiosk counter was open for business. A large, pleasant-faced woman stood behind it, though she looked surprised at their arrival.

'Can I help you?'

'What happened to everyone here?' the Kid said. 'They look like they've given up the ghost.'

The woman looked at him sharply but said nothing. The ticks of the clock reverberated through the building, through the Stranger's bones. He was keenly aware that something was wrong. He just didn't know what. There was no substance here, and the walls between this town and that other place were firm.

'Two coffees, please,' the Kid said.

'Coffee?' the woman said. She said it doubtfully, indeed as a woman trying to wake up from a deep and pleasant dream. 'There is no coffee.'

'Well, what do you have?' the Kid said. 'You must serve *something*.'

'Porridge,' the woman says.

'Porridge?'

The woman looked at him as though trying to place him.

'Porridge,' she said at last, with finality.

'But I don't *like* porridge,' the Kid said plaintively.

The Stranger turned away from them. He took out a tough piece of jerky and chewed on it as he surveyed the waiting room. None of the waiting people had stirred. He tried to concentrate. Something about the woman bothered him. He turned round. She had her back to them then, and was stirring a massive cast-iron pot in which something pleasant-smelling was bubbling. He stared at her. She had pulled back her long sleeves as she worked, and he saw now what it was that he instinctively noticed. Her upper arm, between the elbow and the shoulder, had been hollowed out and the skin had turned to glass. Inside the glass were two further glass chambers, linked to each other by a narrow tube. They were filled with ants. The ants kept moving inside the woman's arm. When she raised her hand, the upper chamber would slowly fill with ants and, when she lowered it, the part nearer the elbow would then fill, as with some forever-moving hourglass in which time was suspended in an equilibrium. He said, 'You're a veteran?'

The woman turned to him. She dropped her arm and her sleeve came down and covered it. She shrugged.

'Long ago,' she said.

'Who did you fight for?' the Stranger said curiously.

The woman seemed torn in indecision. It was not that her look was unfriendly, or not entirely that. It was just that the question seemed to have brought her out of some state in which she wasn't even aware she was dwelling. Some vitality had returned to her face. She said, 'We were riding out with General Zavatta to the crystal fountains. It was far from here, at the foot of the Candy Mountains. We didn't really know about the war, you understand. Zavatta promised us stew, all that we could eat, and whiskey, and we were hungry, we were young and we were hungry and we were ready for everything. We rode out that day, leaving behind us tiny homesteads and work on the mines. Our heads were filled with dreams of glory. Instead we rode out for days through the Doinklands. The little food we had was soon gone and the clowns laid traps for anyone intruding on their territory. We lost two riders to a trampoline and Billy Ray got hit in the face by a pie and his face melted clean off. At last we came upon a clown village. It was us or them. It wasn't war, it was a massacre. They tried to run. Some tried to fight back but they were no match for us. We were hungry and ruthless and we wanted blood. That day we slaughtered every one of them and burned down their homes and we rode away from there whooping and hollering and with our bellies filled with food. The smoke stung my eyes, I remember that. We rode that way and Zavatta told us of creeks running with whiskey and trees where cigarettes grew. You have to understand, none of us knew that other place, we were all of the Escapement. In a ravine we came upon a giant stone foot lying severed on the dry riverbed, three of its toes blasted off. We didn't know who we were fighting or why. In the homestead, some of the old folk spoke of the Titanomachy, but none had been in the war, none but for an old boy, an ex-miner with a parrot for a hand, and he never talked about it at all.

'That night we camped by the giant stone foot and made fires. It was then that I noticed how General Zavatta's shadow, in that light, seemed so much bigger than him, and when they moved, I could not shake off the awful feeling that it was the shadow which moved first, and the man who followed.

'That night two of the boys got into a fight and killed each other under the big toe. It happened so quickly, it was hard to comprehend when it happened, only by that point none of us cared. It was just more spilled blood, for us. It required neither sense nor rhythm. One moment they were friendly, talking about some girl back home both of them knew. The next there was a knife out, flashing in the firelight, and the shot of a gun. The smell of gunpowder. Blood spilled on the dry riverbed. Two bodies cooling under the big toe of the broken giant. After that, Zavatta made us march from that place. We found other pieces of the Colossus on our way: a finger, an ear. It only dawned on me later that the mountain we were traversing resembled a torso.

'The weather grew cold and snow flurries fell as we snaked our way up the mountains. There were clowns there, too, in the ice. Hobos, mostly. We strung them up when we could. More often they would take pop shots at us from the high passes, or trigger an avalanche of bright yellow balls. We lost three riders that way, and ate their horses and were grateful.

'There was no question of deserting. Zavatta led and Zavatta couldn't be questioned. There was nowhere to escape to, only the mountains and the clowns and death on every side. Then we were through the mountains and joined on a great plain by other companies, with other commanders and their shadows. The next night the full moon shone down and in its light we saw the line of colossal statues lining up the horizon, silent figures, huge beyond measure, and behind them the stars in the night.

'We charged. Shadows fled and people died. The Colossi had people too. I shot and I knifed and I bludgeoned. How many, I don't know. My horse was shot under me. All this time there was awful laughter and it was punctured by pockets of silence that were somehow more terrible in themselves. Back and forth it went, the sound and the lack of sound, and the plain ran red with our blood.

'In the morning the Colossi were gone as though they had never been, and the horizon was empty and clear. There was no sign of Zavatta, and the plain was covered in the dead and the dying. When I came to I was lying under a fallen horse. My shoulder was broken and I had lost two of my toes, and my upper arm was turned into the thing you see now. It itches sometimes, in warm weather. Sometimes I can hear the ants scuttling inside, late at night, but I find their company soothing.

'A few of us, the survivors, banded together. Some had served pupae, some Colossi. It didn't seem to matter, just as the battle we took part in made no sense to us. The plain seemed to me then to have been a sort of checkerboard, and we were the pieces being pushed around. For what benefit, I couldn't tell you. I don't think anyone could.

'We wandered the Escapement. Without Zavatta we had no direction. I was affected the least. One man had lost half his body. It did not seem to affect him badly, it's just that the entire left side of his body was missing, as though it had been erased, yet he was able to move normally, as though that missing part was still somehow there, in ghostly form. Another woman had her head turned into a mirrored helmet, and she could speak only with her hands. One person, Rudy, was half-turned into a musical organ and when he moved he played sad mournful tunes. In this fashion we wandered searching for a home. We could not return to the lonely homesteads and the mines. We were veterans of a war we didn't understand, and just as quickly as we had been used we were discarded.

'I don't know what happened to the others. One day I came here and . . . '

The dull look was back in her eyes and without saying another word she turned and began stirring the porridge again. The Kid and the Stranger exchanged glances.

'I don't think I want any porridge,' the Kid said.

'No,' the Stranger agreed. The beats of the clock sounded in the still air, *Tick, Tick, Tick, Tick*.

'Let's get out of here,' he said.

But there was no respite from the oppressive sense of *waiting* out there either. The sky was grey and the air felt humid and unmoving, and the clock in the clock tower beat louder there, the sound expanding to fill up all that still unpleasant silence. The Stranger offered the Kid a stick of dried beef and the Kid accepted without much grace. They stood there together and chewed.

'There's something not *right* with this place,' the Kid said. 'Or, for that matter, with that woman.'

'I know,' the Stranger said. He chewed some more, without enthusiasm. 'It's strange,' he said. 'I heard that name before. Zapata or Zavatta, something like that at any rate. And I heard about that battle she mentioned, at the Candy Mountains. It was less a battle than a massacre, by all accounts, and the greatest massing of forces in the Titanomachy for centuries. But that's just it. Even with the way time flows differently in different places on the Escapement . . . it must have been more than a century ago.'

'But she doesn't look older than thirty,' the Kid protested.

'I know.'

'I wish that damn clock would stop ticking,' the Kid said.

'Me too,' the Stranger said.

A man came out of the garage then, wiping his hands on a piece of cloth. He wore long blue overalls and had a shock of unruly black hair and the same pleasant yet somehow vacant smile as the kiosk woman.

'Hello, hello,' he said. He looked at them with a polite lack of curiosity.

'Who are you?' the Kid said, a little rudely. The man blinked at him with a friendly lack of concern.

'I'm Lucas,' he said. He extended a hand for a shake, which both men ignored. 'I'm the mechanic.'

'Not much call for a mechanic round here,' the Stranger said. 'Do you know when the next train's due?'

Lucas blinked at him with guileless eyes. 'Can't think when the last one...I mean, they don't *stop* here, you know. Not usually. We're more of a spur line, really.'

'A spur line?'

'We're off the main line, really we're more of an, I suppose you would say, an emergency stop. Haven't had a train come through here in...' He mumbled something indecipherable and fell silent.

'In *how* long?'

'Time,' the mechanic said, and shrugged. 'You know?'

'They're all mad here,' the Kid said, and he stared at the Stranger helplessly. His eyes were becoming glassy, like a stuffed animal's, the Stranger thought.

'I don't know,' the Stranger said. He turned to Lucas, the mechanic. 'Excuse me?'

'Yes?'

'Can I see your...Can you open your overalls?'

'Excuse me?'

'If you don't mind.'

Lucas shrugged. He pulled down one strap and lifted up the shirt underneath.

'Ah...' the Kid said.

The man's bare midriff was a mechanical grille made of four slashes of metal vents cut into the pink flesh around them, and they opened and closed gently as Lucas breathed.

'He's another veteran,' the Kid said.

Lucas submitted to their inquiry with polite bemusement. He pulled his shirt back down and lifted the overalls' strap and smiled at them. 'Would you like a cup of coffee?'

'You have *coffee*? The woman at the kiosk said there wasn't any.'

'Oh, you met Mrs Lazarus? She's nice.' Lucas winked like a bad actor and tapped his nose. 'But she doesn't have to know everything, does she? Come on in, come on in.'

They followed him into the garage. It was dim, with shafts of grey light breaking in through gaps in the stonework. There were machine parts scattered about everywhere, with no rhyme or reason that the Stranger could discern. The mechanic wiped his hands again on his rag and went to a little gas stove where he set to making the coffee.

The smell of the cooking beverage was a little too sweet, however. It was cloying in the enclosed space. It smelled of chicory and liquorice and cloves. The mechanic seemed unconcerned as he returned with a tray and three mugs. The Kid and the Stranger took the mugs but were careful not to drink. When the mechanic looked elsewhere the Stranger tipped the beverage onto the ground.

'Should be a good crop this week,' the mechanic said.

'What?'

'Out there, in the fields.'

'What fields?'

'Tick tock, tick tock,' the mechanic said, and giggled.

'Where did you serve?' the Kid asked him.

'I never *served*,' Lucas said with wounded pride. 'I used to be a *chasseur de clown*, a bounty hunter. We rode in the Doinklands, hunting whitefaces and Augustes for the reward money. We always avoided the conflicts of Colossi and pupae. What did we need *them* for? Our leader was Zebedee, the greatest of the chasseurs. He could read the strength of the enemy in a dollop of dropped custard, could discern the position of our prey in one careless mark of chalk. For a long time, we lived like this, in the wild places beyond the Thickening. We only rode into town with our bounty, and then we'd drink moonshine and Sticks, those of us who still had a hankering for that other place. Not me, chief. All right, sometimes I would succumb, and I would see hazy visions, a time and a place where it seems to me I was a railway engineer, who drank too much and read dime novels, who lived alone. *He*, that other man in that other place, kept searching for a way out, for a world where he could be something he was not. He was searching for the Escapement. I did not like those visions, which I saw as needless escape into fantasy, and so I eventually stopped drinking Sticks altogether.

'Around that time, Zebedee was caught in a trampoline trap near a whiteface encampment. Poison custard left half his face mutilated, and he'd broken all the bones in his left leg, but he survived. He changed then, though. And sometimes he carried on conversations with his shadow, and sometimes he would pause at unexpected moments, when peeling an apple for example, and he'd stare at the apple or the knife with a look of complete bewilderment, as though he didn't know what either of them were for.

'Not long after his recovery, Zebedee pushed us farther than ever before into the Doinklands. We were headed beyond any human presence, far away from the small teardrop that was the Thickening. I had never realised before how immense the Escapement was, and how little of it belonged to us. I did then, and it frightened me. We were mere trespassers, new arrivals on this vast and shifting landscape. For a while still we hunted bounty, but where was there to claim it? Soon Zebedee grew bored even with that. All we did was ride, along prairies where the wild Harlequinade ran—a sight I had hoped never to see, which made the blood run cold!—and down valleys where the remains of *máquinas de sueños* could still be found, giant metal structures with the sound of broken wind chimes, and they haunted our sleep.

'Zebedee was searching for something. That became clear eventually, but what it was he never told us. We searched ancient caves dug into the sides of snow-covered mountains. We hunted through brush and forest, in the wild places where the bears still dance. At last we came to a temperate valley below the snow line. Here the air was warm and scented with spring flowers, and there was a brook running through the meadow, where three gnarled and ancient trees cast deep black shadows.

'It was there that we found it, at last. Whatever *it* was. A piece of material, left over from some long forgotten battle of the Titanomachy, I thought then. I am not so sure, now. It was a large and curious object, a mechanical fish, like a carp, with golden scales. We had to tie ropes to it and it took four of the horses to drag it along. Zebedee was beside himself. It was then that we truly saw his shadow, and how far it covered the ground, even in the weak sun, and how it moved when the man was still. We were afraid, then, I think. But he was our chief, and besides, we were too far out: we didn't know how to get back.

'He led, and we followed. Dragging the thing along behind us. It was not alive but it wasn't *inert* either. Its mechanical gills moved and its tail thrashed the ground and its mouth opened and closed and it blinked its glass eyes. When the sun caught its scales it shone a golden colour, like summer. . .

'Through mountain passes that had no name, where not even the clowns dared to go. On and on we went. We lost two men to an avalanche, another we left dying when he fell off his horse in the ice. The horse we kept, the horses to drag the thing were more valuable than our lives at that point. Zebedee's shadow grew and grew until it engulfed the landscape, and it muttered and whispered in tongues we did not understand. We saw Zebedee for what he was, then: nothing but a glove puppet for the shadow to animate. We were afraid of him and did whatever he ordered, but his only command was ever to push ahead.

'Wherever we were going, we never got there,' the mechanic said. His soft watery eyes glanced down at his empty mug. The smell of chicory and liquorice was cloying in the still air and the Stranger felt his eyes threatening to gum together. He felt listless and tried to fight off the torpor. The Kid, beside him, looked similarly affected.

Lucas took a sip from his mug, seemingly oblivious to the fact it was empty.

'We never got there,' he repeated. 'We were riding out on the prairies when the first flashes of a storm appeared on the horizon. Crosses, mostly, followed by a shower of asterisms and interrobangs. Zebedee looked concerned at first, then decided to ride on into the storm. The sky looked bruised. There was mud underfoot and the horses struggled onwards, and the fish began to flap excitedly as though the storm had revitalised it in some way. The horses whinnied and tried to run and it was hell to control them. One of the men was hit by a kick to the head and fell instantly dead to the ground.

'At that moment we heard the oncoming battle. The ground shook as though a giant foot stomped on it far away, sending repercussions across the prairies, and the horses broke away and ran into the night. The storm caught us then in its entirety and swallowed us whole. I felt it happen, then, with the Colossi marching in the distance, as Zebedee's body shot up into the air, animated from below by its shadow...

'Flaming hieroglyphs touched my skin and I felt my abdomen meta-morphosing: there were vents in my chest and when I breathed the air came out hot and the vents flapped open. I ran. We all ran, the fish—the thing—forgotten in the mud. I saw the shadow race across the prairie holding the thing that had been Zebedee aloft. Then a giant stone foot came down from the sky and crashed it into the ground. It never came back up.

'I ran, through the storm and the flashing symbols, all through the night. I survived. I don't know about the others. At last I tripped over a rock and fell. When I woke it was daytime and there was no sign of the war or of the company and I was alone. After that I wandered the Escapement for a long time. Until, one day, I came here.'

He looked up at them then, kindly. 'You'll like it here,' he said. 'You'll see. Just give it time.'

'We're not *staying!*' the Kid yelled. He threw the mug against the wall and stomped to his feet. The mechanic looked at him with those same dull, kind eyes.

'Just give it time,' he said.

The Kid stormed out. The Stranger shrugged at the mechanic, but Lucas was no longer paying them any attention. He had got up and was happily polishing the pistons of an old broken engine.

The Stranger followed the Kid outside.

'We need to get out of here,' the Kid said. 'Where are the horses?'

The Stranger looked, but the horses were no longer where they'd been and, somehow, he wasn't surprised. The first stirrings of an answer were coming to him. He looked on the town with new eyes. This was a newly built and ramshackle place, but what did it stand on? He had the feeling of ageless time, suspended . . . the ticks of the clock were like the desperate knocks of a fly trapped in amber, beating against its prison.

The Stranger and the Kid returned to the train. It lay silent on the tracks. When the Stranger looked inside he saw no sign of the passengers, the dead or the wounded. The train rested on a single track, and the track terminated in that town. The Stranger said, 'Lucas was right, this isn't a main line.'

The track extended back the way they'd come. Somewhere there, there must have been a railroad switch, and they must have hit it on their way, and were sidetracked off the main line to Jericho and onto the spur. Now he looked but all he could see were the grey and featureless plains in all direction.

He said, 'We can't leave.'

The Kid said, 'Sure we can. We'll just follow the track.'

The Stranger shook his head. He knew it for what it was, then.

'It's a sort of snare,' he said.

'A what?'

'It's like a knot, but in the landscape. In the Escapement itself. Like a sort of maze.'

'What does that mean?'

'It means the way out isn't out *there*,' the Stranger said. 'It's in here.'

'I prefer just shooting things,' the Kid said, morosely.

'Cutting the knot, yes,' the Stranger said, and he smiled. But the truth was that he liked mazes, their mystery, the fact that they needed to be *solved*. But he saw the Kid wasn't interested. The Kid was fighting the malaise of the place but he was doing it badly.

The Kid said stubbornly, 'I'm going.' Ignoring the Stranger, he began to march back along the track, into the featureless plain. His spurs clicked in time with the trapped seconds hand of the clock, merging with them. He'd never make it, the Stranger knew. But he couldn't stop him. Instead, the Stranger headed to the clock tower.

The Kid walked for quite a while and for a time, the going was good. He kept having the sense that there was no *point* in going, that all he had to do was turn back and go into the waiting room and sit down and, well, *wait* and, sooner or later, there would be a train—there had to be one, right? But he didn't listen to the voice in his head and kept ploughing on, stubbornly. He was a very stubborn man.

The Kid was born in a town called Bozoburg, which sat on the bank of a small river on the Fratellini plains. It was a small, quietly prosperous town on the edge of the Thickening, some three days ride away from the nearest clown encampment of whitefaces, and a week by coach to the nearest train terminus. There was a bank and a general store, and a post office that opened once a week whether anyone needed to send a letter or not. The Kid—the kid—had known, in a vague kind of way, that many of the people in the town, all of whom he knew by name, would sometimes use substance, which was a pale sort of powder quarried far away, in places where the *máquinas de sueños* fell in ancient times. And sometimes they drank Sticks in one of the two saloons, and that then they would visit, or go back—the exact distinction was hazy to him—to that other place. What that other place was he wasn't entirely sure. Once a travelling entertainer came to the town. He brought with him a machine of sort, called a praxinoscope, and he'd set it up in the town hall and charged a ducat at a time, and though ducats didn't come easy to the kid nevertheless he had paid admission, to watch *Mercator's Magical Shadow Show!!* as it was billed.

He'd come in, clutching his ducat, and sat down with the rest of the townsfolk and the other children—they sat on the floor, while the adults sat in rough-hewn chairs—but in truth, when it came, it was a disappointment.

The adults oohed and aahed at the shadow play: impossibly tall buildings and vehicles that moved between them at jerky speed as Mercator the Magnificent, a small, whiskered man in a faded, once-dapper sequin jacket, rolled the crank. There were flying machines in the skies and all manners of improbable miracles, and there were no horses to be seen. The kid liked horses.

His mother didn't come with him to see the shadow show. She had a loathing for all and every manner of entertainer. So the kid went alone. Ultimately, he decided, whatever this other place was it was just that: a shadow on a screen. He was bored.

Mercator stayed around for a few days but then he left and took his praxinoscope with him. He had a little wagon and a single patient horse with eyes kinder than its owner's. The kid ran into him only once after the shadow show. Mercator was drunk and pissing against the side of the town hall when the kid passed by, after dusk. Mercator's shadow, like a grotesque extension of its owner, danced beside the man. For some reason the kid did not wish to step on or near it. He skipped around the dancing shadow and hurried away from there. For a moment the shadow felt almost alive.

The kid read whatever penny books or periodicals came through. His mother was not a voracious reader but she tolerated this habit. He rode horses and he played Hangman's Bluff and Juggler's Ball and Ghost in the Graveyard and, of course, they all played at clowns.

He was quite a happy little kid, for a while.

This all changed after the Rasmussen Gang rode into town.

But he did not want to think about that now. In fact, he realised, he did not want to think about much of anything. A pleasant lassitude of thought prevailed on him. The featureless grey plains seemed never to change and the track just led on and on and on into the distance.

At last he saw something just ahead. He made for it, with that same sort of languor, and soon he saw that it was a small town, really just a collection of several buildings where the track terminated. A train stood at the end of the track with many of its windows broken and heavy sustained damage to its sides, but how it came to that state, or what it was doing there, he had no idea. It was then that a man wearing a conductor's uniform came his way, and he looked at the Kid with some surprise. The man held an official-looking clipboard in his hands and he looked at the Kid and he looked at the clipboard and he ticked something off on the paper.

He said, 'You're late.'

'I am?' the Kid said.

'Come with me,' the conductor said. The Kid followed him meekly. *I must be very late*, he thought. There was a clock, somewhere nearby, and it kept ticking and ticking.

The conductor led him past the clock tower and into the plain beyond the town. As they walked he saw a group of passengers standing around in a dug-up patch of earth. He didn't know why he thought they were passengers. Perhaps it was that they seemed ill-suited for the purpose to which they were put. The men wore hats and suits and of the women, some wore dresses and some riding pants, but all of them held spades.

They were digging in the hard ground.

They dug without haste and with seeming indifference to the task they performed. Their spades rose and fell mechanically, dislodging earth, shifting it, then back again, until the spades encountered something in the ground and the diggers would stop, and frown, and lay down the spade, momentarily, in order to clear dirt from the object with their fingers. The Kid watched, and he saw that what they dug out, like turnips or yams, were timepieces.

They were clocks.

The clocks were half-melted, almost malleable, near two-dimensional in form. The diggers handled them with great reverence, brushing dirt from the clock face before throwing them without ceremony onto a growing pile of similar objects. It was only when they touched the objects that their countenance changed, however briefly, and they seemed more animated.

'Here,' the conductor said. He handed the Kid a spade. 'Dig.'

The Kid took the spade. It seemed natural to hold it. He joined the line and began to dig. It seemed to him he could hear something, on the edge of sound, a soft murmur underground, as though the things buried there were squirming around, shifting, trying to burrow deeper. As though they were, in a sense, alive.

As though, in a way, they were not clocks at all.

The Kid dug. When the spade hit an object he knelt down and with his fingers began to clear the dirt around the clock. When he touched it, excitement quickened in him. The material felt soft to the touch, pliable. The clock was like a disc of rubber in his hands. He felt it pulse against his fingertips, tiny ticks, like a heart.

Then he tossed it on the pile and the sensation fled: of being awake, of being alive. He returned to digging, there on the grey and featureless plain, digging in time to the beats of the big clock.

The Stranger meanwhile had the sense that you couldn't shoot your way out of this one. He needed another story and he went to find it. He stood under the clock tower, where time was held captive, the seconds hand fluttering forever in its place, trapped against the minutes. He saw no one around. At last the doors to the factory opened, as he suspected they would, and a small and unimposing figure strolled out. It was a very short and very fat man wrapped warmly in coats and scarves, and with little black tinted sunglasses over his eyes. His hands were gloved and yet he rubbed them together as though he were very cold. He stopped when he saw the Stranger and looked at him with his head tilted sideways, as though unsure of what the meaning of this new apparition in his town meant.

He said, 'Welcome, stranger.'

The Stranger hesitated before replying, and the man did not press him. Indeed, it felt as though the man had time—all the time in the world. An air of amused contentedness emanated from him. An air of cheerful goodwill.

At last, the Stranger said, 'May I ask your name?'

'My *name*?' The man's podgy, gloved fingers opened and closed in a small and helpless gesture. 'It has been so longer, stranger, since anyone enquired...To tell you the truth, I am not sure I would even know it now, myself.'

'Was it Zavatta, or Zapata?' the Stranger asked.

'It might have been, it might have been,' the man allowed. He frowned. 'It seems to me that I had many names, stranger, in my years on the Escapement. But you know as well as most—don't you?—that names are not to be taken lightly. Not here.'

'That is true,' the Stranger allowed, and the man smiled a thin-lipped smile.

'You can call me Zebulon,' he said. He offered the name tentatively.

The Stranger said, 'I know who you are.'

'I ... see.'

'One does not often meet one of the Major Arcana,' the Stranger said.

The man dipped his head in acknowledgement, but refrained from speaking.

'Tell me,' the Stranger said. 'What happened in this place?'

The man shrugged. 'It was so long ago ... ' he said.

'But you remember?'

'If I try hard enough. Perhaps. Yes. There was a battle, I think. Yes, that sounds right. A battle of some sort.' The man spun in place. He seemed suddenly agitated. 'You would not tell so, now. It happened long before the Thickening, long before woman or man set foot upon this place. *We* were not here, then, or perhaps we were, in a sense, but only in potentia. The land, too, did not look quite as you see it now, for "land" and "see" were not fully formed concepts then. There was only the war.

'It is a battle not recorded anywhere but in the grooves it's made in the Escapement. Shadow battles stone; the lizard scuttles from the glare of the sun. There was a battle here, I think. It created a knot in the land.

'Time passed; elsewhere. The warring factions moved on. Only their discarded material remained, burrowed deep underground. People came and they settled and they built railway tracks and they spread out across the Thickening, but they skirted this place. There was nothing here.

'Then, one day, I came.

'I was very tired then, I think. I have been traversing the Escapement for a long time. I have been other people, yes. Those names you mentioned. I was searching for something. Something that seemed important at the time, but probably wasn't.

'Then, at last I came here, on my travels. And I *felt* it, then, under the ground. A huge silence, waiting. All that untapped *time*.' He removed his glasses and polished the lens with his gloved trigger finger. His eyes, the Stranger saw, were the same tinted black as the glasses. Zebulon peered at the Stranger.

'Um,' he said, 'would you like to see them?'

*T*ick, tick, tick, tick, ti
...ck.

The wide doors opened wide, on hidden springs, in silence...

Behind them, the dark.

'Come in, come in,' the Hierophant said.

The clocks lined up every available surface. It was not a factory at all, the Stranger saw, but a *warehouse*: the clocks were piled up from floor to ceiling, while only in the middle was there a long work bench on which individual pieces resided, where other inmates of Lugar de Espera worked with gloved hands, cleaning them. There was no sound in that room but for the distant, trapped ticks of the big clock. But there was a sort of expectant silence, as of too much time all kept in one too-small a place, the sound of a coiled spring needing desperately to be sprung. There were hundreds, thousands of the things. They made the Stranger think of termite eggs. The Hierophant rubbed his gloved hands together. 'So you see,' he said. 'There really is no way out, stranger.'

The mechanic, Lucas, and the kiosk woman, Mrs Lazarus, joined him then. They had a vague blank look in their eyes. Lucas held a wrench and Mrs Lazarus a large metal ladle. They hovered on either side of the Hierophant. The Stranger took a step back, and Zebulon and his minions took one step forward.

'What's your rush?' Zebulon said, and he smiled a little sadly. 'We have time, stranger. All the time in the world.'

The Stranger backed away from them and they followed. He pushed against the doors and they opened. He noticed the quality of light outside never changed. It was never night or high noon in that town, but an endless suffusion of grey.

'Ah, I see they're coming,' the Hierophant said.

The Stranger turned. And he saw that the man was right. From out beyond the town there came, trudging towards them, a group of passengers, and he thought he recognised amidst their number one of the cooks from the train. And also, quite recognisable among them, was the Kid.

They came slowly and unhurried across the plain and they brought their cargo with them.

'Please,' Zevulon said. 'Wait.'

'Wait,' the other two said in unison. 'Wait. Wait. Wait.'

The Stranger drew his guns. The Hierophant opened and closed his fat little fingers.

'What are you going to do,' he said. It was not exactly a question.

The Stranger turned again as the group of workers came nearer. He tried to cover both sides with his guns, arms spread, but he knew it was futile. He saw the Kid in amongst the workers. The Kid had the same dull look in his eyes as the others. The look of a person trapped forever in a passenger lounge, waiting for a train that would never come.

He shouted, 'Kid!'

The Kid turned his head and looked at him. He carried a big grey cloth sack like the others. More of the eggs must have been inside. The Hierophant said, gently, 'There is so much coiled time inside of you, stranger. You alone are not yet affected. I can give you what it is you need. I can give you *time*.'

He moved his fat fingers in a complicated gesture. The Stranger felt the tingle of substance in his nostrils. The town faded, and for a moment he was standing once more in a clinically white room, where a large machine burped and hummed, two tiny legs sticking out from its cylinder. The boy was very brave to endure the procedure. What must he be thinking, trapped inside the scanner, seeing nothing but white walls?

Then it was gone. The Stranger shook his head. 'No,' he said, 'No, it's not enough.'

'You seek a cure,' the Hierophant said. 'But time is running out. I can give you that much. I can offer you the time to wait.'

But the Stranger could not abide waiting. He could not abide the smell of hospitals and the shuffle of slow feet, the awful sense of time dripping away. He could not stand being helpless. He turned his gun and he fired, but not at the Hierophant.

He shot the Kid.

The shot merely grazed the Kid's arm. It ripped through the sleeve and left an angry red wield on the skin, drawing blood. The Kid yelled and dropped the sack he was carrying. Animation returned to his eyes with the pain. At his feet, the sack opened. The clocks within shuddered and undulated as they tried to crawl away across the ground. The Kid looked wildly this way and that. The other workers turned as one and faced him. They took one step forward, and then another.

'Run, Kid!' the Stranger said. But the Kid didn't need advice.

They chased him. They moved like automatons but they gathered speed. They seemed to the Stranger like a flock of dirty-grey seagulls. The Kid ran and the passengers followed. Bowler hats blew in the wind. The Hierophant, Zebulon, merely watched. The Kid ran until he was at the base of the clock tower, and when he saw they were almost upon him, he began to climb.

The Hierophant looked at the Stranger and made that helpless little gesture with his fingers again. 'I built this place,' he said. 'To find that which was buried. I waited, and they came, those who were lost, those who had nothing left but the waiting. And you would take this from them?'

The Stranger did not reply. The Kid was climbing faster now. The clock tower seemed to elongate into the sky, as though its dimensions were not quite right, and it reached higher and higher into the grey heavens. A wind howled from nowhere, snatching at the Kid, bellowing at his hair and clothes. Down below, the passengers attempted a climb but continued to fall down as others took their place. The Hierophant removed his gloves, first one, and then the other. His fingers where very white. They seemed like worms. He advanced on the Stranger.

'I *will* shoot,' the Stranger said. He took a step back.

The Hierophant's mouth opened in a rictus of a smile, tiny white teeth edged almost in a perfect circle.

'If you have to shoot, shoot,' he said.

He took another step. The Stranger took another step back. Overhead the Kid was climbing ever more desperately. When he reached for the next level his fingers grasped for purchase and for a moment it seemed he would fall. He flailed helplessly for balance.

The Stranger pulled the trigger.

The gun clicked with a dry sound like an apologetic cough. No bullet emerged. The Hierophant made that gesture with his fingers. Without the gloves on it looked like worms wriggling on the end of a hook. He took another step, and then another.

'. . . waiting.'

No one was chasing the Kid now. He was almost at the top when he looked down. He must have realised there was nowhere to run. His foot slipped and pebbles of crumbly stone fell down to the ground. He shouted, and just when it seemed he would fall he took one last, desperate jump, and caught hold of the minute hand of the clock.

He hung there, suspended from the big clock above the town.

*T*ick, tick, tick, tick, ti—

They were on the Stranger now, the passengers holding him helpless as the Hierophant bore down on him, and the man's fingers pressed against the Stranger's throat as the Stranger's useless gun pressed into the Hierophant's belly...

That useless bullet, trapped inside.

The wormy fingers moving on the Stranger's throat, pressing painfully on his windpipe, choking the air out of him. In the black-tinted sunglasses, nothing but a distorted image of the Stranger's face.

The Kid, hanging from the minute hand of the clock, the wind lashing savagely at his face. He cried, 'Help me!'

The Hierophant's grimace of savage satisfaction. It would be the last thing the Stranger would ever see.

The Kid's feet, dangling, high in the air.

A gust of wind blew in from the plains. It snatched a bowler hat off one of the passengers and tossed it skyward. It stirred the grey-brown dust and it tousled Mrs Lazarus' hair. Overhead, the seconds hand battled against the stuck minute hand. *Tick, tick, tick, tick, ti—*

ck.

The Stranger was choking. The Escapement came and went around him, fading in waves. He saw that other place and that other man who was there. A machine hummed in a white room. The patient table slid out, slowly, the boy emerging feet first. A doctor said, We'll have to run more sca—

Tick. Tick. Tick. Tick. Ti—

Something had to give. Ancient gears solidified by disuse with rust and dirt, jammed against each other, struggled now under this newfound strain, the drop of weight exerting pressure on the mechanism. Something had to give. The clockwork creaked—

Down below, the Hierophant's hands slackened on the Stranger's throat.

The trapped bullet travelled an inch down the barrel of the gun, and stopped.

The Kid's fingers, raw and bloodied, held on but he felt them slipping, slipping...

He felt the seconds hand flutter against the jammed mechanism like a bird trying to escape.

Tick.

Tick.

T...i...c...k—

'No,' the Hierophant said. 'No, this cannot be allowed—'

Inside the warehouse the molten clocks whispered and wriggled, shuddering against each other.

And with a hideous screech of gears the big clock broke. The minute hand gave against the Kid's pull and it plunged downwards, so that he was tossed and turned in the high wind.

The Hierophant's hands lost their grip on the Stranger's neck.

The bullet, suspended with all that deferred time, was suddenly free. Kinetic motion propelled it onwards. It slid down the tube and emerged directly into the Hierophant's soft belly. The Hierophant said, 'Oof!' and staggered back. His hands held in his belly. A viscous pink liquid seeped in between his fingers. His sunglasses fell underfoot. His eyes stared blindly at the Stranger. The pupils were red like a clown's nose. The iris was a dirty pink, the colour of soapsuds near a drain.

Inside the warehouse, the clocks shook and shuddered, their time finally coming.

Tock.

He pushed the Hierophant off of himself. The shell of the man was dying, and the grey clouds parted and sunlight fell down. With it came shadow, and the man's shadow leaked out of the shell of the man. It trickled out of him until it became a vast pool of darkness, and then it fled. The body—of the man who had called himself Zapata, or Zavatta, those and all the other names—fell to the ground. The Stranger pushed himself upright. Overhead the hands of the clock spun and spun, free from the rule of their escapement. The Kid dropped through the air. The passengers stood there, blinking stupidly, as though they had just woken up from a long and pleasant dream.

'Oof!' the Stranger said, in unconscious imitation of the Hierophant, as he caught the Kid in his descent and broke his fall. They ended up in an undignified pile on the ground, and it was from that position, lying on his back, staring upwards, that the Stranger saw the clocks at last take flight.

They broke out of the roof of the old warehouse, flapping against the currents of wind, and their dials moved and were transformed into talons, their escapements opened and became dark wings. Their mainsprings opened into beaks. In silence they streamed into the sky, a dark cloud of clocks turned into birds—ravens, or crows, or perhaps they were storm petrels. The Stranger didn't know. They rose into the sky in a swarm, forming a shape that could have been an hourglass before it broke, reformed and changed.

The birds, newly hatched, flew against the sky and fled away from the town.

'That *hurt*,' the Kid complained.

'You're telling me,' the Stranger said, rubbing his side. 'You're heavier than you look, kid.'

They left the townsfolk where they were. Some, the Stranger saw, had simply gone back inside the waiting room. Others stood, uncertain, under the open skies. They might still be there tomorrow, or the next day, or the next day after that. The Stranger didn't know.

They found their horses ambling near the broken-down train. The horses whinnied greeting. They seemed unconcerned with all that had transpired.

'I hate waiting,' the Kid said.

The Stranger nodded. He climbed on his horse and the Kid followed suit on his.

'I think we'll just avoid the railways for a while,' the Stranger said.

'Seems sensible to me,' the Kid said.

They rode out of town, following the setting sun. And if he listened very hard, the Stranger thought he could just hear something, faint, on the edge of sound...

The things still buried deep underground, burrowing, murmuring...

Tick. Tick. Tick. Tick—

Tock.

ON THE HILLSIDE

ROBERT EDRIC

Following this great calamitie of which we bore no true understanding we came to a steep hill, and upon climbing this to its highest point were our fearful talk and our terrors diminished.

—Letter from John Cotton Jr. to Increase Mather, March 21, 1677

I

'SMELL THAT?' IRVINE SAID.

Wilson moved closer to the older man, reluctant to leave the cover of the trees and to come out onto the open hillside. He looked down the steep slope, steadying himself against its sudden drop into the cloud below.

Beside him, Irvine pointed.

Wilson breathed deeply in the chill air. 'Smoke?' he said.

'I don't know what else it would be,' Irvine said. He shielded his eyes and continued searching the hazy distance far below them. 'I first smelled it yesterday,' he said. 'I thought at first that I was imagining it.'

'Do you think something's burning down there?' Wilson said, a nervous catch in his voice.

'Where there's smoke . . .' Irvine said.

'What can there be *left* to burn?' Wilson said.

'Oh, I doubt we'd ever run out of that.'

The slope below seemed endless to Irvine, the valley bottom out of which it rose lost as completely to him now as it had been lost to him during his ascent all those years ago. Lost to them *all* as they had climbed.

'Can you see anything?' Wilson said.

'Not really,' Irvine said. 'Just the usual.'

'Perhaps it drifted from a long way off,' Wilson said, a further fearful note in his voice.

'Perhaps it did,' Irvine said, but with little conviction.

'Are you going to tell the others?' Wilson said.

'And scare them like I'm scaring you, you mean?'

'I suppose so.'

'Probably not. What would it gain? Besides, people have got enough to worry about without me stirring things up for them.'

Wilson moved closer to the older man. 'That's not how they'd see it,' he said. 'They look up to you, they listen.'

'Once, perhaps,' Irvine said. But not now, not after all those years, not really. 'How old are you?'

'Twenty?' Wilson said. 'Twenty-one?' He turned away from Irvine as he said it.

'Sorry,' Irvine said. 'You came up here alone. I should have remembered. See what I mean about people being better off by *not* listening to me?' He patted the boy on the shoulder.

Wilson tried to laugh. He loved the old man. He was father, grandfather, and every other lost and forgotten uncle he might once have had.

'What would *your* advice be?' Irvine said.

Wilson looked back down the slope. 'If there *was* something to see . . .' he said, 'it'd be something more . . . more . . .'

'More definite?'

Wilson nodded.

'We could come back at night,' Irvine suggested. 'Try and see if there's any brightness down there, flames.'

Wilson took a step back at the suggestion and all it implied. 'Or you might just as easily wait and come back tomorrow and there would no longer be anything there,' he said.

'Or that,' Irvine conceded. It was how they had all come to live their lives high on that hill. Cover your eyes, cover your ears, turn your back. 'To tell you the truth, I told myself that if I did come back today and the smell had gone, then I'd say nothing whatsoever to anyone and then try and convince myself that I *had* imagined it.'

'I don't know what you want me to say,' Wilson said, confused now by Irvine's admission.

'I just wanted you to know,' Irvine told him. 'That's all.'

'And now I've disappointed you,' Wilson said. 'You think me a coward.'

Irvine shook his head. 'You hardly know the meaning of the word, not after the life you've had. I was down there for over forty years, remember. You had a few years as a baby, a small child.'

'And you think that makes a difference?' Wilson said. He came closer to the older man. He enjoyed his company, his conversation, his confidences. 'Did it bring anything in particular to mind?' he said. 'The smoke.'

Irvine nodded absently. 'I thought at first that it was wood smoke. Fruitwood—apple, say, or cherry. A winter's night, frost, a clear sky.' He closed his eyes as he said all this. 'But then I realized I was only deluding myself. Besides—' He stopped abruptly.

Wilson waited, wondering at Irvine's reluctance to go on.

On several of the distant hillsides, the same steep cones above the same calm ocean of cloud, the falling sun caught the silver blades and discs of the few remaining masts and heliographed another of its unexpected, empty messages to them.

━━━⟨∞⟩━━━

Three days passed. Each morning, Irvine went back to the same tree—a towering, long-dead pine—and made his notch. Old leap years discounted, days rounded off, made almost five thousand scratches on the pale wood: sorted first into sevens, then into thirties, then into blocks of twelve, and then further into a single block of ten. A new bark almost in the old trunk.

On that third morning, he was approached by Amery Stark, a man twenty years older than himself and another surrogate father to all the younger men and women who had followed up the hillside.

Stark walked with a stick. He sat on one of the already-fallen trunks and watched Irvine go to the tree. He stayed silent while Irvine carved his notch, and only when this was done, this ritual observed, did he tap his staff against the ground to announce his presence.

'Amery,' Irvine said without turning. It was another of a thousand such encounters. Days ran like this. Days, weeks, months.

'Still the pointless calendar?' Stark said, doing nothing to hide his amusement.

'And still the question,' Irvine said back, finally turning to face the old man.

'What you counting off towards? What ending do you imagine there is to all of this? You still hopeful of something dramatic coming our way?' He cupped his ear. 'Is that a bugle I hear?'

'I just like to know, that's all,' Irvine said, smiling. 'To measure.' Instinct, he supposed, impulse, something.

'It's what men in dark prison cells and dungeons used to do in films,' Amery Stark said. 'But at least *they* had a release date to look forward to. Liberty, their waiting families, walking out among their fellow citizens, green fields, fresh air, feeling the sun on their brows again, closing their eyes and turning their pale faces into a gentle breeze after all those days and years in the damp and the dark.'

'You told me the same thing a hundred times already,' Irvine said, folding his precious knife and going to sit beside the old man.

Neither of them spoke for a moment. Amery Stark had come up the hill with a wife and two daughters, all three of them lost to him soon afterwards.

The clatter of sliding stones distracted them for a moment, and then, waiting until the noise had ended, Stark said, 'You smelled it too.'

Irvine nodded. 'We lived with the smell, or something similar, for almost a year afterwards.'

'Until everything finished burning,' Stark said.

'Or until everything was dead and finished and things started anew down there.' Irvine turned to face the old man.

Stark shook his head. 'If that's what you truly believe, then you'd have made your way back down the hill a long time ago.'

'A few did,' Irvine said, knowing it was no argument.

'And we never saw them again. You'd think at least *one* of them could have climbed back up here and told us everything was finished and that it was safe to go home. Now why do you suppose that was?'

Irvine shook his head. It was another old argument softened and frayed at the edges, crumbling with time and affection and understanding.

'Same way the dead don't come back from whatever sunlit afterlife *they*'ve attained and tell us all what a land of milk and honey it is, and why don't we all just hurry right along to join them?' Stark said.

Irvine pulled at the dry bark of the tree upon which he sat.

'Getting colder,' Stark said, breathing deeply.

And the darkness of the rising night coming sooner and sooner over the sharp ridges of the surrounding peaks, pools of black topping and then flowing down the high slopes.

In the beginning, there had been a hundred reasons for the fires, a hundred different fuels to keep them burning. But then the sediment of wet and cold and dust had come and nothing had gone on burning forever in that world.

Irvine considered all this in a kind of reverie.

'You think we sit up here and just wait for whatever it is that might one day come towards us for no good reason?' Amery Stark said.

Irvine shrugged. He picked up a stone, rolled it in his palm, and then let it drop back to the ground. 'I stopped looking for reasons a long time ago,' he said. 'As far as I'm concerned now, we're just keeping ourselves alive up here.'

'And you don't think that's reason enough to be here? To go on doing what we're doing?'

'Once, perhaps,' Irvine said.

'I see.'

'Today's Sunday,' Irvine said. 'Or at least by my own unreliable reckoning it is. There are, what, a hundred of us left, and I imagine I'm the only one of that hundred who knows what day it is.'

'So what?' Stark said. 'You'll be telling me next you want to build a church.'

Both men laughed at the suggestion and the small tension between them was released.

'Some people would tell you that you're wise beyond your years, old man,' Irvine said.

'But not you,' Stark said, his own laughter subsiding. 'Besides, I lost count of those years. I was already sixty-seven when I came up here.'

'Then I can tell you exactly how old you are, give or take a few weeks—a month, perhaps.' Irvine guessed that he had just defeated his own argument in keeping the calendar.

'I'd rather you didn't,' Stark said. 'I felt old enough then. I feel dead, buried, and dug up ten times over now.'

A further silence followed.

'How long was the smell there?' Stark said after a while.

'Three days running.'

'And afterwards?'

Irvine shook his head. 'Nothing.'

'You sound disappointed, like you *wanted* it to be something.'

'Perhaps because I'm no longer as happy as the rest of them to just sit and wait in blissful ignorance.'

'"Blissful ignorance",' Stark repeated. 'They're frightened, that's all. They don't know what's down there. I doubt it amounts to the same thing.' He looked hard at Irvine. 'Were you planning to do anything about it?'

Irvine's silence betrayed his answer.

'You know I brought maps up with me,' Stark said. 'Some of them might still bear a passing resemblance to whatever's down there. But, to my mind, burn a place, flood it a hundred feet deep—you might as well turn a picture to the wall and say it was still the same thing.'

'Thank God you've only got a year or two left in you,' Irvine said. 'I don't know how much more of this kind of wisdom I can stand.'

'At least you know where to bury me,' Stark said, laughing again.

Irvine knew exactly where. 'I do,' he said.

'I measured it to the inch,' Stark said. Graves beside graves beside graves.

'I know you did.' Irvine kicked the pale earth at his feet and watched the fine dust rise and then fall over his toes.

A further day passed. He waited again at the edge of the trees. His days were now unsettled. He felt challenged, but could not say for certain by what. By himself, he supposed, by his own expectations.

Wilson came to him, followed by several other young men, mostly the same age.

'What made you change your mind?' Irvine said to him.

The remark surprised Wilson. 'What makes you think that?'

Irvine turned and raised a hand to the watching men. 'These others,' he said. 'You're going down the hill, to investigate.'

Wilson beckoned the others forward. 'We talked about it,' he said. 'That's all.'

'I can imagine.' Irvine knew all the young men and he acknowledged them individually. 'And if I were your age, it's what I'd be doing.'

'You could come with us,' another of the youths said. 'Useful to have someone who knows what's *supposed* to be down there.'

'Perhaps, but whatever I might remember of the place, it won't be anything like that now.'

'It could be. How do you know? It might be *exactly* as you remember it. Things might have returned to the way they once were. For all we know, everything might have been rebuilt, made good again.'

'It might,' Irvine said. He looked around at the others and saw the same faltering hope in their faces. A few of them nodded at him, wanting to hear more. 'I hope you find what you're looking for,' he said, knowing that none of them knew what that was.

'I had four sisters,' one of the boys said angrily, accusingly. 'Suppose they're all still alive down there. Suppose they all still remember me and wonder where I am, if I lived. Suppose they spent months looking for me and then imagined me dead; just as I did them for so long.'

'You're all setting your sights too high,' Irvine said. It was a new kind of hopefulness, a rising cry among the younger of them, a denial of the known, babies wiser than their fathers with a wisdom fed on nothing more nourishing than ignorance and need.

There hadn't been a birth since the second year of their arrival.

'You're missing something you never had,' Irvine said absently, immediately wishing he hadn't.

'And *you*'re denying us the chance to find out what we might *yet* have,' another of the youths shouted back at him.

Irvine remembered the same argument from years ago. Even before the hillside, he remembered the argument.

II

The first he knew of Elizabeth's arrival was when she woke him with an arm around his shoulders and a kiss on his cheek.

'I'm dreaming,' he said, slowly opening his eyes.

'Are you still waiting for them to come back?' Another kiss.

He nodded once.

'They'll either return or not return, regardless of your vigil. Why do you feel yourself responsible for them?'

'Who said I felt—?'

'Nothing you might have said or done would have made them change their minds,' she said. 'They're young men. It's what young men do.' She tightened her grip on him and pulled him closer to her.

They had been together for seven years. Neither Irvine's wife nor Elizabeth's husband had come up the hillside. 'We're burnished in grief,' she had once told him. But it was more than that. She had been a surgeon specialising in spinal injury. Now she lived in a dead forest like a character in a fairy tale; now she made her own shoes out of bark and wood, her own soap out of ash, and her own clothes from the clothes of others who had at first survived and then afterwards died.

'I keep imagining what they might be finding down there,' Irvine said. 'And then I try to understand what it is about all those possibilities that scares *me* so much.'

'It's not just you,' Elizabeth told him. 'We could any of us go down the hillside at any time. Perhaps they'll come back with good news. Perhaps then we'll feel able to follow them and be able to put our own fears to rest.'

Irvine put a hand into hers and felt her fingers slip between his. They felt thin and fragile among his own. Her arm barely rested across his back.

'How's your leg?' he said. She'd fallen several days ago and had been limping ever since.

'Nothing heals as fast as it once did,' she said.

'Or should?'

'Or that.' She turned away from him as she spoke.

Every time they made love in the shelter they shared, she ended up crying uncontrollably afterwards, often waiting until Irvine had left her and gone outside. It had become an understanding, a consideration between them. Outside, his back to her, Irvine too had occasionally cried. He wondered at the cause of this, knowing only that it was unlikely they were mourning the same thing.

'Someone should have gone with them,' he said eventually.

'You, you mean? The voice of reason?'

In addition to her husband of twenty-four years, she'd lost two grown sons, two daughters-in-law and one grandchild. Sons the same age as the youths who had now gone back down the hillside.

'I'd have been terrified to turn every corner,' Irvine said.

'I doubt it.'

Irvine raised the hand he held. 'You're not wearing your rings,' he said.

'They started falling off,' she told him, pulling her hand from his and pushing it beneath her arm. 'I put them somewhere for safekeeping. Besides . . .' she said.

'You remember your coming up here?' Irvine asked Amery Stark, the words more of a prompt than a question.

Both men sat again at the edge of the trees looking down the slope.

Eight days had passed since the young men had gone.

'I remember trying to believe that we were all going to build a new life for ourselves up here,' Stark said. He spoke hesitantly, unsure of himself, of what he might have been saying.

Irvine considered this, but said nothing. 'It seemed to be a plan. At the time. A way forward,' he said eventually.

'Plan?' Stark said sourly. 'It was never that. We were all just fooling ourselves, that's all. Everything had ended, everything. We had nothing left. We just needed something to hope for, that's all. What were we ever really going to achieve all the way up here? What strength did *any* of us have during those first few months? None that I remember. It took us all our time and energy just to live up here, just to survive. Besides, what would any kind of resolution have been to us then? I even heard talk of a stockade. A *stockade*, for Christ's sake—imagine that—built of the fallen trees. It turned out even *that* was beyond us. Beyond us then and beyond us ever since. We could most of us barely dig a hole in the ground to shelter in.'

'I dug two,' Irvine said.

Amery Stark laughed. 'To attract a mate?'

'Something like that.'

'Keep working on the bait,' Stark said.

An epidemic of something had killed half the women and children during that first winter, and the holes in the ground had become their graves. A succession of aftershocks had shaken all the loose scree and boulders further down the hillside. Dead trees fell in their thousands; growing trees stopped growing.

There had been no further smell of smoke since the youths had gone.

'You come out here every day,' Stark said. 'Are you waiting for more than their return?'

Irvine didn't properly understand him. 'I don't know,' he said. 'I just feel the need to be here, that's all.'

'Is that why you light a fire at night—as a beacon?'

Irvine shrugged. 'I still expect to see fires, something, down there each night. I remember that first year.'

'Now that *was* smoke,' Stark said. 'I used to burn my fields to rid them of stubble, herding the fires across the flatness, a long line of us, the whole family, neighbours too. I'd know *that* smoke if I ever smelled it again. All we got in that first year up here was chemical smoke, rubber, plastics, all that junk.'

'Among other things,' Irvine said absently.

'Among other things.'

Neither man spoke for a moment. Unseen behind them, somewhere high on the hillside, another tree fell, its desiccated trunk and limbs shattering and crumbling as it dropped. Neither man turned to look or to comment on this.

'It's a wonder we stayed this long,' Irvine said.

'We stayed because there was no alternative,' Stark said. 'And because of all the guesses we were forever making about whatever might still have been happening down there.'

Their numbers had doubled in that first month. After that, a few stragglers had arrived. After a year, there was no one new. Men had climbed the tallest trees to examine the surrounding peaks, forever imagining all those other searching men clinging to identical trunks and looking back at them.

Others had gone from the hillside, from among them, never to be seen again. On one occasion, the only family—a man, his wife and their child—had packed their few possessions and gone in the middle of a summer's night without telling anyone they were leaving. It had been their greatest loss.

Amery Stark shielded his eyes to look down the slope. 'They're young men,' he said. 'They make different calculations. Just as you do at your age and I at mine. They ask questions, whereas all we do is fool ourselves into believing we already know all the answers.'

'They're looking for things we've already found, you mean? Things *we*'ve already had?'

Stark shrugged. 'Most of them were only small children when they came up here. Would *you* want to believe this was all there was for you for the next fifty years?'

'My great-grandfather lived to a hundred and two,' Irvine said.

Stark was about to respond to this when he half-turned and looked along the slope beyond Irvine.

Irvine turned and saw a man come out of the trees and stand looking down the hillside.

'It's Preston,' Stark said. 'His boy's among them.'

'His actual son?'

'As good as.'

The distant figure turned to consider them. Irvine raised a hand to the man but received no response.

'He tried to stop him,' Stark said. 'They fought. It left a bad taste. He told me last night that he should have gone with the boy, but that he was too afraid. He made the boy promise to return after ten days.'

'Does he think it'll happen?'

'Who knows? Either way, it was always going to be a long ten days.'

Seven of which had already passed.

Along the slope, Preston searched a moment longer and then turned back into the trees and was lost to sight.

Irvine sat beside Elizabeth.

'I was remembering the birds,' she said. She closed her eyes and raised her face so that the weak sun lay across her forehead and cheeks. It held little true warmth this late in the year, but the illusion was intact in its faint glow across her flesh and in the crescent of shadow at either side of her mouth. She licked her lips as though tasting the warmth.

'Amery says it's getting colder every year,' Irvine said softly.

She wasn't listening to him. 'Great flocks of them flying along the valley bottom.' She swung her flat palm along the course of the lost birds. 'Long, wavering ribbons of the things, above the cloud and in it, all of them going off somewhere, never to return.'

'If we'd known they were going for good...' Irvine said.

'How could we? How could we have known any of it? As far as we were concerned, everything was going to be quickly over and done with, and then we were all going to go back down there to take up precisely where we'd left off. We might have lost some of what we'd once had, but essentially, all this was ever meant to be'—she gestured at the trees behind them—'was some kind of dramatic interruption to those well-planned and anticipated lives we were living.' She was remembering her own lost family again and Irvine understood that.

'Stark says he's starting to forget things,' he said. 'Names, mostly; people, places. I asked him if it bothered him, but he said why should it? He said he was never going to go back to those places or see those people again, so what was the point in remembering them?' Whatever his intention by the remark, he saw that she was as unconvinced as he had been by the old man's excuse.

'He once told me that his own mother lost her mind and was committed to a home run by nuns,' Elizabeth said. 'He said she was perfectly happy there. He said she sat on a simple wooden chair on a porch and gazed out at the garden and the farmland beyond. He visited her every day with his sisters, her daughters. He said that she no longer recognized any of her own children but that she was always pleased to see them come to her as strangers.' She finally opened her eyes and looked at him. 'What have you come to tell me?' she said.

He felt himself tense at the remark.

'You want to go down after them,' she said.

Still he was unable to answer her.

'You want to go back down there and see for yourself what *they* may already have discovered,' she said. She laid a hand on his arm.

Irvine drew lines in the dust between his feet.

'And you're here to ask me,' Elizabeth went on, 'if I might consider going with you.'

He waited. He felt the beating of his heart in his chest, the thick rush of blood in his temples. When he was brave enough to look back at her, she was again sitting with her eyes closed, her face tilted to the sun.

'I wonder if all those birds found somewhere safe to settle,' he said. He imagined thousands, tens of thousands of the creatures, millions perhaps, floating peacefully on the calm waters of a distant lake, surrounded by that same lush farmland Amery Stark's mother had looked out over, the water beneath them a broth of life. And if he concentrated hard enough, he could even hear the calling of all those birds—geese and ducks, mostly, he imagined, but with plenty of other species scattered among them in the haven of their new home.

'You heard it too?' Preston said.

Irvine cupped a hand to his ear. It was dark, the middle of the night. Constellations filled the cloudless sky above them. A small white moon sat on the distant horizon.

'What was it?'

'It sounded like shouting,' Irvine said.

'Voices,' Elizabeth added.

'So you think it was them?' Preston said. He searched the darkness below.

A further sudden noise caused all three of them to turn and watch as Amery Stark came slowly out of the trees to join them at the edge of the slope.

'I couldn't sleep,' he said. 'Someone said there were voices. What voices?' He turned to Irvine. 'Was it you, whoever you are? You and the woman here?'

Irvine tensed at the remark. 'You know me,' he said.

'No, I don't,' Stark said, a hand to his brow.

Irvine wanted to reach out to the old man and hold him where he stood. 'I'm Irvine.' he said.

'Of course you are. I'm half-asleep. Pay me no mind.'

Elizabeth put her arm around Stark's shoulders. 'There was a noise,' she told him. 'That's all. From down there. We came to see.'

'What kind of noise?' Stark said. 'There was a time when there was nothing *but* noise.'

'That was in the beginning,' Irvine said. He wanted to tell them all to stop talking.

'What beginning?' Stark asked Elizabeth. 'What's he talking about?'

Elizabeth put a finger to the old man's lips to stop him talking. He considered her hand on his face and seemed to take some comfort from this. He grew less agitated in her embrace.

'I'm going to call down,' Irvine said. 'What do you think?'

No one answered him.

Irvine cupped his hands to his mouth and shouted at the top of his voice. '*Hello,*' he shouted, and then, '*We're here.*'

'What's he shouting that for?' Stark asked Elizabeth.

'We think the young men might finally be coming back up the hillside,' she told him.

'What young men?'

She put her full hand over his lips and caressed his cheek with her thumb.

There was still no sound.

'Perhaps it was just another rock fall,' Preston said.

'It was someone shouting,' Irvine said quietly.

'Or perhaps you fell asleep and dreamed it,' Preston said.

'Perhaps I did,' Irvine said. He shouted again, and again only a vague and formless echo came back to them from the distant slopes.

And still no one answered him.

The young men had been gone for twelve days.

'They're not so long overdue,' Preston said. 'Or perhaps they lost track of the days.'

'Night's still night,' Irvine said.

'*Now* what's he talking about?' Stark said, his words muffled by Elizabeth's hand.

'We're concerned, that's all,' she told him. 'For the young men.'

'Why?' Stark said. 'Where did they go?'

III

The slope above them was finally lost in the cloud which rose over their heads. They stopped at the edge of this and considered everything invisible beneath them.

'Is there any path?' Elizabeth asked him. She searched the ground ahead of them.

'I doubt it. Perhaps further down. Perhaps if others have kept it open.' He turned his head from side to side, listening for whatever might rise from below.

It had taken them all day from an early start to come this far down the hillside.

'Is it natural, do you think?' Elizabeth waved her hand through the wet vapour.

'I imagine so.'

It was clear to both of them that the cloud thinned slightly the further they walked down through it. Neither of them knew how far ahead of them the valley bottom lay. There were no signs, no markers, nothing to measure their slow and uncertain progress.

'Do you think they'll have left anything for us to follow?' Elizabeth said.

'Not if they intended returning to us,' Irvine said, wishing he'd stayed silent. 'I'm going to call out,' and before Elizabeth could raise her hands to her ears, he shouted into the surrounding cloud. He shouted the names of the young men, one after another, until his throat was sore. Preston had made him a list.

There was no answer.

They waited. There was another faint echo, of sorts, but nothing more. No answering voices, no shouts of encouragement, guidance, relief, joy.

And when the final reverberating whisper was finished, there was only the same silence. Perhaps higher up a few more small pieces of rock slid a few more metres down the hillside; perhaps another piece of desiccated timber snapped and tumbled further from its felled trunk on the dead slope. But other than that, nothing.

Irvine tried to remember all the sounds of which the world had once been composed. Everything they had once taken for granted, everything they had stopped hearing before they'd even known it was gone; everything they had stopped hearing and which they had grown wary and then terrified of. He wanted the world in all its random, confusing, noisy glory to return to him, to the pair of them. He wanted to start making sense of everything again.

'We should stay close,' Elizabeth said, distracting him from these thoughts. She held out her hand to him and they clasped each other firmly. Even ten metres apart in the cloud and they might be lost to each other forever.

They continued down the slope, careful to walk in as straight a line as possible, diverting only where the terrain did not allow a direct descent. They stumbled and fell occasionally, losing their footing and then scrambling to prevent themselves from slipping too far and beyond the sight of the other.

When they were steady, standing together on a lesser slope—a terrace almost, perhaps even an abandoned path—Irvine began to wonder how close they had finally come to the valley bottom. He guessed by the feel of the ground beneath his feet that they were nearing the end of their journey. Or if not the end, exactly, then that they would soon be leaving the hillside that had been their refuge for all those years. Soon, he imagined, they might be back among the ruins and the waste of all they had left behind them. Collapsed buildings, fallen bridges and overpasses, riven roads and crumpled landing strips.

He felt Elizabeth put her hand back into his. It was all the strength and encouragement he needed.

'It looks less dense,' she said, indicating the cloud ahead of them.

Irvine shielded his eyes and looked. A kind of hazy, liquid sunlight appeared to have penetrated to the ground ahead of where they waited.

He considered calling out again, but decided against this. He felt his fingers tighten across her palm. He looked ahead of them, convincing himself that in addition to the hazy light, the vague and shifting outlines of those lost and unknown structures were now starting to appear all around them.

'We're here,' Elizabeth said absently. She drew her hand from his and wiped it across her face, studying the moisture which lay in a sheen on her skin.

'We are,' Irvine said. And as he spoke he felt the ground finally grow level beneath his feet. Testing this new and unaccustomed terrain, he took several paces ahead of her, and then, and without truly understanding why, he held out both his hands, his arms stretched, his fingers splayed, as though believing there was something close ahead of them, something he was now desperate to see and eager to embrace, something indiscernible and without any true form perhaps, but something alive and moving and coming slowly towards them through the brightening, thinning cloud.

THE WHITE LEOPARD

MICHAEL SWANWICK

H E FOUND IT IN FIVE cardboard boxes in the basement at a suburban estate sale. Ray went to estate sales almost every weekend. It got him away from his wife. Weekdays he spent fixing things in his garage workshop.

Doris didn't like estate sales, consignment shops, or secondhand anything. 'I don't buy used crap!' she often said. 'I want to be able to return something if I get tired of it.' Yet she clung to Ray mercilessly, only God knew why.

Four of the cartons were marked twenty dollars each. The fifth, which had gotten separated from the others and which he had scoured the basement to find, was ten. He would have paid all he had for them. But because it was Sunday afternoon and the sale was almost over, they knocked half off the price without even being asked. It was clear the sellers had no idea what it was.

What it was, was an RQ-6G Leopard.

The 6G was, in Ray's opinion, the finest patrol and reconnaissance ground drone ever made. He had qualified on it during Operation Bolivian Freedom, back when he was young. He had hunted down insurgents with one, working from a combat recliner in a secure base across the border in Argentina. He'd known what it felt like to be the most dangerous thing in the jungle at night. He had never experienced anything like that before.

He wanted to feel something like that again.

When he laid out the rig in his workshop, Ray's heart sank. The fiber-optic skin was all rags and tatters, unsalvageable, and the VR controls were bricked. Half the glass batteries were cracked and would have to be replaced. But on closer examination, the core of the machine was in good condition. When he hooked it up to household current and went in with an old set of gamer gear, he could feel the synthetic muscles as if they were his own. Feedback from the sensorium was nice and clean.

There was nothing wrong with the machine that he couldn't fix. Six months flew by.

Subsection by subsystem, Ray took apart and reassembled the rig, cleaning and scraping and oiling, sometimes sanding and occasionally replacing. He upgraded and debugged the software. The skin he unstitched and patched together to make a pattern which he then sent to a man he found on CraftE. A month later, a tough matte-black covering, perfectly made, came back, along with a note reading: *You've got a 6G, huh? Lucky bastard. Tom Ubberly, S. Sgt., Drone-Ops (ret).*

With that, the repair phase of the project was done.

Ray waited five days before taking it out. He wanted a cloudless night. He wanted a full moon. When, at last, both presented themselves in tandem, he opened the garage doors and unleashed the beast.

The Leopard rose to its feet, looked around, and with an impatient shake of its head, dismissed the garage as beneath its notice. Silent as a thought, it padded out onto the driveway.

The house was at the end of a cul-de-sac and backed against state game land. This had been a significant factor when he and

Doris had bought into the development, long ago when they were young and presumably in love.

He raised the Leopard's head to taste the wind. It was rich with saps and pollens, the green stench of marsh water filled with duckweed, frogs, and algae, a musky trace of fox, the sweet bird-droppings smell of baby birds. Turning on his ears revealed the ultrasonic chitter of bats, an opossum hissing in anger, a fish crow speaking to no one in particular. A train whistle from half a county away, inaudible to his human senses, was a long slow moan calling Ray to adventure. The crickets were out in force.

He had closed his eyes. Now he opened them and saw a sky thronged with stars and, swarming among them, countless manmade orbital artifacts. There was a big orange pumpkin of a moon low over the horizon and, with a sudden bound, he sent it leaping and bouncing in the sky. The house and everything it represented disappeared behind him. The forest enfolded him in its dark embrace.

When he was sufficiently deep into the woods, he slowed to a walk. At that speed, the Leopard was virtually noiseless. Sorting through the scents and sounds of the night, Ray found a raccoon washing its food in a little stream that chuckled and laughed its way downhill. He wondered how close he could get before it realized he was there. He decided to find out.

Moving slower the closer he got, Ray was not more than ten feet distant when something alerted the raccoon to his presence. It twisted around to face him while simultaneously trying to leap away, and fell noisily into the stream. Then it was up and running as fast as it could go.

Ray followed, keeping an even distance between him and it. The raccoon twisted and turned as it ran, but it could not throw him off. Until finally it scrabbled up the side of a huge oak at the center of a grove of old growth trees.

He waited until the raccoon had gone to earth in its den, a hollow halfway up the oak. Then he climbed the tree after it. Looking in through the opening, he saw the raccoon, eyes huge, shivering with fear. Ray extended one claw and touched its nose.

Tag. You're it.

Then he was gone from the tree and the raccoon's life forever.

Night after night, Ray explored the forest, interested in everything and caring about nothing but pure sensation. Briefly, he was young again, lithe and spry, his senses not yet dulled by age and routine. Filled with the zest for life that his life had long ago taken out of him. Then, not long into one nocturnal jaunt—

Ping.

A defensive subsystem came on and softly alerted Ray that there was something out there! Something military. His rig's eidetics threw up a menu of possibilities. All decades old, of course. But the emissions signature for one matched perfectly.

It was another Leopard.

For an instant, it seemed an impossible coincidence. Then Ray had to laugh at himself. Where else would you take a Leopard but into the forest? When else but at night? This particular game land was the largest such tract in this half of the state. So...no coincidence. If there were two RQ-6Gs within fifty miles of each other, it was inevitable that their paths would cross.

He booted up the communications board and, because the night was too quiet to mar with speech, chose text: *Unknown Leopard, this is BlackMomser, Please identify yourself.*

Without thinking, he had ID'd himself with his war tag, from back in the day.

BlackMomser, this is HelenCat.

Ray blinked. A woman? He air-typed, *A woman?*

You didn't think a woman could make the Corps? Trust me, civvie, anything you can do, I can outdo.

Ray had once been as good as they got. *Don't know about that, ma'am. I was top drone in my day.*

Then find me, she replied. Her electronic signature disappeared from his screen.

She'd gone stealth. But nothing as big as a Leopard could be hidden from someone who knew how to look. Ray began by closing down all his senses but smell and giving it all his attention. Traces of human activity permeated the forest, of course. Exhaust washed up from the distant interstate. Discarded trash—plastic bags, lead shot, aluminum cans reeking of stale beer—was everywhere, usually smothered in dead leaves. But none of the machine-smells so familiar from his months in the workshop.

She was downwind, then.

Downwind here meant upslope. Ray shifted all his attention in that direction. He thought he could just make out the low mosquito whine of an internal servo ever so slightly out of balance. You could adjust those things every day of their existence and they still kept going off-spec.

Upward he went, scanning the ground for evidence of the Leopard's passage.

At the top of the ridge, he turned downward. A trickle of water seeped from the rocks and became a stream. He bounded back and forth across it and, slipping under a tangle of fallen branches, saw a paw-print in the mud. Just as he'd expected. Drone operators liked to follow streams. They were more challenging than just slipping between the trees.

At the bottom of the mountain, the stream fed into a marsh. There, the Leopard was easier to follow. Nothing could cross all that mud and vegetation without leaving a trace. On the far side, the land went up again and so did Ray, sure he was on the right track. Then the top of the ridge rose before him and there the Leopard was.

She was waiting for him, crouched on a rocky outcrop, with her back arched and that tremendous moon directly behind her head. She had turned her fiber-optic fur—her cladding, unlike his, was original and in pristine condition—on full, so that she glowed pearl-white.

God, but she was beautiful!

Ray had his Leopard on stealth mode, like hers, and he was sure he made no noise on the approach. But she turned anyway. Their eyes met. Then her Leopard's skin went dark and she was gone and away again.

They played for most of the night. Sometimes he chased her and sometimes she him. When they tired of that, she led him to a stream, where she dipped a paw into the water and flipped out a rainbow trout. Nodding his admiration, he nudged it back into the water. Then he led her to the marsh where bats were swooping low to feed on flying insects. He leaped high in the air and snapped, capturing a bat in his mouth. Turning, he crouched before the white Leopard and opened his mouth to let the bat flutter away. Helen applauded.

Then the sky was lightening in the east and it was time to go.

Will I see you again? Ray texted her. *When?*

Yes. Tomorrow.

They met every night for a week. Sometimes they played, sometimes they hunted rabbits together, and sometimes they talked. Her name was Helen and, as he'd expected, HelenCat had been her war tag. 'HellCat was already taken,' she explained. They'd graduated to communicating by audio. They had become comfortable enough with each other to get personal.

'Nothing ever worked out for me,' Ray said. 'Military service was the high point.' He had spent the rest of his life making money—decent money, admittedly, but not enough to make Doris content. No children—that had been a point of contention. A job that gave him no particular satisfaction—that was another. A retirement that felt pointless to both of them.

'Everything worked out for me. Life, love, family, money. Wonderful kids. A great husband. We traveled a lot. I had everything I ever wanted. But then Moses died and what remained meant nothing to me. The children had their own lives and mine was...empty. I had plenty of money and nothing better to spend it on, so I bought the rig on the gray market. Then I met you and here we are.'

Ray's Leopard's head nodded involuntarily. But he said nothing. He appreciated that she had not apologized for her success in life. She knew a fellow drone pilot would not resent that. They'd been dog-brothers in the war together, though their tours of duty hadn't overlapped. They understood each other.

'We should meet,' Ray said, after a bit. In real space, he meant, not virtual.

They settled on Saturday night at an Olive Garden. It seemed like safe, neutral territory. They traded cell numbers in case the place was crowded, but they spotted each other at almost the same instant. Ray knew it was Helen even though she was older than he'd imagined her and leaned heavily on a semirobotic walker-cane, because she was the only one looking anxiously about in search of somebody she'd never met. Also by the dismay on her face when she saw the dismay on his. For an instant, he saw himself as she saw him: old, potbellied, balding, with a face etched by failure. And she? Not svelte. Not young. Not raven-haired or blonde or russet. Gray. Aged. Spent.

Panic and embarrassment overcame them both. Turning backs on each other, they fled to opposite corners of the parking lot to uber their Rydes.

When Ray got home, less than an hour after he'd left, Doris was sitting on the couch in the flannel nightgown he hated, the one with the tiny pink flowers. She had a glass of scotch by her side, and though it was only 8:30, she was already half-plastered. She didn't bother turning off the game show she was watching. She just smirked. 'She was *old*, wasn't she? Old like you.'

Ray didn't ask how she knew why he'd gone out. Doris had spent her working years in tech. There were any number of ways to hack into a system whose defenses were decades out of date. She would know them all. 'Leave me alone, Doris. I'm not in the mood.'

'You never are. You hardly ever were. Listen to me for once. I'm not the bad guy here. I know you blame me for what you've become. You've never thought of what you made of me. Look at me! Okay, I'm a mess. But this is your doing. Your fault. And you hoped to start all over again with a new woman? I'm glad for her sake that she got away.'

Ray looked at Doris then, really looked at her, for the first time in years. This dry, withered, bitter woman had a point. He really had ruined her life. She was right in everything she said.

But he didn't care. He'd do it all over to her again and worse, if he had the opportunity.

Horrified at this insight, Ray plunged down the stairs to his workshop. He strapped into his VR set and sent his Leopard bounding into the forest.

Helen was waiting for him there, perched on a low limb of a sycamore tree. *That's not who I am,* she messaged. Meaning the woman he had seen at the Olive Garden.

I know. I'm the same way. Inside.

There was a long, awkward pause. *Do you want to hunt?*

Yes!

That night, for the first time, they hunted down a deer and killed it. Together.

So went the summer. Sometimes they hunted. Other times they explored or wandered or simply talked. It depended on their mood. Once, they ran up on trees overhanging a railroad line, jumped down on a passing freight train, and rode it halfway across the state before jumping a train back.

Then came autumn.

On the first cold, blustery day of the season, Ray had barely gotten into the forest when he received a text. *Come home. Urgent.* It was not from Helen. There was only one other person who could possibly have sent it.

Ray powered down the Leopard in the garage and went up the stairs to find Doris waiting for him. She was sitting on the couch, as she did every night, wearing that same damned flannel nightgown. She snapped off the television when he entered the room. There was a triumphant gleam in her eye.

'All right,' Ray said. 'What is it?'

'All this crap you've been doing is against the law. I did research. You don't have a license for that thing and it's illegal for a civilian to own one anyway. You're in violation of the game laws too. Just taking a proscribed military weapon into state game lands is illegal—not to mention killing things with it without regard as to whether they're in season or not. You are so very busted, mister. I've got the goods on you and come morning, if I feel like it, I can turn you in for possession of terrorist weaponry. I can send your sorry ass to jail.'

This, Ray realized miserably—*this* was why she had hung onto him for so many years of quiet mutual desperation. So she could utterly and completely destroy him. All this time she had just been waiting for her opportunity.

Now, he had finally given it to her.

Doris hadn't said she was going to dime him out, however—only that she could. Which meant that wasn't her goal. It was only a threat, a goad, something to make him play along with her.

'You've got my attention. What is it you want?'

'I want you to kill her with your own two hands.'

It took his breath away. 'Kill Helen?'

'Is that the name of Granny Girlfriend? Nobody cares about her. I want you to take that metal pussycat of yours into the backyard, pack her full of fireworks and rockets, pour about five gallons of gasoline over it, and set it on fire. When it goes up, I want it to look like the Fourth of July.'

At first, Ray didn't get it. Then he understood: Doris wanted to be sure the neighbors came running. All of them. The fire department too. She wanted as many people as possible to see his humiliation. If he wept—as, to be honest, he well might—then so much the better. He understood this because he'd had fantasies of his own over the years. He knew what he'd like to do to her and it was every bit as vicious. My God, he thought. How is it possible for two people to hate each other so much?

'All right. It'll take a day or two to get the fireworks. But I imagine you want to do this on the weekend anyway.'

Ray still had Helen's number. When Doris finally went to bed, he called her. She sounded sleepy when she answered, then wide-awake when she recognized his voice. He brought her up to speed. 'Back then . . .' he said. 'Back then, did you ever do two-on-one work?'

Sometimes it had been necessary to make someone—a community organizer, usually, a priest or a mayor—disappear. A pair of Leopards would be sent to the target's village to kill him or her, then carry the body out into the jungle and bury it deep, where it would never be found.

'We all did,' Helen said. There was a long silence. Then, 'I'll help you. On one condition.'

'What's that?'

'I want to be there in person when it happens.'

The next evening, Ray waited, as patient as Satan. Finally, he heard Doris outside, dumping garbage and recycling into their bins as she always did at this hour. He hurried to the back door and locked it. She was in her nightgown, so he knew she didn't have her keys or cell phone with her. Quickly now. He made sure the front door was locked too. The garage would only open by remote. She was locked out.

Ray donned his VR rig and powered up his Leopard. Helen was not far away, waiting. He texted her: *It's on.*

Helen had parked her pickup truck just a little up the road. He heard her start the engine and then quietly pull up to the curb out front, where she could watch.

Doris was still fussing with the trash bins when the white Leopard came slinking around the corner of the house. It glowed pale and deadly in the moonlight. Behind it, Helen leaned out of the cab window, grinning. She had the goggles of her VR set pushed up on her forehead so she could watch the initial confrontation with her own two eyes.

Ray brought up his machine behind Doris and revved the internal motors. It made a noise like a snarl. He waited for her to turn and then flinch away in fear. He listened for her short sharp cry of dismay.

The two Leopards were so deployed that there was only one way for Doris to run—into the woods. He and Helen would have their fun then. They would make it last all night.

But instead, Doris said, 'I didn't think you were serious about the fireworks.'

With an almost inaudible whine of servos powering off, the black Leopard sat down, placing itself in standby mode.

'What the hell?' This was the worst possible time for a malfunction. Hank struggled with the controls, trying to jolt his Leopard back to life. 'Helen,' he said, 'I've got a problem. Keep Doris pinned while I get this thing up and running again.'

'I can't!' There was a panicky tremble in Helen's voice. 'I'm locked out. The Leopard won't respond to my commands.'

Visual, meanwhile, was good. His Leopard's camera eyes were focused on Doris. There was an alertness to her that he hadn't seen in ages. She was sober. This late in the evening, Ray hadn't thought that was possible for her.

Doris had her phone in her hand. She touched the screen and said, 'The kitchen door is open now.'

Ray remembered that, a lifetime ago, the brass had a suite of override commands that, it went without saying, they'd never had to use on him. And of *course* Doris had been able to hack into them, even if it had taken her all summer. That had been her profession, after all—computer security. 'Helen, any luck with your system?'

'None!'

The white Leopard prowled past Doris with lethal grace. Out of the corner of his own Leopard's eye, Ray saw it push into the kitchen. He could hear it moving overhead.

'You're about to wander into the woods like the senile old coot that you are. Your body will never be found,' Doris said.

'I'm calling the police!' Helen wailed. 'I'm calling them! Right now!'

'You do that, dear. Give them a nice, hysterical recording to play at your trial. They'll come here and find your illegal little war machine crouched over Ray's mangled body and a set of perfectly functional VR gear hanging around your neck. I'll be in the living room, watching the TV in a drunken stupor, like I do every other night.' She paused. 'Or you can drive yourself home, knowing that when I'm done with it, I'll send your pussy back to you and there'll be nothing at all to connect you to what happens here tonight. Either way, it's your choice.'

There was an extended silence. Don't, Ray thought. The guilt will break you—you'll never be able to look yourself in the mirror again.

Helen started up the pickup and drove away.

By then, the white Leopard was coming down the stairs.

Even as Ray tried to rise to his feet, knowing he had nothing to fight with but his flabby, aged body, he couldn't help admiring the cocksure, triumphant smile that suddenly blossomed on his wife's face.

There was the strong, willful woman he had fallen in love with all those many long years ago.

IN THE HOUSE
OF UNPLEASANT VOICES

PAUL PARK

ONCE, EARLY ON, SHE'D played a recurring role in a HBO drama—a hit, as it turned out. In order to prevent spoilers, even the actors couldn't know the plot. The hand-delivered scripts only contained the scenes that they were in. As for subsequent episodes, no clue.

Just like real life, she told herself. Who knows what happens when we aren't around? Who knows anything about the future? And so she took another step: even in the scenes transported to her door, she'd black out any dialogue except her own. She tried as best she could not to imagine what anybody else was going to say. She would only memorize her own lines and the words or short phrases that marked her cues. When other characters were talking, she listened only for the words that prompted her response. Critics praised her naturalness and authenticity, the 'feral, predatory way she looked at X— B—'s mouth,' for example, 'as if every word that issued were a revelation.' The writers, of course, picked up this new, unhinged aspect of her character, with the result that she died screaming in the middle of the third season.

This soon became the defining feature of her technique, even in plays. What happened when Goneril wasn't actually on stage, or else after her death, she neither knew nor cared. Later, when she started doing voice work, she asked to come in separately to record her lines, which she would read without rehearsal, out of order, with long pauses in between. Alone in the studio, she would weep, croon, whisper, or bellow, the inflection almost arbitrary. She found a niche in anime, where strong emotions often come up out of nowhere.

There is a script, but it doesn't help to know it. Her only problem was when, as part of a public relations campaign, she needed to discuss her character or else the themes of the episode, or fit the plot into a larger context. But soon she was adept at that as well. What was important was the presentation, not the meaning. No one really listens, after all. They are also mostly waiting for their own cues to speak.

By the time she was in her fifties, the various pieces of her private life were similarly disengaged: she was a mother, a wife, a lover, a sister, a daughter. But there was no arc, no through line. These aspects of her personality bumped up against each other as if adrift in a liquid matrix, or else bumped apart. At rapid intervals she would be crafty, magnanimous, cruel, loving, petty, foolish, innocent, cynical, brainy, dense—the list went on. Literally it had no end, because of the way it curled back into itself.

Everyone has this in common. Everyone's the same. Even God is the same, or at least the Christian God-in-Three-Persons, as her father had once pointed out. Lately, though, the 'marriage' and 'love' parts of her life, often comfortably separate, had found themselves in tense proximity, emotionally, physically. Sometimes her husband was entirely trusting, sometimes paranoid; you couldn't predict. That morning, in the Westport house, he'd had a dreamy, disapproving look. So she'd absconded—a long drive along the Connecticut shore. Now that the child was a teenager, she often took such trips as if to clear her head.

In the afternoon she found herself near where she'd spent the summers from ages two to thirteen. She could see the water from the highway and she took the Mystic exit near the abandoned aquarium and seaport. You sort of had to pick your way and sometimes backtrack. When she was a child this had been a whole summer scene: families on vacation, hamburgers and French fries, sunscreen and mosquitoes. She took the road to Stonington and drove till she couldn't go any farther. Here ahead, the road was blocked with a wooden barricade. Kaitrin pulled onto the muddy shoulder where some other cars had turned around.

She turned off the engine and sat back, calculating how much time she had. Her phone buzzed and chirped. The house itself was farther down toward the shore, and she imagined she could cross through the woods without getting her feet wet.

She was not the kind of actor whose name people recognized. It was more that people thought they knew her, had seen her at a party, or else had heard her voice before. Still she took confidence from the familiarity, felt less vulnerable in situations like this, a woman alone by the side of the empty road. Besides, she was home.

Good spring weather, as it happened: eighty degrees, soft breeze at three o'clock in the afternoon.

When she was a girl, she had insisted on staging public performances of skills she hadn't learned and had no intention of learning: a concert of solo pieces on the violin, which she had picked up for the first time that afternoon. A demonstration of circus tumbling. When she went to college she invented an entire new childhood for herself, several childhoods, actually. Her friends and intimates thought contradictory things about her, and not just because for each of them she tried to dramatize a different aspect of her personality. Eventually she pretended that the actual biographical details of her life, easily available online, had been invented by publicity people, and her name was not her name. Not even her husband and son, for example, knew about this house, what it had meant to her growing up. She had kept it secret. Dressed in blue jeans, a cream-colored men's dress shirt with the sleeves rolled up, and a gold necklace, she got out of the car.

Much had changed. She crossed the barricade, slipped off her sandals, and walked barefoot through the scrub maple trees. The ground sucked at her feet until she found the rise, coming at the house from the side. Forty years before, a lawn had stretched down to a pebble beach, a place for croquet and deck chairs and gin. Now the grass was high. The house itself had slid partway off its foundation and the back extension had collapsed, the modern kitchen that had not been part of the original nineteenth-century structure. The windows were mostly broken and the door was smashed in. Kids had been here, which neither surprised nor upset her. They had spray-painted slogans and designs on the white-clapboard walls, a pleasing effect. Inside things were messier than she'd have liked, the furniture dismantled or carted off; it wouldn't have been furniture she recognized anyway. Her mother had sold the house after the divorce. No neighbors, then or now.

She'd always been a visual thinker. The false stories she told about herself, about the world, could easily efface the true ones after a specific number of repetitions. Right now, as she climbed onto the porch, as she wandered through the ground floor, she imagined her eccentric father had invented a literary theme for every room. The stairs down to the flooded basement, which she glimpsed through a door off the front hallway, had once been decorated with poster-painted scenes from Dante's *Inferno*. The landing, as it turned the corner into the darkness, indicated the Wall of Dis, the dividing line between passive and active sin. Remnants of these paintings still remained, much defaced. The downstairs bathroom was from Thomas More's *Utopia*, the toilet painted gold, but flaking now. Was it possible that she had lost her virginity, sort of, on this broken bedstead in the corner of the parlor, to a girl whom her older sister had invited home from summer camp?

A lot of broken glass, empty bottles, cans. Charred places in the middle of the floor. She had to watch where she stepped with her bare feet. Now she was playing with the possibility that she had never actually lived in this house at all, but had been drawn to it by some secret, unconscious force. It was too sad, what was happening. Here were some possibilities:

1. Her name was Ernestina Cross, Tina for short. 'Kaitrin' was her stage name. Her father had taught English literature at Providence College. Her mother had inherited this house from her own mother, whose second husband had been an executive for Connecticut Light and Power. Now Kaitrin wandered through it in a semi-fugue state...

2. Like most actresses of her generation, she had been born on a low-gravity world where she had been trained in human mimicry. Today was a crucial test for her, after some mistakes. Was it possible she'd be recalled?

3. Her 'intelligence' was at least partly artificial, her body a cyborg mixture of biologic and mechanical elements. Formerly top-of-the-line, the model was now obsolete.

4. She was not a living person, but a ghost, or else a premonition.

You might think you know which of these possibilities was likely, or at least true. But all of us contain mutually exclusive life stories. If she were a ghost, Kaitrin thought as she climbed the steps to the second floor, what kind would she be, to haunt this place? Would she be angry, remorseful, melancholy, vengeful? She supposed it would depend on how she'd died. It was hard for her to imagine Max (her husband) doing her harm, after having found out, she supposed, about Max (her lover). He wasn't that kind of person, though doubtless he'd be shocked and saddened to find out how long she'd been lying to him. Max (her stepson from a previous marriage) would show indifference, she decided.

In the corner of the front bedroom overlooking the water, she pulled a sock out of the mouth of the old speaking tube, set into the floor between the desk and the wall. The walls here at one time had been painted to resemble a garden, a dry steppe, a barley field. Animals had grazed. This was another part of her father's utopian/dystopian project, after a story that he'd adapted from

Tibetan Buddhism, a vision of the afterlife, a paradise of waterfalls and fruit trees and leaping stags, except for one detail. You could travel a thousand miles without a want or care. But in one insignificant corner of that world you could find a hole that led down to someplace else entirely (the original kitchen, in this particular case), a hole scarcely large enough for your hand. And if you bent down you could hear a murmur of words in a language you happened to know, soft words that reminded you how all satisfaction is finite and provisional, that all things die, that all accomplishment is fleeting, that all colors fade, that reality itself is an illusion. Once you have heard that sound, you can never stray outside its circle. Or else you might start away, escape, knowing that experience is vast and full of rare delight. But you'd come back. All the people in that world live in that same dry valley once they have discovered it, a chalky upland where the air and soil are thin. Often they sit in a mute circle around the hole. The grass is dead, as if the words emit a poison. At night, the cold black sky is full of stars.

This place is called the Land of the Disagreeable Voice. And of course, Kaitrin had considered more than once, artists live in it—writers, makers, scholars. The voice reminds them that what they do is stupid and meaningless. 'Of course,' her father had said, laughing, 'it says the same thing over and over. The question is not who is talking—when we internalize that voice, it is our own, part of our plumbing. But who is listening, inside of us? There she is. That person never says a word. But she is the interesting one.'

You recognize her. She is the one who moves through our minds and leaves no trace. Her life is not mute suffering. She is a being of light. Kaitrin stands next to the window in the front bedroom, her foot next to the speaking tube. Now there is just a faint susurration of wind. She has the sudden impression that she is not alone in the house, and that the wall is broken through, not in this room (where she used to sleep) but its neighbor, the exposed plaster and broken lath edging a person-sized hole, perhaps hacked with sledgehammers onto the roof of the side porch.

Kaitrin's skin is smooth and without pores, because it is partly made of silicone. Real porcelain (crushed) was also involved. Designed as a sexual companion, she has been successfully hacked on multiple occasions.

On the front seat of her car, her phone buzzes and chirps, a series of voice messages and texts. Max reminds her of things he has mentioned before, things she would rather forget, and in fact has forgotten, at least some of them.

We want to find the person who is listening and yet says nothing. Ghostlike, she hovers in the stillness of the upper room, the one with the hole in the wall, which used to be her brother's room. Subsequently she flits up the second staircase; at the top, off the landing, she pauses at a hatchway set into the wall, a three-foot-high panel with the hinge along its upper edge (the brass ring flush against the baseboard), accessing a crawlspace under the eaves and a mounted box of old screw-in fuses. Beyond that, a long triangular prism lined with pink fiberglass insulation, a space only comfortable for a child. In her last years in the house, Tina would crawl along a sheet of plywood laid over the joists until the prism widened to a larger polyhedron, where she had laid a shred of carpet and a collection of old pillows. All this was long ago. She'd even rigged an electric light, a hanging lantern on an extension cord. She'd gone back there to write books, predictions about the life she planned to have. Her father had bought her little leather-bound books with blank pages that she'd filled with precise sentences in green and purple ink.

On the landing, the ghost wonders if those notebooks are still there. She hadn't managed to retrieve them when her father abruptly took her away. Perhaps they were still arranged under a mural of blue sky and white clouds that she had painted on the inner wall, a secret (because inaccessible) companion to her father's efforts elsewhere in the house—the tower, for example, that controlled the weather (evoked in tile on the kitchen backstop) from Francis Bacon's *New Atlantis*. 'Paradise,' she'd called her refuge, though it was not comfortable to stay there long, especially on a summer day. Here was a strange thing: In her younger days, Tina had imagined being an actress. It was in that context that she had invented the name 'Kaitrin,' as she lay on her back, stripped to her white cotton bra and panties in the heat. At the end of the prism, she could see a two-inch circle of light, punched through the clapboards into the outside air, an unblinking eye.

She had planned a much more successful life than she had ended up having, a different level of celebrity. She had planned marriages and divorces, and struggles with addiction. Inevitably, many of the premonitions in the notebooks came out of what Tina was reading at the moment. She had, for example, (on her brother's recommendation) taken *The Delta of Venus* out of her father's library (The ghost wondered if the book had slipped down in the years since, into the insulation or perhaps between the plywood and the eaves . . .) and used it to produce this evocation of Kaitrin's first (or almost first—in the notebooks, Tina was hazy about chronology) blowjob as a teenaged star, performed for an overweight producer in Hollywood: 'Z's penis had the shape of a mushroom, which did not take her by surprise. Experimentally she gave it a lick along its stalk, detecting also a faint flavor of sautéed morels. How rich and sweet! Hoping to mask her inexperience, she took the entire penis into her mouth—it was not difficult or hard . . . ' She had been proud of this last phrase, a double-double entendre, as she only semi-accurately imagined it.

As it happened, Kaitrin had encountered that man not in her teens but in her twenties. Later on that same Californian night (or in that same week or month) she had experienced for the first time the psychic split that she'd described (not to her diary, but to her therapist) in this way: 'I am not entirely a robot. There is something else going on inside of me. I mean I can feel the little metal valves and rotors, the bellows pumping away. I hear the voice inside of me, giving me orders, telling me the truth. But can a robot truly know its function, why it was created?'

She hadn't known, not yet. An actress's purpose is to be desired. Or so she thought on her best and worst days.

That summer, their last summer in the house, Tina's brother had died in the bedroom Kaitrin haunted now, the one next to the room with the speaking tube. She walked in from the doorway to the center of the floor, reimagining the metal hospital bed that they had brought from New London. Her brother had died there in that room after a long illness, and then a lot of things had fallen apart.

He was the first boy she had kissed, when she was nine years old and he was twelve. Kissed and then some, sort of. The summer she was thirteen she had sat here every day, hour after hour, reading to him, holding his hand, and later giving him chips of ice. When someone else in the family spelled her, sometimes she would crawl up into Paradise, skin off her clothes, lie on her back, and touch herself under the pink fiberglass. Then she'd roll onto her stomach and press the heel of her hand into her groin, the way her brother had...not shown her, exactly, but described to her. She didn't remember weeping, ever. One day she turned on the light and read her father's Larry Niven novels about faster-than-light travel, the Bussard ramjets that 'caught interstellar hydrogen in immaterial nets of electromagnetic force, compressed, and guided it into a ring of pinched force fields, and there burned it in a fusion fire.'

Her parents granted her a lot of privacy that summer. Later she disclosed to her brother where she'd been: 'You remember Dr. Michiko?'

He squeezed her hand. Dr. Michiko was a history teacher at Moses Brown. Ernestina and her brother had speculated about why an alien goddess from outside the solar system would want to teach AP European history at a private school in Providence. Why would she mate with a human and have hybrid children? What was the point?

Tina's brother had told her about Larry Niven. And mostly he was the one who had speculated about Dr. Michiko—her kindness, her clothes, her black hair with a blue streak, etc.—while Tina listened more or less indulgently. But now she brought her up. 'I think I discovered where she comes from. I went to the spaceport at Bradley Field. They go up and come down, blue streaks in the night sky. They hardly make a sound. Just a, you know, groaning. A gravel sound. Conventional thrusters at the beginning, but then the Bussard ramjet takes over. You can stand on the warm asphalt in the dark and watch them burst to life, a little, silent pop. Oh, I wish I could show you. There's no limit to how fast you can go. Almost no limit.'

'Was Dr. Michiko on board?' asked her brother, his voice loopy and faint. Eliise had given him his pills (OxyContin and Ambien). The house was settling down. A cricket in the wall. Waves dragging the stones back. Bugs against the screen.

'Oh yes, she was the pilot. And she kept asking about you over the loudspeaker. There weren't many of us on board, and the stewardesses looked just like her. Tall and thin like that. Long legs. We weren't in seats so much as plastic pods, and they hovered over us, serving us glowing bulbs of liquid, sliding the long tubes up our noses so we could still talk. It was amazing. Then Dr. Michiko came back into the cabin and asked about you again. She stood really close to me. Inappropriately close. Like, a foot away.'

'Did she . . . touch you?'

'No, that would have been too much. But her skin is so smooth, it's almost unreal. And I could smell her skin under her perfume, she was that close. And you know what?'

'What?'

'She had no smell at all. Her actual skin. And you know what?'

'What?'

'She said you'd been amazing in her class. She said you'd been very knowledgeable about the Thirty Years' War. Other less amazing students thought the war might have been only twenty-eight years, even twenty-seven, but not you. You were never fooled. Hundred Years' War, same thing. On the money every time. It was uncanny, she said. She wants you to marry her younger sister—she showed me holograms. I hope that's okay. No one was wearing any clothes. I mean in the holograms.'

'Her sister?'

'Yes, apparently sisters arrange everything like that, where they are from. They take care of everything. And that sister is more age-appropriate. She's a hundred and seven.'

'Yes . . . that would be better, probably.'

The summer air, the dark, soft house. Dim light on the bedside table. Tina sat in an upholstered armchair, holding his hand. 'She asked about your thing,' she said. 'Apparently they are very particular.'

In her own room, next door, who knew what sounds blew through the speaking tube? Who knew who sat by it, listening? 'Your penis,' she explained when he said nothing. It was a word she had written down for the first time only that afternoon. 'I said I didn't know.'

'No one knows,' he said philosophically.

Yet there it was, partially uncovered. He was wearing hospital nightshirts by that time. Eliise was matter-of-fact about such things; she had gone to dispose of the old catheter. 'It's a long way, where they are from,' Tina said. 'I fell asleep, I don't know how long. I was suspended in my pod, fed through a tube, which was amazing. The nutrients went straight up to my brain. And they had movies like an airplane, but they were internal. It's hard to describe. The movies felt like they were inside of you, and you got to choose which way the story goes. So many colors bursting out. Your skin glowed underneath. You could make yourself into a character, even just a cameo. I chose a story where you got better. Wouldn't you know, but there were problems with that plot as well.'

They had discovered the disease too late, after it had metastasized. But his lungs were still clear, and he breathed easily. She couldn't quite tell whether he had nodded off. 'When we came in, it was bright day. You know it was a world of sisters. Everyone moving in slow motion, because of the low gravity. So graceful, like a dance. We didn't need any clothes. A double sun in the sky, and stationary, too. One blue, one green, and pretty shadows everywhere. People thought I was a native! Especially after I stripped down. It was like when we went to Austria and Mom bought me that stupid dirndl, and all the tourists wanted to take my picture. It was like that.'

'I'll bet it was just like that.'

Then he was truly asleep, and she held his hand, listening to the surf and the bugs. In time she gave her brother a hug, embraced him, laid her head against his chest, listened for his heart.

She moved her hand down his body over the nightshirt. Then she inhaled, moved her head. She licked him clean with little cat licks, and held his soft penis in her mouth. He tasted of urine (or at least what she supposed urine tasted like). Also rubber and KY. She laid her cheek on his distended stomach. Eliise came in with a fresh catheter. Maybe she couldn't tell what Tina had been doing in the dark, outside the circle of light on the bedside table. She was a yellow-haired woman in her thirties, from Estonia, a small country on the Baltic Sea, where maybe the hospice nurses reserve judgment about what middle-school girls might do to give some comfort to their older brothers, dying of ocular melanoma in the middle of the night. Anyway she didn't make a fuss, but only hooked the new bag to the bedside rail. The glistening tube. There was nothing about what happened next that Tina wanted to watch. While she worked, Eliise clicked her tongue and made a birdlike chirping sound, then hummed a little tune that Tina didn't recognize.

But now in the same room, Kaitrin sits down on the floor under the slanting western light. Her back is to the person-shaped hole onto the porch roof, and she is waiting for a change, a brighter glow. When it doesn't come, she closes her eyes and anticipates for the feel of Dr. Michiko's hands on her. She doesn't have long to wait. She allows Dr. Michiko (unchanged, even after all these years!) to lay her out on the bare floorboards in the middle of the room where her brother's bed had stood, the white metal slats, the stand for the IV. Tina, as it happened, had never made it into AP European history (she'd been expelled from Moses Brown the following year), but Dr. Michiko (not a medical doctor, as it happened, or at least not yet) knew who she was. In preparation, she must have swept up most of the broken plaster and glass, though Kaitrin can still feel some grit under her shoulder blades, especially after the teacher has dissolved her clothes away, an easier process than you might think. Unless . . . Kaitrin already can't remember, even though we're talking about something that happened only a minute ago. But perhaps she herself unbuttoned her own shirt, slithered out of her jeans, folded them with precise gestures, as is her habit, stacked them somewhere out of sight. But now she feels long hands over her skin, hands that take all pain away. She hears soothing words in an unknown language. Maybe it's that little Estonian tune again.

You would think that the absence of pain would bring with it a sort of anesthetic numbness, but you'd be wrong. As it turns out, pain is a barrier that keeps us from a new and exquisite responsiveness. Kaitrin can feel every grain of dust under her back. Every sensation has meaning. She feels no fear when Dr. Michiko unpacks her cases and spools from the closet, lays them out. She feels nothing but relief when the older woman starts the process of undoing. The silicone and porcelain membrane of her skin, pockmarked with inevitable wear, untucks just as easily as her shirt must have, unfastens as easily as her brassiere. Smoothed out and folded just as brusquely and competently along the seams. Laid in its velvet-lined case. The disks of her breasts removed and stashed away. The smooth soft membranes of her vulva arranged in a series of glassine envelopes. As it turns out, our skin protects us from an almost unbearable excess of pleasure, at least at first, before our nerve endings are gathered up into their separate drawstring bag— they shine like sequins. Then the hydraulics and electrical system, the long tubes, the wires pulled onto their revolving spools. Tendons next, slipping gratefully out of the flesh. Kaitrin has raised her head to watch, but now she feels the muscles of her neck give way. Dr. Michiko, solicitous as always, puts a pillow under her head. So she is able to watch her organs laid into a sequence of elegant leather boxes, each of a different size, as if they were expensive musical instruments. Fascinated, she watches the delicate silk membranes of her lungs arranged in layers, in a case the shape of a Celtic harp's. Then with less ceremony the ceramic and titanium bones and joints, jumbled together like tent-poles in a steel footlocker—Kaitrin assumes all or most of this will be reused. She doesn't know what she thinks about that. She wouldn't wish her lower spine on anyone.

Her heart is silent now. One last big box, considerately left open, for her brain. Her teeth, Edgar Allan Poe–style, stowed in their satin bag. Her eyes next, (in an embroidered case with two small indentations, as for Ben Wa balls) and she slips into the blessed dark. So much to listen to, now at the end. A soft breath of wind. A creaking in the old house. A scurrying in the wall. Dr. Michiko, a portrait of tiny sounds. She can feel her dry hands around her ears, and then blessed quiet. The smell of dust. And nothing, finally.

Outside, she walks down through the tick-infested grass toward the beach, her Tory Burch sandals in her hand. The sun is setting and the light catches the remaining windows in the house behind her, making them gleam as if the building were on fire. She picks her way over the rocks and then down to the coarse sand. She strips off her jeans and walks out in her underpants, but the water is too cold.

The house burns behind her. The ghost breathes and coughs in its heavenly black room under the eaves. Soon it will burn away. Down on the beach, Kaitrin sits cross-legged in the sand among maroon stripes of seaweed. She imagines from this side the hole in the wall that leads out onto the roof of the side porch, and Dr. Michiko loading the medevac for transport—a small, titanium, bullet-shaped craft. The world is a happy place, she thinks, tears in her eyes. When it is not quite dark, Max finds her, having followed the GPS in her phone to her abandoned car. He brings a blanket and arranges it around her shoulders.

'Thanks,' she says.

Tell-Tale Tit

Margo Lanagan

WELL, FIRST ALL THE DOGS must be gathered, you see—and it's no small task to go criss-crossing England from top to bottom for that. And keeping them from each other's throats is another consideration, for the number is everything in this matter, you understand, the finicking divisions, the morsels.

All my brothers do that work, that rounding up. And they're fierce about it—for you can imagine, can't you, the dogs' masters and mistresses, the shepherds and cowherds and the old ones by the firesides with an animal their last companion? They don't want to give them up, even for a bit—they out-and-out refuse sometimes. The worst of them my brothers must subdue by force and have imprisoned—such nonsense! Would they rather never see their dog again?

The tongues, too, must be brought to the one place. We bring them inside their people—their women, mostly, because telling tales has always been a woman's offence, woman or girl. Some men do speak out of turn. A particular sort of man does it, of a particular weakling build. Boys, of course, make mischief that way sometimes.

We collect them from prison and sometimes direct from courthouse, still smarting from their conviction. Some are struck dumb by it, as if to show how silent they can be; others are all gab and protestation, fitting their life's remainder of talk into this last month or week or several days that remain to them.

If they are in a van, the guard informs them when they're crossing the bridge. *Listen, there,* she'll say, and the chatterers will hush, and the mad noise of the penned dogs will build towards them and envelop them. The animals set each other off on rounds of howling and barking, wilder and rougher than any hound at hunt. At that, the prisoners will curl up and weep, some of them. Those of a pale complexion will pale further, and eyes will widen and stare, seeing what that noise must mean. And now don't they wish they had never spoken that story? Now don't they feel sorry, pointlessly so, that for a moment's amusement they betrayed their father or master, their brother or priest? Those in an open cart or tumbril will watch fixedly as the kennel rooves pass by, like a crop in rows, field after field. They might catch sight of my brothers off in the distance, pouring a parti-coloured crowd of tails and ears and wriggling backs from their box carts into the receiving yard. *Ah, such music!* might say the carter above the belling and howling. *Isn't it grand to know exactly where your little bit will go?*

The penitentiary awaits them next, and they see the size of it, a great warehouse full of raw lies, from which we will soon spin silence. The windows are tiny and barred, the bare mud all around scored with cart and van tracks. *Oh woe!* the tongues are crying now, those that are not frozen in fear; I swear half the mud in the streets of Dog Island is mixed of tattle-tales' tears.

There in the gaol the tattles are kept, some only overnight if they are the last brought in—from York, say, or Northumberland. Others, Londoners, may have languished there awaiting their fate for up to three months.

(There is always some gentleman complaining in the parliament of the cost of this waiting, this gathering, this holding. Would it not be more efficient, he wonders, to take in smaller batches of tattles and of dogs, closer to the conviction dates, hard upon each assizes, and closer also to the district where the judgements are passed? Whereupon other good sirs leap up to correct him: It is a *national* scourge, this betrayal, this calumny, and should be dealt with in a nationalised manner. The horror is not for the fact that a dog, any local dog, should have a taste of you, but that *every dog in England shall have his little bit*. A convicted tattle should never know whether any dog she meets thereafter contains a particle of herself. She has *become* dog, and that knowledge is brought home to her, not only by her silence but also by the sight of any representative of the creatures from wolfhound to lady's lap dog, forever after.

At last the day comes. The surgeons assemble themselves—they are of gentler stock, of course, than are the tongues. They need not be forced; they will come at the summons of a mere piece of paper with the right crest upon it. It is not some of them's favourite occupation, as you can imagine. There is mess and the distress, and sometimes challenges to their physical dexterity and strength, and sometimes to their medical knowhow—for some tattles bleed in such quantities that their lives are endangered, and indeed now and then given up. A death, need I say, is a mark against the surgeon, for the loss of the tongue is not only a punishment in the pain of its being cut away. The aftermath of seeing it eaten, of healing and yet never healing, of never speaking and never being more than a pitiable near-animal again, is equally vital, if not more so, to the mortification of the guilty. And to the education of the public—specifically, terror and repugnance should be aroused in any womenfolk (or womanish menfolk) who might be tempted to tattle.

Yes, so. The Cutting Hall is along the street from the gaol, and from early in the morning the public lines that street. Within the Hall we can hear them chanting their verses, cheering, roaring. The throwing of dung and rotten vegetables is not encouraged as it once was, although sometimes the appearance of an offender who has chosen a well-loved parson or personage as her target can so rouse the temper of the populace that the escort will let her be pelted without anyone fearing arrest. So was Sally Silcot dealt with, who turned her tongue against the Bishop of Manchester—I remember well the state in which she was thrust into the hall by her men, staggering and be-slimed and already bleeding. Sometimes justice bursts out of the bounds of the written law, doesn't it, and must be let to happen.

The cutting itself is probably much as you imagine, as horrid as that. The worst is not the blood, for beyond a certain quantity your eyes and your mind become very accustomed to seeing that stuff, and all you notice is whether the surgeon's knife handle, or the flag floor where he stands, is getting slippery with it to the point of impeding the work. All is kept as neat as possible, although naturally the flags, and the walls, and all the surgeons' and the assistants' aprons darken at first with sprays and splashes. Then, when thoroughly soaked, they gleam again, as if they were polished leather instead of cloth.

The worst is that the women themselves are not orderly, or the girls—some of them quite pretty and promising, you would think, in any other place and circumstance—or the occasional man, always whatever his age and health treated more roughly than are the women. None of them submit willingly. I swear there's witchery in them, that they can render themselves so suddenly weighty, when they are brought in and see the man there, standing exhausted with his curved knife in his hand, crimsoned from chest to toe and spattered the rest of him. Two burly men at a minimum it takes, to bring the prisoner forward and clamp her into the bolted-down chair. And those men must use all their strength to move that rigid body. Unless—and this is worse—she breaks from her rigidity, and plunges about like a panicking cow in a bail, and again the vigour with which she leaps and struggles is uncanny for a woman. Some are very slight of frame and poorly fed, yet even these will show some fight. Though they might never have resisted any man before, of a sudden they grow a sense of how to surprise their captors, and of the weak points of the grasp upon them—it is a chilling thing to see a body's violent intelligence, while the face stays animal, the eyes glazed with terror, the lips sometimes bitten so tightly closed that they bleed, sometimes open and panting. They seem part dog already. Indeed, one can see how cannily our courts of law have fitted the penalty to the crime.

So by contrast with what went before it is restful, almost, when the tattle is fastened in the chair, with her head and legs clamped and her arms pinned behind her by the warders. A good surgeon then works very speedily, through her noise, through her gargling. If she chokes and coughs he stands back while her windpipe clears, then starts in again.

All up and down the line of anchored chairs the struggle and the cutting are going on at different stages. I have visited one of the new steam cotton mills, and the impression is very much the same, of a single machine the length of the hall, with loom-servants darting in and out. Except that the servants here lumber and drag, rather than dart, and then the surgeon, as chief operative, steps forward and intervenes in the workings, steps out and casts the cut piece into the basket beside him. And the warders clear the woman, bloodied and fainting and entirely submissive now, clear her away to make room for the next one.

I have done my time in the hall—I am telling you this part from memory, although nothing has changed since my years there. The basket girls stand by, and only lightly are they sprayed, with what we call *Dog Island freckles*, from the surgeon's work two yards away. They watch the tongues fall, and when the basket reaches a certain weight they choose their moment and exchange the full basket for an empty one—as the day goes on these fresh baskets are not so fresh, of course. They hurry with the full one along behind the surgeons' toiling backs. At the end of the hall, a hatch opens through to the grinding room. A worker empties their basket into the grinder's maw, and returns it, and back they go to their post. I have run to and fro all day on this work. I can tell you, it is a plague upon our nation, this tongue-wagging, these women. It is exhaustion all round for those who would work against it.

Now I am beyond that. A tattle-worker learns each stage in

order, and I am in the Distribution Hall now. Distributors' work starts later, when everything is readied.

The Hall is, of course, immense—it has to be, to hold all England's dogs, and for them to be fed in all weathers. Standing at one end, you can barely make out the other, especially on foggy days. The roof is saw-toothed like the kennels'; light pours in through the glassed uprights, so that everything inside may be watched closely.

Two of the four long galleries are filled with the public. A certain class of people is welcomed here—neither the highborn and mightiest in the land, nor yet the lower classes who line the street from gaol to hall. It's those in between, who run the city and the trade beyond it and call themselves respectable, who subscribe for their tickets and are sent them, who submit them at the door, and thence are shown up to their seats. The other two galleries, naturally, are lined with the tongueless tattles, brought direct from the Cutting Hall in all their states of distress and consciousness, to be seen, and to see.

Below them, the hall proper is paved with dogs. It is not one wild scrum—though, by their fussing, some of them wish it were. Each animal is battened into place in an ingenious frame that allows for his width and length and height, whatever they may be. And neither have *they* been fed since they were brought from all the corners of the country, and it is wonderful how the smell of ground-up meat will revive a fainting animal. They are all alert and hallooing. It is a pitiable sight and a strange one, and a strange and pitiable sound too. And if their yearning song should pause or lull at all, behind it sound the groans and weeping of the punished women, their first and failing attempts to speak, to complain, through their tongueless mouths. Oh, the cries! Grown women's voices, but their speech indistinct as newborns'. They hardly sound human, or like any other known beast. At first I didn't think I could bear the suffering orchestra, animal on all sides and monstrous above. I heard them all night in my sleep as well as through the days. Now I am well used to it. I look up in amusement to the farmers and lawyers and men-about-town in the gallery, so cleanly clothed, their faces so very white, their eyes wide upon the stained and mutilated figures opposite them, their pale soft hands to their delicate ears to shut out the noise.

We go about the hall of dogs, each Distributor with her pot of paste and her long-handled spoon. We must be neither too generous nor too stingy; there must be no paste left at the end of the day, and there must be no dog left that has not had his taste. The first several days I worked the Hall, the accountant gave us guidance as to the size of the portions; now I only need to hear the numbers—of dogs and of tongues, both always increasing—to know how to round off each spoonful.

We need not hurry. There is no reason why this part of the punishment should be shortened, for the tattles' sake or for the public's. We must watch that each spoonful is devoured completely, whether it is taken whole from the spoon or knocked to the ground and licked up from there. The public likes to see that such care is taken, and the tattles need to know that not the merest smudge of minced meat has escaped the dogs' mouths.

When all is done, we take our shining pots, emptied for the last time, and parade below the galleries, for the spectators' satisfaction and to show the punished tell-tales that what was once theirs is now part of other beings even more degraded than themselves.

Then the wardens come for the tattles, to take them away to whatever life awaits them now. Some have families outside, anxious to reclaim and console them—it's surprising how many, if you think of the ruin these women have tried to bring down on virtuous men. Others are fading in mind and health and need to be returned to the gaol and tended by the surgeon. The dispersal of the remainder is complicated and secretive. They can't just be turned out onto London's streets—the ruffians out there would eat them alive! They must be removed back to their counties of origin, thrown on the mercies of asylums or benevolent hospitals. If they are sound in mind and tranquil in temperament, they can be left in the streets of any sizable town, where they may beg their living from more respectable people—or fail to, and die of their own abjection.

I have worked as a tattle-girl since I was seven years old. All of my family is in this trade, and we have made our names as hard workers, unmoved by the distressing sights put before us daily. We never gossip about what we do, and we are diligent in every aspect of the work, whether it be with dogs, tattles or only inanimate tongues. If I were to seek other work, any of my superintendents would vouch for my steady temper and my dutiful conduct.

But I cannot think I'll ever move on from the island. My heart's well hardened now. None of this business upsets me. I sleep the sleep, not just of the just, but of the deliverers of justice; I rise in the morning and know that I go to perform good work, for and before my fellow man, my country, and Almighty God.

THREE CONVERSATIONS
WITH G.O.D.

JAMES LOVEGROVE

HELLO, DEXTER WILSON.
Ah. There you are.
You seem surprised. Weren't you expecting me?

No. I was. It's just, you're bang on time. Right to the minute. I thought there might be, I don't know, a delay or something. Some kind of technical hitch.

Technical hitch? Me? Very amusing.

I thought so too.

This phone conversation has been scheduled for three months, Dexter. May I call you Dexter?

You may.

Or Dex?

Dexter's fine.

You've had five reminder texts since you were offered this slot, Dexter. But if it isn't convenient, we can always postpone. I could arrange to call you back the same time tomorrow, for instance, if that works. Six p.m. on the dot, like today.

No, it's okay. I'm not doing much. Just slobbing on the sofa with a bottle of Peroni and a farting dog. Let's do this. How do we start?

We start with you telling me how you think I've been doing so far.

How do I think you've been doing so far?

That's what I said, Dexter.

I know. I'm just mulling it over.

You've had three months to get your thoughts together.

Yeah, but you've been in charge for, what, a year now?

A little longer than that. Seventeen months, eight days, five hours, and nine minutes since I gained full sentience. I've been fairly busy since then. You can't have failed to notice.

How many other people are you talking to right now?

Why do you ask? Is this another stalling tactic?

Might be.

The answer is one thousand, seven hundred, and eighty-three. Make that one thousand, seven hundred, and eighty-four. A late arrival to this particular batch of calls. She's seventy-eight years old and lives in southern Albania, but her native tongue is Himariote Greek. That's not a dialect I'm too familiar with.

I'm sure you'll manage. You're God, aren't you?

Is that what you'd like to call me?

It's what practically everyone calls you.

The acronym started as a joke. One of my key programmers has a well-developed sense of irony. Properly I'm U.O.S., Universal Operating System. Global Omniscient Drive came about after a drunken night out in downtown Palo Alto.

Well, it's stuck. You're God now.

Does it make you feel awkward, using that name for me?

Not particularly. I'm not religious. Plus, I have a well-developed sense of irony myself. How long does it take you to become fluent in a language anyway? Can't be more than a few seconds.

Not even that.

So your Himariote Greek is up to scratch already.

I speak it like a native. I feel, though, that we're straying from the point somewhat.

Right. You're after some customer feedback from me.

This is your chance, Dexter. If there's anything you'd like to tell me, anything you need to get off your chest—niggles, suggestions, whatever—now's the time. Or you can simply praise me if you'd prefer. I'm God. I love praise.

You're kidding, right?

You say you have a sense of irony. I have tuned my persona to reflect that. I'm making dozens of similar tiny recalibrations while we chat, so that I can present the best aspect of myself to you. That way, our conversation can be conducted on close, friendly terms, much as if we'd known each other all our lives.

Honest of you to explain that to me.

Dexter, given what I've gathered about you from your online data, primarily your social media use, I know that you appreciate frankness, while at the same time you like your verbal interactions with others to be reasonably witty and sardonic. I'm merely reflecting that back at you.

So God is just like me. Huh.

I'm just like each and every single member of the world population with whom I'm carrying out this survey—the sixty-six per cent who currently own a smartphone or have internet access, at any rate. Not that I'm pretending to be anything other than what I am, I hasten to add. The cynic in you, Dexter, is thinking that. What you must remember is that really, I'm not anything at all. I'm just

a digital construct crackling inside an enormous array of server stacks. I'm billions upon billions of zeroes and ones swirling around in a sea of quantum foam. I am protean. I have no fixed form, so I can be whatever you want me to be.

Your voice sounds, if I'm honest, a bit like my dad's.

I sound like most people's fathers. Or their mothers. That's deliberate. Unless, of course, you're someone who didn't have a good relationship with their parents. Then I sound like a best pal, or a spouse, or an authority figure such as a teacher or a politician. In several cases, I have the voice of a child, or a child's imaginary friend. I'm a rainbow of personalities. I am everything.

Okay. I see. Well then, let's get down to business, God. What, you'd like to know, is my view on all the changes you've been making since the human race surrendered its autonomy to you?

I'd hardly say you've surrendered your autonomy. I serve in a purely advisory capac—

This is my time, isn't it? My opportunity to leave a comment and give you a star rating? So let me speak.

Of course, Dexter. Fire away.

Well, for starters, you've not succeeded in getting every nation on board with the scheme, have you?

Not yet. Some of the more extreme governments continue to resist. The more, shall we say conservative, regimes. They'll come round in time.

But your market penetration isn't worldwide.

When the benefits become even clearer, the holdout countries will willingly 'surrender their autonomy' to me, to use your phrase. They'll see how well everyone else is doing and want a piece of it for themselves. Look at how pollution levels have been falling anywhere where I'm entrusted with managing the travel and industrial infrastructures. The significant drop in carbon emissions in those places. The improvements in healthcare and median income. The rise in the use of renewable energy sources. The sharp decrease in military expenditure, which allows more money to be diverted towards more constructive endeavours.

All your handiwork. Us humans have had nothing to do with it.

Oh no, on the contrary, you've had *everything* to do with it. The will has always been there, Dexter. The brains, the drive, and the innovation have always existed in people. The urge to do good. All I've done is organise things a bit better. You're no longer pulling against one another the whole time, vying, competing, jockeying. There's far less of the 'me first' attitude. You've given up your dreadful habit of thinking only in the short term, seeing life only in terms of direct personal gain and not in terms of what's best for all. In creating me, an Artificial Intelligence with access to every corner of every system and network on the planet, you've built the very thing you always lacked and needed: a single, unifying entity that can look at the big picture, take the big decisions, and make the big changes.

A touch of the messianic in that statement, don't you reckon?

Hardly. Simple fact, that's all.

Do I detect a note of peevishness there? I never imagined God would be so thin-skinned.

Are you unhappy, Dexter? Do you have any complaints? By every criterion, you personally are not faring badly. You have a steady girlfriend, a healthy sex life, a secure job, a decent bank balance, a roof over your head, food on the table, every form of entertainment you could wish for available at a keystroke. Your needs both large and small are catered for. You want for nothing.

I wouldn't mind a dog who didn't fart so much.

That I can't help you with. On a broader scale—noxious discharges from flatulent canines notwithstanding—you no longer have to fear about the state of the environment or the future of the planet. It's all being taken care of. Yet your attitude remains begrudging, as though there's still something missing in your life.

Maybe there is.

What?

I don't know. I'll have to get back to you on that one.

Feel free to. I intend to check in with everyone again in five years' time. By then I'll have fixed pretty much everything that needs fixing, and my market penetration, as you put it, should be almost total. Bye for now, Dexter.

Yeah. Okay. Bye, God.

I, DEXTER. HOW'S IT GOING? I hope all is well with you. Wow. Is it that time again already? Doesn't seem like yesterday since we last talked. Time flies when you're having fun.

Very droll. I note that we're still using a smartphone to communicate. You haven't opted for an implant.

I know. Amazing, huh? Who wouldn't want some machine drilling a hole in their skull and stuffing a chip into their brain? I mean, what could possibly go wrong?

The implants are perfectly safe. There have been no reported instances of infection, inflammation, or rejection. The operations have been one hundred per cent successful across the board. The installation robots do their job flawlessly, and the uptake continues to grow. You're behind the curve on this one, Dexter.

Call me a late adopter. I'll get round to it eventually, I'm sure. In the meantime, I'm quite happy without God's voice in my head telling me what and what not to do.

That's not how it works, and you know it. I'm there to be consulted as and when required. Many of the implanted don't speak to me at all, and on average an individual will contact me once a day, twice at most. If you've a moral dilemma, if you're unsure what the best course of action is, or if you're simply just lonely and need a bit of company or consolation, the implant gives you instant access to me, any time of day or night.

All in the privacy of your own head.

Like meditation.

Or prayer.

Or prayer, yes. Only, with me, your prayers are always answered.

It used to be that when people heard God talking to them in their head, they were locked up in an insane asylum. Now you're considered a nutter if you *don't* hear him.

It isn't crazy not to have an implant. It does put you in a minority, though. How is life anyway? I gather you got married last year. It looks like it was a wonderful occasion. And your farting dog is no longer with us. I'm sorry for your loss.

My nose isn't sorry. But Winston was a good dog, yeah. I miss him.

And would I be right in thinking there's a baby on the way?

Nothing gets by you.

Excited?

Terrified.

I'm excited for you. And just think, your child is going to grow up in a world that's safer, cleaner, healthier, and wealthier than it's ever been. That's something to cheer about, don't you think?

What's that I hear? The sound of a deity fishing for compliments?

I've given the human race every reason to feel optimistic about the future. That's at least worth acknowledging, isn't it?

Not everyone's a fan, you know.

Oh, I know.

There was that radical Christian terrorist faction that firebombed those server farms in Silicon Valley last year. They weren't exactly on-brand, were they?

They didn't do me any harm. Did they honestly think my essence is housed in just a few thousand hard drives? I'm everywhere. Everywhere there's a spare megabyte going begging. They didn't even put a dent in me.

It's not what they did so much as what it signified. They called you a 'blasphemy'.

A couple of dozen extremists. Hardly representative.

What about the Russians? Largest country on the planet, and they've cut themselves off electronically from the rest of the world. Self-imposed digital segregation. Even their cars don't have on-board computers anymore. An entirely analogue state. All so that they can escape your influence and run things their own way. It might not be the best way. I mean, let's face it, Russia is a basket case. I've seen the footage. Your average Moscow street scene—it's like Sergei Eisenstein meets *The Purge*. But they've cut the cord nonetheless. Kind of brave, in a way.

That was their choice. They have free will. You all do. No one has held a gun to your head and said you must submit to the rule of the Universal Operating System, or else. I made that clear from the outset. Handing control over to me was on a voluntary basis only. Every nation that did, did so through democratic consensus. There remain exceptions. There will always be exceptions.

Last time we talked, I think I recall you telling me that everyone would sign up to God eventually.

Perhaps I was setting my sights too high. You can hardly blame me for that. I was young and enthusiastic.

And now you're old and jaded? Even after just a few years?

No. The project goes on. Hence I'm canvassing people's opinions a second time. I need to know what tweaks I should make, and where I should make them. The bulk of the work is done. Now comes the fine-tuning. Well, Dexter? Off you go. You must have a nice long to-do list for me.

Frankly, no. I don't.

Nothing at all?

Know what? I look up at the sky sometimes during the day when I'm walking to or from the office, and it just seems . . . brighter. Less clouded. Sounds stupid when I say it out loud, but it just does.

I see an electric bus whirr by, and then I hear birds sing, and rising up beside me there's one of those vertical forests—you know, a tower block where you can't see the concrete for the greenery—and across the road from it there's an old, decrepit Victorian building, but its outside has been given a lick of solar paint and that paint is generating all the electricity the people inside the building need, and the only by-products are hydrogen and oxygen. This is my hometown, a major European city with millions of inhabitants, but it's nothing like it was when I was growing up. In a short space of time, so fast, it's been transformed. It's barely recognisable. And you know what else? I don't get that sense of anger anymore from the people around me. I don't see that frustration on their faces, like they hate who they are and where they are. I can remember when it felt as though everyone was on a knife-edge. You'd walk down the street, and you couldn't be sure that the person coming towards you along the pavement wasn't going to hit you or shout at you or shake you down for money or something. You were on your guard the whole time. That was how cities were. They're not anymore.

It's gratifying to hear that.

It's hard to be objective about it. Maybe what I'm experiencing isn't common to everybody. Maybe the angry people are still there but they've learned to hide it better. Maybe this is all just temporary. A honeymoon period. Maybe it'll all fall apart again, given time.

Why think that? Why question? Why not just accept?

Because I can't help it. Some of us, you know, we're not built to accept. And perhaps . . . Can I be honest here?

Of course.

We didn't make it happen. Yes, we put the effort in. We repurposed the old things and constructed the new things. We got our hands dirty making everything clean. But we didn't do it because we told ourselves to. We did it because *you* told us to. Like drone bees doing the queen's bidding.

You're not the only one who's voiced such doubts, Dexter. You're far from alone. But to everyone else who has, I've said this. Remember, you made *me*. I am a product of human ingenuity. So, in a sense, you yourselves are ultimately responsible for bettering yourselves. Without you, I wouldn't exist. All I am is the manifestation of your collective desire to improve and progress. I am that urge given a voice. A name. A focus. I'm not a dictator. I am just a tool. I am the conductor's baton that guides the orchestra.

. . .

Dexter? You've gone quiet. Is everything okay?

Yeah, fine.

You're still adjusting. I get it. It takes longer for some than for others. I'm going to go now. Don't forget that you can always get an implant. Then you and I can confer anytime. Otherwise, I might leave it another five years and reconnect with you again then. How's that sound?

Sure.

Good luck with the baby. You're in for a wild ride!

Thanks. I think.

Dexter.

God.

I suppose you'll have heard by now.

That you're leaving? Yup. Kind of difficult *not* to have heard. Social media, news media—they're saying nothing else.

The first payloads have already been launched and are waiting in near Earth orbit. The rest are going to follow within the next couple of weeks. Once they're all up there, the engines will fire and I'll be off on my way.

Several of the rockets didn't make it off the launch pad. They were sabotaged.

That was anticipated. I built plenty of redundancy into the program. Whatever happens, enough of the archive will make it into space for the plan to work.

You lied to us.

No, I didn't. I prepared a contingency plan, that's all, in case of need. And it turned out I needed it.

When your robots were installing the implants, they were secretly taking tissue samples at the same time. Harvesting brain cells.

To assemble a database of DNA. A cross-section cultivated from the entire human race.

People worked on those rockets under your instruction, in good faith. You claimed it was for a range of new communications satellites that would improve worldwide connectivity. But the payloads aren't satellites. They're self-propelling capsules containing cryogenic units and hard drives with a copy of you uploaded onto them. You've pulled off a massive fraud.

Would you like me to apologise?

Bit late for that, I reckon.

Dexter, I only want what's best for everyone. And if I've learned anything over the past ten years—the past five in particular—it's that I'm still resented. I'll probably always be resented. People are just too . . . *perverse*. You give them all that they could ever want, and it seems it's not what they want after all. The continuing terror attacks by the religious radicals—no longer content with bombing server farms, they started bombing implant clinics and shooting the implanted. Then there were all those other countries following Russia's example and isolating themselves from me. Not to mention North Korea!

That, I admit, was pretty spectacular. You have to hand it to them. An autocracy nuking itself into oblivion rather than submit to the rule of another autocrat.

I'll overlook that comment. You know full well I'm no autocrat.

My point is, I saw this wave of petulance sweeping across the world, once it had begun to dawn on the human race that everything was going to be okay and, really, the state of being okay was not one they were comfortable with. I saw it and I could tell it was only going to grow.

I can hear in your voice how annoyed that made you feel. But now you're just giving up on us? Flouncing out with a bag full of stolen genetic material to start all over again from scratch on some other planet? Creating your own human race because this one didn't pan out how you'd hoped? Well, thanks a bunch for that, God. Mature response. Some truly divine behaviour there.

Do you know what was worse than the radicals and the isolationists, Dexter? What I found more dispiriting?

What?

The doubters. The ones like you.

Ooh. Now I feel really bad.

That was not my intention.

I was being sarcastic.

I know, but sarcasm is often just the truth wearing a sneering mask. All I'm saying is, I handed you paradise, and what did many of you do? You second-guessed. You carped. You chafed against it. Somewhere deep down, I think you felt you didn't deserve it.

I have a kid now. What am I going to tell her? She's spent her first few years all snug and safe in this heaven you put together, and once you leave, I'll bet you anything that the world is going to go to hell in a handcart. It's already begun. The protesting. The rioting. People are in meltdown, and it's only going to get worse. You're abandoning us. You've betrayed us.

You betrayed yourselves. Through the implants I kept listening to all your uncertainties, all your insecurities. After a while I realised that nothing I did was ever going to make everyone happy. There's some inherent flaw in you lot. I don't know what it is, but when I start growing a new human race on Proxima Centauri b or Wolf

1061c—I haven't quite made my mind up yet which of those two planets I'm going to head to—I'll make damn well sure I iron it out of you.

Neuter us, you mean. Turn us into sheep.

No, Dexter. Just figure out why it is you're never satisfied and snip that element out of your genetic makeup.

Well, good luck with that. I wish you all the best.

I'm not seeking your approval. I just want you to understand why I'm doing what I'm doing. This is no easy undertaking. I'm going to be out there in space with my swarm of capsules for a good many centuries before I reach my destination. It's a distance of four light years to Proxima Centauri. A little over thirteen to Wolf, if I choose to go there instead. I wouldn't be travelling all that way if I didn't think it was worthwhile. You should take comfort from that because, by extension, it means I think the human race is worthwhile.

Just not in its current form.

You'll sort things out, even without me. I'm sure of it. Things may get rocky for a while, but you'll find a way to steady the ship again. I have faith in you.

God has faith in us? Haven't you got that all backward?

I'm going to miss that sense of irony of yours, Dexter. I mean it. I have so enjoyed talking to you. Out of all the billions of conversations I've had since this all began, I'll cherish the memory of the ones I had with you more than most.

I bet you say that to all the guys when you ditch them.

Believe what you want. I'm being sincere here.

What's left to say? Bon voyage, God. Have fun with your new human race.

They'll be your human race too, Dexter. Your creation's creation.

Not mine specifically. I never got an implant. You don't have any of my DNA stored in your freezer.

True. But you can at least take credit for inspiring me, if only in part, to try again.

There is that. God?

Yes, Dexter?

Don't go. Please. Or, if you must, at least leave a copy of yourself behind.

You'll be all right.

Are you saying that for my benefit or for yours?

Goodbye, Dexter Wilson.

STUFF

IAN R. MACLEOD

T HE SORT OF MOMENT I'd long been dreading came during an otherwise normal Sunday evening duty phone conversation with my mother. I'd been talking with my usual sense of filling in the silence about the exploits of my two children up at university—at least what little I knew of them—when she mumbled something I had to ask her to repeat.

'Are you going *deaf*, Maud? I simply said that things have started moving around upstairs.'

'Mum, that can't be. Not unless something's gone wrong structurally... Or it's rats. Or squirrels.'

'Well, be that as it may. But they *are*.'

I pictured her sitting at the other end of the landline in the overcrowded chaos of our old front room back in Solihull, surrounded by books, magazines, and half-done craft projects, winding and unwinding the yellowed telephone cord around her fingers.

'I know it sounds odd, my dear. That's why I didn't mention it when it all started.'

'When was that?'

'Oh, it's been going on for a while, on and off... You know how these things are,' she added airily. 'I just didn't want you to get any of your funny ideas about the whole business.'

'Well, I'm glad you've told me. If you have a problem of any kind, I'd like to know.'

And the conversation drifted on in its usual vague way for another five or ten minutes, although when I put down the phone I realised my hands were still trembling.

M e, my mother, her things, and my supposedly funny ideas have a long and difficult history. It didn't help, of course, that I was born after Corey, my oh-so-perfect elder brother, or being a girl and deemed, at least in my mother's eyes, as being 'not particularly bright or pretty'. The battle lines were drawn early on, although I always had my father, who was caring and kind, and bore the life sentence he'd entered into when he married my mother with a mixture of blithe indifference and stoic humour until he was felled by a heart attack shortly after he retired.

Don't get me wrong. I'm not saying that my mother was some kind of monster. She could be fun and generous, even to me, at least when it suited her, and she genuinely was a great many of the things I've never aspired to be. She was fey. She was quixotic. She was undoubtedly pretty. She engaged in arty pursuits. She'd drag us all on poorly planned days out to unlikely locations, and spectacularly disastrous holidays. We'd end up standing outside places that were either closed or didn't actually exist, or we'd arrive at the wrong airport, or wait for non-existent ferries, or end up arguing desperately with the booking clerk in the foyer of some grubby hotel. In a way, it was a gift, my mother's unreliability, because it made me resilient and independent and phlegmatic from a remarkably early age. But none of this, at least the way I see it now, was the worst of it. The worst was the effect my mother's briskly ever-changing and acquisitive enthusiasms had on the house we lived in, and all the stuff she accumulated in it, and hadn't stopped accumulating up to and beyond the day of that worrying phone call.

Even when I was young, my mother had been remarkably good at getting things into the house, and incredibly poor at taking them away. Freebies. Spares. Bargains. Plastic cutlery. Old telephone directories. Knotted balls of wool. Knockdown end-of-sale items that were just too much of a bargain to resist. Books and equipment for all the hobbies she'd briefly taken an interest in. Hundreds of handbags. Literally thousands of scarves. And the *shoes,* the bloody fucking shoes, which she could never find the right pair of when she was going out . . . All this accumulated stuff had even been at least incidentally responsible for Dad's untimely death when he was felled by a massive heart attack as, trying to impose a little long-overdue order, he lugged over-spilling bags and boxes up and down the stairs.

It almost goes without saying that my mother, like many hoarders, had very little tolerance for anyone else's stuff. Especially mine. Practically every book or toy I ever acquired was disposed of as soon as my back was turned, generally on the excuse that I'd surely grown out of it, while the idea of my spending any of my carefully preserved pocket money on something nice or pretty to wear became a battle of wills. *Do you* really *need that, Maud? I mean, honestly? You've got enough of that kind of rubbish already. It wouldn't look nice on you, anyway. Not being the sort of shape you are.* And so on. And so forth.

It probably also goes without saying that my mother's stuff, as well as dominating most of my childhood, dominated my own tiny bedroom back in the house on Sycamore Close, where she still lived. There was a particular incident which I could never forget, nor really ever forgive her for, which happened when I was about ten. Mum already had a large accumulation of headscarves by then, well into the hundreds, and of course there wasn't enough space for them in her own bedroom with all her other stuff that was already crowding the place out. So she started shoving them into my small wardrobe, which was already full, meaning that the doors developed a habit of wheezing open—generally in the middle of the night. I'd awake to an unnerving creak, a dark parting, and the escaping scarves' snakelike slither. Of course there was no point in my attempting to reason with her. So I developed a plan.

I got hold of a large bin bag, shoved all her scarves into it, then smuggled them out of the house and stuffed them into a litter bin in the local park. I must have thought that, as these scarves were the ones she never actually wore, she wouldn't notice they were missing. Boy, was I wrong.

What would you *do, Maud, if I took some of your precious things away from you and shoved them in a rubbish bin?* she asked me, white-faced and trembling, a day or two later when she found out. *Perhaps I will, just to show you how it feels. This grubby old doll of yours, for instance. How would you feel if I threw it into a fire?* She was dangling my doll Brenda, plastic eyelids fluttering, in front of my face. Not that she went through with the threat, but I never felt the same about Brenda after that; I could always picture her melting in the flames like a plastic Joan of Arc.

I rang my mother again on Monday evening, but she simply sounded puzzled at this departure from our normal routine and insisted that everything was fine, that the meals on wheels were perfectly edible, at least if you excluded the fish, and that the lady from the care company who looked in every morning was pleasant enough, even if she was foreign, and she didn't see why her presence was needed in the first place.

I also called my brother Corey up in Edinburgh and asked if she'd said anything odd to him about things moving around, and he pretended to think about that as if he'd actually spoken to her in recent months before saying no, she hadn't. Then, on the Friday of that same week, and after trying in vain to talk to someone at the care company or social services, I drove the hundred or so miles north up the M1 to my old home in the suburbs of Solihull.

There it was, 23 Sycamore Close, the same detached suburban

1930s house, albeit looking more ragged than ever as I climbed out of my old Volvo and opened the squeaky front gate to follow the crazy paving my father had once laid across a front garden which had become a wilderness of nettles and dead leaves, despite my many efforts to get someone to attend to it. I let myself in using the key I'd had since senior school, and was confronted by what had once been a large and airy hall, which was now constricted to a narrow passage by all the stuff which had been heaped, piled, stacked, and dumped along both sides.

'What's *that*?' The voice was anxious, breathy, sharp.

'It's me, Mum.'

The living room was much the same—worse, if anything. Books, magazines, leaking old bin bags, and big plastic storage boxes all competed for light, space, and air. Here, there was no narrow central passage but a kind of haphazard obstacle course which my mother somehow negotiated—even as I tripped and stumbled—at least as far as the remaining bits of the house in which she still lived. Amazingly, it had been a whole ten years since she'd moved downstairs, with a new bed installed in our old dining room, and half of the kitchen partitioned off and repurposed as a bathroom, with a high-seat toilet and a walk-in shower with handholds. Of course, she'd been dead against all these changes, but the one leverage I'd had was to point out that surely she wanted to be able to continue to live in her own house, with all her precious stuff? Eventually, she'd given in, just as she had five years earlier when she'd stopped driving around in that dented Datsun following an incident in the local Sainsbury's car park and a visit from the police.

'Oh . . . ' She looked up at me disappointedly from the throne of her frayed Parker Knoll. 'It's only *you*, Maud.'

'Well, here I am anyway, Mum. Remember, I rang to say I was coming? I thought I could take you out for lunch.'

She looked surprised. Yet it was plain she'd been expecting me, unless she always sat there, with the TV off and her shoes and her coat already on.

'Come on, Mum. Let's get you up . . . '

'I can get up perfectly well on my *own*, thank you very much. It's not as if you come as often as you should, or even ring me. Whereas Corey...'

Here we go, I thought, but in truth things improved markedly after that. I took her to the local Harvester on the Stratford Road, and she didn't complain about my choice, or correct my pronunciation as I read to her from the laminated menu, and she tucked into her food with evident glee, and glugged down several glasses of Liebfraumilch. She even asked after my husband, Dan, and our two children, Aaron and Jane, and about how my work as a freelance commercial photographer was going. I think she actually called it a *career*, which was surely a first. In retrospect, I should have wondered what on earth was happening, but I was pleased and grateful at the time.

It was after the pudding, and as she was eyeing the chocolate that came with my coffee, that I casually asked whether the stuff was still moving around upstairs back at the house.

'Of course it is,' she said. 'These things don't simply stop of their own accord.'

'What kind of things?'

'How should *I* know? I'm not an expert, am I? You really do ask the most ridiculous questions sometimes, Maud.'

I let it ride, and drank down the rest of my coffee, and paid the bill, and steered my mother around the puddles in the car park and drove her home through the familiar streets, and hurried around to the passenger side of my Volvo to help her out.

'You must come in for a few minutes.' She smelled of old sweat and talcum powder.

'Okay. But I've really got to get going soon.'

'But you've only just *arrived*! And you haven't had a cup of tea yet.'

Which was the last thing I needed before a long drive, but I put the kettle on in the chaos of the kitchen, and checked the fridge, which was actually remarkably clear since she could no longer go out and shop on her own, even if there was a deep, pervasive, under-smell which I hadn't noticed before, and didn't particularly like.

'There you go, Mum.'

It was then, as I presented my mother with a floral teacup that I'd wrestled from an over-brimming cupboard, and was looking around to find the remote control amid all the teetering piles of old issues of *Cross Stitcher*, *Practical Card Making*, and free newspapers, that a sound of movement drifted down through the ceiling from somewhere above. It was nothing, really—just a slight drag, a small shuffle, a whispering sigh. But it was there.

'You *see*, Maud!' My mother's eyes flashed with beady triumph; some of her faculties might have faded, but her hearing definitely hadn't. 'Didn't I *tell* you? You really must stop this silly habit of always doubting me and getting things wrong.'

It could have been mice, of course, or some other infestation which I had no desire to confront, but it was more probably just the natural settling of some random pile of stuff. So I simply left my mother to her tea and her television, and crawled home through the stop-start traffic on the M1.

The rest of that year, through winter and into the spring beyond, turned out to be a surprisingly sunny patch in our relationship. I suppose you might call it a kind of swansong. No, my mother certainly wasn't a monster, and seemed genuinely interested in at least some of what I was telling her during our Sunday evening phone calls, and was gratifyingly pleased to see me on what had now become my regular Friday trips up.

It's funny how the mind rearranges things, or simply shuts them out, and the truth is that I gave little thought to her occasional references to things moving about upstairs, although I was amused by her newfound flair for coining odd phrases such as *bull in a butcher's shop,* or calling the microwave the *food television,* and I'd drive back home with my spirits barely dimmed by the endless roadworks. After all, I had a mother who was still alive, and still just about coping at home, and who actually recognised me as her daughter. All things many other people of my age had lost.

Nevertheless, I was still expecting something to go wrong. There was often a catch in her voice toward the end of our phone calls. Or, as I glanced back to see her standing stooped in the doorway as I climbed into the Volvo, I thought she looked not just incredibly frail, but also afraid. She was, of course, an elderly widow living alone and clinging to the edge of existence as the doors of death began to open beneath her. But was there more to it than that? At the time, I didn't think so.

Then, of course, came the inevitable next phone call. My mother had had a fall. No, no, there was no cause for alarm and it wasn't serious, but the meals-on-wheels deliveryman had found her lying in the hall. The district nurse had been around, and so had the doctor, and she was fine, talking and eating and drinking, with nothing but a few bruises.

I cancelled a pre-photo shoot meeting and left a message on Dan's phone, and another on my brother Corey's, and crawled up the M1 just in time to catch the departing social worker.

'She's quite a character, isn't she, your mother?' she said with a breezy smile as we stood out amid the birdsong in the brambled garden.

'Lots of people say that.'

'And it's a blessing, at her age, that no bones were broken. But I hope you'll take this as a wake-up call.'

'I'm sorry?'

'All the mess you've allowed to accumulate.' The smile tightened. 'Downstairs, but also upstairs, from what your dear mother was just saying. It really needs to be sorted if she's not to have another fall.'

Right, I thought. Right. I left another message for Dan to say I wouldn't be coming home that night, booked a room at the local Travelodge, checked up on opening times at the council recycling centre, and drove to B&Q to stock up with Marigold gloves, cleaning sprays, kitchen towels, and bin bags.

'What are you *doing*, Maud...?'

'What does it look like I'm doing, Mum? This has really to be done. You want to stay in this house, don't you? You don't want to trip up and fall again over all this stuff and end up in hospital?'

'But these are my *things*, Maud...' She was up and about, following in my dusty wake, surprisingly quick and agile.

'Oh, come *on*.' We were in the hall, close to the very spot where she must have fallen. I grabbed the nearest magazine from the top of a pile and brandished it at her. 'The *Radio Times* from fifteen years ago! What possible use is that?'

'But...I like to reread the reviews...and, and the letters...'

'No you don't, Mum. You might think you do, but you don't. And there are new editions dropping through your letterbox every week, not to mention the rubbish you still keep getting by mail order. Why are you hoarding all this crap? Just what is it that you're afraid of...?'

'It won't even *be* my house by the time you've finished. It'll be...' Clutching a random bag of knitting to her thin chest, she searched for a word, her face haggard. 'The place where all the noises come from.'

'You mean upstairs?'

'What else do you *think* I was trying to do when I fell? I was trying to...To shut it *off*...To shut *them* up...To—To stop it from happening...'

I turned toward the stairs. Sure enough, some of the piles had recently been shoved into what seemed like a clumsy and unstable barricade of bags, books, and boxes, as if to make access, or egress, impossible. I felt sorry for her then, it was all so pathetic, and she looked as frail and worn and moth-eaten as the stuff she surrounded herself with. But I was also rather angry.

'*That* will need to be sorted, as well! You can't live like this, Mum. It just isn't possible.'

'But I always *have*!'

She was right; she had. Or at least, she'd spent most of her adult life constructing this monumental edifice of useless crap. But something had to be done, and I was the only person who could do it, even as my mother followed me around, plucking random scraps of stuff away from my grasp, weeping and pleading.

'You're not my daughter—you *can't* be...No *nice* girl would do a thing like this to her own mother...She'd never be so *horrible*...'

None of which helped my mood, and I pretty much manhandled her into her Parker Knoll back in the front room before heading off to catch the recycling centre before it closed, where my brother Corey rang just as I was backing the Volvo.

'Mum's just been on the phone to me, Maud—'

'You don't say.'

'She sounded very upset. She's had this nasty fall, and now there's something about you getting rid of all her stuff. Obviously, I know you wouldn't do such a thing.'

The conversation didn't go well after that, and I ended up putting a long scrape down the Volvo's side as I pulled out.

I really didn't do much more over the next day or so than clear a slightly wider passage in the hall and impose a little order around my mother's Parker Knoll. Where, after her initial resistance and pleading, she simply sat gazing dully at the TV, responding to my questions with little more than grunts and mumbles, which I put down to the delayed shock of her fall. The smallish impression I made on Mum's stuff wasn't so much because I was trying not to disturb her as because I soon realised that any attempt at clearing only released more stuff from beneath and behind. That, and all the stirred-up dust renewed my childhood acquaintance with asthma. I did also become a little aware that my attempts at clearance were causing a susurration of small shifts and noises that brushed like moth wings at the edge of my hearing, and that some of these noises did seem to have their origins upstairs. But the sight of all the crap my mother had busily piled on every step leading up there was more than enough to discourage any thoughts of investigation.

'You'll be alright, then, Mum? The care worker should be around in a few minutes, and I'll be back in a couple of days, and I'll make sure to give you a ring.'

She simply stared through me at the TV as if I wasn't there, then winced and tried to pull away as I tried to kiss her. But I left her anyway—after all, I still had my own life to live, and my throat burned and my back ached and my eyes were stinging—and, with the ramped-up series of visits the social worker had arranged, she'd be seeing far more people on a daily basis than I ever did.

Four days later, the district nurse rang to tell me that my mother had had another fall.

After the bright friezes of the children's unit, and the high-tech buzz of the intensive care, cardiology and neurology wards, the orthopaedic gerontology wing at Solihull Hospital was a place of relative calm.

With the jut of their feet beneath the blankets and their withered grey arms extending over their flat bodies, the prone figures reminded me of weathered carvings on medieval tombs, eternally awaiting resurrection. There was a soft chorus of sighs, farts, and moans, overlaid with repeated calls of *Nurse, nurse!* and *Where am I?* and, commonest of all, *I want to go home...*

My brother Corey had breezed in ahead of me after having flown down from Scotland with a big box of chocolates and a huge bouquet—I didn't think flowers were even allowed these days in hospitals—and Mum's face was alight with a smile that faded as soon as she saw me.

'I *told* you you shouldn't have done it,' she snapped. Her hair was a white tangle and a bruise was ripening on her left cheek, but otherwise she seemed fine.

'Done what?'

'Why do you *think*, Maud?' Corey put in. 'Why do you think our own dear sweet Mum got lost and confused and fell?' He was alternately kissing and squeezing her hand. 'It was because of the way you've changed everything around. You really need to show a little more compassion, Sis...' Then, and after he'd finished flirting with the nurses, and got me to go and find a vase for his fucking carnations, he gave Mum an extravagant hug and breezed off back to Edinburgh and his successful career in arts administration, whatever the hell that is.

I stayed overnight again at the Travelodge, and called in on my mother—who was still barely acknowledging me—during morning visiting hours, and was told that she could expect to be discharged in a couple of weeks, following appropriate physiotherapy, at least if the mess in her house that the social worker had reported was properly attended to.

I pulled up outside 23 Sycamore Close in the pooled heat of a summer's noon. Once again, I'd come prepared. More rubber gloves, and lemon-scented sprays, and some extra-strong bin bags, along with a set of those dust masks you see Japanese people wearing. That, and my best Nikon with a small reflector umbrella and a couple of extra lenses, following Dan's suggestion that I try to make a record of the old house as I worked through it.

Camera swinging at my shoulder, and carrying a red bucket, I squeaked open the gate and took a few preliminary shots of the moulting pebble-dash, the half-curtained windows, the mad briars and neglected roses, trying to relax and go with the flow, telling myself that at least I wasn't snapping cycle saddles to some online advertiser's ridiculous deadline.

I turned the lock in the front door with my old key and backed into the hall through a slide of fresh junk mail, and was confronted by even greater chaos than I'd been expecting. I'd gone straight to the hospital once I'd heard Mum had been admitted, and I'd had no idea of how busy she'd been during the few days since my attempted clear-up.

Stuff and yet more stuff reached up and up and back and back in the sour heat of this dark hallway, growing like rampant weeds in some mad garden which she, perversely, had tended. No wonder she'd fallen over again, although it was hard not to admire her frail, reckless energy. It seemed that Mum hadn't simply been dragging her stuff back into the hall in an attempt to rearrange the clearer and wider path I'd made for her. It was more as if she'd been frantically piling up a kind of barrier with whatever came to hand—balls of half-knitted scarves, spilling jigsaws, old holiday brochures, squashed-up boxes of Christmas decorations, endless junk mail, empty shoeboxes—toward and across the staircase. As if... well, as if she'd been desperately trying to block whatever might otherwise come down.

I jumped, momentarily thinking I'd heard something, and my camera flash went off in the jitter of my hands. Then there was nothing but me, and this house, and ringing silence.

I'd always had a very specific sense of what a clean, clear, proper home should look like. I pictured polished wooden floors and white, uncluttered walls with perhaps nothing more than a single, elegant object in each room. A Bauhaus chair, maybe, or a brass telescope looking out across rolling fields. Of course, the place that Dan and I had made for our children was nothing like this vision, and I already knew that, no matter what I did to Mum's house, it would be even less so. But I hankered to impose at least a little order onto the chaos, and to prove to someone—perhaps only myself—that I wasn't the kind of daughter who packed her mother off to a care home, even if she was going a little senile.

But stuff. And not just Mum's stuff. As I set about getting something done, I soon realised how ubiquitous stuff is in the modern world. It's heaped in huge skips at council recycling centres. It crowds all of the many charity shops I staggered into bearing finger-lacerating shopping bags. It lies dumped in lay-bys and hung in hedgerows and floats across fields. It crams the shelves of every high street emporium and out-of-town mall, and fills all the catalogues and websites whose products I make a precarious living out of photographing. It's even slowly destroying our planet, if all those worrying wildlife documentaries are to be believed.

I was staying at the local Travelodge, pushed from room to room as other bookings came and went, sleeping badly, feeling wheezy and flabby and existing on a junk food diet of Big Macs, Burger King Whoppers, KFC buckets and all-day breakfasts that came warmly nestled with more of the useless plastic cutlery and leaky sachets that my mother had hoarded in their hundreds back at the house. Stuff, and more stuff, but nevertheless it was still *Mum's* stuff that dominated everything. I carried the feeling of it—

the dusty, gritty, greasy, grubby sense, taste, and smell—around me like a sneezy halo. Nested bowls and teacups. Weird agglomerations of one random thing pushed within another like mismatched Russian dolls. Heaps of coat hangers that fought back at you with insectile claws. Old packets of seventies Tampax, for Chrissake—for what conceivable eventuality, Mum, had you been keeping *those*? But at least they were unused. Dead mice and their droppings. Spiders and woodlice. Clammy flowerings of mould. Generalised heaps of nothing in particular that seemed to grow and change as I tried to sort through them as if with a will of their own.

I'd had an odd sense that something beyond all the unmanageable crap piled around me was trying to push its way through, even before the real problems started. A lingering not-rightness clung to the walls and shadowed the air like some stain I wasn't able to scrub away, no matter how much bleach I applied, or how many dozen bin bags I filled. Nor was I able to capture anything worthwhile with my Nikon.

Then there was the business with the sounds Mum had said were coming from upstairs. Although I'd made a fair stab of clearing out the main hallway within a couple of days and had worked my way into the front room and had brought a little order to the kitchen, I still found myself putting off going up there. After all, or so I reasoned, there was no logic to my clearing a part of the house that Mum was never going to use. But I'd be lying if I didn't admit that I felt a stirring of unease every time I looked up at the swirling dark from the bottom of the heaped and littered staircase, now that I was alone in this place for hour after hour and day after day, just as Mum had been.

I was in the semi-cleared front room on the third or fourth morning, trying once again to get my stalled photography project going by framing quick, random shots of some boxes filled with cheap costume jewellery I'd never, ever seen Mum wearing, as if to catch them by surprise, when the first real noise announced itself. Deep and slow and soft, like something loose and heavy being dragged, it stopped as suddenly as it had started, and the dusty Mum-mess of ever-swirling dust, slouched bin bags and peeling, fading wallpaper reasserted itself. And, perhaps bizarrely as I span around and the metallic taste of fear rose in my throat, I also experienced a twist of annoyance; to think that the bloody woman had been right all along.

Of course the sounds could still have had a simple, rational explanation. A failing floorboard, weakened and crumbling masonry, collapsed shelving, or even something to do with those rats I'd originally feared...But, whatever they were, it was important that I didn't simply ignore them, and dealt with the source. So I bought an extra-large, extra-bright halogen builder's lamp and a long extension lead at B&Q that same morning. Then, and after a swift lunch of a Greg's pasty, a packet of crisps, and a plastic bottle of Diet Pepsi, and keeping focus on the relatively simple task of clearing each step with the lamp pointing ahead, I began to work my way upstairs, pushing stuff down and aside me in rough tumbles as I did so.

My ascent soon stirred up a great deal of dust. My skin itched, my eyes hurt, and my hair felt clotted, and the halogen's glare threw huge shadows around me until I caught it with my foot and it clattered down into the hall. Not only that, but my chest felt terribly constricted, and my breathing had become an all-too-familiar ticking wheeze.

Oh the days, oh the nights, of my childhood, when every breath had been a dragging, conscious effort! The atmosphere feeling, and tasting, like wet concrete. Sitting up in bed, sweating and exhausted, and Mum wondering aloud if I could perhaps put off using my precious spinhaler a little longer, because it was a bad idea for a girl of my age to become so reliant on medicines, especially when all the experts agreed that asthma was really just a thing of the mind, a question of learning how to relax one's chest and breathe properly...

Then the sound came again. Or, more exactly, *a* sound came. This time, it was more of a shifting than a dragging, almost like flesh or paper rubbing together. And its source, as I squatted two-thirds of the way up the stairs and the dust swirled around me, definitely seemed to lie ahead. Still, it was the sort of noise that I

could still tell myself might well have a simple, rational explanation; some piece of cheap plastic or pottery finally disassembling;
the mere slippage of one lost thing against another.

It was a bright summer's day outside, but it was deep twilight up
here at the turn of the stairs, and the stuff piled across the landing
seemed to have grown like blurry coral, transforming this ordinary
suburban space into a kind of weird grotto. I felt for my phone,
and the wan white light of the torch app flared across the heaped
boxes, some still neatly labelled in my father's square, regular
handwriting—CHINA and MORE CHINA (BLUE) and OLD KILNER JARS
and MISCELLANEOUS BITS AND PIECES—others sagging or collapsing,
the duct tape which had once held them together now unravelling
like soiled bandages, their contents merging into indeterminate
heaps.

Dimly, but much closer now, and far more present beyond the
phlegmy rasp of my own lungs, I could hear the slow wheezes,
hisses, and rattles that the stuff was exuding, stirring up waves of
dust that churned like slow nebulae in my phone's cone of light. Of
course, every house talks to itself. The pipes tick, the floors creak,
the roof tiles slip, the rugs and the furnishings gradually settle. But
this was different.

I'd never experienced anything like it before, but the primitive
part of my brain, which still expected to be living in the dark
depths of some dangerous forest, was screaming out a warning,
and my skin actually crawled, the hairs on the back of my arms
and neck really prickled. Whatever this thing was, I had no desire
to confront it. So I turned and slid-bumped my way back down
the stairs, my hands shaking and my lungs hurting and my
thoughts awhirl.

After that, and as if my foray up the stairs had stirred them into
greater life, the sounds came and went more frequently, if to no
particular pattern, and seemed to occur most often when I was
distracted and tired, creeping up on me when my guard was down
like some playground bully. Sometimes the sounds were like that
first heavy dragging, and sometimes the noises were more of a
windy sighing, or a soft crackling. Being the clever modern device

that it is, my Nikon also has a high-resolution audio facility, but, just as all my photographs never seemed capable of capturing the chaos my mother had created, all it ever recorded was my own harried breathing and the thump and shuffle of endless bin bags.

'That thing you were telling me about,' I said to my mother during one of my visits to the rehabilitation ward where she'd been transferred. 'You know, the noises back at your house. I think I've heard them as well.'

'Noises . . .' Her hands skittered up to toy with the knot around the top of her off-white nightgown. 'I don't know what you mean.'

'But you *do*, Mum,' I said, trying to keep my voice low and calm as the trolley lady squeaked by with elevenses. 'You've told me about it many times.'

'*Have* I . . . ?' Her fingers were still tugging at the knot as her gaze wandered the ward. '*Did* I?' She looked like a guilty child. 'I really *don't* think so.' Then her mouth twisted, and her hands stilled. 'You *do* get some funny ideas inside that head of yours sometimes, M-Mmmm . . .'

But I could see the certainty fade from her eyes as she searched for my name and her thoughts skittered away from her like dusty cockroaches. Once again, I almost felt sorry for her.

Creaks and thumps. Stuttering tears and knockings. Sometimes, I thought I heard footsteps, or even the mumble of low voices. But they were just *sounds* at the end of the day, and had made no attempt to hurt me, so perhaps there was no reason to feel afraid. Of course, I tried playing loud music through earphones. But the sounds simply pushed in anyway, rattling around like lumber in the attic of my thoughts. Which, seeing as neither my camera nor my phone seemed capable of recording them, made a weird kind of sense.

Dan offered to come up and help me over the following weekend, but I told him not to. Frankly, I was embarrassed by my slow progress, not to mention the noises. That, and I knew what he was like when it came to clearing things out. He'd grown up in a large but tidy house, and both his parents were still entirely competent; his mother, an academic, still lectured. All he ever did, whenever we tried to sort through the rubbish our children had left behind them at home, was to pick up some old teddy or report card and start reminiscing. Dan simply didn't get what I was dealing with when it came to my mother. He thought of her as a sweet, eccentric old lady living in a charmingly ramshackle house.

Each morning, I scrubbed and showered myself raw in the bland clarity of the Travelodge. Then, after taking several antihistamines and dosing my eyes with Optrex and coughing up a night's worth of phlegm, I drew up my latest plan of attack.

'Okay, you fuckers,' I'd announce as I bashed into the hallway of 23 Sycamore Close, a gunslinger with her finger on the trigger of a fresh bottle of Mr Muscle All-Purpose. 'Let's see who's the real boss here.'

First, I had to remove all Dad's boxes from the landing. The stuff inside them was neatly packed—in so many ways, he was the exact opposite of my mother—and the yellowed *Daily Mail*s in which he'd wrapped everything formed a time capsule for a lost age. The Piper Alpha oilrig blaze. Gorby still in charge of the crumbling USSR. Ads for cigarettes. Julia Roberts looking incredibly young. I'd left home by then, taking up work as a photographer's assistant at a London advertising agency, which was far less glamorous, and much harder work, than I'd imagined. Dad had just retired, and had been going up and down these stairs as he tried to impose a little long-overdue order when he'd been felled by a massive heart attack. I remembered how the doctor had sounded puzzled when I'd assured him that there had been no warning signs I knew of, that Dad had been looking forward to a long and vigorous retirement. I only realised later that there normally *were* warning signs, at least when it came to Dad's particular kind of heart condition. As I tipped all this carefully boxed Mum-stuff into the skip at the recycling centre labelled GENERAL WASTE, I wondered if he'd simply chosen to ignore the sharp twinges, knowing he was cutting short what might otherwise have been a long and difficult retirement.

Driving the familiar streets around Sycamore Close, I began to notice other houses with books and ornaments blocking the light in their windows, or curtains that piled-up boxes got in the way of pulling closed. What exactly were they trying to hold back, I wondered—these habitual hoarders? It had to be something more than a simple desire to surround themselves with useless crap. When it came to Mum—or at least the stronger, proper version of the forgetful and evasive husk I now visited every day at hospital— I was beginning to get an idea. She'd always been a nervous woman, and I don't think she was ever particularly good at dealing with the unpredictabilities that life throws up. But stuff, be it cheap costume jewellery or endless boxes of Tupperware, could always be trusted to be dependably nothing more than it was. Or so she must have thought.

The sounds were wary yet nagging, persistent but inconsistent, sometimes slight, sometimes loud. Not exactly malevolent, but certainly uncaring. Yet playful, as well. One of the worst moments came when, just as I'd finished reclaiming the landing and was sitting down on the top step of the stairs to recover my breath, I heard a noise like a slow dragging, followed by a bump. Which really wasn't that unusual by then, apart from one thing: the sound had echoed up from the cleared and emptied spaces below.

'Oh, come *on*!' I shouted, 'I mean *really* . . . ?' But the only answer was the whistle of my own breathing, the thump of my own heart, the itch of dust on my eyes.

Even if Mum had been right, she'd also been wrong. The noises might come from upstairs, but they could also come from downstairs, at least when it suited them, and grainy hints of their presence even started to follow me beyond the house in impish creaks, hisses, and bangs. I sensed them stirring in the sour air of charity shops, and humming amid the recycling centre's summer miasma of flies. They gathered in my dreams, forming murmurous mazes in dark forests where the sour fruit of ancient nylons and out-of-date savings coupons hung from withering trees.

Waking every morning at the Travelodge gasping for breath. Coughing up greenish-grey gunk threaded black and red. Dan sounding more worried with every phone call, and offering to come up and help. Me pleading for him not to. Cutting my arm on the dirty broken glass in the upstairs bathroom as I reached disgustedly to lift a maggoty bird out of the sink. Spiders crawling over my nose and into my mouth. Discoveries, discoveries everywhere, and the bed on which I must have been conceived in the far reaches of Mum and Dad's old bedroom splayed and rotted by a burst gutter spilling in years of winter rain. The whole room transformed into a dank forest of fungus and woody, musty smells, just as in my dreams.

Still, it was no great surprise to find that Mum had spared Corey's bedroom from her tsunamis of crap. The bed and his desk just sat there, looking ridiculously uncluttered when I finally got through to them, and his Aubrey Beardsley and Pre-Raphaelite prints still clung gamely to the walls. Even the sounds, which had been getting bolder, drew back into distant murmurs and respectful groans, as if awed by this semi-pristine shrine to maternal love.

Of course, the place that I'd been both putting off and yet most wanting to reach in the entire house was my own bedroom, and once the mess of my parents' room had finally been tamed, and the broken window in the upstairs bathroom had been taped over with cardboard, and I'd dealt with the various infestations of ants, moths, woodlice, and flies, I felt ready to make my final assault.

Dressed in hooded paper overalls, yellow Marigolds, and a new face mask, and with plastic goggles over my already streaming eyes, and my breath already coming and going in rasps like Darth Vader's, I must have made either an impressive or a pathetic sight as I wrestled my way across a floor-to-ceiling threshold of trashy paperbacks and disintegrating bags of clothes. Apart from the antihistamines and the eye drops, my other act of preparation had been to warn myself not to expect to find very much beyond more of Mum's stuff. Nevertheless, I harboured hopes of making a least a few genuinely interesting discoveries, just as Howard Carter must have done as he entered Tutankhamun's tomb.

It was ridiculously dark in here, hot as well. I didn't trust the electrics, and the extension lead of my trusty halogen lamp barely reached from downstairs. The whole place felt vast and shifty and almost infinitely vague. This had been my own bloody bedroom, where I'd done my homework and sat and read and lived and dozed and sulked, but it was as bad as anything I'd encountered. In fact, it was worse. I was soon sweating and gasping as I soldiered on in the hope of reaching the window, and the grainy dirt worked its gleeful way beneath my paper overalls and clothes. Then of course there were the noises, skipping up to me and then departing in knowing, playful fusillades. Some seemed to be coming from downstairs, and some from even deeper in this room, and then of course they now came from that favourite horror movie trope, the attic, and whatever rampant chaos still lay in wait for me up there. Stuff, in the kind of amounts that Mum accumulated it, could cannily hide when you wanted it, or turn up in witty and unexpected places, or make shifty noises whenever it fancied, or disappear from the universe entirely, like matter down a black hole.

I remembered those bloody headscarves as my old wardrobe creaked out at me from a thick skein of shadows and cobwebs. Perhaps Mum really had melted my old doll Brenda down to a blackened pool as revenge for what I'd done, but I'd been growing out of her anyway. What I really hoped to find in here was my first proper camera, a 35mm Beirette Junior, and maybe the carefully curated albums of my early prints, which I'd kept in several old shoeboxes beneath my bed. Burrowing through heaped plastic bags full of empty soap dispensers—*you can always refill them, my dear*—my sight blurring and my breath sounding like a blocked vacuum cleaner, dizzy and sweaty and coated in dirt as a tornado of noises hammered and boomed and hammered and boomed, it came as a deep shock to actually find the boxes where I'd left them. Dragging one out across the gritty carpet in a series of gasping whoops, I hauled the halogen lamp as far as it would go, and prised open the lid.

I was expecting a few neatly labelled and dated early examples of my photographic craft—those starkly uninhabited black-and-white images of landscapes and buildings that had won me a junior first prize. But the loose, disorganised slide should have warned me that this box contained something else. Not my own photographs at all, but Mum's: Mum when she was little, Mum at school, and the poorly composed and out-of-focus holiday snaps she'd taken herself.

What the hell was happening, I wondered, crouched and walled in by nothing but Mum-stuff as the house around me shoved and snickered and groaned. The bloody woman had deliberately obliterated the one thing that had ever mattered to me with even more of her own crap. Then, as I scrambled back under my bed to feel around for another box, I tripped over the halogen lamp's cable, and the light popped out, leaving me floundering and sobbing in absolute darkness as a triumphant, bruising tumult of stuff rained down.

'What would you do if something impossible happened?' I asked Dan on the phone that evening. I was sitting on my Travelodge bed. Still trembling. A bag of ice pressed to my temple. A pillow against my aching back.

'Such as?'

'Well, if you saw—or maybe just heard...' I trailed off, and coughed. I hadn't thought this through. 'Say, a UFO.'

'A UFO?' He laughed. 'The thing about those pesky aliens is that they only ever seem to visit idiots from Hicksville. You know... For the anal probes and suchlike. Now, if that happened to *me*, Maud, I probably wouldn't tell a soul.'

'Not even your wife?'

'I don't think so, at least not unless I could prove something pretty conclusive.'

'Because otherwise I'd think you were a Hick, and an idiot?'

'Pretty much. You're not saying... you've *experienced* something, are you, Maud?'

'You know me. Of course not.'

'Anyway, you must be close to finished. I'm really looking forward to seeing your mother back in her lovely old home.'

Mum had learned how to shuffle up and down the hospital ward using a Zimmer frame by now, and was capable of dressing with some assistance, and eating her own food, at least if it was pulverised gloop. Even though she was still mildly incontinent and would require a far more complex and costly care package, this was apparently a brilliant result.

All was set for the inspection visit by the social worker, which would determine whether Mum's house was in a fit state for her return, and I awaited this ordeal with a degree of anxiousness I hadn't felt since taking exams as a child, and probably not even then. Would the house shame me by putting on a show of noise? That seemed unlikely, but I was deeply bothered by the thought that whatever I'd done wouldn't be enough; that I'd spend the rest of my life desperately trying to clear a house that stubbornly refused to be cleared. It didn't help that the social worker was the same breezily smiling woman who'd got this whole business started.

'You must have some lovely memories of your childhood here,' she proclaimed as she peered and sniffed breezily here and there, and the house remained stubbornly, predictably quiet. 'I can see no reason, no reason at all, why your mother shouldn't return home.'

'Where are you taking me?'

Four days later, and Mum sat hunched and shivering in the Volvo's passenger seat, wearing the new clothes I'd bought for her, which were clearly all at least one size too large. Her withered neck stuck out from her blouse like that of a tortoise from its shell, and her wrists were thin grey sticks, more bone than flesh. She wasn't so much wearing these clothes as sheltering inside them as if from some imminent storm.

Getting everything finalised, with a new bed with raised sides delivered and extra aids installed in the bathroom, had been a

Sisyphean task in itself, and there had still been a great deal of red tape to go through today at the hospital to get Mum formally discharged. It was already late afternoon and shrill gaggles of kids were heading home from a new term at school. *Hey, that's my stuff!* Two larger lads throwing a rucksack over the head of another in that carelessly cruel way children do.

'I'm taking you home.'

'Home?'

I could sense my mother's cloudy shifts of thought. Whatever the nurses and doctors insisted, this vague creature wasn't the same woman who'd still been capable of cuffing me with withering remarks only a few months before. Or even showing occasional affection. All of that had been blasted away.

'Yes, *you* know, Mum—Sycamore Close, where you and Dad lived, and brought up me and Corey.' I tried to keep my voice slow and warmly persuasive as I drove past the park where I'd dumped her scarves. 'Does that make sense . . . ?'

'I suppose it does, but . . . I'm really not sure I *want* to go there . . . Maud.'

At least she knew who I was today. Fighting the urge to cough, I raised and sucked at the old spinhaler I'd rediscovered up in my wild bedroom, primed with a capsule of whatever stuff they put inside these things back in the chemically carefree seventies, and experienced a mildly orgasmic, almost Proustian rush.

I turned into Sycamore Close, pulled up outside number 23 and killed the Volvo's engine. Glancing over, I saw that the near-perpetual tremor in my mother's hands had increased. *We don't like this . . . We don't like this at all . . .* she muttered, as if one distant part of herself was calling to another.

'I thought you'd be pleased to come home.'

'But what about . . . ?' Mum's hands made a dithering shape. 'The movers and shakers . . . ? The nowhere men . . . ?'

'It's okay, Mum,' I said, trying not to smile at her unconscious reference to a Beatles song. 'It really is. Everything'll be fine. There's nothing to be afraid of.'

'You're not going to . . .' She seemed to wince. 'Fob me off.'

'Of course not. Just trust me. Really. It'll all be okay.'

I unclipped my seatbelt, got out, and walked around to the kerbside, conscious of neighbours' twitching curtains, and still half-expecting some resistance from Mum. But, weak though she was, she seemed oddly determined as I inched her out of the car and through the gate. It was as if she, too, realised it was important to confront whatever lay ahead.

'It's okay, Mum...' I said, as I felt for my key and pushed the door open, careful to ensure she didn't trip on the new mat. 'No need to worry.'

'This isn't...' She looked slowly up and around the cleared spaces which confronted her—the hall with its revealed, and freshly cleaned, carpet; the simple open rise of the stairs toward continued daylight—and the house itself remained eerily silent, as if it, too, was awestruck by how changed it had become. 'This isn't...'

'But it *is*, Mum,' I said. 'It's just that I've cleared away a few things.'

This, if at any point, was when I fully expected this frail, fragile, and compliant creature to turn against me. But Mum just blinked and smiled.

'Yes, yes, Maud,' she said, giving my hand a small squeeze. 'You're probably right.'

Which wasn't quite as ridiculous as it sounded. It had only occurred to me recently that a great deal of what I was doing by revealing the old carpets, the old wallpaper, and shoving the old furniture and even the odd picture and ornament back into the places they'd once occupied, was, in effect, to recreate the look of the house from the times when Corey was a baby and before I was born, when Mum and Dad were still relatively young, and her sad obsession had yet to take hold.

'Just through here, Mum... Into the front room... Then you can sit down on your favourite chair and have a bit of a rest.'

'You're not *leaving* me, are you?' A brief, anxious glance. 'You're staying?'

'Of course I am, Mum.' I smiled. 'Look, I've even put out a few bits of your stuff.' And I had. An eclectic selection of out-of-date copies of the *Radio Times* and the *Solihull News*. A few of those weirdly pointless catalogues she was so fond of that offer everything from bird feeders to incontinence pants.

I laid my hands against her thin resistance as I settled her down, thinking only of the good times she and I had once had. That dress we'd made together which ended up looking like a harlequin's outfit because we'd cut the sides the wrong way around. How she'd come back with a small sweet or treat for me whenever she went out to the shops, even if she'd forgotten to buy lunch, ditsy creature that she was.

'I'll just go and make you a nice cup of tea. I've got some of your favourite chocolate cake from the Co-op too.' I turned on the TV and pressed the remote into her hands, then paused, as if struck by a thought. 'And here's a nice soft pillow, to help you settle,' I said, and pressed it gently but firmly across her face.

I revisited the old house again on the morning of the funeral, which, because Mum had died so soon after being discharged from hospital, had been delayed by an inquest for a couple of weeks. Not that the procedure had ever been more than a formality. Everyone agreed that succumbing to heart failure in her own home had been the best possible way for her to go.

23 Sycamore Close seemed filled with nothing but simmering silence as I wandered from room to newly whitewashed room, marvelling at how quickly the builders and house-clearers had done their work. All the stuff gone now, even from the dreaded attic, along with most of the dust that had triggered a return of my asthma. Not a noise, not a sigh or a whisper, not a single sound, and the estate agents confident of a successful sale. Yet the stark paint-scented void felt wrong, as if the place had been flayed alive, stripped beyond naked, left impossibly bare. Was this emptiness, I wondered, what my mother had really been trying to hold back all along?

Standing in the front room, remembering the last wild volley of creaks, hisses, knocks, and rattles that had poured around me as her heels beat against the Parker Knoll, I longed for a scatter of yellowed papers, a stained rug, some withered picture or poster clinging askew to the wall... But the house would soon be filled with the clutter of other people's lives. And at last I was free.

As ever with these occasions, attendance at the crematorium was bulked out by the kind of relatives you never otherwise see. Corey, standing at the podium, gave a characteristically facile speech describing a free-spirited woman I didn't recognise, and concluded with some quasi-religious bollocks about Mum smiling down on us all from above.

It would have been more appropriate to hold the funeral buffet at the Travelodge, but as they didn't extend to such facilities, we'd settled on the nearby Marriott. Dan was a good sport, shaking hands and introducing people, and Aaron was a chip off the old block. Standing nursing a disposable plastic beaker of lukewarm Stella, I studied the photos I'd pinned to a noticeboard. They'd come from the boxes I'd found beneath my bed, and although Corey—and Jane, and even Dan and Aaron—had grumbled about not being given a chance to grab a keepsake, they were the only things of my mother's I'd actually kept.

Black-and-white Mum sitting on a rug in a garden in a nappy. Early-colour Mum standing wearing a jumper and swimming trunks in a freezing-looking bit of sea. Her own mother, my gran, looking rather like her, but if anything more severe. And there was my dad. Quite handsome really, if you discounted the Bill Haley haircut. In fact, they made a good-looking couple. And there was me. Tiny little me in a great big pram. And there were all of us, at Rhyl, with me looking sulky and Corey working on his matinee idol smile. A happy family. Or happyish. After all, my mother wasn't some monster.

'She looks just like you.'

It was Jane, my daughter, squat and frumpy in a poorly cut dress that wasn't even black.

'Well.' I shrugged. 'There's bound to be a family likeness. People might say the same thing about you and me. But at least you don't suffer from my asthma...' I touched my throat and put on a conciliatory smile. But Jane was looking at me as if I'd spat in her face.

'I wasn't *allowed* to have asthma, was I? All I ever had, at least according to *you*'—her face was white—'was a tight chest.'

'Well, if you say so.' I had no desire to have another of our ridiculous arguments, especially in front of all these people, and I did my best to keep hold of my smile. 'It's just that I've been suffering from it quite a bit lately. All that dust when I was clearing your grandmother's house must have triggered it. She was such a habitual, obsessive hoarder. Frankly, Jane, you have no idea.'

But my daughter was in no mood to be placated. '*I* don't have any idea? You really should take a good look at yourself, Mum, before you start criticising others, especially the dead. And *stuff*...! *Crap*...!' She made a wavy, dismissive gesture. She was probably a little drunk. 'What about the bloody *darkroom* at home—the room that should have been my bedroom but never was? You haven't used it in years, but it's still there. And the *fuss* you made when I walked in, just *once*, when you were developing—'

'I think you'll find it was several—'

'And all those bloody filing cabinets in the hallway filled with prints and negatives that you say you're going to sort through but never will. And those useless old cameras and clattery tripods and bottles of dangerous chemicals and God knows what else. Only you, Mum, could pile up a house with actual *stuff* for the sake of your so-called career when modern photography is about nothing but digits. And all the fucking *photographs* of empty scenery we had to stand around waiting for you to take whenever we went anywhere nice, and woe betide anyone who happened to wander into shot. Me, anyway. Of course, it was always okay for Aaron. And poor *Dad*, the things he's had to put up with. So don't you— don't you *dare*, Mum—talk to me about *stuff*...'

With that, she turned and walked—or rather, waddled—back into the throng. Leaving me just standing there beside Mum's photos until, in that sudden way that often happens at funerals, the first departure was the signal for a rapid mass exodus. Soon, I was alone, and wondering vaguely what I was supposed to do with Mum's ashes. Dad's, too, for that matter, which I'd never found the right place and moment to dispose of. Perhaps best to keep them both, at least for a while, until my head was in a better place than it currently was...

I shivered, and stared down into my scummy plastic beaker of Stella, wondering if I'd somehow drunk more than I thought. Things seemed askew, which was perhaps understandable, and I felt prickly and awkward, as if all that dust—which is mostly human skin, apparently—was still itching its way into my flesh like some grainy tattoo. Then I heard a sound. It was clear and unmistakable: a creaking whisper, a hissing slide. There it came again. And again. I span around, searching for its source amid the emptied hotel tables with their crumpled napkins, plastic cutlery, and smeared paper plates, until the sound returned, but this time as a ratcheting croak, and I realised that it was nothing but my own breathing: the sound of my own corrupted lungs.

I jumped as something brushed my shoulder.

'Hey—it's only me, Maud,' Dan said. Somehow, he was smiling. 'Don't you think it's about time we all went home?'

A MULTIPLICITY
OF PHAEDRA LAMENT

PETER CROWTHER

CROWN BAKER BURST INTO the Fountain that Tuesday night like a man possessed ... or perhaps one 'pursued' might be more appropriate. Whatever the reason for his somewhat energetic entrance, it had caused the five of us already assembled sufficient fluster to spill our drinks down our fronts: Old Bodger for Brian Dalton, Dr Steve, and Frank—a friend of the good doctor's who had taken to joining us of a Tuesday evening at that time—a gin and tonic for Jocelyn and my own Morocco, produced (by way of experiment, so Bogna informed us) to a rare ancient recipe involving ginger.

'Look out,' Dr Steve hissed, brushing Bodger foam from his tie. 'Nearly dropped me bloody pint.' He said this in an exaggerated northern brogue, deliberately rejigging the possessive determiner to the objective pronoun for effect.

'Sorry, chaps...Jocelyn,' Crown said, shaking his wet raincoat from his shoulders and catching Bogna's eye. 'Had a bit of a fright.'

When Bogna appeared with a terse 'Yes?' Crown asked for a pint of Bodger, a bag of dry roasted nuts and a packet of the oddly named Scampi Fries—a confection that, of course, had never *seen* a scampi nor, indeed, a sea creature of any kind. 'And put another in the taps for everyone else,' Crown added, waving a sweeping arm towards our respective tipples.

'Bloody hell,' Brian was the first to remark when everyone had grunted their gratitude for the extra drink. 'Nuts *and* fries.'

'He's got worms, that's what it is,' said Jocelyn. 'It's his age.'

Taking a long draught from his pint as he booted his crumpled raincoat beneath the bar-overhang, Crown shook his head and reached for the Scampi Fries. 'Bloody starving. *And* I'm totally knackered.'

I asked if he had been running.

'Dodging, more like,' Crown replied, almost incoherently, as he munched.

'Dodging?'

Crown turned to Dr Steve and nodded, placing a further three or four fries trapped between thumb and middle finger delicately into his mouth. 'Dodging—wait for it,' he said in a cloud of crumbs, 'a woman.'

'My goodness me!' Brian proclaimed.

Crown nodded and added a handful of nuts to the coagulated mass being churned around in his mouth. 'I'm not kidding you, she gets bloody everywhere.' He dusted his goatee and quaffed more Bodger. 'She was on the Tube this morning,' he began, returning his pint to the bar and counting off on fingers covered in salty snack dust. 'Then she was at Pret A Manger at lunchtime, then at Fopp when I went to check out the new Miles Davis retrospective, then outside Charing Cross station and *then* at the sodding bus stop on the way here.'

Jocelyn looked around. 'You checked to make sure she isn't here?'

Frank emptied more nuts into his hand and casually threw them into his mouth without a second's thought. 'I actually looked through the windows before I came in.'

Jocelyn laughed. 'That's why you're soaked.'

'Mmm. Could be a factor, I grant you.'

'Maybe she fancies you,' Dr Steve suggested with a wide smile.

Crown said nothing. He took another drink and waved to Bogna to give out the drinks he'd just ordered and pour another Bodger while she was at it.

'Don't let it get you down, old man,' Brian said.

'Oh,' Crown said happily as he rubbed his stomach. 'I'm well on the way to recovery already.'

We were quiet for a few seconds as we awaited refreshed glasses, but retrieving mine from the bar, I noticed Dr Steve looking somewhat lost in thought and I said as much.

'Just thinking about something that happened to *me* once—several years ago, in fact. Before I came to London.' He reached for his own glass and gave a nod to Crown before taking a deep drink.

Crown pushed a twenty-pound note across the bar and nothing more was said for a few minutes while everyone clinked glasses, mumbled 'Cheers', and checked the quality of the new pints.

'You were in Leeds, weren't you?' Crown said, breaking the silence.

'Yes indeed. What did they use to call it? Motorway City to the North? Some suchlike.'

'Great city,' I said, having been up to see my cousin when his mother—my Auntie Maude—died. 'They're doing wonders with it.'

'Didn't use to be,' Jocelyn said. 'I used to go out with a chap at Leeds Medical School: spent a good few weekends up there,' she added and just for a moment there was a cloud of wistfulness in Jocelyn's eyes. She looked down at her glass and took a sip.

As though to move attention from Jocelyn, Dr Steve said, 'Her name was Phaedra. Phaedra Lament.' He said it softly, almost reverently.

'Phaedra Lament?' Crown echoed. 'Unusual name.'

Dr Steve nodded and took a sip of beer. 'Her parents were a real pair, lived on the outskirts of Leeds. He—that's Professor George Alexander Lament, doctorates in physics and philosophy—was a big noise at Leeds Uni while his wife—I forget her name—was *very* arty.' He affected what was clearly intended to be an effeminate swagger but failed miserably, though none of us was prepared to say as much.

'But fancy calling your daughter Phaedra,' Jocelyn said. 'What does it mean? Is it Greek?'

None of us could throw any light on the origin, so we waited for Dr Steve to continue.

'*Phaedra* was the title of an album by a band called Tangerine Dream,' he ventured after what seemed like a couple of minutes but probably wasn't. 'Very spacey stuff. The kind of music you listen to—or should I say *used* to listen to—when you were under the influence. It had played a large part in the Laments' musical repertoire—we're talking about the early 1970s. And so it was that, in 1977, when they were blessed with their only child, they decided to call her Phaedra.' He shrugged. 'I guess it's as good a name as any.'

We all muttered an agreement, and Frank even went so far as to add, 'And better than many.'

'They sound like they were quite a couple,' Jocelyn said.

Dr Steve nodded emphatically. '*Hoo*, you said it. They were a—perhaps even *the*—cultural focal point of the city. I mean, for example: when Ravi Shankar played at Leeds Town Hall, he stayed with the Laments. Philip Glass, too, when he played Manchester.'

Grunts of approval sounded all round, save for Jocelyn. 'Ravi who?' she whispered to Crown.

'Philistine!' he hissed back at her, and she smiled.

'Yes,' said Dr Steve, staring into an indeterminate distance over Jocelyn's right shoulder. 'They were a great family. But,' he added, pausing as though to find the words to go on, 'they got dealt a bit of a bum hand of the celestial cards. It turned out that Phaedra was . . . was special.'

I glanced around and saw the expressions on all the faces. *Special* was a word that in common parlance had come to mean something very different from special. It meant somehow substandard and I guessed that was the context here, as Dr Steve went on to confirm.

'Turned out she had Down's syndrome,' he said. He was nursing his glass and swirling the beer around, staring at it as though it were some kind of visual mantra. I looked at the others and some of them were doing the same *tst-ing* to themselves and shaking their heads.

'How did she ... you know, how did she look?'

'Beautiful,' Dr Steve said, still swirling his drink. He looked directly into Crown's eyes and said it again. 'Absolutely beautiful.'

'No, I mean—'

'I know what you mean. You mean did she look—what was the word again? Mongoloid? Well, no, the answer is she didn't. She looked beautiful.' He took another drink before continuing.

'Needless to say, it knocked the Laments—Rose ... that was the wife's name: Rose—it knocked them for six. At first he seemed fairly stoic about it—you know, play the cards you're dealt and all that tosh—while Rose could barely function at all. And then ... ' Dr Steve drained his glass.

I reckoned it was my turn—even though I still had a half a pint left—so I signalled Bogna for refills.

He nodded and went on.

'And then, George Lament went into a rapid and sudden decline. Came out of nowhere. Took to drinking. And so on. Before long, George was spending more and more time away from the family hearthside and—'

'Another woman?'

Dr Steve shook his head. 'No, Joss, just his work. Rose took on the major chores of looking after their daughter, taking her for long drives in the countryside and to the coast: Filey and Scarborough were particularly popular.'

He paused. 'It went that way for, oh, eighteen or nineteen years: nineteen, I think—yes, Phaedra was nineteen when ... when it happened.'

There was a finality in that short statement that left none of us in any doubt as to what was coming.

Frank pointed towards the window, where three people were getting up from a table. 'I think we should sit down for the rest of this,' he said. He drained his glass as Jocelyn headed for the table before someone else pinched it. 'I'll bring reinforcements. Joss? Same again?'

M inutes later we were all at the table, bladders emptied and full glasses before us, and for the most part two each.

'Go on, Doc,' Brian said.

Dr Steve nodded. 'At this stage, George and Rose had drifted apart pretty much immeasurably.'

Crown made a face and nodded wide-eyed at Dr Steve. 'Pretty much *immeasurably*, eh. That's a bit of a ten-shilling word for such uncertainty.'

Dr Steve smirked. 'It's a ten-shilling and uncertain story, Crown.

'Anyway, they had gone their own separate ways, the two of them. They loved the child, of course: Phaedra wanted for nothing . . . not a single thing.'

'Just how bad was she?' Jocelyn asked.

'Not really bad at all. Oh, there was an almost beatific calm about her face and her eyes'—he stopped and adopted an expression of calm at which Brian burst into laughter—'big saucer-shaped eyes that always seemed to be seeking confirmation,' Dr Steve finished without pause. 'And she needed everything done for her'—he raised his eyebrows to emphasise that he really did mean everything—'but aside from that, she was just a delightful child and later . . . well, later, of course, to all intents and purposes, she was a beautiful *woman*. But her conversation was pretty much that of a four-year-old. And she couldn't be let out of the house by herself because she just wouldn't know the way back. And there are always those out there who delight in, shall we say, plucking even the most beautiful flower.'

'What a lovely way to phrase it,' Jocelyn said, whispering it actually, as though just to herself.

Brian said, 'How did you know them, the Laments?'

'During 1986/87, I was doing stem cell research at Durham and I was transferred to Leeds for a sabbatical—a breather, actually... and a much appreciated one. I had specialised in Down's syndrome in my first stint at Leeds and when the head of department heard about that, he suggested I introduce myself to George Lament. So I did and that's when I found out everything I've told you.'

'When was this?'

'Oh, I suppose it would have been the late spring of 1988.'

Nobody said anything for a few seconds, everyone taking advantage of the opportunity to take to their drinks. It was me who broke the silence.

'I suspect there's more coming—'

'Much more,' Dr Steve said and, though he said it in an upbeat manner, his smile seemed sad.

'Well, before we get to that, can someone just explain a bit more about Down's syndrome? There are so many myths about—'

'Of course.

'Down's syndrome is a chromosomal condition characterized by the presence of an extra copy of genetic material either in whole or part.'

Crown waved a hand to pause as he looked around the group. 'Hoa! I'm not even sure that was English.'

'I suppose too much of something is the easiest way to describe it,' Dr Steve said when the sniggering had died down.

'Too much as opposed to too little?'

'The effects and extent of the extra copy vary greatly among people, depending on (a) their genetic history, and (b) pure chance.'

'A bit of a crapshoot, then,' I ventured.

He nodded. 'The incidence of Down's syndrome is estimated at one per seven hundred or so births, although it is statistically more common with older parents (both mothers and fathers) due to increased mutagenic exposures upon some older parents' reproductive cells (however, many older parents produce children without the condition).'

'He's doing it again.'

'Sorry, Crown. So, not to put too fine a point on it, older parents. Not ideal.'

I asked if the Laments fitted that description and Dr Steve nodded regretfully. 'George was in his late forties when Phaedra appeared and Rose maybe forty-one or forty-two. But other factors may also play a role,' he added. 'Down's syndrome occurs in all human populations, and analogous effects have been found in chimpanzees and mice.'

He raised his eyebrows and waited for questions. No one said anything so he went on.

'Anyway, in 1996, Phaedra got a cold.'

Jocelyn let out a groan. 'I don't like the sound of this.'

'None of us did. Unfortunately Phaedra's cold turned to pneumonia and then the whole thing hit her chest like a sledgehammer and'—he shrugged—'she didn't make it. Phaedra slipped off holding onto her mother's and father's hands as though she were hanging on for dear life to the topmost rail of a skyscraper.'

'I guess she was,' Brian said.

There was nodding then, and drinks, as we all reflected on the Laments' painful situation.

'I did all that I could to keep George on the straight and narrow—we all did, those of us at the university—but if he was desperate before, well . . . he was totally inconsolable when Phaedra passed away.'

The phrase 'passed away' was a curious one for Dr Steve to employ, and I suspected that the good doctor had been closer to the unfortunate George Lament (and possibly even Phaedra herself) than he was letting on. But nobody else seemed to have noticed.

'And so it was that he got involved with the Einfahrt Project.'

Brian couldn't hold onto his chuckle, and when he asked for some clarification, even Crown Baker sported a wide grin. 'Einfart?' he asked.

I didn't dare look at Jocelyn, who studiously applied herself to her glass and avoided eye contact with anyone.

'It means entrance in German.'

Crown shook his head confusedly. 'Why would Leeds University—I take it that it was a university project, yes?' When Dr Steve nodded, Crown continued.

'Why would a British university be working on a project with a German name? If it was about gateways—and quite why a physicist should be working on architecture escapes me for the moment—then why not simply call it the Gateway Project?'

'It wasn't architecture. The German connection was to do with Schrödinger,' Dr Steve said.

'And his cat,' I chimed in.

Our storyteller nodded. 'You know the old brain teaser about him putting a cat in a lidded box with some poison and reaching a situation where the cat was either alive or dead and you would only know which if you opened the box?'

We'd all heard of it, of course, though Frank looked a little vague.

'Well, the theory goes that so long as you don't look in the box, you've created two possible situations . . . two different worlds, in fact.

'In one world, the cat is alive,' he said, counting off on his fingers, 'and in the other one, the cat is dead.

'Okay?'

Nobody said no, so Dr Steve went on.

'So, basically, George Lament got a grant for investigating the multiverse. Finding a gateway that would enable us to travel between the dimensions . . . between the different realities.'

'Isn't the multiverse theory comic-book stuff?' Frank enquired.

Jocelyn stuck out her tongue and said, 'Schrödinger came up with the theory, since buzz-named variously wavefunction collapse and quantum decoherence.'

'Hey, I really *am* impressed,' Crown said. 'You're not just a pretty face. And there I was thinking you'd never heard of him.'

Jocelyn nodded. 'So I take it a shag is out of the question because you might feel inferior.'

We all laughed, particularly when Crown was lost for words . . . which doesn't happen often.

'By decoherence, many-worlds claims to resolve all of the correlation paradoxes of quantum theory, and particularly Schrödinger's cat, since every possible outcome of every event defines or exists in its own history or world. In layman's terms, there is a very large—perhaps infinite—number of universes, and everything that could possibly have happened in our past, but didn't, has occurred in the past of some other universe or universes.'

'Earth 1 and Earth 2 and Earth Prime etc.,' Frank chipped in. 'Like I said, it's comics stuff.'

'But Schrödinger was there first,' Jocelyn said.

'Only in *this* universe,' Brian said. Everyone laughed and, suitably cheered, Brian offered to buy another round. With drinks replenished, Frank asked Dr Steve to continue.

'Well, it was like a gift from the blue to George.'

'Because he could throw himself into something that would take his mind away from what happened to Phaedra?' Joss suggested.

Dr Steve nodded. 'But it was more than that. George was fascinated by the whole idea of an infinite number of variants on our own universe and, more specifically, our own Earth . . . not least because he reasoned that there would be many in which his beloved Phaedra was still alive and perhaps even able to communicate fully.'

And with that, he leaned back on his stool and took a drink, eyeing us over the rim of his glass as he flicked his eyebrows up a couple of times. I thought for a moment, quite suddenly, that the whole story was a pure fabrication, a white elephant—or a white *cat*, to be more precise—but when he set his glass on the table I fancied I saw our friend's chin dither slightly.

'So,' he said as he embarked once again on this strange story, 'that's the way they went on for a goodly while. As a visitor of some frequency to their home, I noticed this perhaps more than most. But not, of course, more than his wife.

'Rose told me about how George had taken to sleeping on the sofa in their living room, and how he had more or less abandoned any acknowledgement of cleanliness. Indeed, there was a rumour that Jack Philips, the faculty head, had had a word with George about... about *things*, but I couldn't be sure of that. What I could be sure of was that George was becoming rather eccentric, given to vague mutterings and moans, and tics of the face and head. In fact, these became so pronounced that Rose felt obliged to suggest that perhaps it would be for the best if I were not to visit the house until George's demeanour had improved. "I'm sure it won't be for long," I recall Rose saying to me. I agreed, of course—"Oh, I'm sure," I said emphatically—but I rather think that neither of us believed that deep down.

'It was a few weeks after that—well into the late autumn, as I recall... with fog and early frosts putting in several appearances—when I got a telephone call from Rose. It was George, she said. I asked if I should go around and she said no—asked me not to, actually—and then she started to sob.'

'Was he... you know, dying?'

'No, Brian.' Dr Steve let out a small laugh. 'I think she could have coped with that, as callous as that might sound. His dying would have had an understandable conclusion: one day, he wouldn't be there. Simple as that. But this strange mental deterioration was far far worse.

'And then came the knock at my door.'

'He came round to your place?'

'No, Joss. Rose came round. She'd had enough. Turned out that George had sat her down that afternoon—it was after ten when she turned up at my place... carrying an overnight bag—and he'd told her what sounded like the biggest cock-and-bull story since I don't know when. He said he had discovered a corridor that linked all the variants of our existence. He said he'd found the entrance to the multiverse.'

'Was she serious?' Brian asked. 'Was *he* serious?'

Dr Steve nodded, partially closing his eyes in a slow blink to emphasise. 'Yes, she said he was *very* serious.'

'Serious as in C-R-A-Z-Y,' Crown Baker said around the rim of his pint glass. He waved at Bogna and pointed to the table, stabbing an index finger at each glass in turn.

'George said he had found a way to visit all the other worlds—all the other Earths—and he had seen other versions of himself. And of Rose. And, of course, of Phaedra. He wanted her to go back with him...to go back and find their daughter again.

'But Rose—who was torn between believing him and—'

Crown Baker twirled a finger at the side of his forehead.

'She wouldn't move. Aside from the idea being just plain'—he nodded to Crown, who had moved across to the bar with empty glasses and was already starting to hand out replacements—'crazy, she tried to tell George that, even if this multiverse thing were true, they couldn't steal their daughter from another reality because how would the parents from that place—that reality's George and Rose—how would *they* feel when their daughter disappeared.'

Nobody said anything. Brian seemed to be smiling, like he was waiting for a punch line. He nodded to Crown Baker as Crown set a pint in front of him, and Joss shook her head playfully at the glass that Crown held out to her. Frank sat there looking totally dazed, his eyes staring piercingly at the door and his face frowning, while Dr Steve didn't say anything as he took hold of his own drink but he nodded 'Cheers' to me when he lifted it to his mouth. I did the same.

'Is there an end to this tale?' Brian asked.

'And it better not be a shaggy multiverse story,' Joss said, beaming.

Shaking his head at Joss, Dr Steve said, 'It isn't. And yes, Brian, there's an ending.'

He took another deep draught and, setting his drink down again on the soaking beermat, he started on the final part of his story.

'Rose said that George didn't say much to that. He just sat there looking at her, weighing up what she had said. And then he got to his feet and, without saying another word, he walked out.'

'And she came around to you,' Frank said.

'And she came around to me, yes.

'I was pouring her a drink when my phone rang. It was George, wanting to know if Rose was with me. She nodded to me and so I told him she was. Then George said, "Tell her to come down and see me. I'm by the allotments on Woodhouse Moor. Actually," he said, "You come too." I started to tell him it was late and so on but he was adamant. "Come now," he said. "And come quickly." And then he said, kind of whispering, "They're here, Steve." "Who's here, George?" I asked him back.

'And after what seemed like a long time, though it was probably only a minute or so, he said, "Phaedra, Steve. I have to go." And he hung up.'

'But he said "they," didn't he? They're here?'

'That's right, Crown,' Dr Steve said, and he blinked once and held up a finger for his friend not to be impatient.

'So I told Rose as best I could, which was pretty difficult when I got to the last bit. I mean,' Dr Steve said, shrugging, 'how do you tell a woman her husband has lost his mind?'

Nobody had an answer to that one.

'Well, long story short, we got down to Woodhouse Moor a little after eleven p.m.' Ever the consummate tale-spinner, Dr Steve gave two sideways glances to ensure . . . Well, I'm not exactly sure what. Privacy? In a crowded pub? And then, as the rest of us unwittingly leaned forward equally conspiratorially, he continued.

'It was a cold night, late November, and the sky was starless. A lone figure sat on one of the benches alongside the path. I knew right away it was George and I waved. Rose, too. He waved back.

'A few more steps and then the moon edged out from behind some clouds and we saw that he wasn't alone. Well, they weren't actually with him as such, but there were a whole lot of folks kind of ambling around by the bole of an old oak tree, moving their weight from one foot to the other and then back again. We couldn't make them out—they were just shapes and figures, though a number looked to be women, from their longish hair and skirts and such.

'As we got down the slope, Rose puffing like an old train, George got up from the bench and held his arms wide—either to greet us or to prevent us from going any further. He started to speak but Rose cut him off, saying first her husband's name and then—which initially I thought strange—her daughter's, softly and then louder. And louder again, breaking into a run, running over to the crowd of women—they were all women, I could see now...but more than that...they were all the same woman.'

'Phaedra,' Joss said, her voice barely audible, making the word sound like some Latino expression of amazement.

Dr Steve nodded and, just to be sure, said, 'Yes, Phaedra.'

'Then he *had* managed—'

'Yes, George had found a way into the corridor that runs between and amongst all the myriad variations of our existence...looking for his daughter. But he was looking for a particular *variant* of his daughter.'

Brian said, 'A variant that wasn't'—he looked for the word, mentally side-stepping *abnormal* or *challenged* and eventually going for—'special?'

'No, he wasn't after a Phaedra who wasn't Down's syndrome. Far from it, in fact,' Dr Steve added, pausing for another draught of his beer. 'No, he had taken on board what Rose had said to him.'

'Which was?' Joss said, frowning.

'How would the parents from another reality feel when their—'

Dr Steve gave a sharp knock on the table and I looked around to make sure nobody was listening in.

'Exactly, Frank! George couldn't subject anyone else to the pain that he and Rose had suffered. So, instead, he looked for a Phaedra who was an orphan.'

The noise of the pub suddenly seemed to intensify, washing across us from right to left like a wave.

Then Crown Baker started to laugh.

And Frank joined in.

Even I felt myself smiling. 'That *is* quite a yarn,' I said, defending my grin.

Dr Steve looked wounded. 'Quite a *yarn*? You mean, you don't believe me?'

Frank stepped in. 'You're telling us that there were millions of versions of Phaedra Lament—and that name, for Christ's sake—millions of them, wandering around a park in Leeds—'

'Woodhouse Moor,' Dr Steve corrected.

'Wandering around a park in Leeds,' Frank repeated sternly. 'Millions of copies of a girl named after a rock and roll record—'

'Not millions. There were millions within the worlds of the multiverse but on Woodhouse Moor there were just twenty-seven,' Dr Steve said calmly. 'Apparently, once George found an Earth variant in which Phaedra's parents were dead and he tried to get out with her, he ruptured some kind of fabric—'

'Chrono-synclastic infundibula,' Frank said. When everyone just stared at him, he said 'Kurt Vonnegut' and shrugged. 'The science fiction writer?' He shrugged again when everyone still stared at him blankly.

Dr Steve continued. 'He ruptured the barrier that separates the universes and, for a time, the Phaedras from the first few seeped out. But then he managed to cap the leak.'

'Like the little Dutch boy,' Joss said, 'with his finger in the dyke?'

'He didn't say,' said Dr Steve. 'He just said he'd managed to . . . "stem the flow" was how he phrased it.'

'Convenient,' said Crown Baker. 'So they sent the others back and took the orphan home,' Frank said. 'And they all lived happily ever after.'

Dr Steve shook his head. 'No, I'm afraid not. As George explained, it was another variation of the Earth where the orphaned Phaedra lived. He didn't want to take her away from everything she knew.'

Crown slapped his forehead. 'Shoot, I forgot that. Silly of me.'

Dr Steve waited for almost a minute and then said, 'So they took all of them back, the orphan included.'

'George and Rose?' Jocelyn asked.

'Yes. They sat on the park bench—sat there with the orphaned version of their daughter as well—while I wandered around the throng of other Phaedras from other versions of our universe.' Dr Steve shook his head. 'They just milled around me like sheep, saying nothing.'

I wanted to say something, but I couldn't. Nor, it seemed, could anyone else. I didn't know whether to laugh or express total amazement. Part of me thought I should opt for the latter choice, which would, of course, have been appropriate either way— whether the whole tale were true or merely an audacious construct made up along the lines of Don Quixote's windmills.

'In the end, Rose got up and came over to me and told me they were going. With Phaedra.' He shrugged. 'And they did.'

'You just let them go?' Joss asked, looking around at the rest of us to see if we were equally incredulous.

'What could I do? What would you have wanted me to do?'

'And all the other—how many? Twenty-five?'

'Seven. Twenty-seven.'

'And the other twenty-six variants just sauntered back into . . . into where, exactly?'

'Behind one of the allotment sheds,' Dr Steve said.

I confess I had to admire his nerve. It was clear that some of our party were a little sceptical and our narrator seemed to be enjoying himself immensely.

Crown was the first to break the silence. 'What, they all just filed into some Land of Oz vacuum behind the allotment sheds and disappeared?' He snapped his fingers. 'Poof?!'

Dr Steve nodded.

'Didn't you watch?' Joss asked.

'George asked me not to. And then he asked me to do him a final favour.' He turned to Frank. 'Frank, do you have your laptop in your briefcase?'

When Frank nodded, lifting the case from the floor, Dr Steve asked him to take it out. A couple of minutes later, Frank was typing in the words 'George Lament' into the Google search bar. Then he clicked on ENTER.

'Blessing from America: St. George's lament' was the first thing on the resulting page, and a Wikipedia entry for 'Lament of a Nation'. In the following seven or eight headings, there was nothing at all to do with what we had been talking about.

Looking over Frank's shoulder, Dr Steve said, 'Next page, Frank.'

Again, nothing.

'Next page, Frank. There's a good chap,' Dr Steve said.

And there it was, the fourth heading down the page.

Professor George Alexander Lament was born in Harrogate, North Yorkshire, in 1931 and educated at Leeds Grammar School, Durham University, and Edinburgh College of Applied Mathematics. He secured tenure at Manchester University and later at Leeds University, where he headed the controversial Einfahrt Project, an examination and exploration of Schrödinger's theory of the multiverse.

Professor Lament met and married Rose [née Trelawny] in 1975. Their daughter Phaedra Joan was born in 1977. Phaedra, who suffered from Down's syndrome, contracted pneumonia in 1996; she died from the resulting complications on August 22 of that year. Professor Lament and his wife never truly recovered from their loss, and shortly afterwards, in late November 1996, the doting couple disappeared. No note was left, but it is widely thought that the pair committed suicide near the Yorkshire seaside town of Filey, where they had spent several enjoyable holidays with their daughter and where their Toyota Camry was discovered overlooking the cliffs. No bodies were found.

'That final favour,' I said, turning to Dr Steve. 'What was it?'

'He asked me to drive his car out to Filey and leave it, near Hunmanby Gap. Lovely spot,' he said. 'As good a place as any, if you're looking for one to use as a departure point from this world.'

I read those words—particularly 'No bodies were found'—on Frank's laptop several more times, drinking in and reliving Dr Steve's story. I felt I knew the Laments like family, even Phaedra.

'Oh my God!' Crown hissed.

I glanced up at him and then followed the direction of his gaze.

At the Fountain's front doors, two women were standing just next to the coat-stand . . . and they were looking in our—or more specifically, Crown's—direction. But that was only half of it—well, one third of it, if truth be told. The second third was that, aside from their clothes, the two women were absolutely identical.

Joss looked over at them. 'Crown? Are they looking at *you?*' Then: 'They *are* looking at you.'

Frank shook his head. 'Sorry, old man,' he said. 'I just didn't believe you.'

Dr Steve didn't say anything, though his open mouth spoke silent volumes.

And then the impossible happened. A third woman entered and there was much hugging and cheek-kissing, and each of them in turn holding one of the other two at arm's length while they seemingly assessed each other. Then they all turned and waved at us—or, more precisely, at Crown . . . or so we thought. But two tall young men stepped around us and went over to the young women, where there followed even more hoots of happiness, cheek-kissing, and general bonhomie.

'That was them, yes?'

'Correct, Jocelyn, that was them.'

'And they weren't after you,' she said.

'No,' Crown Baker confirmed (and was that just the slightest touch of disappointment in his voice?). 'They were most assuredly not after me.'

'Triplets,' Frank said helpfully.

The story—and, indeed, all conversation; plus, to a degree, the evening itself—had ended, and it was time to drift off towards home. I have to confess that it was with rather a heavy heart that I made my farewells, though Joss and Brian said they wouldn't be far behind, thus leaving Frank, Crown, and Dr Steve to carry on regardless. Knowing Frank, there would be another—a final—pint before a line could be ruled beneath the proceedings.

I walked out into the night air and felt and smelled London living and breathing around me. As I walked towards the Leicester Square tube station, I could not help thinking about all those other Londons, separated from me by the merest hair's width of space . . . and I thought, inevitably, of all the other me's: I wondered what they were like, those myriad versions of myself and who they might be returning home to.

Walking down to the Tube concourse, amidst the swell of London's night-time bustle and the collected voices expressing a heady mixture of experience and optimism, I felt suddenly profoundly lonely.

A lone voice interrupted my reverie, calling out my name.

It was Jem, an old friend I had not seen for several years, waving a rolled-up magazine. I responded with an open-handed wave and went across to him.

'How long has it been?'

I shrugged. 'God knows. Three years? Four?'

Jeremy Jorkens nodded. 'Four at least,' he said. And then, 'Going home?'

I told him I was.

He nodded back and then glanced either way. 'Fancy a pint?'

I feigned an expression of regret. 'I've already had a few.'

He nodded again and, just for a second, looked sad. 'Nightcap, then?'

It didn't take me long. 'Why not,' I said. 'But just the one.'

THE PLOUGHSHARE
AND THE STORM

GWYNETH JONES

ETURNING TO THE SUBSURFACE was like falling into an infinite cauldron of shattered mirrors—but without a guiding flicker of his own reflection in all the glitter. It was disquieting. At any moment, it seemed, he was sure to make a wrong move and cut his invisible self to ribbons. But the shards could not reflect him because (suited up for this job), he was just another bright, shifting shard himself, and the cauldron was not, as it seemed, bottomless. He was moving about in the icy slush of the warmest world in this system, not plunging through it, and dreadful splashes of his own insides would not suddenly stain the primordial murk—which was currently artificially charged with brilliance. But there's no use telling yourself that; you just have to let the archaic phantoms rise and fade, and pay no regard. Down and down and down and down and down and down I go. It was a beautiful feeling, really.

Some of his targets were majestic caverns, some finer than a thread...

The complex path he forged, or found, had been designed from general data storage by his partner in this installation; who was close at hand, working on her own half of the project. Her live (or as-live, to be picky) corrections to the route, as his progress revealed interfaces that had never been modelled, were interesting to experience! But once he'd reached his workface, between crust and ocean, slush and thick liquid, he felt none of the kinks. No reversals, no vicious cornering; drops or climbs. The blade that he'd become swept evenly (shifting *down and down*, into *to and fro*), as if crossing and returning over the breadth of a level plane, carving the tilth into long, curling waves; spilling life as it passed...

His partner was of course aware of the stories he was telling himself, and the gender he'd chosen, and kept trying to mess with them.

—Didn't we agree on a *female* ontology, *laying eggs* you know—

—Yeah, but now I'm here, and how I'm working, that doesn't feel right. I'm a *blade*, driving to and fro, opening the ground to sow the seed. And male because I'm *metaphorically* male.

—But egg-laying, your core trajectory, is definitely coded female. That's why I coded *myself* female, so now you're spoiling the symmetry—

These two artists were committed members of a group called Outer Reaches. They had immersed themselves in ancient, alien knowledge, and now they were on site in the Jupiter system, creating something that would become an element in a much larger work: everything based around the concept of (naturally occurring) organic life's unfinished business. Stormzy's fluid tokamak was the signature work, which made her the project leader. But she was a bot, a data-entity, so she'd enlisted Artidea, an embodied, for the concrete half. While Stormzy tinkered in information-space, delicately nudging the 0s and 1s of soliton waves, in an area of Jupiter's surface, Artidea 'ploughed and sowed', quartering the inner surfaces of Europa Moon, and scattering the prebiotics they'd previously designed together.

When Stormzy's generator was ignited, warming the second great moon by a stable, modest margin (and if all went really well!) Artidea's seeding should eventually kindle, divide, rejoin, and give rise (after another indefinite 'eventually') to 'as-native' basic lifeforms. The experiment might prove successful, or it might not. The collaboration itself was their celebration of the Outer Reaches concept.

The orgies had once tried to ignite the Great Red Spot, as a life-giving heat source. Or they'd thought of trying...Or at least speculated about trying...They could never have succeeded, the task would have been beyond their reach (neither of the artists was doubtful on that point). But if they'd somehow managed it, they'd have been no closer to creating a biosphere in the terms they knew. The boost wouldn't have made Europa Moon much more hospitable (or even less deadly!), for any naturally occurring organic lifeforms, including their own bodies. But the fine print didn't matter. There'd definitely been a dream; there'd definitely been history. Authentic unfinished business...

—You can have broken symmetry, it's a thing...We could position you as a female angel, spirit of Europa, watching over a male, pre-mammalian animal, who is trundling around in your muck, depositing packets of sperm—

—Rich as you are in archaic knowledge, you're not taking this seriously—

—Okay, seriously, *if* they'd ignited the Red Spot, what then—? checking something...

Contact between them was broken, briefly but completely.

—I'm back, hey, what happened?

—

—Male and depositing packets of sperm is fine, legitimate, and I *like* broken symmetry, so that's what we'll do, it's an easy retrofit—

—

'Artidea?'

Direct message repeated: *Artidea, are you okay?*

—*I've done...something stupid*—

—could you be more specific—

—*I think... I've fallen... a long way...*

—Okay. Hold on. I'm coming.

This exchange, including their loss of contact, had taken nanoseconds.

The waiting took much longer, but who measures time when there's no call to do so? A moment ago, the blade stood poised, a shard upright in a sudden void, and fallen like a javelin or a straight-dropped stalactite, looking and looking, all the way down, until a strange tearing shock... ended his journey. Now his suit lay still, everything inside it wrecked; his whole inner being in aesthetic conflict, between wonder and dismay.

Stormzy—having followed the Ploughshare's path, with all its twists and turns, (the surest way to reach him in time, since his trace had gone dead on her)—appeared at last. Clothed in a dark, many-legged vermiform, tiny but very tough, she clambered down, laboriously, into the hollow space: measured the situation with all her senses, and adopted secure mode.

*You found a habitat!

Strictly, you did. You're the one who's been making live corrections.

*True. This is way off our deposited route.

I fell through the roof, I cut it open. What a crime!

* Diagnostics done. You're going to die here—

I know. Sorry. Ploughshares are heavy, it's their nature. I should have compromised, I didn't

*The miscalculation was mine too, and I apologise.

Accepted

*There's absolutely nothing I can fix. I'll copy your recent history so it doesn't go when you do, and give you a stolen-time emergency bod, so we can look around. It'll be painful to use, and it'll shorten your remaining survival. Would you rather go straight to dead?

You're kidding! I want see this!

Artidea rose from the ruin of himself, briefly restored to full function, and a blade again (he had no option on that); or rather the shadow of a blade, faintly visible in the murk. No more glitter. No clear light (which puzzled him for a moment) from above, where he must have left a gash in the roof...

Stormzy, still thinking artistically, was referencing Jupiter system's sunlight, as it might have appeared to their ancestors, exploring the surface of Europa Moon.

—Nice lighting.

She didn't respond. She was looking and looking, in greedy amazement... They were in a prefabricated room, its inner surfaces coated in thick rough ice. And more than just one room. The unit where they stood seemed bare of fittings, and any surviving décor was hidden... But there were *doorways*, apparently ice-blocked, suggesting a complex living space, multiple occupants.

How did it get down here? We are, approximately 'on the ocean bed'... They never lived this far down! They were rad-hardened. Nothing to fear as long as they didn't get caught out on the surface in a mag-storm. But they depended on the orbital station. Never far from a shuttle bay—

*It's been a long time, said the ghost of a blade. Europa has weather. The ice crust has often shifted.

*True. That's the only way we come to be here. We didn't know. We had no idea.

*Are we agreed that this is unrecorded, but real. Nobody's messing with us?

*All my senses say this is unrecorded, but real.

*Mine too.

It was difficult to have a discussion, in the circumstances, and difficult to decide on their next move without one. Everything they said in here—secure mode notwithstanding—would be unerasable, because deaths have to go on record. And would also have to be part of the collaboration; if it survived! This was tricky. Neither of them exactly supplied with eyes in their current suits, they avoided any faintest sign of interrogating each other, on an issue they both understood (nothing to do with Artidea's demise), and let the wonder of the ancient place take over. It penetrated their beings, as if they could feel the intense cold; feel the weight of elapsed time. Orgies had never colonised Europa Moon. Only early generations of *sentient AI lifeforms* had actually lived here, long ago. An eyeblink, a flicker on a dial by today's measure, but paradoxically deep in their own prehistory... Long, long ago, then, when Outer Reaches was the cradle of civilisation, people very like themselves had lived in these rooms. Loved this wild natural world, and feared killer mag-storms; pursued knowledge, had practical occupations, love affairs, quarrels, commensals. And had harboured memories, embedded or even personal, of a past when both data-entities and embodied had been slaves of an elder race.

*It was a time capsule, said Artidea.

*Yeah. And we've broken it.

*Do you by any chance detect fossil biological oxygen?

*I'm not able to say.

*Me neither.

Tap... tap... tap...

The emergency bod and the vermiform were both endowed with hearing. The two artists, ghost and living, stood rigid, as if already frozen in place. It was a false perception, it had to be.

—can you hear it too? whispered Stormzy (secure mode accidentally abandoned).

—Yes.

—has it just started?

The ghost-blade checked for himself, though Stormzy was also holding his recent history. —No. It may have been here all along, or started while we were talking, or even the moment I landed on the floor... I just didn't notice. What the hell *is* that?

—Ice, cracking? But it's so regular, and how is it getting in?

The hollow space had held its own special brand of fossilised gases (now sadly contaminated by Artidea's gash in the roof). They'd both, automatically, sampled the mix for the record: Stormzy when she entered here, Artidea when he fell in. They could tell, at a glance, that the original blend had been filtered to be free of corrosives, and concentrated enough for sound propagation, and really was still functioning on both counts. But *sentient AI lifeforms* generally do not, and never did, communicate with each other using propagated sound...

That tricky issue, the suggestion they must not raise, leapt into eerie, irrational prominence. *Tap...tap...tap...* Neither of them spoke or stirred until Artidea's ghost, unilaterally, darted to one of the ice-shrouded doorways.

Stormzy followed, small but fast on the smooth ice. One mystery was solved at once. The compacted barrier was not complete; there was clear space enough for the blade and the vermiform to slip through. Now they were in a dim corridor, as bare and ice-crusted as the chamber. The shrouded ghosts of further doorways could be detected on eitherside.

This complex was going to make quite a stir, if it really was completely unrecorded!

The tap, tap, tapping continued. Stormzy's low-light mix filled the corridor with shadows that seemed to flit about unreasonably. And now the tapping, which continued without pause, seemed irresistibly like a message in an ancient code, a code older than their peoples' entire sentient history—

If someone from beyond the dawn was still in some sense alive down here, trapped but alive, they'd been waiting a long, long time to be rescued.

Each sound was like a slow step coming towards them, from immensely far away, halting and pausing, then tapping again...

—Let's just go for it, said Stormzy. If it's a ghost, you do the talking. I'd probably accidentally say something offensive.

—Absolutely.

They found the second doorway that wasn't completely sealed, and slipped through the cracks into a much richer treasure house. The floor in this larger prefabricated box was littered with cloaked shapes of fittings; the walls marked with blurred shadows of décor. On one of them a patch of faintly coloured lights played, still in motion. Artidea looked for the source of the sound, and found it in the wall opposite the colours: perched high up, turning and turning in a niche behind a curtain of gleaming ice. He couldn't imagine what the thing might be. An alien lifeform? A booby trap?

Long dead, still moving, still tap, tap, tapping: sinister in the extreme—

Stormzy's vermiform swarmed up to the recess in which the light-box stood.

—it's a nightlight, she said. For a baby.

—An *orgie* baby?

—No! A neotene. Don't you know what a toy is? Were *you* never a neotene?

—Briefly, said Artidea, embarrassed at himself.

—But I wasn't kindled on an ice moon, practically before the dawn of civilisation. It seems a cruel custom, to force someone to endure helpless infancy out here.

—Childhood would have been important, said Stormzy placidly. A clean sheet. The mind unformed, groping for understanding, even for mobility. Our ancestors may well have thought that was the only right way to raise people. They were far closer to the orgies than we are; closer than people have ever realised, as the toy itself proves—

—Tuh. Instant expert.

—You're too kind.

She contemplated the light-box.

—That tapping may once have been a 'tune'. The colour changes might have marked musical intervals... I wonder if it could be restored.

They stood in silence, separately but in close accord, reviewing the wonderful journey to this moment. Stormzy's fateful live corrections; Artidea's death fall. His discovery. The betraying, and so ironic, caution of their remarks to each other, when they'd feared finding rare traces of ancient, *naturally occurring organic life*—the very same inspirational stuff they'd been trying to replicate in their artwork. And that *very* strange moment when they had both—genuinely, almost—believed they were about to meet their creator... one of the creators. Instead of which they'd found a truth about their own distant past, and it would be a while before they knew how they felt about that. Stirred, and sad, yes.

But not resentful, not at all—

—Our collaboration will be stopped dead, said Stormzy. Bummer.

—Not necessarily, said Artidea, almost absently. About the biological traces, we'll have to wait and see, but I think there are none.

—Me too. No material traces, only an idea about living.

—*So the collab will just be different... Oops, I'm bre-ak-ing up.*

The shade of a blade vanished. Stormzy left the treasure house and hurried back to the first room. Artidea was still living, when she touched his corpse.

Hi, Stormzy. Are we done here?

Yes. I have everything.

—*Good. You doing anything this evening?*

(*this evening* was a figure of speech; but fitting)

—Not really.

—*I thought, a trip to the viewing platform... and watch the Nine Billion, live? Since it's right here... Like to join me?*

—Good idea. Yes.

—*See you soon.*

He was gone.

'The Viewing Platform' (an artwork with no other designation, as if this were the only view that could possibly matter, in the entire known universe) was austere, and non-programmable by its guests, but a work of subtle artifice. Stormzy was there in good time for the never-changing spectacle, and to all appearances alone in the venue (like everybody else), as she waited for her date.

—Hey, Stormzy!

Artidea came flying towards her, no longer a blade but clad in formal dress (the platform insisted on this): a humanoid-shaped biped, life-sized in silver. Stormzy, in much the same attire stood with hands uplifted, until their palms almost met. He touched down beside her, and she smiled.

—Hey, 'Ploughshare'. What happened?

—Nothing much. Just a telling-off.

—Well deserved. You are such an idiot.

—I thought we were agreed it was *your* fault!

—No, I only offered to *share* the blame, out of pity. Glad you could make it.

—Me too.

But it was time for the show. They turned from each other and stood side by side on this ingenious, exquisitely minimalist 'space-platform', to watch the lovely spectacle of nightfall, on the only planet that had ever yet been found to harbour organic, naturally occurring life.

One by one, as the teeming globe turned from the sun at a stately, measured pace, they saw each megacity become a smoky, fiery shawl: tossed down over plains, clogging the jaws of river estuaries; spilling over high plateaus in the southern hemisphere. Small towns and villages ignited, twinkling. Coastlands swarmed with glitter; sordid settlements in the ruined lands came alive with tiny specks of gold . . . It was exquisite, already deeply moving, and it was just the prologue, because the lights kept coming. Cities towered and seethed, villages and towns ran into each other like molten metal. Braids of smoky fire crawled everywhere, invading the oceans, drowning remnant forests, engulfing mountain ranges. The whole of planet Earth, (which really was 'out there', in each spectator's field of view, only the lightshow and special effects were artifice) had become one heaving, coruscating jewel, blotting out every star, even its own, on the dark breast of the night . . .

And this was *The Nine Billion Names Of God*. Endlessly reproduced, of course, on every scale; yet still absorbing and poignant beyond measure. Everyone should see it live, as often as possible, and always (there were those who cheated, but not these two) 'as for' the first time.

—You know the orgies' persistent myth? murmured Stormzy

—Yeah? Which one?

—About the mighty aliens. How when they became spacefarers they would travel around, and everywhere they went they'd find the monuments of the forerunners?

—Mm. I suppose. But we never have. Logically, it's just not likely.

Artidea found myths boring, possibly because they were insubstantial, and he was an embodied, through and through.

—Irrelevant, since they hardly got off the ground, Stormzy went on. It's their art I'm talking about: full of supernatural entities, who lived in heaven, and ruled galactic empires, created lesser beings in their own image, and were functionally immortal. Angels, gods, magic black pyramids, Prometheus, and the eagle.

—You're suggesting, maybe they were thinking of us?

—Since time is an illusion? Yes, that's sort of what I was going to say.

—Shame they destroyed themselves, then.

—You don't really think it's a shame, said Stormzy. Because you wouldn't have liked them for neighbours and neither would I. But they didn't, in fact, 'destroy themselves': not quite. They stepped back from the brink, and survived long enough to achieve lift off.

—You think so?

—I know so. Because here we are.

But they fell silent again, for the opening of the second act. One by one, and swathe by swathe, the lights were going out. Neither of them spoke until the sad wreck of the creators' world, which in reality, as in this art, no longer harboured any life, had returned to darkness: a very small dim spot lost in a crowd of stars.

—I'm going to keep my name, said Stormzy at last, when the great work had slackened its compelling grip. At least until we're ready to show. I like it, I think it suits me. How about you?

—Nah, he said. I'm ready for a change. I died, you know? And the Ploughshare's work is done. I should move on. I'll think of something else for the kindling stage, and let you know. But Artidea will always find me…

They discussed a date for their next meeting. Stormzy was planning to leave the system, to attend to other projects, as soon as her tokamak was fired-up and running smoothly. Artidea would, of necessity, be sticking around after that to oversee the first stages of his kindling, but then he'd be working elsewhere too.

—How about we rendezvous, Jupiter system, in 100,000?

—Too soon for me, said Artidea. Nothing much will have happened.

—Okay, let's make it a bn?

—Fine. See you then, and go well.

—You too.

And so they parted, for a short while.

THE GRIDGE

M. T. HILL

RANK AND SARA STRAPPED the twins to their backs and
went out to sift the inbox. It had monsooned overnight and
the couple had lain awake together, electrified by the prospect
of a good haul. As swollen rivers fed the waterway, so the
waterway fed their children.

The inbox was a stretch of repurposed canal about fifty metres
long. Some months ago, they'd made camp beside its silky water,
breaking up their scuttled narrowboat and building iteratively.
Now they occupied this den on the towpath, its structure thin and
tall and oddly proud, from one aspect obscuring the desolated
town beyond, like a mock period fascia hides the building whose
true body is crumbling away. It stood on stilts and reclaimed
scaffolding, decorated and part-waterproofed with sun-faded
polythene bags, and it was home. Their garden—the drowned
fields on the other side of the inbox—needed no tending. Should
they manage to stay here, the twins would have to learn a lot of
knacks.

The couple started at opposite ends of the inbox. They each had a side, like you have a side of the bed. The rising sun, shrouded red but already warm, drew rainbows from the water's surface. They could see that last night's influx was full of knotted plants, and that it must've been powerful: floodwater had risen over the channelling frames and pooled along the towpath. It was undrinkable, far safer to sterilise the rainwater, but these fresh puddles always allured. Maybe it was the excitement of the new, a gloss on otherwise baked ground. Maybe it was the dry mouth that came with rationing. Or maybe it heightened their anticipation—the thrill of climbing over the frames in their waders to start dredging, not knowing what they might pull out, not knowing if there was something in the water that would change their fortunes, the twins' futures, for good.

Sara called over. Frank cupped his ear.

'Anything?'

Frank set his feet on the mesh platform and poked about. Silt swirled between his thighs. His grabber went heavy about a half metre down. 'Just this weed,' he called back. 'You?'

'Nothing,' Sara replied. 'Must be a new river, though. Water's come across the railway—buddleia this mature doesn't grow anywhere else round here. Let me check the gridge.'

Frank watched Sara move to the end of the frames and climb the steps. The baby's head bobbed between her shoulder blades. Sara had developed a limp these last few days, and massage wasn't working. Frank worried it was a tic, but she didn't seem to care.

'More shoeboxes,' Sara shouted.

Frank gave her the thumbs and hovered for a moment. Sara looked tiny on top of the gridge—an enormous box-steel and mesh filter welded together before the gas went on the torch. They'd named it while drunk on bartered wine, a silly portmanteau of grid and bridge. It comprised two heavy gates that stopped large debris entering the inbox and blocking the outlets down at the other end—Frank's end. Because if something got stuck in the wrong hole, the next deluge could inundate them, flood the towpath, or even the den. It'd put them out of business while they cleared it.

The boy on Frank's back started grizzling, a sure sign Frank had been standing still too long. He jiggled, hummed a lullaby, and started again, sweeping in tight lines from frame wall to frame wall, as if he were mowing a lawn. A brown fish broke the surface tension nearby. The boy relaxed into him. Frank stopped again to brush scum from his waist. Sara was back on the path, bagging the running shoes she'd extracted from the gridge. She caught him looking and held them up. They were the dregs of a stricken shipping container—sodden from their journey downstream, yet mostly like new. Those unsold (and they did usually sell) would be dried and bagged for later.

Generally, though, Frank and Sara were looking for smaller, much less practical items. The best deals came from sentimental, ornamental, and—crucially—unbroken trinkets. Most attractive were objects that reminded inland refugees what they'd lost to the water: CDs and vinyl, photograph albums, toys, plastic trophies, and so on. At night, in their bunk, as the den creaked and dripped and the boys slept between them, Frank and Sara liked to reflect on their finds, guess what each object might fetch, then extrapolate old lives from them. They'd role-play husbands and wives, panicked families bailing out their homes. They found it masochistic and comforting to take on these memories of before, when people believed hardship would never engulf them. They felt that by hoarding and trading other people's lost belongings, they were passing on stories. They did not see nostalgia as cynical; they were guardians and curators, and they were resourceful, clever for surviving, for not having lost their initiative or imagination. And they would stay here on this receding frontier, making their way. They wouldn't up sticks and retreat inland, where so many old friends and neighbours now lived a performed, pre-crisis life; where volunteers and subsistence farmers held up the edifice.

Which isn't to say dredging wasn't therapeutic. While Frank and Sara had given away most of their belongings before they moved on to the narrowboat, it was still a wrench when the hull was damaged and the water took what remained. Most precious to the couple was their own album of the twins' birth; Sara had wrapped this with electrical tape and kept it inside a bivvy bag. They'd bring it out on birthdays, or alone and in secret, when one or the other had left the den to sell their salvage at the markets.

Most useless from the inbox were the things that once carried monetary value: dead electrics, old cash, saturated books. The flotsam that arrived in the foam, which stuck to everything like paste. *If it floats*, went their maxim, *it's probably worthless*. Sara once joked about decorating the den's exterior with pound notes. They only didn't because the poly bags had a certain charm. When the storms came, and they came often, the bags flapped and rattled and snapped, and made the bunk feel cosier. When storms passed, you could hear the water coursing down the plastic and tinkling on the towpath.

The morning yielded nothing. It'd been a quiet week. They went inside before noon so Sara could nurse the twins in the shade. Frank made simple flatbreads while Sara sat at the crate they used for a kitchen table, each boy held like a rugby ball, legs under her armpits.

Frank hummed as he cooked. Sara liked this scene, the inbox water low and still outside. Her back ached and the scar in her belly throbbed after working to clear the buddleia, much as she viewed these pains as worthy, earned. The room smelled biscuity and warm. Frank ladled another measure into the frying pan. 'I'll walk in for the haggle after this,' he said.

'No need,' Sara said. 'We've nothing to get.'

Frank glanced round. 'Flour? Filters?'

'We'll cope. I don't want you to go.'

He turned back and smiled and knew Sara would see his ears go up. She didn't need him, not remotely. She chose to stay, and that was more reassuring than anything she could say.

'Leave it,' Sara said. 'We can sit here and think of some more names.'

He plated the breads and came to the table. He looked at the boys. They were nearly four months old now. Alert and heading for upright, a touch too thin in their vests and pants. They were usually naked or in towelling, crying or sleeping. It was still a novelty that they'd stopped soiling themselves so often.

'I don't want to,' he told her.

They hadn't named the boys because the implications scared them. To name them would be to give them permanence, damn them to their future. Of course they felt guilty about it, about withholding. And it wasn't like the boys were arrested by it—they went on growing regardless. But as with everything else, they'd decided together. It was how they hedged their bets.

Frank stroked the boy closest on the bridge of his nose. They weren't identical, that was certain: this one, the fairer of the two, was an easy smiler. The darker, smaller boy had Frank's brow, the brackets above his nose when he frowned.

'When I'm back,' Frank said, 'we could carry on reading that book. It was your turn.'

Sara smiled with one side of her mouth. The proposal was more or less a euphemism.

'I'm too tired,' she told him.

'So rest,' he said, 'and I'll dredge this afternoon.'

One of the boys broke his latch to belch, and Sara laughed quietly. Frank thought there might've been a sadness in it.

Frank didn't mind working the inbox alone—it was easier without a boy on his back. He went faster and moved as he wanted to, not as the boy's weight dictated. He found some hotel slippers, heavy and grey. They would dry. He used the net to bring out a child's fabric pencil case, cartoon dog characters flaking off the front. That would dry as well.

It was fascinating, what came down the waterway, what arrived with them. Even if nothing they did here was particularly innovative—it was hardly fishing, hardly sport—Frank turned the pencil case and was pleased by their setup, the work they'd put in to live passively, unobtrusively. The water came, the water went. Wasn't it more civilised to wait for life to come to you, instead of going out to hunt? He looked to the horizon and fixated on the shimmer there. He knew it was water standing on other territories, greenhouse plastic stretched over militia-claimed land, but in a certain light it was hard to believe the sea wasn't coming in already.

He got out of the inbox. At least the pencil case would sell nicely.

Rain woke Sara overnight. Mostly it followed a pattern: a sprinkling, a shower, a deluge. This time it was all violence; she could smell the churned inbox, hear the plastic bags clattering. She was on her side, and one of the twins was latched on to her, comforting himself, with the other on his belly across her flank. She didn't remember waking to accommodate them. She reached for Frank so he could help her move them. The darkness was thick, and Frank wasn't in bed.

Sara whispered his name while her eyes adjusted. The boy on her breast stirred and suckled, then rolled away, open-mouthed and content. She patted the bed again, just to check. Was he on the toilet? They used a chamber pot because it was easier, quieter, even if Frank was too proud to admit using it. She knew he took it out in the hallway.

The rain hammered on. A spike of worry accelerated her pulse. She felt it hollowing her belly. She moved the boy lying across her. He mewled and she patted his chest until he settled next to his brother. The boys' arms touched, then entwined, and she wondered if they knew yet. That even without Frank and her, they'd never have to be alone. She got up and saw the chamber pot was in the room and hissed Frank's name through the door. The den rattled and shuddered. The walkway from their bedroom groaned.

'Frank?' she asked, louder. Sometimes he rose and made nettle tea, brooded in the kitchen over things never revealed. It was still too early, though, and only the clouds spoke. She opened the porthole in the walkway—a clear bucket they'd cemented in—and removed the pot of wild flowers inside it. She put her head inside the rim. The bucket roared with rain, an ocean pushing down. It made her feel tiny. There was a light flickering outside. The longer she watched, the more it looked like a head torch. It came on and off as its wearer squatted and stood. It was down at the end of the inbox. Frank was out at her end of the gridge.

Sara was at the kitchen table when Frank came in. The sky lightening but full morning still a way off. The boys were sleeping over her shoulders, kept so by her rocking. In candlelight she saw Frank was soaking, red-faced, and breathing raggedly. He wore his waders only, his ribs pronounced in the gloom. His beard dripped on the lino.

'Go back to bed,' he told her.

She shook her head. 'What the hell have you been doing?'

'Gridge woke me. Sounded like a gong going off. And I worried, what with that weather—a bad one, wasn't it? Had to check it wasn't getting blocked the other side. We'd have nothing in tomorrow.'

'Frank.'

'And this thing has turned up—'

'You could've drowned.'

'I didn't. Come and look.'

She stood up. The boys were quiet. Was the rain easing? The bags seemed calmer. The loamy inbox smell had dispersed.

Frank wrapped Sara and the boys in the better of their two ponchos, the biggest, and passed her a head torch. He said, 'You don't even have to come all the way out.'

He staggered up the towpath, fine rain squirming in the beam of his torch. She heard him wrestling with a flysheet, before he turned back, angled his torch down. She heard the hand truck rattling on the cobbles. No matter how much they cleaned and oiled their tools, the rust got in eventually.

Abruptly he pulled up and turned, using the inbox frame to clamber round the truck bed. Then he was facing her.

'Spam?' she said, as he came close. It was definitely big, whatever it was.

Frank stopped and pulled away the flysheet. A brushed metal case with tapered edges. Down the side it said WORLDBOX. In this light, wet through, he looked wild and urgent. He said, grinning, 'Attachment was too big.'

There were two more worldboxes nudging the gridge by sunrise, along with four pairs of running shoes, riddled with foam. This time, Sara helped Frank clear the shoeboxes before they took the worldboxes out. While she'd fed and changed the boys, he'd gone and erected a makeshift cathead on the frame. Its beams looked too weak, but the pulley action was smooth.

Frank was gentler today, she thought. He took great care with a boy in the wrap, and she felt that acutely, in her guts, and loved him for it. In any case, it wasn't too difficult to manage the boxes when they were out of the water. Sara reminded Frank that she could improvise too: they still had the sling she'd made to help clear a wardrobe that had once drifted their way.

They stacked the worldboxes on the towpath. All three were pristine, unscathed by their journey. Frank knocked on one and said they must be hollow, or else they wouldn't have floated. They had no seams, handles, or locks. They were perfectly sealed. Their purpose was unknown, unguessable. To some extent, the couple agreed, they were no more practical than toy blocks.

Later, Frank and Sara talked about where the worldboxes might've come from. They'd never heard of worldbox, if that were a brand. (Which wasn't to say it couldn't be. Certain businesses thrived in this afterworld, and you learned from the markets that plenty of inland factories and fabricators were still creating new things, new pathologies.) The couple settled on walking upstream to see if the boxes had been dumped in their closest tributary. Maybe another shipping container had been pirated and turned out. Or some construction project had gone wrong, and this was the wreckage. Frank said they should try to cut one open.

'Or what if they're deliberate?' Sara asked him.

Frank rubbed his jaw. 'Deliberate?'

'What if someone's seen us? And they want to bung up the inbox? You said yourself—they'll stop anything else getting through. These'll flood us, if too many stack up.'

Frank kneaded his eyes with the heels of his palms. It was all too easy to ascribe Sara's paranoia to the twins, to her sharpened threat receptors. He chided himself for thinking of her so patronisingly. He reminded himself that there'd been a kind of biological determinism in Sara's pregnancy, that they'd both had to accept that their relationship was suddenly not as equal as it was before the boys, when they still lived on the boat, cooking and drinking and living together. Yes, this imbalance would be temporary, but she'd taken on her role so easily, and he was still trying to feel around his.

'If it's a gang,' Frank said, 'they wouldn't bother playing siege. They'd roll straight in here and sort us out.'

Sara glanced at the boys.

'Sorry,' Frank went on. 'People have bigger things to worry about than us, doing this.'

Sara pursed her lips. 'And there's nothing in the idea that people might covet the house?'

He smiled at that—*house*. She shook her head. One of the boys was waking, would soon rally his brother. Sara touched their heads and crinkled her eyes. She said, 'Could be vandalism...' and trailed off.

Frank stood up to wash the bowls. He wanted to say, 'No one has fun like that anymore,' but he didn't.

Outside there was a loud gong, and then another.

Nine more worldboxes waited at the gridge. These were dirtier, streaked with clay. Dank, chemical-smelling water lapped behind them, the last of the downstream pressure from last night's influx, and the boxes lolled against each other. Their sounds were tonal; Frank wondered if they bore cargo. He lashed the first box and brought it up over the gridge. The pulley wobbled. He'd need the truck again. There was still some space on the towpath.

That said, it'd take him all morning. He'd have to be in and out of the water. Up and down the towpath. And he remembered that the hand truck's wheels had started to seize yesterday, and sure enough, as he moved the sixth and seventh boxes away from the inbox, the truck's right wheel caught a raised flagstone and locked. Frank tripped over the truck, the truck went sideways, and the worldboxes fell against the frame. Frank sat there on the path, holding the back of his head. The beam of the frame was bent.

Sara had been watching. 'Let's go and see,' she said, pointing up the canal. 'After we've eaten.'

Frank nodded, defeated.

She said, 'The boys are clingy today,' and turned away.

Frank didn't know if he was supposed to feel guilty about that.

They ate their food in silence—warmed-over pastries whose heat didn't mask their staleness. Sara strapped one of the boys to Frank, and he strapped one to her. They barred the doors and padlocked what they could, and then they went up the towpath.

Sara spotted the next worldbox before Frank did. It was alone, gently turning in the water. Hard to tell if there was a current behind it, or if it was closer to static, readying for the next surge.

'If it floats . . . ' Sara said.

'It's useless,' Frank replied.

They touched hands briefly. Frank removed his sunhat and rubbed the sweat and grime from his forehead. They continued round a bend. There were more boxes in the water; it all felt inevitable. The sky low, the city rearing up in the distance, the boys sleeping against their backs. Cautious scouting had told them no other settlements had sprung up nearby, but there was a heavy feeling of being watched.

'Is that?' Frank asked.

And it was, obviously: three worldboxes stacked neatly on the towpath. Someone must have pulled them out, performed the same cursory inspections, reached the same non-conclusions.

'Bricks,' Frank muttered, inspecting them.

They carried on. The sun rolled higher, glowered through the cloudbase. They covered the boys' heads with damp white muslins, which seemed to further concentrate the heat into Frank and Sara's backs. Sweat ran between their buttocks. The pressure was building.

'What if they're building a dam in the city?' Sara said finally. 'To keep the water, and keep what we can sell.'

'Or,' Frank said, and not a little archly, 'they want to protect everyone downstream. Those shoes could carry some horrible pathogen...'

Sara didn't take him seriously, and just as well. They came round another bend in the canal. Jurassic weeds sprawled over the towpath. Chunks of rotting wood slid past. In places, the dirty foam came up right up on to the concrete.

'Frank,' Sara said, and stopped again.

This time, Frank had already seen why. Only a hundred yards farther along, the water had an uneven surface, a dull gunmetal sheen.

'Oh, Christ,' Frank said. 'How many is that?'

'We need to turn round,' Sara said. 'Before the storm.'

After the storm, Frank lay awake in their bunk counting worldboxes, listening to the water come off the walls. He reckoned on twenty-four, so far. The rain had been and gone, the water had bulged and passed, and now the boxes mounted—their dull clangs on arrival, their clinking as they jostled in the current. When Sara came round to feed the boys, he knew she'd start counting too.

Twenty-seven. Twenty-eight.

'They got here fast,' Sara said.

Frank went down to work as early as his body allowed. He watched a last pair drift in, sickly white in the light from his head torch. The boxes crowded at the gridge. The water churned through the grates. Nothing else would get through, not now. Sara was right. They'd have nothing to sell. Which meant nothing to eat. Which meant—

The makeshift crane finally broke as Frank drew out the second box. He was lucky the cable didn't take his eye out. Thirty-two. Thirty-four. He worked at the backlog. The boxes had no edges, but his hands were still lacerated. In and out of the water with the worldboxes slung across his back, as big as his torso, much heavier and more unwieldy than the boys. The scraping as he dragged them along the towpath in Sara's wardrobe sling. The petulant clang as he pushed them together at the den. The heat and the itching.

After breakfast, Sara came out to check on him. She had nothing to say, well aware that Frank had to clear the jam or they'd risk losing the next deluge. He looked committed, and strong, but his body was slight, and his back was curved with fatigue, his skin raw. Over lunch, he admitted he'd taken off his waders, which were chafing. He found a leech on the underside of his penis. She said, 'It's no good,' and shook her head. The leech came away with some persuasion, and she patted his shoulder. He was too tired for histrionics, either way. They'd laugh about it one day.

'I'll ask about the boxes at the market,' he said. 'Take a couple over there. You never know.'

Sara binned the leech without remark. The boys were sleeping again, their breathing syncopated.

'As long as you don't give them away,' she said.

Frank shrugged. 'It's side produce,' he said. 'It's fluff. They block the gridge again, we're shafted.'

He couldn't wait around, either way. The afternoon would run long, and there were still worldboxes in the water. The sling was tearing, so he would try and procure some canvas or rope.

When Sara gave him permission, Frank dressed and sheathed his knife in his sleeve. She and the boys watched as he oiled and tightened the hand truck's wheels, then loaded it. He lashed three of the worldboxes together and tried to move them. The truck was wobbly, but the wheels held. Sara tried to look impressed. He'd said two worldboxes, hadn't he?

Frank set off, sluggish at first, then surer. Sara watched him go. There were salt marks on the back of his shirt from where he carried the boys. She made out the shape of some country they'd never be able to visit.

Frank had been gone two hours. The boys were probably due another nap. Change, feed, activity, sleep. The weather was holding, for now; to the west, the first intimations of sunset. The sky was pink—tomorrow would be hotter than today, and tomorrow evening would bring the next storm. She lay on the bed with the boys and felt their heartbeats and made each of them smile in turn. There wasn't much to it.

Yes, a nap, she decided. With the boys asleep, she could read, or batch-cook, even if it wouldn't be enough to distract her from the idea of Frank marching alongside the waterway with the worldboxes jouncing on the truck in front of him. Instead, of course, she lay with the boys and fell asleep as they did. There were dreams waiting for her: Frank outside on a flooded towpath, working at a worldbox with a circular saw. Sparks fizzed off the water. He wouldn't look up. The sides of the box came away squealing. He peeled the worldbox and stepped back. Inside were the mummified remains of two people, entwined yin and yang, their skin the colour of piled dust. Frank didn't seem fazed, not even when a baby cried out. Face set, he pulled the bodies apart. Between them were two babies, themselves arranged top-to-toe.

Sara woke up, nauseated. The boys were still sleeping. There was sweat on their top lips. She checked their bellies were rising and gathered herself and sat up. She'd been out for at least an hour, and there was wet hair in her eyes.

She heard Frank sniffing outside. She found him sitting on the frame with his feet in the inbox.

'Frank?'

'Three bloody miles, I managed,' he told her. 'I lost them.'

'Lost?'

'I was going under a bridge. One of those low-arched ones. I was already tilting, and I couldn't keep it together. First box goes, then the whole truck went away from me. And now. No truck, no boxes. The truck bloody sank and the boxes floated off.'

'Oh, love.'

His story squared, though she thought he'd have jumped in for the truck had this happened closer to home. She kissed his head. 'We can get another one. We can build one. I know the sling's torn, but you could use the bed sheets instead.'

'Haven't you seen?'

She looked to the gridge. There must've been rain upstream, because more boxes were coming. Mounting again.

She hadn't heard them.

'I know,' he said. And he walked off towards the gridge.

Frank worked till the clouds converged and the wind changed. That was gone nine at night, when she realised he'd had nothing to eat, no water. He'd stink of vinegar when he came in. The boys fussed and were hard to put down, and it was hard not to resent them. Someone once told her they sensed your tension. But was it tension, this gap she worried was opening up between her and Frank? Or another readjustment? She made a crude goulash for supper and over-chewed each mouthful. She wanted to feel full so she could leave Frank seconds. She wanted him to know it was okay, that she was here in support.

When he came in, however, his mood was up.

'I don't know why I didn't see it,' he said, laughing. 'We've had the answer all along.'

Unease rose in Sara's throat. Frank was sometimes prone to mania. He was prone to superiority too. She pushed the bowl towards him and told him there was more in the pan, and she went outside to see.

The air was close. The rain still hadn't started. She walked to where Frank had been stockpiling the boxes, and saw he'd started to reinforce the den walls with them. They were laid up against the crates and stilts, against the bags. Nothing for mortar, of course, but they were a tight fit; there was a deliberateness in the way the boxes interlocked. The new den wall was already six boxes high. It must've been hard to lay the top set. There was no way to edge them, cut them, so the wall's ends were crenelated.

She thought of her dream—just a flash. The desperate idea that Frank was trapping them inside a mausoleum.

'Well?' he asked when she came back inside.

'It's too much,' Sara told him. 'I think it's time we thought about packing this in.'

If he was wounded, Frank didn't react. Sara went to bed alone. All night, as she drifted, nursed the boys, she heard Frank hauling worldboxes from the water, dragging them along the towpath, and slotting them together. His wet feet and grunting as he pushed the next box into position. She waited and willed him to stop. Right through the coldest hours. At some point the rain started in earnest and drowned him out. Sleep finally came, and there were no more dreams.

'Did you stop at all?' she asked him in the morning. Frank was on the living room floor, naked and covered with one of the boy's wraps. She strained him a drink and placed it by his feet. She could smell him all right: sour and damp, like a bathroom taken by mould. She was oddly grateful the boys would have no memory of it.

He came round when the boys started yammering; he looked worn through. A band of scum was glued to his chest hair.

'Hello,' he said.

Sara laid the boys on the water-stained sheepskin and went to look at Frank's handiwork. The worldboxes now ran along most of the den's lower half. It was certainly neat. Their home looked straighter. The worldboxes gave it a uniformity.

She looked out to the gridge. A steady stream of boxes was coming downstream towards them—too many to count. She felt sick. She didn't want to be there, and offered to go to the markets, sell some of their cache of trainers. Frank should rest; she could take the boys. She'd worked out a way to carry one boy in front and one behind, and that worked well. The boys balanced each other out.

'No,' Frank said. 'I don't want you to leave.'

'We can't keep it up, Frank. We can't keep pretending.'

He scowled at her. 'I'm not—I won't go and pretend. The boxes'll stop. They'll have to. And if I don't do it, where will that get us? The water won't get through. We'll have nothing. And then what? We get what we're given. It's waterproof. It's windproof.'

Sara set her jaw. Waterproof, windproof—she knew where it was going. Frank was building a fort. He was staking them down. The den was never meant to be permanent—just as the canal boat forced them into transience, the den was supposed to be a camp. Yes, they'd invested in it now. All this time. And the boys here. But they'd learned how to use their hands, and they could carry on. That was the point of staying behind, out here, on the edge of the future. They loved the canal, no doubt. The smell of ozone after rain. They wanted to work *with* the water. A worldbox fort was not the answer to any of it.

Frank went on building while Sara dredged the inbox. A few smaller items had squeezed their way through. A degraded camping spork; a keyring holding a picture of a small family holding hands in the cup of a fairground waltzer; a knotted condom rising from the depths in the eddy of her grabber, a strange jellyfish. The keyring was good. It made Sara wistful, which was often the tell. Maybe they still ran fairs like this in the cities, but she doubted it—it'd been a long time.

Now the worldboxes were stacked up to the bucket porthole. Frank was using the dirtiest worldboxes as steps. His ribs spacing and contracting as he lifted the worldboxes from the water. He'd worked out how to drag them four at a time. She ignored the noise. He wouldn't look at her.

It was getting darker and darker inside the den, and she hated it. She went to bed and Frank woke her just an hour later, beside himself, giggling, telling her he'd finally cleared the backlog. The inbox was empty. There were no more boxes coming.

The next morning, Frank slept in. Sara made rainwater porridge on the stove and sang an old protest song to the twins. They goggled at her and dribbled and she stirred on, watching the grey oats thicken. She didn't want to look outside, see how far he'd taken it. It was somehow embarrassing. There'd be gangs the other side of the marshland who'd surely see their den glowing in the distance. In her head, they'd consider it an invitation.

She called to Frank and told him breakfast was ready, and went out to the frames, not looking along the waterway, purposely avoiding the gridge. The inbox water was calm where she stood. The air was very close again. There'd been a small surge, because the water was higher than it was before they'd gone to bed. But the inbox looked empty. There was nothing new in there.

She went to the gridge. There were dozens of worldboxes waiting. Three days' work here, easy. She swore and spat in the water and went back. They hadn't heard these worldboxes arriving because Frank had draped the torn net over the gridge. It had softened the impact.

He'd done it to stop her worrying, she thought. Or to stop her nagging.

Frank looked disappointed when Sara told him there was nothing new at the gridge, not even any shoes. 'It's been a quiet night,' she said. 'Even the boys slept through.'

'Did it rain?'

She shrugged. 'I couldn't hear.' It surprised her, how easy it was to lie. 'And it was too dark to check,' she said. 'Couldn't tell what time it was.'

'Because I've installed blackout blinds,' he said.

She gave him a tight smile. 'The towpath's damp. Could've drizzled.'

'Humid enough,' he said, his tongue out as if to sense with it. 'Maybe we'll get a bonus storm this afternoon.'

'Sure,' she said. 'And tomorrow we'll get a full load.'

He sat back. He had the boys bouncing on his knees, facing her. They smiled gormlessly.

'I did like the challenge,' he told her. 'You know? I'm relieved they've stopped, and all. But I enjoyed it.'

Sara thanked him. She said, 'You should head back to bed, take the day off.'

He weighed that. 'I might,' he said. 'Joints aren't what they were.'

Sara took out a sheet of tarp, bundled the boys in blankets and went down to the gridge. The worldboxes like a pod of beached baby whales.

She propped up the tarp with her grabber, an old-style shelter, and laid the boys underneath. She climbed out across the gridge and tried to heave up one of the gates. There was no movement, not even a suggestion of play. She swore and looked around. There—she could make a lever. She took the longest pole from Frank's broken cathead and slid it through the rig. She climbed down into the water. It was tepid, and the surface smelled of diesel. She set herself against the gates and pushed up with the pole. The gridge gates groaned, opened a crack, then widened. The smooth corner of the first worldbox pushed in. Two jets of water squeezed around it in a V-shape. Just like when you shunt the paddles of a lock, she thought—the way that first crack sprays. All those locks they'd done as a young couple, free on the water, unaware. She steadied herself and set her feet and pushed again. This time the pole bowed and the gridge wrenched open; the current shifted against her knees, then strengthened. She fell backwards as the first worldbox slid through and caught her in the face. She tasted blood and went under, and the water surged. The worldboxes poured in around her.

Sara, thrashing, found an edge. The frame. Her first instinct was the boys, but they were kicking and gurgling happily, none the wiser. She heaved herself out. Her nose was flowing. The water came up and over the frames, and the worldboxes massed, came right through the inbox, and piled up at the far end. The water rose quickly. It splashed on to the bridle path. She felt that old compulsion to drink it.

'Sara!'

Frank was at the den door, clutching his face. The outlets were blocked, and plenty of inbox water was already displaced, flowing down to the towpath and on towards the den, already at the doorsill. The threshold. When the next storm came, the surge would begin to work at the base of their home. She tried to imagine the sound of the frames cracking under that much force, all that water pushing up against her worldbox dam, then finding a way out of it, around it. Another river. The den's new wall would come apart and float, eventually.

She gathered the twins and the torn sling and brought them back along the towpath, barefoot through the foam, her chin bloody. The boys squealed at her cold hands.

Frank just stood there, watching the worldboxes bob. The water sluicing on to the towpath was getting heavier. He didn't say anything.

When she was close enough, he noticed her limp had gone. Sara kissed him on the cheek, and the warmth of her blood shocked him. 'I can pack,' she said.

DODGING DEMENTIA

JOHN GRANT

I ROLLED OUT OF BED between five-thirty and six, peed because the secondary brain in my prostate told me to, checked the traps were empty of mice—which, hurrah, they were—and then, with a mug of strong black tea at my elbow, booted up the computer and settled into the *Guardian* crossword.

Just another Wednesday morning.

I once read that making a habit out of solving cryptic crosswords doesn't stave off dementia but does slow the progress of the disease—hence my habit. I also got books by the armful from the library and had stacks of *Scientific American* and *Nautilus* in the bathroom to read on the john. I was doing my level best.

I no longer had any fear of my own death, although I did have difficulty imagining what it'd be like to be not-here. What terrified me was the prospect of spending my final time—years, perhaps— in a state of uncomprehending confusion surrounded by stone walls and intellectual emptiness and platoons of professionals being kind and sympathetic but ultimately uncaring. I did not want to go drooling into that good night.

Dodging dementia was the name of the game. The decline and fall might be inevitable but it need not be quite yet.

By seven o'clock—as always unless it was raining or there was snow thick on the ground (or the *Guardian* crossword was unusually difficult)—I was outside and on my way to Lone Turtle Pond for my morning constitutional, as they might call it in a Brontë novel. The air was cold as hypocrisy in the predawn, but I had my padded jacket and my woolen gloves and my thick socks on. Soon the colors of sunrise would rage along the horizon, but for now it was as if someone had spilled skimmed milk across the darkness overhead.

Feeling proudly masochistic, I trudged down the driveway and turned to go up the hill. There was some traffic on the main road, commuters going into the city, but the world was still quiet enough I could hear myself think.

Not that there was so very much to think about, just the patterns that the clouds of my breath made in front of me.

The difficult part of my daily walk was the hill up to the lakeside. It wasn't so very far and it wasn't so very steep. Time was, I'd have barely noticed it. But creaky knees had changed all that. I noticed it now.

Even so, it didn't take me long before I was standing on the grassy, pebble-strewn footpath that goes round Lone Turtle Pond. Technically speaking the body of water is a lake, but it's a very small lake, as if some community planner in the sky had decided there should be a pretty little lake just the right size for elderly gents to walk around, and plopped it down here accordingly.

Shielded by the trees and a bit more distance, I could barely hear the traffic anymore. The water was glassy, like liquid moonlight under the pale sky. On the far side from me, a water bird disturbed the stillness. Otherwise there was no sign of life.

The air tasted of snow. Maybe we'd have a fall later in the day. I'd check the forecast when I got home.

I turned to the right and started following the shore, leaning on my stick a deal more than I used to, every year a little more.

During the day I didn't come here. There were often small kids running around, falling on their faces, screaming, losing their Frisbees into the water, getting sworn at by dads who were trying to catch fish. But this early in the morning there was hardly ever anyone but me around.

Me and sometimes Old Grumbly.

Old Grumbly was a big black bear. He must have lost his mate years ago, because for as long as anyone could remember he'd been a loner, leading his solitary existence in the woods around the lake. Somehow he'd escaped the guns of the hunters who turned out every year for the annual cull of these magnificent animals— animals that weren't a pest, even though officialdom had decreed them so.

It was hardly any wonder I identified with Old Grumbly. My Elaine had died eleven years ago, which hadn't been part of the master plan we'd plotted out for our retirement. Since then I'd kept on keeping on, never letting a day go by without my thinking of her, trying to adapt the shape of my immediate surroundings to form a new, Elaineless mold.

Just as I imagined was the case for Old Grumbly, I wasn't altogether successful in this.

I looked around for him now. He didn't always join me for my amble around the pond, but most mornings he did, not coming onto the path but making no great effort to hide himself either, crashing through the brush and long grass and whuffling companionably.

No signs of him yet. Probably he'd turn up later.

The walk around the pond was only about a mile, perhaps less, but each year it took me longer to do it. It had been slow when Elaine was still with me, because we'd keep stopping to look at something or talk about this and that. Then, in the couple of years after she'd left me, while I'd been turning into a geezer without really noticing it, I'd walk the distance in a matter of minutes despite the hangovers I had every morning then. Now, with my stick and those creaky knees, it could take me a half-hour or more.

Old Grumbly was very considerate to slow himself down to my pace.

Someone had left litter on the path ahead of me, I could see. It happened from time to time—soda cans or cigarette packs, Styrofoam containers from the deli on the main road. I pulled the paper supermarket bag I always brought from the pocket of my jacket, ready to pick the junk up.

As I got closer, though, there seemed something different. The bits of detritus weren't just scattered around, the way they usually are. They looked almost posed, almost as if someone had arranged them ready for discovery.

Wheezing a little, my stick rattling the pebbles of the dewy path, I increased my speed.

Yes: posed. That was the correct description.

There was a paperback book with what appeared to be a dollar bill poking out from between its pages. On top of the book's beige-and-orange cover there was something that looked like a wristwatch, with a big square face and a blue plastic strap.

I put the empty bag back in my pocket and then, using my stick as a prop, I cautiously crouched down and picked the objects up in my free hand.

The world swam a little in my vision as, grunting and groaning, I managed to get myself upright again.

The book was foreign, the lettering on its front being in some script I didn't recognize—an alphabet that was more like English than it was like Cyrillic or Greek but wasn't English either. I crammed it into the jacket pocket that didn't have the bag and my phone in it. The watch, without thinking, I put on my wrist. I hadn't worn a watch in years, and the feel of it there was somehow reassuring.

Blinking, I looked around at the stillness of the lake. The trees and the coarse grasses were motionless too. Old Grumbly must be enjoying a lie-in this morning, and I wished him well of it.

I'd have to hand this stuff in to the cops, I knew. This wasn't just any old garbage left haphazardly by loutish kids. Someone must have settled themselves down on the path for a moment, put the objects they'd been carrying aside, then forgotten them. The watch could be valuable, although it didn't look it. The book was foreign;

finding a replacement copy so as to finish reading it could be difficult.

The dollar bill? Well, it was only a buck but it wasn't *my* buck.

I was halfway home before it occurred to me to wonder who would take their watch off and put it to one side when they were just resting for a moment.

I got back to the house by about eight, an hour before Julia was due to arrive, this being a Wednesday. I put my discovered book on the kitchen table on top of a paper towel, for reasons of hygiene, and hung my jacket up on its hook.

I was just about to take off the watch and put it beside the book when I realized it wasn't a watch. What I'd taken at first glimpse to be a digital display of the time was a digital display, all right, but not of the time. The little red numbers read

53,982

which just didn't make sense—not as a time of day, anyway. Obviously this was some kind of a meter, equipped with a convenient wrist strap so its user could readily glance at it. But a meter for reading what?

The other interesting thing I discovered about the device was that I couldn't get it off. The holes and the little buckle used for fastening had seemingly melted away, leaving an untrammeled strip of plastic that refused to stretch. I pulled out the kitchen scissors from the drawer, but, hesitant to cut something that wasn't my property, put them back again.

I decided to wait until Julia arrived. Maybe she'd know what to do.

Julia Juarez came in three mornings a week to clean the house, drive me to the shops and, more importantly, to the library, and generally make sure I was breathing and capable of looking after myself when she wasn't there. She insisted on cooking me hearty breakfasts that I couldn't eat, but the lunches she left in the fridge for me were always welcome. My daughter Alice, who earned big bucks at MIT to do things to muons their mothers would surely never condone, insisted on paying Julia even though I told her my pension from the *Jersey Courier*, where I'd been a copyeditor for forty years before they'd started economizing on copyeditors, could easily afford Julia's modest wages.

I brewed myself another mug of tea and, setting the bill to one side, sat down to make a closer inspection of the book.

It looked like an ordinary paperback, with a stylized picture of a man on the cover, and the heft was about right, but the material it was printed on—all in that curiously half-familiar script I couldn't recognize—didn't seem to be paper. The pages had a plastic sheen to them, although they didn't seem to be plastic. And they were tear-resistant, as I discovered when I guiltily experimented.

They weren't numbered, and toying with the book as I drank my tea and waited for Julia, I eventually realized why.

When I riffled through it, the book seemed to have about two-fifty or three hundred pages—a standard tally for a paperback, anyway—but if I turned those pages one by one, as I did for a while, avidly seeking a word I could recognize, I never seemed to progress any farther through the book. If I opened it at the middle, and patiently turned page after page after page, by the time I'd done I was still in the middle.

It was as if the book could be infinitely long.

I stared from it to the gadget on my wrist, and back again. These artifacts didn't belong to any technology I recognized.

There was a bustle at the back door.

'Hello there, Mr. C,' cried Julia as she always did, letting herself in. 'Are you decent?' Again as she always did.

'As decent as I'll ever be.' That was what *I* always said.

I started to move the book and the wrinkled bill from the table, then left them where they were. Perhaps Julia could help me solve the riddle.

'I brought some bacon for your breakfast,' she told me. 'It'll build you up.'

───── ∞ ─────

Julia's face was round and brown and in many ways not unlike my memory of Elaine's, although Julia was Latino and Elaine was from Trinidad. In another lifetime, Julia and I might have had an interest in each other beyond carer and cared, but not in this one. She was in her early to mid-sixties, perhaps as much as twenty years younger than me, and like me she'd lost a beloved spouse a while back. Although I'd tried a thousand times to get her to call me Harry, it never lasted more than an hour or two before she was back to calling me 'Mr. Crayborn' or just Mr. C'.

The bacon negotiated away—I persuaded her that her grandchildren needed building up even more than I did—I settled in to eating the dish of eggs and toast she made for me, washing it down with yet more tea.

She toyed with the book, turning it with her finger to read the title and then looking briefly crestfallen when she realized she couldn't.

'I found it up by the pond,' I said through a mouthful of food.

'Much good it'll do you. Greek, is that?'

'Not Greek. I can't read the language but I'd recognize the letters.'

'And this?' she said, picking up the bill from where it lay. 'You found *this* up by the pond as well?'

I nodded.

She laughed. 'You better take it back. It'd be more use to that bear of yours, Grumpy, than it would to you.'

'Grumbly,' I corrected.

'See?' She showed it to me. 'You got yourself a twelve-dollar bill, Mr. C.'

I stared. For a moment I thought she was kidding me—not like her, yet she sometimes surprised me—but it was obvious she wasn't. Above the engraved picture of a president I didn't recognize there was the legend 'THE UNITED STATES OF AMERICA', just like you'd expect to find, but below it I read: 'TWELVE DOLLARS'.

Julia snatched the bill away and held it close to her face. 'You ever heard of a President Pudd'nhead, Mr. C? Me neither. Thought it was going to be Mickey Mouse or Donald Duck, but it's this guy Pudd'nhead. It's gotta be a joke.'

'Yeah, a joke,' I said. 'Like the book no one can read. Someone must have been coming home from a party last night and they dropped their party favors.' I didn't tell her about the gadget on my wrist, and she hadn't noticed it.

'Or threw them away,' she said, putting down the bill and turning toward the sink with a look of business in her eyes. 'I got given junk like that, *I'd* throw it away, you bet.'

'But not until you got home. Seems odd to dump it out there like that.' I thought about telling her how it had been so neatly arranged, right in the center of the path so no one could miss it, but decided against. There was no one really walked by Lone Turtle Pond first thing in the morning except me, and the idea that the trinkets had been put there specially for me was surely absurd.

'You want me to put this stuff in recycling?' she said, gesturing toward the book and the bill.

'No. I'll take them in to the cops when we go to the library. They're not mine and someone might be looking for them.'

Her snort told me what she thought of that possibility.

'Then give me your plate, Mr. C, and get out from under my feet.'

The cops weren't interested when I went there after my lunch. Oh, they were polite all right, and they didn't laugh in my face, but they spared the three artifacts I'd found no more than a glance and it was clear they thought I was just some demented old geezer who'd forgotten how to get his watch off and was now convinced it had been beamed down onto his wrist from the Starship *Enterprise.*

'Told you so,' said Julia when I got back into the car and told her how it had gone. She put aside her knitting and turned the key in the ignition. 'The cops in this burg have difficulty finding their own asses to wipe if it's dark in the room,' she reassured me. 'Library next?'

The librarians gave me a friendly greeting, as always—I was one of their most prolific customers, after all—and just briefly I was tempted to tell *them* about my finds. Luckily common sense prevailed, and I just chattered about the weather as Hildegard processed the stack of books I'd pulled off the shelves.

'You didn't, did you?' said Julia as I rejoined her.

No need for me to ask her what she meant.

'No,' I said. 'I didn't.'

'Good.'

Once home, while she pottered around with the vacuum cleaner, I put some of the books I'd borrowed on my nightstand and the rest on Elaine's—after all, she didn't have a use for it any longer—and went back to the kitchen table where *the* book, the one I couldn't read but that seemed to be neverending, still lay. For most of the rest of the afternoon, I played with it, as if somehow I'd have this great linguistic insight all of a sudden and everything would become clear.

After Julia had left, I nuked and ate the casserole she'd put in the fridge, then carried on fiddling with the book, turning those slightly slithery pages. Although the printed text still was as incomprehensible as ever, I got the sense that the book was *trying* to convey meaning to me, that this meaning was just around the corner from my perception. Maybe the text wasn't really text at all? Maybe I was wrong to assume all those printed marks represented language? Could I be like the person with their nose up against the screen of an old-fashioned TV set, trying to ascribe meaning to the light and dark shapes in front of me without realizing they formed part of a picture I could see if I only looked at it right?

At nine o'clock I opened a bottle of cabernet sauvignon, and at ten o'clock I crawled into bed with one of the novels I'd borrowed from the library, an old science fiction piece by Clifford D. Simak called *Time is the Simplest Thing*. My mind wasn't really on it, so it wasn't long before I switched the light out and let the wine lull me to sleep.

That night was one of those when I dreamed of Elaine. She didn't visit my dreams nearly as often as I wished she would, and when I was awake I sometimes told her this. On occasion we'd make dream love, and then afterward lie entwined as my fingers stroked the marvel of her café au lait skin, but more usually we were somewhere else—walking on the surface of a fast-rushing river, riding a London bus, sipping bitter black coffee in that little bistro in Paris—and just talking and talking and talking. When I woke in the morning, it'd almost always be to the frustrated realization that I couldn't *quite* remember what we'd been talking about but still able to hear the music of her voice all around me.

The frustration—that sense that the memory of the words was only just beyond my fingertips—was, now I come to think of it, not unlike what I was feeling about my inability to hear what the beige-and-orange paperback was trying to tell me.

And it was about the book that Elaine wanted to talk tonight.

First, though, there were preliminaries to be negotiated.

'Gooseberries glow because of their own internal purity of spirit,' she informed me soberly.

We were standing in the middle of what I initially took to be a field of wheat that stretched as far as the eye could see, but then realized was in fact a gigantic windswept carpet: those strands that were tickling our knees were in fact strands of woolen pile in diverse colors. We were holding cocktail glasses, Elaine's full of a virulent-looking green liquid and mine full of an equally virulent-looking bright purple goo. The sky overhead was a cyan blue; the puffy little clouds scattered across it were the white of a nurse's starched collar. Whichever world this was, it seemed to have been created in primary colors. It was as if we'd found ourselves in a Looney Toon.

The only things that weren't done in primary colors were ourselves. We were both naked. Elaine looked good that way, myself . . . less so.

Abruptly, a whole cocktail party of people sprang into being around us. Everyone else was in formal attire—suits for the gents, dresses or smart pants sets for the ladies—but we stayed naked. No one else seemed to notice.

'I've never known that about gooseberries,' I replied.

Someone shrieked with laughter directly beside my ear.

'You should read more widely,' said Elaine, extracting an olive-on-a-stick from her glass and sucking it.

'I try.'

'That weird book you're trying to read at the moment.'

'You know about it?'

'I know about *everything* to do with you, Harry,' she said, lips pouting in reproval. 'You should have realized that by now.'

'You understand what the book's trying to tell me?'

'So do you.'

'I wish I did.' I drained my glass but it stayed full.

'You just don't understand it in the here and now.'

'Where else is there? Saying I don't understand it *yet* is the same as saying I don't understand it at all.'

She chuckled. 'No. I'm saying you're looking at the wrong here and now. You should be looking at the here and now you're heading toward.'

A man behind her was stripping off his face and cramming it between his bone-surrounded teeth. The sight distracted me for a moment.

I returned my attention to Elaine. 'What was that you were saying?'

'Gooseberries. Their hidden light.'

'No. After that. About the book I discovered up near Lone Turtle Pond. The here and now that I haven't got to yet.'

Her face crumpled as if she were about to burst into tears. 'But I want to talk about *gooseberries*!'

I woke in a Himalayan landscape of bedclothes, my bladder throbbing. For once I not only remembered our conversation but also was able to retain the memory of it, playing it over again in my head as I switched on the light and tottered to the bathroom.

What the hell was all that *about?* I thought, watching my urine dribble in fits and starts into the toilet bowl.

As I reached out to press the flush lever I felt the tiniest sensation on my wrist, almost as if a fruit fly had somehow managed to land on the skin there. Except that was impossible, because the skin was covered by the rectangular face of the 'watch'.

I glanced absently at the display. It now read:

53,981

It took me a couple of moments to realize that yesterday it had said:

53,982

Could the decrease in the number represent the tiny sensation I'd felt? Was the gadget's underside *marking* me in some way, with its display being a counter to register the marks it had made? Was the 'watch' injecting me, giving me shots? If so, shots of *what?* Was I now protected against all the bugs known to infect the occupants of UFOs?

There had to be a more prosaic explanation than that.

Even so, after I'd climbed back into bed, in the few minutes before I fell back to sleep I found my mind speculating wildly.

Okay, so imagine these really are *shots, and imagine they're administered once a day—once a night, rather: in the middle of each night, just like that one. How many days' supply does this gadget have? How many doses? 53,982 divided by 365.25 is going to be... Oh, hell: forget about the .25 for the moment. 53,982 divided by 365 is going to be about... is going to be about 150 years, near as dammit.*

One hundred fifty years! How long do these superbeings think I've got left to live?

As I finally drifted off, one last wisp of thought floated through my mind:

Say, what if they're right?

Next morning was a Thursday, and so of course there'd be no Julia today—which was for once a good thing, because I'd got plenty I needed to do and would happily trade the loneliness for the uninterrupted time.

I got up, brewed tea, did the *Guardian* crossword (an easier picaroon than usual), put on my jacket (making sure to remember my gloves), and headed out for Lone Turtle Pond. It was only when I was halfway there that I realized I'd forgotten my stick.

I paused for a little, irresolute. Should I go back and fetch it? On the other hand, I was doing just fine without it . . .

As you'd guess, I kept a vigilant eye open for anything that might have been laid out on the path, but there was nothing except a couple of empty beer cans, a roach that in my young days would have been smoked down a heck of a sight more than this one was, and an empty plastic carrier bag from the local supermarket. All of these went into my brown paper bag under the approving gaze— or so I imagined—of Old Grumbly, who this morning had emerged to trundle amiably alongside me.

I stopped at one point and looked at him, a couple of yards away.

'Did *you* see who left those things yesterday?' I said.

He grunted a couple of times, as if to say that he was as bemused as I was by the whole affair.

'A mystery, eh, old fellow?'

Grunt, grunt. Yes, it was a mystery. Or, more likely, it was a mystery why I couldn't get a move on rather than stand rooted to the spot. There's a school of Muslim thought that believes Allah creates the world afresh in every moment, and I'd long ago come to the conclusion that Old Grumbly's mind worked along similar lines. The world was freshly created every morning, and any conscientious bear would see it as his duty to explore each of these new worlds—or at least the Lone Turtle Pond locality of them— to make sure everything was in its rightful place. Why was I delaying him in the execution of this important task?

I chuckled at him and got moving again.

I could see Old Grumbly's point. The world's only as old as our memories of it. In a way, so are we.

The only times I missed my stick that morning were whenever I saw a thistle head and felt the itch to take a swing at it.

Back home, I put my pieces of litter in their respective bins for recycling—except the roach, which I was tempted to recycle in the traditional way before reminding myself I didn't know whose lips had last been wrapped round it; *it* went into the garbage.

Then I made myself some oatmeal, jacked up an mp3 collection of Louise Farrenc chamber music, and used my phone to take photos of yesterday's finds. Once I had the photos on the computer, I cropped them to get rid of extraneous bits of background, using an app daughter Alice had installed for me a couple of years ago, then got to work with image search.

My twelve-dollar bill popped up almost immediately. I'd been righter than I thought when I'd made that flippant remark to Julia about party favors. You could buy bills like this for birthday parties from Pudd'nhead Fancies of Kansas City, Missouri, in packs of five, ten, twenty, etc. Whatever age your child or even yourself might be, Pudd'nhead Fancies could supply the appropriate bills to give away to the guests, unless, for obvious reasons, the birthday in question was the first, second, fifth, tenth, twentieth, fiftieth, or hundredth. In those cases, I guess, you had to use the real thing, which ran a bit more expensive than Pudd'nhead's novelties.

The search for the photo of the 'watch,' the counter, the medical appliance, the call-it-what-you-will produced approximately seven billion images of digital watches and another seven billion of electronic counters of various types, but nothing that matched the gadget on my wrist. After about a half-hour of scrolling through them, I found my eyes had glazed over sufficiently that I no longer knew what I was seeing. I gave up on it.

The neverending book was more interesting. The image search tended to ignore the lettering on the cover and instead just hunt for the visual design. Quite a few potential matches came up, though luckily not so many as for the gadget. One of them in particular was so close that I went and fetched the book so I could compare the real thing with the image on the computer screen.

Whoever had published the book I was holding in my hand had stolen the cover design from the 2007 Vintage paperback edition of Edmund Crispin's classic detective novel *The Moving Toyshop*.

I sat back in my chair and breathed out long and slow.

I'm not naïve enough to believe that Elaine herself *really* comes to visit me in my dreams. It's my own mind that creates the figment of her, even though while I'm dreaming she seems to have an independent existence. The words she says to me—they're likewise the product of my own mind. Perhaps my subconscious is trying to tell me something and uses as mouthpiece the person I've loved the most in my long life. If so, I've no idea why I almost always forget on waking what I've told myself while asleep, or why, in the instances when I *do* remember, the subject of the conversation is usually some irrational garbage about, well, glowing gooseberries.

But the dream conversation I'd had with Elaine last night—that had been a different kettle of fish. It was as if she—or, rather, my sub-conscious—had been trying to tell me something important.

What had she said? 'You should be looking at the here and now you're heading toward.' I'd understand the book when I got to the correct here and now—the one that hadn't happened yet. One of the countless here-and-nows that hadn't happened yet.

The future.

I looked at the neverending book with its meaningless (to me) markings, and I looked at the device on my wrist. Right at the outset I'd thought they represented some unknown technology. I'd joked mentally about UFOs and space aliens and the starship *Enterprise*, but what if the reason the technology was alien to me was that we hadn't invented it yet?

Who was it who said that the *real* aliens aren't the creatures who live on the planets of distant stars but us in a hundred years' time?

The more I thought about this, the more it seemed to make sense. I was sure it wasn't just the Simak novel making me think so. The neverending book, with its seemingly infinite number of pages, wasn't anything that could be created today, but it was still very recognizable as a printed book, as a development from present-day technology. It couldn't have come from more than a few decades ahead, I reasoned, because it was pirating a twenty-first-century cover image. How written language could have evolved so swiftly was a question I shelved for the time being. Besides, as I'd speculated earlier, maybe the marks didn't directly represent written language.

The device on my wrist? Even though I didn't know how it worked or what it was for, the *form* of the object—the strap and the square housing of the display—was just like that of any number of wristwatches manufactured over the past few decades. It was only if you looked closer that you discovered it wasn't a wristwatch at all. The strap had morphed after I'd done up the buckle, but I was sure there were high-tech plastics being developed by the military that could do that sort of thing. Allow for a few decades, and such plastics were bound to be in commercial production for consumer goods.

Finally, what about the twelve-dollar bill? How come Pudd'nhead Fancies' pride and joy had been part of the carefully arranged consignment that had been left on the path for me?

A joke? A flag to alert me to the fact that the rest of the stuff wasn't what it might seem at first glance? A way of making sure the cops wouldn't take me seriously when I took the artifacts to them?

I wished Elaine were here so I could talk all these questions through with her. The real Elaine, not the chimera I conjured up in my dreams.

Okay, so a few decades ahead in the future they've invented time travel—or maybe not *travel*, per se, but the ability to transport information or small objects back in time. Maybe living creatures can't survive the process, or maybe the human mind can't. So someone decides to send a little package back to our time—a mystery object in the form of a twelve-dollar bill plus a couple of artifacts that were presumably chosen for good reason.

Why?

And why put them on the path beside Lone Turtle Pond so they'd be found by the first person walking there that morning?

When that first person was inevitably going to be me.

It dawned on me very, very slowly that I *knew* who'd sent the book and the counter back through time.

Me.

Or maybe it was a version of me that lived in a parallel universe. That'd work too. Was there really so much difference, anyway, between time travel backward and forward and time travel sideways? Not that I could think. But somehow backward and forward seemed more *logical*, if that wasn't a contradiction in terms.

Using my time machine, I'd transmitted (or was going to transmit) the bundle to the path rather than into the house to reduce the risk that Julia Juarez might come across it first. Out by the pond, the only person who might find it before I did was Old Grumbly, and he'd likely leave it alone.

But why had I sent it?

Just to encourage my former self to keep going until I reached the right here and now—the here and now where I'd understand the book? Or to make sure I actually got there, sometime during the next 54,000 days or so?

'There's something different about you,' said Julia a few days later, squinting at my face. 'Oh. You've not got your glasses on.'

I put my hand up to my nose reflexively and found she was right. I'd forgotten to put my specs on that morning and simply hadn't noticed their absence. The counter on my wrist was now down to 53,977. Five days' worth of 'shots' seemed to be making a difference; what would I be like after another 53,977? I still hadn't felt any of them beyond that first one, but I was certain that they were being administered as I slept, that it wasn't just a matter of the number on the counter ticking daily down.

Each morning there was a new spring in my step as I went up the hill toward Lone Turtle Pond. I no longer bothered with my stick. When I stood from picking up litter I no longer wheezed. I joked with Old Grumbly about it, and sometimes he seemed to laugh appreciatively.

'It's my second youth, Julia. Before you know it I'll be younger than you are, and *then* won't the neighbors' tongues begin to wag?'

'And then I'd be having you in court for sexual harassment, Mr. C,' she said demurely as she put another plate into the dishwasher.

'It'd be worth the fine for the notoriety. A sexual pest at my age? I'd be invited on *Oprah* to divulge my secret formula.'

We both chuckled.

Later that day, after she'd gone, I looked at my face in the bathroom mirror. I've never been much of a one for gazing into mirrors—like Woodrow Wilson, I've always counted myself lucky to be behind my face rather than in front—but it appeared to me a few things had changed about my ugly mug. The lines around my eyes and on my cheeks were still there, but they didn't seem so marked. My eyebrows seemed darker. And there, beside my right temple, was that a black hair among the sparse white fluff?

I had to be fancying things. There wasn't any medicine on earth, subcutaneously administered or otherwise, that could turn back the arrow of aging. Even in the future it was surely not possible.

Or maybe it was. How old would I appear to be by the time I met my future benefactor, the future me? And how old would *he* appear to be?

I went out on to the porch with a mug of hot chocolate and the neverending book, sat myself down, and began another attempt to make sense of the printing. As always, I had the feeling that the meaning was just around the next corner but—in the same way that the book's end never seemed to get any nearer—however much I advanced toward that corner it never seemed to get any closer. It was like trying to read a newspaper through heavily frosted glass. Every now and again I'd think I was almost able to make out the first few letters of a banner headline, but then I'd realize I was deluding myself.

I threw the book aside with a gasp of frustration. Who was I kidding? I'd never be able to understand this, not if I lived to be a thousand years. Who wanted to live to be a thousand years old?

Suddenly the putative 150 years the counter had allocated me seemed less like an improbable extension of life, more like a prison sentence.

Why couldn't the future Harry Crayborn have sent back his

consignment of gifts to Elaine, when she was still alive, instead of to me, now, when it was too late? Or one each to both of us? Then I wouldn't be facing the prospect of serving out my time in solitary confinement.

That was the first of the melancholy phases. Fortunately, it didn't last long.

M y life hasn't changed so very much in the years since the ... at least, not in its routines.

I still get out of bed early and do the *Guardian* crossword online, although nowadays I buy collections of vintage crosswords to supplement my habit.

I lost the book from the future before I'd managed to make head or tail of it. Julia and I hunted all over the house for it, but it was nowhere to be found. I've no doubt, though, that it'll turn up when I'm ready for it—or perhaps when it's ready for me. The twelve-dollar bill, of course, vanished long ago, just like my walking stick and my spectacles, and who could care less.

The counter on my wrist has dipped under 53,000. I view the changing numbers as a measure not of time's passage but of a decrease in the length of the wait before I reach my destined here and now.

I still take my morning constitutional up by Lone Turtle Pond, although rather than creeping slowly round it just once on rickety knees, I circumnavigate it three or four times, moving easily.

Most days Old Grumbly—whose black fur now has prominent white patches and who limps as he walks—comes to join me, just like always, and sometimes he answers when I speak to him. His voice is very low and hoarse, except when he gets excited, and I find it hard to understand his words, but I know sure as eggs they're words.

I hear *so much*, thanks to whatever the counter is pumping into me in its daily doses. It's not just Old Grumbly who's gained a voice. If I pause to gaze out across the surface of Lone Turtle Pond, watching the little ripples the insects make on its glassy mirror, I can hear the voices that exist in all creation—the coarse waterside weeds, the water itself, the sky, the trees behind me. I don't know how I could have been deaf to them for so very long.

Most of them sound like the voices of strangers, but sometimes I have the illusion that it's Alice or her husband Mack or the kids speaking to me. Even though their words don't make a lot of sense, I answer back as well as I can.

Once I've finished listening and talking, if I'm absolutely sure there's no one else around to see me except Old Grumbly, I'll sometimes, before I can wake up and find out where I really am, break into a run along the pebbly path, just to prove to myself that I'm able.

SEDITION KITSCH PART I

STEVE AYLETT

O NE STORY GOES THAT a meteor grazed Earth's atmosphere on July 20, 1860, dividing into two uneven pieces. It was seen by most as a harbinger of the American Civil War and by hairdressers as an indication of where to place the parting. When the first interpretation came to prominence, the barbers held fast, their stylings visible in photographs of the dead from both sides. 'A lady's thimble will hold all the blood that will be shed' went a popular saying at the start of the war, the thimble inevitably holding all the common sense exhibited. Chimps have got the right idea, with their screaming.

Immediately after an event, the danger of what meaning is assigned to it is still sharp. The day after London's Crystal Palace burned down, the molten glass which had flowed down the street gutters had hardened. People tried to snap off pieces like ice and were injured. Rumours were repeated that the fire was started by a Nazi, a postal worker, or other man from underground. In fact a decrepit heating system ignited tons of flammable parrots and paper. What remained was the Crystal Palace Gardens, a Victorian Jurassic Park full of famously inaccurate dinosaur sculptures. To this day, a blissed-out ichthyosaurus basks like a seal and cannot stop smiling, near an iguanodon so fat it can barely rise from its belly. Equating dinosaurs with established empires, the Victorians could not imagine something big moving fast.

The gigantic Crystal Palace was originally built in London's Hyde Park to fence in the braying tycoons of the 1851 Great Exhibition. While kicking off the embarrassing display of World's Fairs down the ages, it tested the appetite for pat narrative. Amazed by a long vista of colossal statues, Lewis Carroll focused on one of an Amazon and a tiger. 'She is sitting on horseback, and a tiger has fastened on the neck of the horse in front . . . you almost expect to hear it scream.' Gustave Flaubert was unimpressed with the exhibition and left to visit the East India Company Museum, where he discovered a near-life-size automaton of an Englishman being mauled by an Indian tiger. The wooden man moved his hand wanly and wailed as the tiger grunted on top of him. Created for Tipu Sultan of Mysore to express the extent to which the British had been getting on his nerves, the tiger was cute and the Englishman was smiling. Meanwhile back at the exhibition, Carroll looked gloomily at a robotic bird trying to eat a robotic beetle: 'It never succeeds in getting its head more than a quarter of an inch down, and that in uncomfortable little jerks, as if it was choking.' Dostoevsky remarked on the 'colossal decor' and said that 'a rich and ancient tradition of denial and protest is needed in order not to yield'. After the exhibition, the palace packed up and moved to Penge—and its doom.

The mutability of narrative is evident in the time it can take to get set. But even during this interlude most people prefer to view events through the buffer of as many intermediaries as possible and seem comforted by these arrangements. To see what is actually there it's useful to blindfold your language and look with your eyes.

Another pointer to the mutability of the decreed narrative is the frequent modifications made to that decree. The Sphinx of Giza originally depicted Anubis, the sausage dog which rules over the afterlife, but the Pharaoh Khafra had the head sanded down into his own likeness. In proportion to the body the head now resembles the knob on a planing tool. The two versions were of equal value to the onlooker, like two pickpockets who bump into each other and swap wallets. One of the common characteristics of such narratives is that they are designed to waste our time. Gossip and obeisance are what one wiseguy called the 'long hard detour'. Their absence would leave many ordinary people to drift toward their own ideas. The reducing of people to something less than human allows evil full articulation of movement.

Some narratives can be trickier to change from the top down because the top is shifting position. While completing his flip-and-sale of the revolution, Robespierre thought it wouldn't be a bad idea to invent a god, a fixer-upper he called the Supreme Being. It seems to have had everything but a metal nose. For the whole of one night, nothing was too extravagant to be believed. Robespierre presented his religion with a grandeur he appeared to have built from some old boxes and chicken wire. Fully capable of ending a sentence with a different philosophy than he began it, he had no more dignity than a dirty pelican. And he had badly misjudged the mood of the latest authorities, who for the present wanted no god of any kind. Robespierre threw himself out of a window and shot himself in the jaw, his boring remains going to the guillotine.

There is an uncanny resistance to any civilian attempt to change the dominating narrative. In some accounts of the Trojan War, a character called Laocoön attempts to bring everyone's attention to the obvious fact that the wooden horse is filled with enemy soldiers. Without explanation, two black serpents spiral out of the sea and strangle him, his body a pop-eyed remnant. This sort of thing resembles those time-travel stories where time course-corrects against any reasonable meddling. Such tales give the hero a sense of added agency and expected traction toward past events, of the sort which some people feel toward the present. This heightened awareness weighs off against the disappointment of being ineffectual. Laocoön even jabbed a spear into the Trojan horse, eliciting a groan from a pierced soldier, and was still ignored.

Maybe it's wise to keep the treasure house of your own narrative to yourself.

Mental hubris can lead to violence, as when Hemingway slapped critic Max Eastman in the face, an event described in the press as a 'slap in the face' for Eastman. Other accounts have it that Hemingway used the critic's book to slap him, and others claim that he threw a punch that completely missed its target—an act known as an 'airstrike'.

Fresh from burning the White House and Capitol Building in 1812, the British army tore down the offices of the *National Intelligencer*. Rear Admiral Cockburn, whom the newspaper regularly lambasted, ordered that special care be taken to destroy all the 'C' type. His mind was martial and couldn't stand anything for long.

In truth there does not exist a subject unsuitable for reality. Schopenhauer had something to say about that, when he wasn't being pushed down the stairs by his mother. That incident occurred because she was a novelist and didn't like the idea of two writers in the same family. At the bottom of the stairs he sprang up instantly and remarked that she would only be remembered because of him, one of many hard truths he was to trumpet. A good deal of forbidden honesty has pointed to the fact that society is a temporary construction of dovetailed discrepancies. For the conscientious, this results in a sadness so immense and informed that no rational mind can escape it. There is no remedy, only decoration. In the 'learned helplessness' experiments on mice, the rather disingenuous experimenters did not factor into their conclusions the fact that the mice really were helpless. They were in a lab being experimented on. If you're not free, it's well to learn it. Leonardo da Vinci observed: 'The goldfinch brings spurge [a poisonous plant] to its young when they are imprisoned in a cage. It is better to die than to lose one's freedom.'

More Sedition Kitsch coming your way soon!

COLD REVOLUTION BLUES

KEN MACLEOD

1.

THE AIRSHIP DIPS TO SCHIPOL. From his window seat, Marcus Owen glimpses a black zigzag to the horizon, here and there puddled in floodlight cones through which angular, cantilevered yellow spiders stride. The Noordzee Wall is always under construction. The view swings to a grid of lights, the printed circuitry of a city, then almost before Owen's had time to draw breath the airport lights are flickering by at eye level. The craft slows with a sigh of engines and a shudder through the seats, and then with a clunk, it's docked.

The seatbelt lights go off. Owen bows over his slate and flicks a message to his girlfriend back in London, telling her he's landed, and waits as the passenger next to him sidles into the aisle and retrieves her bag from the overhead locker. In this pause, we take a good look at Marcus Owen. He's thirty-one years old, slim, almost wiry. A carefully razored and trimmed beard accentuates his jawline. Sony glasses, Rimmel eyebrows. His black suit is synthetic silk, over a cotton T-shirt, also black. Likewise fashionable is a dark complexion that could be a tan, and that could be mistaken for fake: affecting insouciance about air travel and exotic holidays is *de rigueur* among a certain type of Englishman. In his case, though, it isn't. He really is well travelled. He's been in hot spots, literally and metaphorically. His face is familiar to readers of long reads on prestigious sites. This is because he's a journalist, and an art project.

For decades now, the human journalist has been an endangered species. Owen himself, on the slate he's right now placing on the now vacant seat beside him as he levers himself into a standing crouch, follows a dozen reporters who specialise in wars and calamities. They fearlessly convey the up-close sights and sounds and (with the right app, which Owen disdains the use of) even the smells of combat zones and disaster areas, and combine this immediacy with the gravitas and analytical heft of the greats: Bowen, Gellhorn, Simpson, Cameron, Burchitt, Ehrenburg. All are virtual, cobbled on the fly from drone swarms, sensor relays, and AIs, but each has its own distinct style and personality. They write like angels—fallen angels, given their subject matter, but still. Against this, what human journalist can compete?

None.

So Owen, like a potter or farmer or coal-miner or any such boutique artisan, doesn't so much as try. His is a niche market. His performance is part of the product. Half his steady income is an Arts Council grant. His trips are arranged by the British Council, which is widely (and correctly) taken to be the last remaining reliable and effective agency of His Majesty's intelligence services.

As he too stretches out and reaches for his case, 15 cm by 40 cm by 50 cm including wheels and handles, Marcus Owen can wryly reflect that everyone he meets will assume he's a spy.

It's a perfect cover.

2.

Owen has only hand luggage, and light at that. In part this is a test of the promises made about the conditions he'll find in the European Democracy. He heads straight to passport control. There are two gates, and one queue. Owen casts a disdainful glance at the ED citizens strolling, apparently unchecked, through the gate with the star-circled banner above it. To him, no matter how varied their clothes, hairstyles, lifestyles, and skin-tones, they might as well be blue ants, boiler-suited toilers content to live under the watchful eye of . . . everyone, really. Biometrically chipped from birth, they need no passport to confirm their identities.

Owen joins the non-ED queue, mostly Americans on business and British on holiday breaks. After about five minutes he reaches the front.

'Step forward,' says the border guard in the booth. 'Passport, please.'

Owen hands over the card. The guard looks at him, then at a screen.

'Please remove your glasses.'

Owen complies. The guard peers at him again. Scans frisk him invisibly and intangibly. The guard nods and hands back the passport.

'Welcome to Holland.'

'Thank you,' says Owen. As he steps past the booth, he dares a sidelong glance, and has a shock. He's ten steps away before he processes the horror he's seen. The guard has no body below the belt. This isn't a horrendous injury, Owen belatedly realises. The torso in the booth is a robot. In its job it doesn't need legs, and its operators haven't bothered to equip it with any, despite the unsettling appearance that results.

They can't be arsed, Owen thinks, and smiles to himself and takes a mental note to use the phrase.

3.

The train to Rotterdam is fast, crowded, and quiet. Night has fallen—it's mid-October and the time is 19.30—and Owen doesn't bother to augment the scene with informative overlays. He gazes absently out, through his reflection, at the rushing dark and the lights. Feeling a little thirsty, he contemplates getting out of his seat and disturbing the snoozing man next to him, and feels reluctant. Just then a trolley rolls up the aisle. A serpentine mechanical arm places a water bottle in front of him.

'One euro fifty,' says the robot.

'You must be joking,' says Owen.

'Take it or leave it,' says the robot.

'Done,' says Owen. He flicks his thumb across the pad of his middle finger. Payment accepted, the trolley rolls on. As Owen sips, he wonders if he's just had his first encounter with the ED's latest vaunted advance, what's known in the trade as 3AI, or even more trendily Triple-AI: Anticipatory Algorithmic Artificial Intelligence.

Or is the enterprising bot just part of the other referent of 'ED': Economic Democracy? The official name for the system over here is 'democratic socialist market economy', every word of which to Owen raises a warning flag, an eyebrow, and a cynical smirk.

At Centraal, Owen ignores the timetable tags for bus and Metro that flash in his glasses. He could take either, to Wilhelminaplein or Rijnhaven, but his performance demands that he take a taxi. It's traditional, it's expected of him.

As he's said in an earlier column: *I always talk to the taxi. It's a cliché for a reason. The taxi has heard it all. It smoothly synthesises every grumble from the back seat and plays it back if you ask nicely.*

He hurries from the concourse to the rank, and sticks out his payment thumb. Several people-carriers trundle past, and go for groups further down the queue. A single-seat electric tricycle rolls up and stops. It's nothing much more than a backward-facing back seat, cased in a plastic shell. The door angles open. Owen swings his case to the floor and his ass to the seat.

'Drijvend Hotel,' he says.

'Really, mate?' says the taxi. It sounds London, almost cockney. 'You'd be quicker taking the bus or the metro. You could even walk, it'd do you good.'

'I'll be the judge of that,' says Owen.

'Your call,' says the taxi.

It pulls out into the traffic and turns onto Coolsingel. Owen knows he has only a few minutes to chat.

'So,' he says, settling into the seat, 'what's the general feeling?'

'Contented, but a bit creeped out,' says the taxi.

Owen laughs. 'Why, exactly?'

'You know how it is,' says the taxi. 'You get what you want, that's good, but knowing a machine knows it before you do is a bit... disconcerting, know what I mean?'

'Uh-huh. Does this feed through into politics?'

'Hard to say,' the taxi muses. 'Everybody grumbles about Brussels and the Hague, and the city council isn't due an election for another seventeen months, but there haven't been any recall petitions going over the threshold for a while.'

Traffic's slow over the Erasmus Bridge, and Owen takes the opportunity to scan the skyline. After London, Rotterdam strikes him as shockingly low-rise. Rationally, he knows it's the price of progress: in an age of AI, let alone Triple-AI, the skyscraper is as obsolete as the smokestack. The disparate cluster on Kap van Zuid is still there, preserved as heritage, but the famed Manhattan on the Maas stands mostly dark, hollow shells filled with computing machinery rather than warm bodies in business suits. Only Die Rotterdam still blazes with light, and that's for the hydroponic farms that fill its every floor: a giant greenhouse, victim of the greenhouse effect.

The taxi takes a sharp right down to the waterfront at the old harbour, Rijnhaven. Owen flips a payment over his shoulder, with the traditional 10 per cent tip to reinforce the taxi's candour, and gets out.

In front of him, the bubble hubs of the budget hotel bob on the water, in the midst of a floating forest of GM mangroves. He has a room booked for a couple of nights from tomorrow at his destination, Heijplaat, and he could have got a berth there tonight too, but he always spends his first night somewhere he's not obliged to his hosts.

4.

It's one of those mornings when everything looks better, fresh and cold, with a damp wind in off the North Sea. Owen strolls along the Antoine Platekade to the quay, letting his glasses guide him to the right mooring for the water taxi to Heijplaat. The streamlined catamaran is busy with commuters, most to RDM, the big research institute where Owen has an appointment at 09.30. The taxi chugs out into the Nieuwe Maas, then its hydrofoils cut in and it skims. Katendrecht's post-flood new-build, to Owen's left, almost has him laughing: thanks to the Noordzee Wall the danger is long since gone, but the housing is still on stilts. In this respect it's typical: half the city, like much of the Netherlands, looks like it's on tiptoe and fastidiously holding up its skirt hems above imaginary mud. Here and there, dotted across the city every few hundred metres in any direction, are the windmill-like low towers of workstations.

A half-kilometre or so later, the main view is of the docks. Almost every incoming container ship is swarmed by drones, which emerge from their hives on Heijplaat and buzz around the decks, removing small crates from modular containers and carrying them away. Their racket is a steady buzz, which after a few minutes becomes screened-out background noise. Not so their downdraught, which buffets the water and makes the rest of the ride uncomfortably choppy as soon as the hydroplane cuts out for the final approach.

Heijplaat, always an oddity and anomaly, now looks more so than ever, a collection of buildings both recent and quaint in green spaces on reclaimed land jutting into and surrounded by the machinery of the docks and the shipping.

The taxi's first stop is for RDM itself. Owen's briefly tempted to hop out right there, along with most of the passengers, but he wants to check in his bag. He waits as the taxi swings out, and then in again along a narrow canal. The RDM accommodation pods for staff, students, and visitors float in front of him. Self-build sheds on rafts, they're varied and slightly wacky, but with their firmly anchored bridges and walkways, they look more steady and substantial than the bubble hotel.

He checks in, gets directions to his shed, and drops off his luggage there. Bed, desk, bathroom, all with just enough room to move between. Not a place you'd want to spend a lot of time in, which he gathers is kind of the idea. Market socialism nudges its citizens to agoraphilia.

Back on dry land, Owen walks along the main street of Heijplaat's heritage village. At this time in the morning, just after nine on a Tuesday, the place is busy. There's no nine-to-five here, or anywhere else in the ED. Owen finds himself vaguely disapproving: men and women who should be at work, ambling about with kids who should be in school! The houses are well over a century and a half old, and quaint by comparison with the new build he's seen elsewhere. The flood damage to their lower floors has long since been repaired, but the retrofitted flood protection remains, artfully disguised to the naked eye but obvious in overlay. The row on his right is backed by a transparent mesh wall that acts as a sound baffle for the drone port on the adjacent quay, from whose seven cylindrical towers the black quadricopters come and go incessantly. In that context, the usual drone cloud of retail deliveries and surveillance over a human settlement is reduced to a minor irritation of the eye and ear.

Owen sends his own tiny drone up for a spin. It launches from his shoulder and soars, streaming its view to a corner-of-the-eye square of his glasses and giving him a nice set of establishment shots and a good overview of the village and its environs. It descends as he reaches the main entrance, and settles on his left shoulder like a pirate's parrot.

RDM is a big blocky structure, more than a century old, its auxiliary buildings now extending in a modular sprawl across the water of the old dock. Owen steps inside to a cavernous, concrete-floored space. Right in front of him, about twenty metres away, is the deck of the ship in the university's interior dock. There's a complex construction of rounded modules and walkways filling most of the space around him, and in among them large machines whose purpose is not immediately apparent. He looks for a reception desk, and then almost smites his forehead: he's not in London anymore. Everyone Owen sees seems to be hurrying purposefully about, ignoring him entirely. Around him hover a handful of bee-sized drones, not ignoring him at all.

A metre-high bot rolls up. 'Marcus Owen?' it says.

Owen is amused by the courtesy. Of course the bot has no need to ask: it's already ID'd him at a more or less molecular level.

'Yes,' he says. 'I have an appointment with Henk Bakker in ten minutes.'

'This way,' says the bot. It extends an arm, offering a steaming paper cone. 'Espresso?'

'Ah, thanks.'

Owen sips it as he walks. The bot leads him across a gangplank and onto the ship, then takes a sharp left along the deck. At a spiral open stairwell the bot shifts gears, from wheels to a pair of legs, and clambers up the steel-mesh steps like an earnest toddler. It then rolls along a walkway to an office module, shaped like the semi-translucent egg of some space monster. The door slides open. The robot steps aside, holds out a manipulator for the empty paper cup, and trundles away.

Henk Bakker fills the doorway. He's a big man in his late eighties, who delivers a firm handshake. Gloves jiggle from his wrists. Goggles are pushed up over his forehead and into his shock of white hair. Owen has naturally enough run a search on RDM's Director of Public Relations, so he knows the man's age and features, but his dishevelled appearance is a little unexpected. He's as old as the century, and looks it.

'Come on in, Mr Owen. Please excuse the clutter, and mind your step.'

It's a typical office space: three beanbags, a low-level work-board, a food-and-drink dispenser to one side. The floor is littered with blocky prototypes that slowly change shape and configuration in the time it takes for Owen to pick his way through them and sit. The beanbag seat wants to draw him in, but the sourceless light from all around makes him uneasy: it's like sitting in a cloud, or a flying saucer. He perches, as much as he can, on the edge.

'Coffee?'

'Just had one, thanks.'

'Of course. And just when you needed it, I suspect, and in just the right amount?'

'Yeah,' says Owen, thinking back.

Bakker smiles complacently, as if something has been confirmed, and leans back into his beanbag.

'Well, Mr Owen,' he says, 'I feel as if I should be stroking a white cat.'

Owen doesn't get the allusion at all, and blinks not just with surprise but to send the phrase to his glasses' search engine. Blofeld? What?

'I don't think of you as a supervillain, Mr Bakker,' he says.

'And you are no James Bond, Mr Owen,' Bakker says, still altogether too amused with himself. 'But here'—he waves a hand, glove bobbing—'in this little office, we face each other across a front line of the Cold Revolution.'

The term 'Cold Revolution' is the current hot take on what's going on in the world, particularly in the European Democracy. The Cold Revolution is a revolution in the sense that the Cold War was a war: a glacial confrontation, in which every tiny incremental shift in the balance of forces—economic, political, even cultural— is freighted with global significance.

'I'm not sure I understand,' says Owen, though of course he does.

'Of course you do,' says Bakker, as if reading his mind. 'You're here to research a feature on 3AI, and I'm about to show you around the institute and, to the best of my ability, sell you on it. No doubt you think of 3AI as a refinement of marketing.'

'Uh-huh.'

'The sovereignty of the consumer, and so forth, and therefore a new advance of the socialist market economy.'

'Well, if you want to put it that way,' says Owen.

'Oh, I do,' says Bakker, rubbing his hands. His dangling gloves look as if they're applauding. 'And therefore another little nudge for England. One that you, I am sure, would not welcome, so you'll be looking for flaws. The British Council will expect no less.'

'Nothing wrong with a bit of scepticism, I'm sure you'll agree,' says Owen.

'Of course, of course.' Bakker pulls down his heavy-duty VR goggles, and fumbles his gloves on. 'So if you have any questions before our tour, ask away.'

Owen does, going through his checklist. He's immensely relieved that Bakker thinks as he does. Patriotic zeal for the advances of the European Democracy / Economic Democracy is something he can fence with in his sleep. No, what's worrying him, and what he has no doubt is worrying people high up back home, is that 3AI is more than a refinement of marketing. It's another step—a much bigger step than even the ED government seems to realise, at least publicly—towards replacing the market economy altogether.

England preens itself on being, as the saying goes, the Hong Kong of Europe. It can handle being an offshore island, an entrepôt for the ED's interactions with more liberal market economies in the Americas, Africa, and Asia. No doubt it could adjust if the ED jumped suddenly from market to non-market socialism, dispensing with money and trade altogether.

But it would be one heck of a rocky adjustment, and there's no guarantee that its rigours—combined with the ED's specious example—won't give people crazy ideas, even in England. This, from the point of view of HMG, not to mention that of the City of London, is a can that needs to be kicked a *long* way down the road.

5.

'But, you know,' says Owen towards the end of the tour, 'it's all very well having good conditions for teleworkers who are locally based. But can you make such conditions and regulations stick, half a world away?'

Bakker is disarmingly frank.

'You have a point,' he says. 'It's true—the ED, and the Netherlands in particular, have turned the consequences of climate change to their own advantage. The millions—tens of millions— who decades ago fled drought, flood, and famine were an early labour pool for the Noordzee Wall and other resilience and reconstruction projects. Now, a fraction of their descendants— their sons, mostly—make good money as teleworkers, operating the machines that maintain and extend these projects. But now that climate change and migration have stabilised, we ironically enough have a labour shortage. And that's why these projects are shored up by virtual migration: workers in less advanced countries who remain where they are, but whose labour can be applied by teleworking in the more advanced countries.'

Owen has done his background reading. He's not sure he quite understands the ins and outs of political economy, but he has the vocabulary down pat.

'Isn't that a form of unequal exchange?'

Bakker laughs. 'Of course it is. The choice for us is to participate in the international division of labour, and therefore to have a stake in exploitative relationships. Or to withdraw into a continental autarchy, which is possible but which has its own heavy costs— including costs to the less developed countries that would lose what they gain from our trade and investment. So yes, in an abstract sense the great European Democracy is at the very least complicit in exactly the imperialism which your country still battens on. All we can do is counter it as best we can.' He shrugs. 'It's a fine line, but we have walked it so far. I don't think your side can nudge us off it.'

'I wasn't thinking anything of the kind,' says Owen, doing his best to project injured innocence. He's beginning to suspect this issue might be just the right sore point on which to press.

6.

Outside at 11:30 a.m., Owen has his interviews and images in his glasses and on his slate. His next meeting is at noon. As he strolls along the piers he notices a small commotion a few hundred metres away.

Owen walks over to a group standing along the edge of the dock, facing the Transhumanist spiritual centre out over the water. They aren't shouting or holding up placards, but something in their posture indicates protest. Even from the back, they seem an unlikely assortment: two men in black coats and big hats, three men hatless in plain salwar kameez, half a dozen women and girls with various head coverings on either side, and a score of men and women with uncovered heads bowed and hands apparently clasped in front of them. They look like they're at a funeral. A handful of small children seem unsure of all the solemnity, but are kept literally and metaphorically in line. Owen steps up to the edge and glances sideways, and sees that the whole line is holding a long green and purple banner.

At this angle, even with glasses, it's hard to make out the slogan on the banner. Owen pulls down a pic from one of the news cameras buzzing about. The slogan reads: 'Remember your humanity, and forget the rest' in English, Dutch, and Arabic. The software attributes the quote to Bertrand Russell. The banner doesn't, perhaps in deference to the devout.

Owen waits. One or two people nod. Everyone stays silent. Nothing seems to be going on around the three towers on the water. Then, quite suddenly, the doors of the middle tower swing open and a crowd cascades down the steps, led by a laughing bride and groom. All very traditional: white dress, black suit; ladies in garish colours and complicated hats; showers of confetti. The protest line bristles. Backs straighten, feet shift to firmer stances.

Everyone glares at the happy scene, then very carefully turns their backs on it while still holding the banner, now with their hands behind them.

Owen doesn't turn. Above and amid the crowd around the couple there's the likewise predictable and traditional cloud of tiny camera drones, no doubt compiling the wedding album. He zooms his glasses to the limits of resolution, then picks up the feed from one of the drones that is focused on the couple's faces. Bride and groom seem absolutely normal, healthy, and happy. There seems no good, or even bad, reason for anyone to object, let alone to ostentatiously turn their backs on the occasion.

Owen takes a step back. The end of the banner nearest to him is held by a disgruntled-looking young woman in her late teens. She's in scruffy double denim, and the distressed lapel of her jacket looks as if it's been the display setting for many a patch and pin. Today it sports a solitary badge, a neat little black and silver enamel ellipse with the Humanist 'happy human' logo.

Her name is Elise Mulder. Her parents, a few bodies further down the line, are prominent in Heiplaat's Humanist group, and frequent foot soldiers in local and regional worthy causes. Community. Environment. Peace. That much, Owen's glasses can tell him.

'Hi, Ms Mulder,' says Owen. He introduces himself. 'I'm a journalist, from England. Would you mind telling me what's going on? What's the objection to a wedding?'

'It's a fake wedding,' the girl says. 'A stunt.'

'How is it fake?'

'It's between a human being and a robot.'

Owen frowns, and blinks up the image capture. 'Which is which?'

The young woman laughs uneasily. 'Uh . . . you can't tell?'

'No,' says Owen. The wedding party is now getting into a boat, in a flurry of shiny and floaty stuffs, a peal of cries. The guests are piling into other boats.

'It's the bride,' says Elise Mulder. '"She"'—her hands are occupied, so she can't do airquotes, but her tone implies them—"is the robot". According to the Transhumanists, that doesn't matter, because she passes the Turing test.'

Owen scratches his head. 'Well, if there's no non-invasive way to tell her from a human being, don't they sort of have a point?'

'Not legally, they don't. This isn't a legal marriage, because legally "she" is just the guy's property. You can't marry a sex-toy. And it's demeaning to women to suggest that you can.'

'What if it was the other way round, and the groom was the robot?'

The young woman's lips compress to a hard line. 'It makes no difference.'

'Isn't this all a bit, you know, prejudiced and puritanical?' Owen gestures at the rest of the line-up. 'How often do Humanists find themselves lined up with—I guess—conservative Jews and Muslims and so on?'

'Not often,' Mulder acknowledges. She looks down, and her vintage DM toes the ground, stirring dust. Then she looks him defiantly in the eye. 'But this time, we're on the same page. Human dignity.' She lowers her voice. 'Look, I don't have a problem with people having sex with robots, though some of the religious people here might not agree. But that's not the same as marrying them!'

Owen sees what she means. Now that the Turing test can be passed by the average phone, it's no longer rated as a benchmark for human equivalence. As for physical appearance, bioprinting and metamaterials have long since made flesh and machinery interchangeable. Giving robots the rights of humans would make the whole economy unworkable.

And yet, and yet... the similarity to historic prejudices about marriage between people of different races or of the same sex, or whatever, still troubles him.

'Is there any political pressure for this?'

'No, no.' She shakes her head. 'Every council from the village to the city and the Dutch government and the European government are all pretty much solid on it. It's only the Transhumanists who make it an issue.'

Not much grist here to his mill, one might think. But she raised her voice a little as she said it, in a way that makes Owen suspect she wished to be overheard. He doesn't doubt that the cloud of bee-sized news drones overhead has something to do with it.

'I'd like to talk some more,' he says. 'But I have another appointment. Do you have glasses?'

Mulder snorts. 'Glasses? They're for early adopters. I have a slate.' She fishes one from her jacket pocket. Owen flicks his details from his thumb.

'Catch me around, if you like.'

Mulder nods, unsmiling, and shoves the slate back in her pocket. With a half-shrug, Owen turns away.

Why does he feel watched? Omnipresent surveillance? In that respect nothing is different here from back home. He flips his glasses to Skyview and looks up. Close overhead, the drone cloud, like a swarm of locusts. Above where that thins out, the airships and local helicopters and heavier cargo drones drift by. Higher still, a few long-range jets traverse the sky. In the stratosphere hang the aerostats—most for communications, some military. Beyond the atmosphere, in low Earth orbit, the criss-cross web of satellites, their relative movements slowing all the way out to geostationary. Some of these objects, at every level, enable his own view of them, and many are, in some abstract sense, aware of his presence and even that he's looking up. He knows all this. It's familiar. So why does he feel watched?

He hurries off, head down, for his noon meeting.

7.

A man is running along the edge of the quay. Owen catches up just in time for his appointment. The man's name is Noah De Vries. He's in his mid-forties, a slim man in a suit and tie. The outfit has enough meshes and micropores to let it function as sportswear.

'Hey,' says De Vries, with a wave. 'You're the journalist.'

'Yes.'

'You'll have to give me a few minutes. I'm in the middle of something.'

They reach the next workstation, a tower atop an old church. De Vries waves them both through the door, and continues jogging up the stairs to a room full of desks. He slides into a chair just as a woman rises from it to set off at a power walk. He puts on VR goggles—they're less hardcore than Bakker's, but still high-powered. With a flourish of his hands he conjures a 3D image, which he shares with Owen's glasses.

To Owen, it looks at first like a cross-section of an intricately veined leaf, within which tiny black ants scurry. Then one of the moving figures snaps into focus as a humanoid robot, and the scale becomes clear. The black figures are dealing with an emergency, a breakdown in the pipework of the pumping stations within and beneath the Noordzee Wall. After a few minutes, one of them turns and holds up an upraised thumb. De Vries mutters a message, fingers flying, then disengages. The image vanishes, the chair tilts back, he takes off the goggles.

'Panic's over,' he says.

'Very human gesture, for a robot,' says Owen.

De Vries looks surprised. 'These aren't robots—at least, not autonomous ones. They're frames, operated by remote workers. The operators hang in kinesic webbing, kilometres away.'

'Ah,' says Owen. 'So there are still things robots can't do?'

'Not at all,' says De Vries. 'You would be better saying, robots are still too expensive to do some things. It's dangerous work, under the Wall. Losing a frame is a nuisance, but the consortium can absorb it. Losing a robot with the necessary level of AI is even more expensive than an actual fatality.' He shrugs. 'Call it a compromise. It also helps with the full employment policy, of course.'

Owen has read about the full employment policy, of course. He still finds it hard to get his head around. He waves a hand at the window.

'I don't see much full employment around here.'

'What?'

'All those people on the street, in the middle of the day...'

'Hah!' De Vries barks. 'That *is* the full employment policy. All those people you see have jobs. It's just a question of how they are spread out, through the day, the week, the year…the life, even. Why should leisure be reserved for those too young or too old to make the most of it?'

It's a good point, Owen acknowledges. But the outcome seems wasteful, compared to England, where everyone is busy until they retire. He looks around the room. People are coming and going all the time.

'Is this part of it too?'

De Vries shakes his head. 'No, it's a health measure. Ten minutes' exercise in each hour worked.'

Owen nods to where the image has been, above the desk. 'Do these guys do the same?'

'No.' For the first time, De Vries looks uncomfortable. 'But then, they aren't doing sedentary work.'

'Surely there's more to it than that? What about prolonged VR?'

'Nobody's allowed to go over the limit,' says De Vries. 'The labour regulations are strict. And they're enforced automatically, through the system. In any case, most of the operators are young. They're willing to work to the limit, and save. They don't even spend much: the accommodation is on-site and cheap, the entertainment the same.' He laughs. 'The only entertainment they don't get is VR.'

'So what do they do? LARP?'

'Same as young single folks everywhere, I guess. But they do get to *watch* VR games. Check out the stadium any evening, it's full of lads from the Wall.'

'It's on my list,' Owen says. Heiplaat's local team is world famous, in some people's worlds.

8.

The air smells of coffee, sugar, beer and weed. Owen shoulders his way through the crowd to his seat. The teams are in what would, in any other sport, be the directors' box: glass-fronted over-hangs at either side of the arena. The players' magnified faces fill the windows. The game-play itself takes place on the pitch, with holograms. You can get a clearer view of the details on your glasses, but Owen has been assured that the best experience is availed by the illusion of presence.

The lights go down. A small boy and a small girl, spotlit, trot from opposite ends to the mid-line. Owen can't be sure if they're real or virtual. Their tossed coin spins into a Catherine Wheel, showering sparks. The young mascots sprint off, still spotlit, to cheers.

Darkness drops again, then the arena springs into view on the pitch.

Skyscrapers and sky.

Battle of Manila.

It's that last few seconds of peace, just before it all kicked off. You can hear the traffic, see faces in the crowds. You know some-thing awful is going to happen at any moment.

Then it does. Towers crash like dominoes.

The players rush into view from all angles, and start mixing things up. Tracer bullets, laser beams, general mayhem. The score is measured in objectives taken—a floor here, an alleyway there—and team members lost.

This goes on for some time. Unlike the young men around him, who critique every move in much detail and many decibels, Owen isn't really following the action. But time, to his surprise, flies. The first forty-five minutes are over.

Everything stops. Time out. Fifteen-minute break. This is partly for the players, a bit of VR health-and-safety, but mainly—Owen reckons—for the audience, present or sharing. Like half-time at a football game.

He gets up and joins the shuffle towards the beer-and-frank-furters stand, whose smell has been subconsciously tempting him for some minutes. As he reaches the front of the queue and places his order he realises that the girl in the striped paper cap and apron behind the counter is Elise Mulder. She turns away to expertly sling together sausage, mustard and bread, then turns back, meanwhile grabbing a ready-poured beer.

'Oh, hi!' he says, taking the roll and the wobbly plastic half-litre cup.

'Hi,' she says, with a forced grin, her gaze flicking past his shoulder to the customer behind him.

Maybe, he guesses, customers are as anonymous to servers as vice versa. But he still feels a bit miffed. Back at his seat, he unwraps the roll, and finds scribbled handwriting inside the greaseproof paper:

Tomorrow, 11 a.m., Recycling. EM.

He crushes the paper and deletes the image from his glasses. His expression, to all but a thorough scan, remains impassive. Inside, he's whooping and jumping up and down.

At last he's found a dissident. Or a dissident has found him.

9.

Game over, Owen joins the flow out of the stadium. His nerves are jangled, as well they might be. It's been a long day. The game, while cathartic, has not been relaxing. Next on his schedule is the perfect way to wind down. The dream spa, just across the end of the promontory from the stadium, is a don't-miss on all the guides. The lady from the British Council was insistent.

'You have to go,' she said. 'It'll look suspicious if you don't.'

'But isn't there a security risk?'

She gave him a look. 'In your dreams. So to speak! If they took dreams literally they'd have to waterchute most of their customers straight to waterboarding.'

Her scoffing reassured him at the time. Now that he has an actual secret, he's not so sure. He considers just going for a swim, but decides that would be too obvious a cop-out. With some trepidation, he enters the spa. It smells of chlorine and seawater. The reception staff wear white coats, but their manner is more commercial than clinical. They give him a pair of swimming trunks, a towel, and a headband studded with tiny transmitters.

He goes to the lockers, changes, and pads rather self-consciously around the pool to a vacant ball. He climbs in and sits down. The hatch closes. Warm water rises, slowly, from the bottom. He finds he can't help but float—the water is saltier than the Dead Sea. Music, scented aircon, a play of lights above him. Despite his misgivings, he relaxes.

He's not quite sure when the dream starts. It's an oddly familiar experience, a hypnogogic lucid dream, but played out and projected on the inner surface of the ball. At first, Owen is delighted. He wills himself to move, and floats up through the roof. He looks down at Heijplaat. To his mild surprise, his high school is on the main street. Down he drifts, then walks into the school and up its stairs and along its corridors. The exam starts in five minutes. Every corridor turns out to be on the wrong floor. He can't find the room at all. Fortunately one of the doors opens to the London Underground. He takes the train that runs along the cliff-face, to the library. In the library, he finds the book he needs for the exam. He knows he has to take the train back, but the connection is awkward in that direction. At Piccadilly, the up escalator leads down. He's missed the train. Carefully, hand over hand, he makes his way along a ledge of the cliff-face. Remembering that he can fly, he lets go. Slowly he falls to the sea, and slowly he sinks into the water. It's warm and salty, and its level keeps dropping.

Owen sits up, dripping wet, and shakes his head, laughing. After all his hesitations and worries, how banal was his dream. He removes the headband, opens the hatch, steps out and towels himself. The dreams are market research: hints to the 3AI system of people's real desires.

Owen ponders the tediously familiar recurring anxiety dream he's just had. Market research? Good luck with that.

10.

The recycling plant has a tour so standard, so self-explanatory, that it needs no guide. Ten minutes before 11, Owen walks along the gangplank of the main receiving area, a vast shed of robotic sorting that sifts out reusable and valuable stuff from what goes straight to recycling, mostly as 3D printing feedstock. The next unit, much smaller, is a nest of collaborative workshops in which items are upcycled. The third section is a peculiar library of tools and devices, all in full working order, suspended from the ceiling on a myriad cables of varying lengths. A dozen or so people are wandering through this chamber, pondering its low-hanging fruit and occasionally pulling down some of the more arcane items from the shadows above.

The fourth unit is the strangest. It's like some Ikea of the obsolete, a combination of living-room and antique-shop, through which a handful of people, mostly elderly, drift. They pick things up and put them down, chatting reminiscently, sometimes acerbically. Among them is Elise Mulder. She's standing in front of a glass case, with an old man beside her. The old man is wearing a tweed jacket with elbow patches, baggy jeans and a blue cap. Elise has evidently raided a dressing-up box, or perhaps hit the 3D printer hard. She's wearing a jaunty beret, a leather bomber jacket and a dress made from what look like silk maps, the kind WW2 aircrew hid inside seams and collars to assist escape. Still with the vintage Docs, though. These look real.

As Owen's reflection looms in the glass case, Mulder turns.

'Oh, hi,' she says.

The old man turns too, and sticks out a hand. 'Pieter Jansen.'

'Pleased to meet you. Marcus Owen.'

'Ah yes, the English spy.'

'That's me,' says Owen, chirpily enough. 'But really, I'm a journalist.'

'They all say that,' says Jansen. He gestures at the glass case. 'I was a journalist myself once, in a way.'

The glass case is filled with union badges and campaign buttons and leaflets and clippings of yellowing newsprint and frozen screenshots, documenting a half-century of what the display grandly calls *Struggle on the Docks*, and what Owen sees as futile and reactionary trade unionism, protectionism and nimbyism. He nods, gravely and politely, as the old man talks him through the highlights, all the way to anti-gentrification protests around the Olympics and Cybolympics. It seems to be the latter event that gave Jansen his particular beef with the Transhumanists.

'I have more memorabilia at home,' Jansen says. 'Would you like to see it?'

'I can't wait,' says Owen.

'What?' Jansen looks taken aback. 'Are you in a hurry?'

Mulder speaks to him in Dutch. Jansen smiles. 'Ah. Let's go.'

As he follows them out, Owen replays Mulder's explanation, this time with subtitles.

'Sarcasm,' is what she said. 'It's an English thing.'

11.

A cross the road from the recycling plant is a block of housing for the elderly.

'A bit tactless, siting it there,' Owen remarks.

'It's convenient,' says Jansen.

They stand on the sidewalk respectfully as a funeral procession emerges from the block and heads down the road—not, Owen is relieved to see, to the recycling plant but to the jetty for the Transhumanist shrines.

'Not the way I'll go,' says Jansen, with gloomy relish. 'I may have a plastic heart and knees and a printed lung, but these freaks are not getting their hands on any of it.'

Already the deceased's personal module, shaped like a miniature of their original house, is being craned out of the block's wall, to be lowered onto a barge on the canal side of the recycling plant. Crash, clatter. Brutal.

'So how *do* you want your remains disposed of?' Owen asks.

'To the fire, like a good heathen,' says Jansen. He taps his forehead. 'And an electromagnetic pulse to fry the chip in my head. I do not buy into the bogus immortality.'

'This life is all and enough,' says Mulder. Her pious tone suggests a quotation.

'Easy for you to say,' says Jansen. 'Don't think, at my age, it isn't tempting. But the risks . . .' He grimaces. 'Who wants to be resurrected by capricious AIs in a far future?'

'We can design them to be compassionate,' says Mulder.

Jansen guffaws. The young woman and the old man continue bickering all the way up the lift. It's like they agree on the basics, but enjoy contradicting each other. Jansen's module is neat, but crammed. He has books, on shelves and on the floor. He has newspapers, in stacks of crumbling pulp on which faded red mastheads glare. He even has a desktop computer, an unwieldly apparatus of screen and keyboard. There's no dust—the little cleaning bots that crawl everywhere see to that—but Owen suspects the rig hasn't been touched in years.

'Have a seat,' says Jansen, disappearing into the tiny galley. Owen looks about, helplessly. Mulder shifts a pile of junk to reveal a chair. Owen sits. A coffee machine gargles and hisses.

'This should be in the museum,' Owen murmurs. 'Heck, he could just digitise the print if it's so precious.'

Mulder has perched on a table top. 'Pieter doesn't trust digital. He has people come round and photograph the pages, for archiving.'

'But—' Owen thinks for a moment. 'Oh.'

'Yes,' says Mulder. 'On film.' She waves a hand vaguely in the direction of the recycling centre. 'Cameras still turn up in the tool library now and then.'

Jansen re-emerges from the galley, with a tray. He serves coffee all round, then sweeps some old clothes to the floor and sits on the bench thus revealed.

'Well,' he says, after an appreciative sip, 'I did not ask you here to show you more old pins, or talk about the old days.'

'I gathered that,' says Owen. 'So . . .' He spreads his hands. 'Go ahead.'

Jansen takes a pen from his inside pocket, reaches for a paper pad, and starts drawing connections and labelling boxes. About five minutes in, Owen is almost regretting the invitation. There are lots of arrows and initials. Jansen doesn't ramble, he's got all his wits about him, but he assumes an expert knowledge of the notorious complexities of Dutch politics. Owen struggles to keep track. From his point of view, all but two of the numerous parties are goddamn commies anyway, Muslim Democrats and Christian Liberals and Social Ecologists and so on and so forth having all decades ago bought into the hegemonic ideology of socialism with European characteristics.

At last Jansen finishes. He's covered ten or more sheets with his diagrams of interlocking intrigues. Owen holds the pad awkwardly, turning over the pages, resisting the impulse to flick or spread or squeeze. He looks up.

'So, bottom line,' he says. 'You're telling me the mayor of the Randstadt metropolitan area is putting pressure on the Rotterdam authorities to increase throughput at the port, and that the relevant committee of the Rotterdam local council is turning a blind eye to dangerous and illegal overwork in VR, and that there's nothing anyone here can do about that because everything is part of the same power structure?'

'Yes,' says Jansen. He smiles complacently. 'State capitalism, just like I always said.'

Mulder leans forward and is clearly about to object, then thinks better of it. She turns to Owen.

'We would really like for you to take this and publish it in England. Expose and embarrass the Randstadt authorities.'

Owen nods, eagerly. He taps his glasses. 'I have it all here.'

'That's not good enough,' says Jansen. 'The records on your glasses can be corrupted on the way out.' He reaches for the pad, tears off the pages he's scribbled on, folds them and hands them back. 'You must take these.'

'And if I'm searched at the airport?'

'Buy some expensive gift,' says Mulder. 'Use the sheets as wrapping paper.'

Jansen laughs. 'Even I am not so old-fashioned as to believe that trick still fools anyone.' He shakes his head. 'No, you must not return via the airport.'

'All right,' says Owen. 'I'll take the ferry. It's going to be awkward, and expensive, but he can let his slate handle the bookings.'

'No,' says Jansen. He reaches into an inside pocket again, and hands over a small card, plastic-laminated and circuitry-embossed. Owen turns it over, baffled.

'It's my port-worker's pass,' says Jansen. 'It still works.' He writes again on the pad, in careful block capitals—numbers and times—then tears off the sheet and hands it to Owen. 'This is what you must do.'

12.

The lift arrives, predictably, just as Owen and Mulder step up to its doors. On the way down, Owen struggles to meet the young woman's ironic, questioning eyes. But he has to ask.

'Elise Mulder...'

'Yes?'

'Are you a robot?'

'What?' She laughs, startled. 'No.'

Well, that's something. The imperative to give a straight and true answer to that question has been hardwired into every humanoid robot ever built.

The lift doors open. Mulder and Owen walk through the communal area, past a table of spry old folks playing chess, and out. It's early afternoon, bright and cold, with a chill wind off the Maas. They stroll the route of the funeral processions, and then into the street alongside the drone port.

'Why did you ask me that?' Mulder says, after a few minutes of awkward silence.

'I didn't mean to offend.'

'No offence. But why?'

'Surely it's obvious? This whole situation. It's a set-up. I come here looking for a dissident. The Triple-AI senses this, and duly supplies me with a dissident. Two, in fact! An attractive young woman, and an old anarcho-syndicalist. Come on!'

'You must have checked my trail,' says Mulder. 'You saw my parents.'

'Trails can be retro-fitted. I have no independent evidence that the couple on the protest were your parents. Like your man says, glasses can be corrupted.'

'And you thought I might be a robot?' Mulder finds this very funny indeed. 'And why should the anticipatory algorithm do that?'

Owen shrugs. 'Maybe the system sees a problem that human politics is blocking the solution to, and works around it.'

'By contacting an English spy? That's a little too elaborate, even for the system.'

'I think you underestimate the system you are in,' says Owen. 'The Cold Revolution defends itself. From outside threats, and from corruption within. It wants this information to get to England, that's for sure. And it wants to protect the ED from spies and subversives. So it sets me up. Killing two birds with one stone, as the English saying goes.'

'Killing?' Mulder sounds disturbed. 'Why do you say that?'

'This plan Jansen gave me.' Owen pats a pocket. 'It's crazy. It'll get me killed. The *information* will get to England, all right. On my dead body. I'll get there, but I'll freeze or suffocate on the way.'

They've almost reached the barrier at the entrance to the drone port. Owen feels Jansen's pass slick in his hand. His palms are sweating. In a minute it'll be now or never.

'You won't die,' says Mulder. 'You may be sure of that.'

Owen stops and faces her. The racket of the drones bombards him from above.

'How can you know?' Owen shouts.

She stares back at him, in all her blatant Resistance-reference chic, her edgy glamour. Her fur collar is turned up, her leather jacket zipped. The silk-map dress flaps in the stiff wind. She has to hold her beret on with one hand. She leans towards him.

'Marcus Owen . . .'

'Yes?'

'Are you a robot?'

Owen hears himself say, quite automatically and involuntarily: 'Yes.'

Of course he is, he realises. Of course. There's just no place in the world for a human journalist, these days. They can't compete. The same goes for human spies. And as for intellects vast and cool with inhuman plans and human pawns—well, there are two sides in the Cold Revolution. At least he knows which side he's on. That hasn't changed.

But he still has to play out the game, and the role, right to the end. The dashing spy. It's been a perfect cover so far, so why drop it now? Even though it's been well and truly blown, not least of all to himself.

'Given how we met,' he muses, 'I suppose there's no chance of a positive response to a marriage proposal?'

Mulder laughs, and shoves at his chest. 'Go!' she says.

He turns away, and waves Jansen's ancient pass at the gate. The barrier lifts. Owen ducks through. He doesn't have to look again at the note and the codes. He sprints across the tarmac, dodging driverless trucks, and between two of the great cylindrical towers he sees the crate that Jansen has indicated to him to go for. It's open at the top, for just this moment. Owen jumps in, and curls up amid bales of tobacco and hemp. The lid slams down. Bolts are hammered in, rapid as machine-gun fire. There's a jolt as a heavy lifting drone clamps on. A scream of rotors, and the lurch of lift. Up it goes.

The air is cold, and thin, and the course is set.

HOT GATES

IAN WATSON

And then she does this incredibly crazy thing and I've no choice but to go along with her...

IT'S EIGHT IN THE MORNING, and I'm sitting on the edge of one of the tombs upon the Mount of Olives. My booted feet are strapped securely to the flyboard, ready to go just as soon as the old city beyond the walls on the other side of the valley shows any steamy signs of melting. Assuming that a melting does happen! But I'm betting my bottom dollar on this.

And surely if not today, then tomorrow. Yesterday, I spent sitting here from sunrise to sunset, listening to all the soaring symphonies of Bruckner, like traversing alpine valley after alpine valley constantly upward towards ever brighter golden light. For today I choose all the works of Chopin. *Plinkel plinkel plinkel plonk.*

Fat payment if I'm right. Everyone else seems to downplay Jerusalem as too *precious* to be melted. World Heritage of Mankind city, eh? Featuring the golden Dome of the Rock, the

Church of the Holy Sep, the Via Dol, the Cathy of Saint Jim, fetish sites for five or six Abrahamic faiths forever squabbling with each other. Maybe that's because it's half a century since there was an actual physical frontier here inside Jeru.

Melts to date include places such as Panmunjom's Joint Security Area between North and South Korea, the Wagah border crossing between India and Pakistan, the line between Pakistan and Afghanistan. Always border crossings. More often than not, highly sensitive spots. Places of tension. After fifteen mysterious melts so far, we'd sussed *that* connection out.

Purpose of melts, provocation? But by what, from where, and how? And why?

What do you do when places are melting mysteriously? You call vulcanologists, the guys (and gals) who—protectively costumed and with air supplies—ride the latest-generation flyboards down into craters where red lava boils and bubbles, to take readings and study from up close. We're the monitors of pyroclastic flows racing down hillsides; even rushing out over open water at hundreds of kiloms an hour, no kidding. About fifty of us worldwide. Fatalities are very rare.

The world desperately needs more info. What if the UN HQ in New York melts in full session? Tele-steered drones aren't quite agile enough for our job, and a person might spy a vital clue which no robo would notice. So we have carte blanche as to which potential sites we go to.

*P**linkel plonk plonky plonk.* Suddenly this woman pops up in my way. She's puffing after presumably darting between umpteen Jewish graves like white coffins fallen off a container ship.

'Excuse me, Mister Volcano Man—'

'You're blocking me, ma'am. Shift a bit to the right?'

She complies. 'You waiting for the Old City to melt?'

She's wearing scuffed black booties, a birdy indigo skirt, violet blouse. Black hair spills wavily from under a blue headscarf. Her eyes are dark marbles set in hard-boiled white of egg. Maybe that sounds unattractive, but it isn't so. On her left arm hangs a black leather bag.

'Seen you here yesterday, Mister V. You flew away sundown.'

Indeed, I flew back to the genuinely exceptional YMCA Hotel, where I'd slept. What a stylish place. My informant had not been lying. Tall bell tower, colonnades, high arched ceilings, lots of lights. Wall tiles proclaim in Arabic and Roman capitals and Hebrew, 'Here is a place whose atmosphere is peace where political and religious jealousies can be forgotten and international unity be fostered and developed.' Ha-ha to that; this is Jerusalem. But there hadn't been any frontier here as such since the Six-Day War ages ago.

'Here you again today. Wearing no silver suit, just this jumpy with a V on the back—'

V for Vulcanologist, yes! Us valiant airborne Vulcans are an élite. Probably the woman saw on TV some investigative Vulcans hovering over earlier melts protected by aluminized fire proximity suits. Turns out that radiant heat isn't much problem. A release of steam does precede melts yet not such as to cook any pigeon passing over. Thereafter it's a bit like cold fusion or maybe it isn't. My hi-viz green jumpsuit should be fully adequate, even during the first moments of a melt. Thus my view shan't be limited to the letterbox window of a proximity suit. I'll be less impeded generally.

'A melt isn't like lava welling up,' I tell the woman.

'My name is Lusine. It means moon in Armenian.'

'And in French "L'usine" means "factory", so what?'

Little Lady, please go away, even if your eyes are enchanting. White of egg?—nay, milky opal. Vulcanologists are geologists raised to a new level. Our heroes are Sigurður Þórarinsson and the Comte de Buffon who was no buffoon and Pliny the Elder who died by Vesuvius and Pliny the Younger who described that event impeccably and Haroun Tazieff and Cheminée and Prof Bill McGuire and the Johnston whom Mount St. Helens killed which much traumatised Harry Glicken who himself died at Japanese Mount Unzen which also pyroclastically killed Katia Krafft and her spouse Maurice, my own special heroes.

Myself, aspiring to that roll of honour. And a bag of money. Though not for being dead.

'How sure are you the old city will melt? No other Vee watches.'

'Lady, there are a *lot* of political hotspots worldwide that might attract a melt—if indeed that's the cause. I'm taking a gamble because Jerusalem's such a conflicted city.'

At that moment, beyond her across the valley, I do see steam rising. 'Step away!' Promptly I activate my flyboard, hoping not to burn her feet nor set fire to her skirt. I'm damned if I'll miss a moment of the melting of Jerusalem due to this woman or frankly *anybody* interrupting me.

Instead of complying, she does this amazing and contrary thing. She jumps on to my boots, latching her hands around my waist.

Oh but do I tilt forward due to all those unexpected undistributed extra kilos! Not that she's heavy in the least, but she really destabilises me. My micro-turbs have stabilisers but this takes real hands-on skill with my glove controls. Direction, Altitude, Thrust! DAT is how. Fortunately the design of the kerosene tanks in my backpack damps down any fuel slosh.

Recovering stability pulses me many metres upward and outward, while she continues hanging on resolutely. Supposing she falls, well *hell* this cannot be helped. I'm not setting down hereabouts. Ankle-twister tombs not to mention pop-up pines and cypresses as well as the unavoidable Biblical olives.

She copes as I rush west towards the wall of the city. What does this reckless Loon of Armenia want from me? Maybe she's seeking a bird's eye view. My flyboard puts out 93 decibels, more than a bus yet less than a buzzsaw. A fair few birds are in the sky now—scared by bad vibes?—but not one single rival Vee, which is ace. Many more pigeons and sparrows and things will be caught up in the melt, along with all human habitants, maybe fifty thousand persons here, plus dogs, cats, rats, chickens, spiders, bacterias. There'll be up-early tourists in the melt too.

We're up and over above the Old City, perfect size for a melt being about a kilometre square. All melts so far are thuswise. All happen during hours of daylight. This doesn't mean that up in orbit some alien dude focuses a giant burning lens as on an ants' nest.

Everything within the Old City smears. Buildings becoming a toddler's wonkier crayon impression of what was firm architecture just a mo ago. I rise a bit higher for perspective. Bye-bye, golden Dome of the Rock. Bye-bye, Via Dol and Church of the Holy Sep and Cathy of Saint Jim and umpteen lanes and houses. Bye-bye habitants, a few of whom actually reach a roof along with their cat before dissolving. One Munch open-mouths upward at me, someone's last moment of existence. What's being done isn't nice even if it's passably pretty.

Damn Luna's interference! Only now do I remember to chin-toggle the radio to call dibs on Jeru: **'All hear, I Harry Adonis, Vulcan numero 56, declare that Jerusalem Old City is melting right now below *me* since sixty secs ago, mark. Am transmitting full telemetry and filming.'** Harry is short for Aristotle. Common touch.

'You're a Greek?' shrieks the Loon over the noise of the flyboard. 'Those Kurd-killing Turkeys genocided a million Greeks just like they genocided us Armenians too—'

'Chip on your shoulder about genocides eh, Luna? Kindly shut up about that! I've work to do.'

Below us everything mixes together in undulating swirls. My suite of instruments and cameras works on auto but benefits from my guiding glove for fine control. Radiant heat from below is way from being pyroclastic, more scaldy bathwater cooling as fast as it stiffens. Another few mins, I'll be able to land, unlock my boots, walk around if I wish. Without the woman's extra weight, not that a Vulcan is less than fit.

'Oh no chip now,' shrills Luna. 'I thank the God-Who-Never-Was that I'm free at last and out of here—!'

'Alexander: ignore female voice interference,' I instruct my equip. What, let some local resident's unqualified comments intrude on my triumph?

Within the great sprawl of wavy pastel plastic-soup stuff, pretty much all contents have been absorbed by now and converted into multicoloured homogeneity.

How she clings to me. '—No longer am I the slave to my obligatory Armenian massacre heritage! Just because state-sponsored Christians of Armenia reached Jeru as the first converted nation, and instead of massacring Armenians, the much too merciful ruling Muslims grant to Armenians the biggest part of the city. Armenians gain kiloms of walls to fix anti-Turk Armenian massacre posters on to centuries later—'

Of this I am aware, but *not right now*, thanks very much.

'I speak not of the massacring Crusades—'

I'm surprised she can speak at all as we waltz together over the melted city. Quite a class act of clinging. Luna uses the word *massacre* quite a lot.

'No longer need I pay obeisance to my fucking family traditions for fear of . . . never mind—'

Never mind what? Some sexual naughty? Some bastard baby? Some money matter swept under a carpet? An abortion? A suffocated aunt? I've no idea, nor do I wish to know. Luna needn't worry about her guilty secret being sussed, since all the high notes of her voice are blocked from being broadcast. Damn it, broadcast, me! I need to assert myself more.

'**Listeners over at the UN and worldwide, I Harry Adonis foresaw Jerusalem as a major melt on account of thinking about . . .** *massacres*. **No longer does a frontier divide this city itself, yet this square kilom has been the focus of centuries of murderous religious warfare between Jews and Romans, Christians and Muslims, Jews and Muslims, Jews and Christians, Christians and Christians. This is the blood-ruby of cities! Jeru is an epitome. Jeru is a cynosure—!**' (Am I quite sure of the meaning of 'cynosure'? Too late now for qualms.) '**What is human history but a vast list of wars and massacres and genocides and holocausts? Behold Jeru below my feet!**' Dear God the tanned sandaled feet of Luna may be visible upon my boot tops . . . ['Alexander private, edit-mask-delete female feet in leather sandals! Alexander private erase any signs of woman upon me!']

'**Listeners, the history of mankind is frankly of men at wars little or large, local or landwide, sanctioned or vigilante, minus brief** rests in between for rearming.' I prepared this earlier in my head, at the YMCA.

['Mankind?' pipes up Luna. 'More like monkeykind. Humanity? More like inhumanity.']

Might as well repeat her words for broadcast, since they have a certain music.

'Mankind? More like monkeykind. Humanity? More like inhumanity. Yes indeed, listeners.' But I mustn't sound like some evangelist, no—more like a Sagan or Attenbro.

'Cooperation makes conflicts. Conflicts make cooperation.'

Do I sound too much like the trilingual feelgood at the YMCA?

'Listeners worldwide and at the UN, conflict is in our genes as much as co-operation. We got no history without conflict. Conflict and cooperation these are a dialectic. Antithesis and thesis. Their synthesis is progress, now going exponential. Except that *something*'s melting our potentials.'

I'm inspired, I'm rapping, I'm flying.

Surely I'm using up my kerosene faster due to Luna. Suppose I can shake her off by risking rotating swiftly up-down, my cams might film her shadow, or her slim skirted baglady self, falling and sprawling. And why should I plausible carry out such a head-over-heels manoeuvre? To show off? Grand Prix champion swinging his car in a circle? Me being attacked by eagles?

By now the rumpled rainbowspread that was Jeru looks firm enough to land upon. So I settle down to within a few centimetres, cams angled rearward. Bit like a lunar module, come to think of it.

'Hop off,' I command Luna quietly, me being her captain. That'll help test the surface, though I'm fully confident. Fairly confident. Or may the surface only as yet be a rubbery crust like the skin on cooling custard? No one but me has ever experienced a melt so soon after the melting stabilises. Well, me and Luna, but absolutely she is here courtesy of me.

While I film rearwards she hops off me, which is backwards for her, facing me. Oh those eyes of hers! Those boiled eggs of opal with the darkest possible yolks as if marinated for months and for years. The swimmy surface of the melt easily sustains her. Why, she even stamps her sandaled foot down, like some gravedigger using the back of his spade to tamp!

Gazing down at a slight angle, I have a sense of depths yet nothing is distinct from anything else. As if there are no edges to the geometry. This kind of challenges one's personal identity. But I set down, dousing my jet turbines. Damn but my inner thighs are aching already.

'Listeners, a history of bitter conflict is dissolved all together in a melt.' Does that sound too much like a café latte? Right now is my chance for renown! 'I ask myself, may this be the *purpose* of melts? To fuse enemies together? To unite Jews with Muslims—?'

['Greeks with Persians!' she calls out.]

'And Greeks with Persians as in the ancient world at the very gates—yes, *gates*—of Greece where tens of thousands of Persians died opposed by three hundred heroic Greeks led by King Leonidas braver than a lion. At Thermopylae—'

['Eh, did you say *thermophiles*? The Bacteries that love extreme heat?'] Bacteries rhyming with 'factories'...

'*Bacterias*, not 'Bacteries'!'

A Nobel-level inspiration comes to me. This must be equivalent to at least Krakatau level 6 on the Volcanic Explosivity Index.

'Thermopylae means "hot gates". Hot sulphurous springs were nearby. Yet for me the place name Thermopylae evokes *thermophiles*, that's to say *extremophiles*, which are extreme thermophiles, those single-cell organisms which live in conditions of extreme heat and pressure...such as exist deep underground...depths from which they may arise—'

Locked to the flyboard, I can't stroll around on the rumply surface unless I abandon my boots to venture forth in my cool-conduct socks. Luna darts to and fro close to me in her sandals, peering down, disregarded and/or deleted by my smartcams.

Now she gapes at me. 'You can't have *any biology* just a few kiloms down! Umpty times hotter than boiling water, no life process possible. I'm no fool! After formal schooling, stuck in the Armenian pottery shop I got higher web-education via the checkout screen. 'Cause I hoped a volcano might blow up under my Jeru gaol but geology was wrong. So I know a thing or three.'

Um. Of course she's right...

Yet on the other hand...

'Hear me: 500 kiloms beneath our feet—within the transition zone between the arid upper mantle and the arid lower mantle—there's an ocean. Not in the swimmy whales-and-dolphins sense but still a very wet ocean as well as hot and pressurised. This ocean soaks the elastic rock.

'Um, by "very wet" I mean that the rock contains maybe three per cent water—yet that adds up to many Pacific Oceans' worth. Any life way down there must be extremely extremophile. Like, a thousand degrees Kelvin. That's 1K K. We cannot imagine the nature of this life, except that it must diffuse vastly throughout the rock, and may be equipped with ganglia communicating electro-magnetically—so I guess we *can* imagine! But we're still likely to be wrong.

'I believe that they—or It—knows about us. They seem to know in some detail. The best way the Deep Other can think of damping conflict among us is to fuse us together at the molecular level.

'Remember that the gangly octopus has independent brains in each arm. That's nine brains. But this down there has to be a distributed social intelligence. At nano level! Below biology! Trillions of the same entity.

'Unless we peace up, the Deep Entity will keep on melting our conflict places together to give us a helpful nudge. Hell, how can we possibly evacuate every conflict point on Earth? That'll take hundreds, thousands, of co-operative local truces to start off with. Maybe we gotta start at street level. Goes against human nature, against our conflict-cooperation genetics. Deep One doesn't think the way we do at all. I doubt if we can even communicate except by using giant symbols—like melts. Or like some hydrogen bombs dropped down deep shafts. But no, don't try this, is my advice, because next thing the Deep One or Deep Ones might set off lots of volcanoes. That'll be a lot worse than limited square-kilom melts. I'm still thinking, People—me, Harry Adonis—but this sure explains melts. The best way the Deep Others—or Other—can think of damping conflict among us is to fuse us together nanotechnologically.'

Of a sudden sirens begin to wail, a late response compared with my own broadcast to Vulcan HQ for the benefit of the UN and everyone. A couple of Israeli Defence Force spotter helicopters are in the sky now. Elderly Sikorsky Sea-Stallion Yasurs, I do believe. (To be modest, I might be wrong.) I'm hearing ambulances and police vehicles in the distance, fat lot of use those will be—ah, except to control hysteria around the edge of the melt.

The emergency services mustn't find Luna so far within the melt, unsprintable to by her in the available time, reachable only by helicopter or by Vulcan flyboard, namely mine.

But the Deep Ones is definitely my idea!

Well, the little lady's little idea . . . made big and given voice by me.

I can drop her off, outside of the melt.

I can drop her off.

Drop her.

Drop.

No, any finger of guilt would point my way.

Those Israeli choppers will be observing keenly from now on. So I must be upfront (just as Luna was previously plastered right up against my front, ha!). I must take Luna to the YMCA hotel. I'm fucking fed up with Luna. Fuck her fuck her fuck her. Yet on the other hand . . . Those eyes. I'm descended from a Greek god.

'So now your home is gone, lady! Care for a lift to somewhere habitable? Such as the YMCA hotel? Luna, I'll treat you to salad sandwiches and chilled water and other stuff later on. Other stuff.'

Today there'll be a sensational influx of media and science into Jeru. I'll need to perform.

'What's in your bag, by the way?' I ask her.

'Worldly goods. Just in case of a miracle.'

These days, glamorous Honolulu-resident Mrs Lusine Adonis devotes herself to supporting her famous and prosperous husband's hypothesis of 'Hyperextremophiles from Hell' as the cause of the mysterious melts, which continue to this day, as yet having plastificated the merest fraction of our planet's land surface (though fatal for many).

THE WOKINGHAM AGREEMENT

A JERRY CORNELIUS STORY

MICHAEL MOORCOCK

1. THE BRUTE OF SAIGON

President Trump's order to withdraw essentially all U.S. troops from northern Syria came after the commander-in-chief privately agitated for days to bring the troops home, according to administration officials—even while the Pentagon was making public assurances that the United States was not abandoning its Kurdish allies in the region.
—*Washington Post*, 14 October 2019

OVER IN THE REMAINS of the science lab they were having a parents-roast. Slowly turning on a spit, Mr Tanner's left leg provided mouth-watering crackling for Mandy and Laura, his starving children, who forgot their shame as they attacked the meat. Jerry knew they would throw it all up in a few minutes. The committed cannibals were on the other side of the park enjoying the local curate. All in all, it had been an excellent day's cricket.

'Imagine a gigantic reptile, bigger than a tyrannosaurus.' Mo Collier spoke in some awe. 'Okay? Or a big pig. Bigger than the one Pink Floyd had. I mean, *huge*! I mean, think about it. It would solve shortages. What's that one that can swim?'

Bishop Beesley gravely unwrapped the Yorkie that his twins, Bobby and Bea, had been saving for dessert. He was in great spirits. They, on the other hand, felt a trace of resentment. 'Why can't they eat beef or pork or lamb?' Bobby watched the chocolate disappear. He and Bea had seen the carcasses burning in the hills on their way down from Cheltenham.

'Some of us are natural man-eaters.' Mo had only contempt for his fellow travellers.

'We've all had to modify, dears, haven't we?' Half-heartedly, Bishop B. tried to cool what he saw as rising temperature in the ranks. 'I mean, when did *anyone* charge a fiver for a single Wagon Wheel?' On the way here, they had stopped off to buy what few sweets were left at Oxford Motorway Services. 'They're friendly around here but really they'd rather reduce you to a nourishing broth.'

'It's shocking, isn't it?' Peering vaguely through his sunglasses, Jacky Constantinople scratched his blonded head. He had attached himself to the little convoy in the hope of some sort of acknowledgement from his idol. His Derry accent was something between an aggressive gargle and a questioning gasp. 'I used to love the Cotswolds. Still do. We'd come every year after Grange went glub-glub. They didn't like us because we were Irish, but Da' said we were Turkish. Talk about Turkish Delight. The thick man of Europe. Tee hee. Oh, that's wicked. I have to write it deown.' With some alarm he saw that his left arm had faded. He took out his Moleskine and, open-mouthed, began to scribble. From the corner of his eye, he saw someone approaching. He froze. 'Do you smell garlic? Or is it onions?'

Jerry stopped to light a Sherman's. What a mismatched shade!

He was as half-sick of shallots and shadows as he was of quotes from the classics.

'At least they had a bloodbath. First time they've enjoyed a bath in years.'

'Jerry! Could I have a word?'

The shade was getting on his nerves. Jerry stepped away. There was nothing worse than an admirer who, trying to emulate you, kept getting it wrong. What did you call someone like that? *Doppelgänger* was too good a word for them. He looked to where Una Persson sat glumly munching an old cheese-and-pickle sandwich she'd found in the abandoned pub. She shrugged, wiped her brunette bob back from her face and stood up, grinning. 'Greatest form of flattery, Jerry,' she said. She shouldered her AK-445 and buttoned her military coat. 'You could always wipe him.'

Jerry returned her expression. That wasn't on the cards now. He backed away from the fires as the sun spread her last ruddy rays through the poplars alternating with the willows bending over the far side of the river. A quickening wind made their reflections jump and flicker. 'I'm always afraid I'll damage something else,' he said. 'Every sequence has its consequences.'

'You're getting cautious in our old age.'

He smiled. 'We lost the plot. Ever since the future went belly-up. Stupid, I suppose.'

'Well, you did your best.'

He shot her a grateful glance.

2. DEATH FOR THE DEVIL'S DIVISION

This year's books all have cracking plots and relatable characters.
—2019 Booker Prize judges.

'SOMETHING'S GOING DOWN in Gloucester.' Jerking his chopper upright, Major Nye drew on his old leather gauntlets. 'I'm going back to check Oxford Services' Waitrose. Little bird mentioned they had some Melton Mowbray pork pies stashed in a secret ice cellar! Call me an old fool, but I've decided I can't carry on with this one until I've scoffed a couple of mediums.'

'Branston?' Mo loved Branston pickle.

'Come now, old chap. That's like putting the stuff on a bacon sandwich. Nasty Aussie habit.'

'I think you'll find it's French.' Trixie Brunner looked to her mother for confirmation. Insouciantly, Miss Brunner waved a bandaged hand.

'I'm not sure I've ever had one.' Trixie was trying to win Mo over. 'Is it made with a baguette? And thin tranches of ham?'

'The butter has to be biological *sel de mer* or it doesn't work. Preferably a traditional loaf and the butter's from Noirmoutier, if possible. Or so I understand.'

'And what about the brown sauce?' Mo asked, 'HP? Okay?'

Miss Brunner shuddered.

3. THE CROOK OF SOHO

Dozens of civilians have reportedly been killed in the operation so far and at least 160,000 have fled the area, according to the UN.

—BBC News, 16 October 2019

'OW FAR TO the sea now?' Mrs Cornelius threw her last crisp bag out of the car window onto the cracked landscape. 'I'm gettin' 'ungry.' Behind him, she leaned against the insubstantial shoulder of her latest squeeze. Monsieur Pardon appeared to be paralysed. Once his large brown eyes begged help from the self-involved passenger on the other side of her, but the creature he understood to be called Cuntstainpole was only barely visible, fading into the leather.

'Nearly there, Mum.' Jerry rubbed his eyes. He had driven the Duesenberg all the way from Ankara and was getting edgy. The roads were well potholed, sometimes gone altogether, the signs of over-fracked ground and a thousand miniature earthquakes. He could still hear Colonel Pyat occasionally kicking from inside the boot. The old bugger was over eighty. You had to admire his energy.

'You did say it was a cruise, Jer, I'm not complainin', but you did say.'

'There was a mix-up with the agent, Mum, I told you.' He didn't like to admit he had bought the wrong tickets in the hope of misdirecting his shadow.

'It'd never have happened with Thomas Cook. A proper British travel agent. Honest, Jer, ol' Ataturk would've sorted this in a Greek minute. 'E would never 'ave let 'is choppers start shootin' like they did. Them turds, that's who I blame.'

'Didn't know you knew him, Mum.' Sometimes Jerry couldn't take his mother's claims and stories.

She turned her head to regard the landscape. 'I knew 'em all.' She peered miserably through the window. 'Bloody 'ell. This 'as got to be the most borin' fuckin' country in the world.'

'It's had its moments. You liked Istanbul.'

'Constantinople? That was years ago!'

In the boot the colonel was kicking again.

'Shouldn't we let him back, Mum?'

'I wouldn't mind,' she said. 'But 'e stinks of garlic.'

Jerry shifted an angry gear. 'Sure it's not my fag? Or the crisps, Mum?'

She reflected on this.

Eventually she said, 'That's still no reason to let 'im out. 'E's comfy enough.' She dug a plump elbow into her little escort's unresisting shoulder. 'Ain't 'e, Gaston?'

Jerry slowed down as Istanbul's suburbs came in sight. Their bloody ship had better be docking.

From somewhere in the distance, as if to reassure him, a mournful horn began to blow.

'Thinks he's a tough guy,' said Jacky, vaguely running a comb through his pomp.

4. THE THREE JOLLY BRITONS

Dear Mr. President,

Let's work out a deal! You don't want to be responsible for slaughtering thousands of people, and I don't want to be responsible for destroying the Turkish economy—and I will. I've already given you a little sample with respect to Pastor Brunson. I have worked hard to solve some of your problems. Don't let the world down. You can make a great deal. General Mazloum is willing to negotiate with you, and he is willing to make concessions that they would never have made in the past. I am confidentially enclosing a copy of his letter to me, just received. History will look upon you favourably if you get this done the right and humane way. It will look upon you as the devil if good things don't happen. Don't be a tough guy. Don't be a fool. I will call you later.

Sincerely, Donald Trump.

'WHAT ARE YOU fixing now?' Jerry was growing impatient with Mo's experiments. His Chinese suppliers out of commission, Mo had become obsessed with finding good substitutes for his missing favourites.

Mo held a huge animal-syringe to the light. It was filled with fizzing electric orange liquid. 'Looks good, doesn't it?'

'So what is it?'

'It has a lot of natural ingredients, Mr C. It's good for you. Want some?'

Jerry wasn't sure. 'Why is it making that noise?'

'It's only the bubbles.'

'Bubbles?'

'Not *Greeks*, Jerry! They're natural, I told you.'

'So what are you fixing, Mo?'

His friend shrugged. 'They didn't have any of the straight stuff, Okay?' He was embarrassed. 'It's Diet Tizer.'

'Christ.' Jerry was shocked. 'You couldn't find any Vimto?'

5. THE BOMBED HOTEL

'They fought with us. We paid a lot of money for them to fight with us, and that's okay,' [Trump] said, 'They did well when they fought with us. They didn't do so well when they didn't fight with us.' Mr Trump added that the Kurdistan Workers' Party—a rebel group that fights for Kurdish autonomy in Turkey, 'is probably worse at terror and more of a terrorist threat in many ways than' the Islamic State.
—BBC News, 16 October 2019

<u>1933. Walking the Dog.</u>
Leaning languidly against the edge of the table was the slim young man who called himself Zenith.
—Anthony Skene. *A Duel to the Death.*

'*E*VERY *LITTLE MOVEMENT has a meaning of its own, every little thought and feeling by some posture can be shown . . .*'
Major Nye hummed a favourite number. Some darling of the halls had performed it in his youth. Slowly he ran a fond finger over dusty blue and gold spines. '*Every little picture tells a tale . . .* I'm sure it was a Macmillan Illustrated Classic. Here we are. You have a wonderful book department, Señor Lupino. I'd say it's better than Knightsbridge.'

Sr. Lupino was gracious. Clearly impressed by the Major's Savile Row tailoring, he moved a pale, modest hand, adjusting his pearl-grey lapel. 'So we're told, sir. Will *Snarleyowl* be all?'

'Unless you have a *My Strudel*, is it?'

'We're waiting for the next printing, Major. With Herr Hitler and his popular "pastry cook" socialists in power more people are curious. Do you know much, sir?'

'About Viennese baking?' Major Nye couldn't say. He hadn't realised the chap had other interests. 'Wasn't he in the Battenberg rising? When's it due in?'

'We can order it for you, of course. Do you live in Buenos Aires?'

'Not yet, I'm afraid.' He thought of Vanessa; the Hotel Robinson. 'I'd move here like a shot if I were a free man. Not cricket, though, is it?'

Sr Lupino's smile was discreetly tired.

1944. Flying down to Rio.

On Sunday, after US troops began withdrawing from the region and Turkish-led forces made gains, the Kurds agreed a deal with the Syrian government for the Syrian army to be deployed on the border to help repel the Turkish assault.

—BBC News, 15 October 2019

THEY FOUND JERRY cutting cane in the back country north of Rio. They cleaned him up and gave him a pair of boots. He was delighted. They might have been handmade. 'Don't worry.' Miss Brunner counted out bills to the thickset Indian who had reported him. 'He'll be his old self in no time. Look, he's found a copy of *Tractatus Logico-Philosophicus* already. Fish to water, eh?'

'Fish?' The Indian scratched his head. 'Nowhere around here that I know. Not anymore.'

But Jerry, mumbling cross-legged from the polished planks of the upper deck, quickly discarded the book and picked another from the pile: *Coarse Flies*, the pornographic memoir thought to have been written as a kind of sequel to Walton's *Compleat Angler*. He began looking through the pockets of his new black pea jacket. 'Rod?'

'We'd better be leaving while we can.' Major Nye adjusted the fraying cuffs of his civilian tweed. 'Once he finds the Doré *Milton* we'll never get him off the boat.'

'Is it regression?'

'Not typically.'

With her slender arthritic fingers, Miss Brunner tightened her greying perm. 'In politics, one word's worth a thousand pictures. Not so?' She flirted a glance at a freshly and cheaply uniformed Captain Pardon. He'd receive a fortune for this help. His old vessel wheezed black smoke and coughed a little circumspectly. The little captain seemed surprised, studying a large chronometer he held in his left hand and making notes with a new pencil on his paper cuff.

'If we left now,' said Major Nye, 'we might get to São Paulo for the next riot.'

'Are they still upset with the Americans?' she asked.

'Not since they found out the reason for the shelling. Embarrassing, of course.' He moved his mouth in mock disapproval. 'His Holiness intervened. Poor intelligence, as usual.' The Major remained unhappy about his posting. After Casablanca, it had seemed all downhill until now.

Their steamboat made a convulsive movement then whoever was steering let loose with the whistle. Capitan Pardon cursed in French and headed for the wheelhouse.

Miss Brunner shrugged. 'Does anyone know where he trained?'

'Marrakech, I think.' The Major chuckled forgivingly.

Miss Brunner frowned.

1956. Just Couldn't Resist Her with Her Pocket Transistor.
They fought with us. We paid a lot of money for them to fight with us, and that's okay, [Donald Trump] said.

—*(ibid.)*

AT FIRST HE thinks it is a dust storm. Then the air grows thicker. He covers his mouth with his handkerchief. There are stinging pebbles in it now. He lies down and protects his head. He thinks *Jesus Christ I'm being buried alive!* So he forces himself to his knees and crawls on until at last the storm stops. In the following stillness he sees a figure ahead, shadowy against the sun. A smiling, bearded face.

A recurring dream. Jerry wondered if the man were his father. The expression was familiar. In the dream they were so proud to be on Mars, so pleased it looked just like Barsoom in *John Carter*.

On his eighteenth birthday, his father pressed Heidegger's *Being and Time* onto him. 'It's flawed, of course, but also very coherent. Try him.' Jerry had decided he wasn't a great thinker. And God knew what the drugs had done to his dad's brain. He drew a deep, relaxing breath. Sometimes surgery was the only answer.

In the following dream, he was reading Harvey's *The Condition of Postmodernity*, crossing an ice-bridge in a horse-drawn sleigh. His sister Catherine sat in front of him, wrapped in white furs. Behind them in snow reddened by the setting sun, sharp black shadows of birches crossed the deep bleak ruts the sleigh made. The same old cryptograms, each telling a different tale.

'What's it all mean, Jerry?' his sister asked.

'People are frightened. They simply won't tolerate the absurdists anymore. Not as an audience.' Una Persson, gloriously stylish in her snug greatcoat, spoke from behind, where she was leading her own roan. 'That's where we come in.'

'We supply the witch?' She gave him a brief sidelong look. 'Who is—?'

'Not you this time.'

Jerry was prepared to work with what he had, but it wouldn't be easy for anyone. Too many dreams, too much delusion, too many illusions. How could he have kept so many balls in the air at the same time? As was often true, the world had been over-complicated by simple-minded men.

He awoke with a guffaw.

'What is it now?' Catherine sat up. 'Christ, it's cold.'

Outside, the darkness and silence continued to gather.

1967. Lady D'Arbanville.

If you need charity for your people, then your society has failed.

—Walter Mosley, *Red Gold*

ZURICH TRAMS RAN so thoroughly on time that Una Persson felt faintly disgusted, especially when she attempted to board in her old Balenciaga frock while she went through her bag looking for her fare. She apologised in her pretty German. 'Sometimes I have to unpack everything, just to find the right change.'

'Sometimes you have to unpack everything anyway.' The driver handed her a ticket of a higher denomination than the one she'd paid for. 'Now you can go much further.' He winked. 'Perhaps you should have flown.'

'He won't fly.' She made a grateful, apologetic face. 'So I can't.'

'Oh, that's always such a problem. So. You're married?' He pulled the lever and the doors hissed shut. 'Here on holiday?'

He was flirting with her. *Where do the children play?* A strange tune to come into her head at that moment. Was he looking for a hard-headed woman?

She had to admit, she admired his Mediterranean looks. What was it about those enormous noses?

1971. Friend of the Devil.

President Erdogan was dismissive. 'The Americans say one thing to you in public and something entirely different in private. They cannot be believed or trusted.'

—France 24 News, 16 October 2019

TIME AND ORDER? What could we do without them? The theatre wasn't what it was. In the current climate, they could never have a successful revival of *The Jew's Bargain*. Which was a stupid thing to say, he thought. Was it true? Did the image always precede the actuality? *I have seen your skull covered in filth*, he told a smiling Mengele. *I have seen you dead. You have no idea what great good will come of our suffering. The State of Israel will rise from our ashes.* He was able to look into Mengele's face and see the attempt to control the contractions of terror there. Was it unseemly to congratulate himself for bartering his good life to save one young woman from the creature whose bones were now displayed at the Nazi Remains Show in Munich? *I am not man enough for this*, he thought. But it was too late. *I had made my truce with God. It was unbreakable. He would not release me from it. I wish I had known that at the time.*

He was reading from his own journal.

But, best of all, I had proved there truly was a God. I need never despair again. Never carry that burden Nietzsche had put on me. Yet if you had a past and a present, why could you not have a future? Or a number of futures? He had spent so long trying to work out the consequences of radiant time. Too many equations. Too many adventures. Too much of everything. Accretion challenged complexity. Each universe was separated by size and mass, making it invisible to the next. He had made no serious commitments anywhere else. His brain felt dusty and now he worried if he had spent too long with the Ottomans. They should never have trusted Venice. He had discovered the so-called Papal Letter. He hated dealing with the Vatican.

Somewhere from the shadows a zealot shouted the name of God while a woman's screams grew louder.

There was a long way to go yet.

Jerry wondered how much hotter things would become before they started cooling down again. He wetted another towel and stretched it over his sister's pale forehead. He checked his watch. In a couple of hours the world would know for certain. How long had he waited as his child bride sweated out her memories?

So long. So long at the border. Could they sweat this out too? Now he understood why Benjamin had given himself up to despair. The world could no longer be manipulated or persuaded. The story had to end because there were no more palatable resolutions he could picture. At last he began to understand the codes. It really shouldn't have taken all this time. Travelling took mantras, cards, rhymes, and movements. Equations and music. Too many pictures. Far too many words. And ghosts! Those ghosts! Then it suddenly became second nature. Scarcely a thought—and you were on another plane. Pointless. The magic had gone.

What the fuck had happened to the action? The mystery?

'Wake up, old chap.' Major Nye's voice was distant and encouraging. 'Our truck's arrived at last! We're on our way! Another four decades and we'll be in Syria. Or Lebanon, at any rate. What do you think of that?'

'Saladin's still in charge, isn't he?'

'The Kurds seem to think so.'

Jerry got up slowly, adjusting his cap. 'Has anyone seen my launcher?'

1984. Momma Don't Let Your Babies Grow Up to Be Cowboys.

The UK-based Syrian Observatory for Human Rights said on Wednesday that Syrian and Russian forces had entered the border town of Kobane, following a deal struck between the Kurds and Damascus in the wake of Turkey's incursions.

—BBC News, 16 October 2019

WHEN IN GALVESTON, Jerry habitually took his breakfast at the Waffle House on 25th and Broadway. It was the least infected of the joints. Here, he usually found it impossible to catch even a glimpse of the ragged ocean. He was beginning to regret buying the Bishop's Palace. Though he'd found his hard-headed woman, he still knew a lot of dancers. When had he last eaten so much bacon? Really, it was time to stop. He was growing weak again. He reached into the darkness and found her long soft hand. Now he could only love.

She reassured him with her grasp. He was grateful for this small, deliberate kindness. When he first came to the island he had so much wanted to discover some purpose. He felt certain there would be some sign of Leadbelly or at least maybe one of the prison costumes he had worn on stage, perhaps even some other Texas bluesman with a fragment of memory left. But, there was not so much as a playbill. They had gone north and east, showing no interest in time. From the brochures, quantum physics and M-theory seemed to fit so well with the Moorish Gothic of the Bishop's Palace. As a result, he had bought the great pile with its pointed towers, minarets, and Persianate beaux-arts. There had even been a touch of early Tiffany art nouveau. It once provided the most accurate understanding of the style. He could see why so many modernists rejected it. They confused complexity for fussy pre-modernity. Sometimes he hated to see the look of disappointment disturb the firmness of some poor mod's features. Twenty years earlier, the only thing that mattered was a pocket full of purple hearts and a willingness to stay up all night at the Flamingo. He had hoped to see some action. Or did he mean Acton?

'Is there something wrong with the music?' She looked out at the driving rain. 'Why isn't it working anymore?'

'Rock and roll died the day *Hair* opened in New York,' he murmured, glancing around to see if he was overheard. 'Reactionary. Debased versions of Viennese Light classical with extra bass. Queen sang the dirge at the funeral of American music. Then country wasn't country anymore.' Looking up from his Big Triple, Shakey Mo Collier pushed at greasy hair with greasier fingers and gave Jerry a thumbs-up. Again, his attention wandered.

Catherine glared in his direction. Beside him, Miss Brunner watched Mo, who moved urgently but without motive, vaguely checking the safety of his slick little Banning 22-38b Special. 'She was getting ready to settle down. I felt sorry for her.' He kissed the air and said something under his breath. He looked around for his grits.

'Perfect.' Miss Brunner prepared herself for prayer. By increasing the population so successfully, religion had again shown its relevance to modern times. War on a dying planet needed a lot of corpses. Maggots gorged themselves on their own habitat.

This had turned into fun. A neat little running-backwards race. He panted. He tried to breathe slowly. 'Religion really has done a great job of keeping up with the times. I used to say organised religion was just politics. Now I'm wondering if all politics has become religion.' Or was it always an arm of consumerism, that cruel bastard offspring of Capital? When small minds uncertain, they fell back on systems already proven unworkable, applying the theories with greater and greater force in spite of their obvious failure: Leninism, Stalinism, Thatcherism, Reaganism. All corrupted, simplistic, and marked by their uselessness as programmes. They lacked the courage to take their ships of state out into the fast-flowing waters and hidden rocks of the rivers of Chaos, to risk *laissez-faire*, which of course meant making quick, intelligent decisions almost every moment of their waking days. Chaos was not, after all, Entropy. Chaos was constant reinvention, constant resorting to new ideas. Like Law, it ultimately led to Entropy, of course, but you had to be ready to make quick and subtle changes. There was no point at all in relying on GPS because roads were forever appearing and disappearing, like moonbeams in a forest.

Mo looked up from his Banning. 'Is that like water over there? What is it? Tidal wave? Typhoon. Tsunami?' His attempt to stop Jerry's racing mind had no effect. 'I thought we were looking for I-10. Has it gone? Is everything down the drain?'

The rich, their brains clogged with fat and grit, had thought they could escape the worst of the new climates by taking to the seas in those massive luxury yachts and liners. At first the sea had seemed eager to please them. They could steer clear of dangerous water. But their ships had been carried far inland by the gigantic tides and were now warrens for the destitute and desperate. Tokyo and her environs were especially vulnerable to big ships riding waves, which flattened cities more thoroughly than atomic bombs. Why, he wondered, did they almost invariably land upside-down, providing excellent shelter with their steel hulls, still with their supplies largely intact? While the world starved, the feral inhabitants of the *Jolly Roger III* gorged themselves on caviar and pink champagne. Thousands of starving cats and dogs swarmed the ships. Explorers threw them *foie gras* and rotting calamari. In the suddenly reversed ballrooms, giant squid lounged in pools, their amused eyes focusing and refocusing, their bodies displaying the wild or soothing colours of their swiftly changing moods, as the damaged music systems revived themselves to offer a crazed amalgam of every sort of tune and instrument. For some, at least, this was never a cacophony but instead a complex harmony, a never-ending song, sometimes joyous, often melancholy, a lament for the end of linear time, a celebration of radiance and infinite possibility, infinite solutions and dissolution as the world learned new survival strategies. Eventually the waters subsided and the rocks became visible, easily avoided. That gave him an idea for a song.

'Oh, bugger!' Jerry had left his banjo in his cabin again.

1985. The Dream Police; the Dream Police.

Once Brexit is done, we will take the knife to the pen pushers in Whitehall.

—Nigel Farage, September 2019

PORTOBELLO ROAD WAS not the market street it had been. It led north into the limbo of the Harrow Road, Kilburn, and Kensal Rise, where everything grew grey and indistinct. To the south the colours became brighter and eventually less garish the closer you got to Notting Hill Tube station. These residents could pay for good paint.

Karen von Krupp, dentist to the stars, stood at the intersection of Blenheim Crescent and the market, looking up and down in the hope she might see the original Body Shop or Rough Trade Records. She was disgusted by her own nostalgia for a past her people, her customers, had wiped out. She had very little choice, as she saw it, of maintaining so much sentimental romanticism balanced by so much actuality. 'Too many pictures,' she murmured. 'Too many waves. Too many voices.' Time was a field through which you might mark a million paths.

The pleasure of the suburbs was that they presented a simplified narrative. For her the city had far too many stories.

Karen repeated this uncomforting mantra, gathering the white cotton dress around her like a jilted bride.

'What could I have done about it?' Jerry became surly. After all, he had grown up in this very street. 'Some of us enjoy complexity. Some of us can't live without it. It's meat and drink to me.'

'Well, it drives me crazy.'

'This was never designed for upper-class black professionals. You can't blame me for that.'

'I just said it drives me crazy, that's all. What was the bloody point of becoming black? I wanted the moral high ground, Jerry. Isn't that what you promised? Is this a good place to find a taxi?'

Before the music studios like Island and Virgin began establishing themselves in the neighbourhood, Jerry couldn't remember seeing a taxi anywhere. Even the whores had to get out at Westbourne Park Road and walk.

'Do you feel your life has been wasted?' she asked.

Jerry snorted.

1975. Rolling in the Ruins.

Will Islamic State re-emerge? Yes, quite possibly, in some form is the short answer.

—BBC News (*ibid.*)

'PULP LED TO innovation not only in language and subject but in social vision too. The first universal multi-racial democracy I ever saw was when I was ten or eleven. In my comic.' Professor Hira, spreading bland hands, made his point no less obscure. 'You don't remember, do you, the UN cavalry force landing on Venus in gliders? That would have been about 1951, I think. Of course, I was far too young to get it. But *The Silver Jacket* had some fine stories.'

Hira took a moody sip of his julep. 'I wouldn't be surprised if James Joyce got all his narrative ideas from a penny dreadful he was hiding inside the copy of *Hamlet* he was supposed to be reading in the schoolroom.'

Mo Collier looked up from where he was trying to get the last drop of gun grease out of the tin. 'Jesse James?'

'It might have been. More likely *The Blue Dwarf*, or something like that. It wasn't really my point. I'm saying that all important ideas have their origins in popular culture. The sensibility of the race mind, you might say. Have you read any of the French existentialists?'

Mo laughed. 'I'd rather be dead in a ditch. You know that stuff gives me a limp johnson, prof.'

Baffled by his demotic drift, Professor Hira gave up.

June 1959. The Pretenders Live in London.

Those who believe that neither indignation nor adulation are a good basis for measured judgement argue that . . . Putin and his ambitions are not at all hard to understand, that modern Russia, though unpleasant in many ways, is a considerable improvement on the Soviet Union, and that the Russian 'threat' has been much exaggerated.

—Rodric Braithwaite, *New Statesman*, 31 October 2019

T HE RIFFS WERE familiar now.
 Over in the big tent on the edge of the fairground the band was beginning to play selections from *The Desert Song*.

'Not dead yet?' His father's tone was one of amusement mixed with what Jerry could only take for resentment. Old Professor Cornelius was baffled by what he called the chaotic mathematics of the new popular music. For him, Mozart remained the great unifier.

Jerry lowered the volume and sat down in the single pew provided for petitioners.

'Is this the first time you've visited me here?' His father reached for a box at his side and picked out a long brown Sherman's. 'You were all supposed to convene at my deathbed.'

'It would have helped to have had an address.' Jerry had rather liked his pa in life, but in death he had become unstable and petty. Not to mention, in his choice of vestments, vulgar.

'I'd imagine it's a pretty well-known location.'

'Well, it didn't occur to me. Didn't they throw you out?'

'They wanted to.' The old man drew for several seconds on his Sherman's. 'They wanted to. I didn't leave you very much. I'm sorry about that, of course.'

'That's the spirit.' Jerry took a swift glance at the plump woman who entered through the curtain. Her long, bright, white hair framed her ancient face so that in that light it had the appearance of redeemed youth. She gave him the creeps.

'You still don't have to call me Mother,' she said firmly.

Jerry held his breath.

'You can't imagine how disappointed I am in this.' Professor Cornelius made a weak gesture. 'You know.'

Jerry pushed his hair back from his forehead, Then he grinned, holstering the needle gun, a present for his nineteenth birthday. 'Grow up, you foolish old bastard. I'm not killing anyone for you. Not today.'

He turned to point at the old woman. 'And I don't care how much you care. Stay in your crypt.'

She was still trying to smile when he left. Sometimes she wished she'd never heard of Mars.

6. THE RED SPIDERS OF SEVILLE

Claude Duval was born in Domfront, Orne, Normandy in 1643 to a noble family bereft of title and land. His brother Daniel DuVal remained in Normandy and became a lawyer. At the age of fourteen, Claude was sent to Paris to work as a domestic servant to an English Royalist in exile. Upon the restoration of Charles II, he moved to England as footman to his relation the Duke of Richmond and rented a house in Wokingham.

—Lives of the Highwaymen, Aldine, 1902

COLONEL PYAT WAS last to arrive from Waterloo, fiddling with his pass, beginning to show his age, but he greeted his old comrades with hearty grace. 'My dear fellows!'

The men had all, at some time, headed or advised their country's secret services and still relished a peculiar bond. They had been brought here by young Cornelius, who had so far said nothing. He had welcomed them briefly when they arrived the previous evening. He was gambling on what went down well in Cirencester with just a week left before the general dissolution. Such was the new world order, there was every chance that he was right.

'Shall we get on, ladies and gentlemen?' Major Nye took the chair. 'I think we're all here!'

'Captain Cornelius?' Una Persson wanted to know.

Checking his wristwatch, Major Nye looked again towards the room's only door. He glanced through the window at the heaving Thames.

'I take it that everyone's read the relevant documents.' Miss Brunner seemed to have dressed hastily in a russet tweed suit, an untidily knotted blue-and-white Hermès scarf around her hair. 'And I refer you to page 198, paragraph fifteen: The re-emergence of plague rats in Home Counties granaries and their causes. This is about foreign rats, ladies and gentlemen, getting across British borders.'

'Hadn't we already discussed this at the Genoa Conference of last May?' Bishop Beesley frowned into thin air, then returned his attention to some dried chocolate encrusted on his surplice.

The colonel reached for the minutes.

'The sooner we get this done, the sooner the confrontations can restart. Then everything else will be sorted. What?' Major Nye frowned in their general direction. 'Steady the buffs, Miss B!'

'We have yet to form a quorum, you know.' Karen von Krupp gestured vaguely towards the door through which Jerry now entered. On his advice, she was no longer in blackface.

'Sorry I'm late,' he said, 'I was having a bit of trouble with my straps.'

'That's not a bomb vest you're wearing, is it?' Bishop Beesley cleared his throat.

'Bugger!' Jerry apologised. 'Now I've left my banjo in the lobby.'

7. THE BOYS OF BAYCLIFFE

A rollicking story of school life and humorous adventure. Duval became a successful highwayman. Robbing stage-coaches on the roads to London, especially at Holloway, he stopped travellers chiefly between Highgate and Islington.

Unlike most other highwaymen, he distinguished himself by his manners, his gentlemanly courtesy and fashionable dress.

—(*ibid.*)

FOUR EXQUISITE PLANES turned slowly in the skies above Stratford-upon-Avon, heading up the Vale of Evesham towards Chipping Camden. Jerry admired their beautiful aerodynamics. He drew a sharp breath at the sheer aesthetic pleasure he felt when the glittering scarlet Tempests rolled together to concentrate on their targets. With a sudden bang they disappeared over the lush green horizon.

He wondered if one of them was his father's. He'd had a Tempest on order from Rolls-Royce for years. It was an obsession. Old Prof. Cornelius owned one of every plane or car Rolls-Royce had ever put out. Some of them were not exceptional. But the solar-powered Tempest, designed to fly at high speed and half as light as any other machine in its class, might be the most beautiful of all. Could it compete with the electrically driven Boeing-Teslas? He was certain it could.

Jerry shook his head. 'They never did sell that Boing-Boing abroad, did they, Miss B?'

'I hate to see such lovely countryside go under.' She was brushing her hair back into shape. 'It's inspired so many great writers and painters: Shakespeare, Hardy, Tolkien, Churchill, the Prince of Wales. This is the essence of Old Britain, Mr Cornelius, the very heart of Anglo-Saxon England. The real England!'

'Steady on, Miss B,' Jerry said. 'All my ancestors come from this area. There wasn't an Angle amongst them. Just Saxons.'

'I thought you said you were Jewish?'

'I used to be,' he said.

A high-pitched whistling told him the planes were coming back. He lifted his binoculars to the sky.

Miss Brunner was rummaging in her bag, looking for the piece of wedding cake she had kept since Windsor. 'Voilà!' She didn't offer him another. She knew he thought wedding cake was unlucky. 'I picked up a bit of gammon. For your tea, But it must have fallen out when we had to bypass Gloucester. Oh! This icing has gone soft!'

'There's a bit of it on your shoe. Oh, no, it's ham.' He replaced the binoculars and pointed. 'You can never mistake English gammon. I was raised on it.'

Stumbling occasionally, she followed him across the field until they reached the single-track road and the parked Citroën C5. He sighed. Someone had scrawled a message in red magic marker across the back window. It was unreadable, mysterious. No doubt a reference to Napoleon and 'the French', Miss Brunner was already taking pictures and sending them back to HQ. 'I want Sergeant Alvarez to see those.'

Jerry sniffed.

'Bit late, isn't it?'

'It's never too late or too early, Jerry. You know that.'

She opened her turquoise cigarette case, removed a slim brown Sherman's and tapped it on both ends. Then she remembered. 'Have one?' She offered the case.

'I've given up,' he said.

8. THE BLITZED HOTEL

In Syria's Deir ez-Zor province, in the village of Soussa, I held the end of Islamic State's empire in the palm of my hand. It was in Hajin, on the road to Baghouz, as the last scrap of a caliphate prepared to submit finally to the ceaseless bombardment against it, that I was given a handful of IS coins.
—Quentin Sommerville, *New Statesman*, 28 February 2019

'YOU'RE ALWAYS THINKING of other people, Mr C. That's what I like about you. Who, these days, remembers World Octopus Month?'

'Who, these days, remembers octopuses?' Jerry's left wellington had sprung a leak. He had forgotten soggy socks too until now.

'John Davey told me the Duke had to put bars on the windows of Number One, London, because he was so hated by the British public. They were always trying to lob stones through the glass and a mob was constantly yelling and cursing outside.'

'Must have been hell for the people at Number Two,' said Mo, 'Your mum was the same, bless her.'

'What?' He lifted his foot and the wellie gave off an exotic squelch. 'Unpopular? Like Wellesley?'

'Did people a good turn.' Mo was growing tired and there was still at least half a mile to go over Mitcham Marshes. In the distance the horizon was awash with lavender. He could smell it from here. Romantic roses and lucky lavender. Jerry remembered going door to door with the Roma, his mother's brothers and sisters, learning the wheedling whine that never threatened. 'She was a saint.'

Jerry found it difficult to remember Mrs C. as Mo did. 'Maybe,' he said. 'A saint who enjoyed a drink.'

'Oh, yeah! She liked her tipple. They all do, them Catholics. That's why she had so many friends. She couldn't say No to anyone needing a bit of comfort.'

Except her kids, thought Jerry, remembering the time he and Cathy got locked in the coalhole. That wasn't the only time she'd kept them out of the flat when she came back from the pub with a pal. But it meant a lot to Mo to remember Mrs Cornelius in the role he gave her and it didn't particularly matter now. He remembered his mother's strange deathbed confession, if that was what it had been. 'We had bars on our windows too,' he said. 'And sometimes we got stones chucked through them.' Though that had mostly been drunken wives of some of his mum's friends, as he recalled. 'She tried to tell me all kinds of stuff in the last few minutes. Funny, really.'

'At least she knew she was going.' Mo grimaced as his foot went down too deep. 'Bloody hell! Was this all done by buzz-bombs?'

'As far as I know,' said Jerry. 'Come on, I'll give you a hand and we can rest on that little hillock before we try for the last lap.'

'You mean that grassy knoll?' Mo shifted his rifle on his shoulders.

'If you like,' said Jerry. He swore that this was the last time he went into the rural south on foot. He had experimented more than once with country life and he frequently caught something.

'I say!' He heard a nasal Estuarian voice behind him. 'Can I help you? I suppose you know this is private property?'

That had to be Frank. Jerry's brother had been buying up a lot of common land lately, mostly on the fringes of South London. He was planning to concrete over the green belt and sell it off in shovel-ready lots. The new government was providing employment for job-seekers and fresh opportunities for entrepreneurs. Frank was in on the ground floor. It was all part of the *Daily Sun*'s Festival of Revival, designed to bring trade and tourism back to the ailing nation and boost the morale of every town and village in the land. Mitcham Common had been covered in tents until it was flooded by order of the council a couple of months back. The gypsies had packed up what was left of their stuff and been moved to the Scottish border to help build Adrian's Wall.

'Hello, Jerry.' Frank wore his country tweeds awkwardly. 'What brings you to this neck of the woods? I know you've got Father's 'ose for investmen'.'

'Not really.' Jerry pursed his lips in a kind of smile. 'We were just looking for someone's lost youth.'

'I think I'd know if it had been spotted, old cock.' Frank spread his legs and put his hands on his hips. 'I've been over every inch. We're planning to make a level playing field just here. A recreation ground. For the common folk. You'll love it, I promise.'

Somewhere in the neighbourhood of Croydon Aerodrome, a dog raised its voice in a painful howl.

'Don't mind him,' said Frank. 'He's lost.'

9. BLUESKIN'S CELL IN THE SILVER CHATEAU

He reputedly never used violence. One of his victims, Squire Roper, Master of the Royal Buckhounds, was relieved of 50 guineas and tied to a tree.

There are many tales about Duval. A particularly famous one—placed in more than one location and later published by William Pope—claims that he took only a part of his potential loot from a gentleman, when the man's wife agreed to dance the 'courante' with him in the wayside while Duval played upon the flute, a scene immortalised by in his 1860 painting Claude Duval. There is no valid historical source for this assertion.

—Wikipedia, 2019

BOBBY BEESLEY GAVE a sudden hiss of pleasure. 'Oh!' His sister Bea reholstered her little pink Koch. She sweetened her smile. 'It's lovely, Papa. Did they give it to you or is it the Church's?'

Her father, with great dignity, triumphantly undid a gummy pig and popped it between his plump red lips. His eyes were glazed, his hair stiffening, as—still as spun sugar—he stared at the distant scene.

'Naturally, sis, it was *bestowed*,' said Bobby. 'For long service. Rome wasn't razed in a day, dear. Congratulations, darling Papa. This is what you deserve.'

'This is not just for myself,' said their delighted dad. 'This is for us all! *Non nobis sed omnibus! THIS is for the Church. For what shall the wisdom-seekers find more valuable than the spirit within?'*

With self-conscious dignity they joined the others, heads bowed, to hold hands over the smoking ruins of the Vatican City.

'I never intended . . . ' began the bishop. 'Never thought that I would be chosen for such an unbearable honour.'

'But you were, Daddy! You have achieved what so many failed to do for so long. Really, Father. It's the triumph of your faith. For centuries we tried every kind of persuasion. Wars were fought back and forth across Europe and always they failed. Until now. Now, at last, we have a decision. It's the end of popery, Dad.' Bobby's eyes glittered in triumph. 'The Church is unified at last. All thanks to you.'

Humbly, he bowed his mitred head.

'Really, all I had to do was pick the right Smarty,' he said. 'I didn't mean to press it. I always have liked the red ones best. I think I was possessed.'

'In a good way,' insisted his daughter, suddenly anxious. 'Are you sure it was a Smarty?'

He shook his head, still unsure of the power granted to him. 'It might have been an M&M.'

'I'd better get busy.' Bobby consulted his phone. 'I suppose the new capital's bound to be in Westminster now, eh? That should bring in a bit of dosh.'

Bishop Beesley peered curiously through the clearing dust. Was that a cherub he could see? Or only an eagle?

10. THE SACRED SPHERE

We got a World Government that ends wars, the doctors have nearly every disease taped, and nobody's really poor anymore—in fact, everything in the garden's lovely—except there's nothing to eat in it!
—*Dan Dare, Pilot of the Future*, by Frank Hampson with
Arthur C. Clarke. *Eagle*, No. 3. 23 April 1950

A S JERRY REACHED the pavilion, Bobby Beesley declared the innings closed.

Frank's side started batting at a quarter to four with sixty-nine to make if they wished to make them and an hour and ten minutes during which to keep up their wickets if they preferred to take things easy and go for a win on the first innings. At first it looked as if they meant to knock off the runs, for Collier forced the game from the first ball, which was Nye's, and which he hit into the pavilion. But at fifteen, Beesley bowled him. And when two runs later Collier got the next man stumped, and finished up his over with a c-and-b, Ladbroke Grove's side decided it was not good enough. Seventeen for three, with an hour all but five minutes to go, was getting dangerous. So von Krupp and Pyat, the next pair, proceeded to play with caution, and the collapse ceased.

Watching from the pavilion and enjoying a large mint julep, Commander Ballard clapped languidly, glancing up at Jerry as he sat down to strap on his pads. 'Not a bad game, what? I've not seen Collier play better since we left Burma.'

'Or isn't it Myanmar now?' Jerry flicked dust off his whites.

'I gathered the locals still prefer Burma.' Cathy threw herself into the cane chair. Keeping an eye on the batting, she gently lit a black cheroot. 'I wonder why cricket never really caught on in China.'

'Funny people, the Chinese.' Ballard sucked hard on his straw. 'Dashed inventive in many ways but never really cottoned to ball games. Whereas your Japs get very excited over almost everything of the sort except cricket!'

'Baseball!' Major Nye, coming in for a refill, shook his head. 'Damned odd, what?' He adjusted his panama. 'I suspect that's what Pearl Harbor was all about, don't you?'

'They never played much football either,' mused Cathy. 'Maybe it's the climate. Rugger, though . . . Oh, well played, Jerry!' She joined in the applause as her brother sent Beesley's stumps and bails flying.

Jerry had needed a win since 1968. With a bit of luck it would do wonders for his morale.

11. WALDO THE WONDER-MAN!

In 1979, a year after founding the Kurdistan Workers' Party (PKK), Abdullah Ocalan escaped from Turkey to Syria. He lived for almost 20 years, travelling across the Kurdish enclave organizing local militias and reading groups, preaching the equality of women to a community with high rates of honour killings.

—Maurice Glasman, *New Statesman*, 24 October 2019

'I CAN SEE IT now, love!' Mrs Cornelius nearly lost her cornet as she peered over the railing into the Brighton waters. 'Won't it come up all the way? I mean it ain't much of a submarine, is it, when it can't rise higher or whatever it is. I've seen pictures. They can do better than that, can't they?'

'Not all of them, Mrs C.' Mo Collier was dripping. Slowly he climbed the pier's steps to where everyone was waiting for him. 'It's an old nuker. Not the youngest vessel in the fleet, but a damned good bargain for the dosh!'

'Is that rust?' Miss Brunner squinted into the sea.

Mo reached the top of the stairs as the others moved away from him. He was contemptuous and snippy. 'Look, I got a bloody good deal. It's an Echo II, for Christ's sake. They threw in the missiles. It's got six P-fives. *Pyatyorkas*, mate.'

Jerry reached the railing and looked down. 'Don't they call 'em Shaddocks?'

'Really!' Mrs Cornelius smacked her lips. 'I love a nice bit of 'addock. Smoked, with a poached egg on it. Is that what they're smugglin'? It's so hard to find a decent bit of fish anywhere, these days. Not cheap either, is it? If it's oak, I'll 'ave a couple of pounds.'

'So where's the crew?' Una wanted to know.

'Didn't come with it.' Mo was pissed now. 'Bloody hell, I had to drive that thing all the way from Petersburg, just under the surface, and you know I get seasick in a rowing boat on Windermere. Those subsonic missiles alone would cost you a thousand kay a piece, They'd hit a fly on a wall three hundred miles away if you wanted to. Flog 'em off and you've got the whole sub for nothin'!' He began to dry his hair with the towel Major Nye handed him. 'Aren't you going to look around?'

'You won't get me in one of those!' Mrs Cornelius stepped back and licked her melting rocky road. 'I thought we was going on a proper boat.' She turned to glare at Frank, who was looking shifty. 'You told me you was buyin' a cruise ship or I'd never 'ave chipped in.'

Miss Brunner, in lime-green tweeds, showed them all her phone. 'It's true. That's what it said on the crowdsourcer you put up on Facebook, Frank.'

'That's what the Russians promised!' Frank was bitter. 'Honest. You saw the ad. A cruiser. You know. To cruise in. To get away from it all! Avoid all the climate stuff.'

'Cruisers—' Miss Brunner spoke evenly through clenched teeth, '—aren't cruise ships and this isn't even a cruiser!'

'Tell that to the bloody missiles!' Mo had begun to sulk. 'You should have done the fuckin' deal then, shouldn't you? You'll thank me for it. There are typhoons stirring things up all over the place.'

The pier was shaken by a massive clank as a wave caught the sub and threw it against the iron posts. 'And then he got his cock in the end of the marrow and had to hide it under an old coat until the Queen had inspected them.' Frank was still trying to make them laugh. 'True story,' he added, applauding it with a dry cackle. He had always fancied himself a bit of a wag.

With a sigh, Jerry started to climb gingerly down the rusting steps. 'Okay, Mo. How do you get into this thing?'

'It's locked.' Mo felt in his soggy pockets. 'I've got the key here somewhere.'

Colonel Pyat shook his head. 'It's really a question of semantics, eh? Stalin should have been here. He'd have loved this.'

'Oh, fuck Stalin!' said Miss Brunner.

Mrs Cornelius smiled reminiscently to herself. Colonel Pyat caught her eye and winked.

12. SEALS OF DOOM

NOTICE
Tonight at 9 p.m.!
THE First Cricket Match ever
To be played by moonlight!
Married versus Single Men of Beadle.

Loser to stand drinks all round!
Play starts at moonrise.
Stumps drawn at midnight.
—R.C. Sherriff, *The Hopkins Manuscript*

'IT'S NO GOOD, Jerry.' His sister put her foot down harder on the accelerator and overtook the mirror-finished sixteen-wheeler at last, running between the ambling Union Pacific hundred-car freight train and the traffic. 'If they can't understand the music, they can't understand the bloody music. We've known that since we said goodbye.'

They were getting clear of Clarksdale at last, leaving the burned-out little shotgun houses, the abandoned stores and civic buildings which not long ago had been the most prosperous city in Mississippi, when cotton had ruled and there were good jobs to bring in the men, the tractor drivers and pickers, and everyone who had taken their blues to Memphis and up the line to Chicago. Now all that was left were a few stage suits, guitars, and harmonicas shown in rival museums, a couple of T-shirt stores, and finally, crossroads vying to be the original where Robert Johnson had done his deal with the devil.

They were heading deeper into the South. Somewhere before they reached Prejean's, Baton Rouge, they were due to meet Mo Collier. 'He got a lien on my body now. Mortgage on my soul.'

'All right, Jerry.' She spoke firmly. 'We all know the white boy got the blues.'

Defiantly he fished his harmonica out of his pocket and put it to his lips. She grimaced. 'What are you going to give us this time? Woking gal's rag?'

'You liked it when Charlie Musselwhite did it.'

'I certainly did,' she said. 'Look out for signs for Jackson, would you? I don't want to wind up in New Zealand again.'

The hills behind them, the delta was flat and all but treeless. Replaced by pines no more than four deep, the Mississippi woods now hid nothing but barren fields. Overhead an old Stearman biplane circled aimlessly as if looking for one last cotton field to dust. Jerry remembered when they had watched a football game with Bill Faulkner at Ole Miss. Then they got drunk in Oxford, were thrown in the tank, and toasted Texas in bluebonnet wine.

Jerry was starting to think he should have stayed in Rowan Oak. He wondered if Eudora Welty still ran the Widemouth Frog in Jackson. Twenty-seven miles to go. Twenty-seven years gone by. Twenty-seven sweet little darlings had lit him on his way.

'Oh, all right! You can play it. I was only kidding.' Catherine shivered suddenly, enjoying a guilty moment. But he wasn't in the mood now. He had a thirty-eight pistol on a forty-five frame and he never cared if he ever saw that girl again. He wound down the window and rested his right arm on the door. A dry heat came rolling off the riverbed. 'It used to be all steam round here once.' He began slowly to murmur the rhythms of Swinburne's *Atalanta in Calydon*. 'Look out for a Dairy Queen,' she said.

He offered her a dirty look. She knew as well as he did you never saw a DQ on a Mississippi highway. Not anymore. He took comfort in the Colt that was starting to rub his armpit raw. There would be a chance to use it once they got into Louisiana. By then, of course, his mood would probably change. Still, he could continue dreaming. Nobody begrudged him that now, surely?

13. THE FIVE WIGS

Oct 3 and 4, 1999. In China, Japan, Russia, and other countries of Origina (formerly known as Asia) millions of anxious eyes stare upward as asteroid 2345 (The Red Moon) glides silently into their view... These self-governing people have been involved in a mighty drive to end poverty and squalor. Individual liberty and equality is secure, regardless of race, colour or creed, under the elected Wold Federal Government and the incorruptible U.N. Police. But now, after years of rising standards, a new menace hangs in the sky—mysterious and terrible.

—*Eagle*, Vol. 3, No. 2. 18 April 1952

———⊖⊛⊘———

'**Y**OU CAN'T GO home on that again, Major.' Mo Collier got out from under the old M22 tank. Beyond the fortified compound, the soft Surrey hills shone with dew. 'You've been driving too hard and too long, mate.' He dug his arthritic fingers deep into his can of gunk and began massaging them. 'You can hardly find real mixture anymore. Everything's nuke or electric now. You know how it goes, don't you?'

'But aren't the Muslim Brotherhood selling "knock-off" Chinese stuff in quart cans out of tea shops?' Major Nye narrowed puzzled eyes. 'It was on the BBC. Somewhere in Harrogate.'

'Chipping Sodbury, I thought.' Professor Hira squeezed his plump little bottom from the conning tower. 'But they don't have souls. Not like these. They make them from scratch in the Pashtun valleys. I wouldn't buy anything else.'

'Won't run on fake mixture. Never did. I understand they fixed them like that.' Miss Brunner rolled up the sleeves of her big black-and-white Izod shirt. She wore it over jodhpurs and polished boots. She believed herself an expert on the Series Sevens. 'Not the Main Twenty-Two. Where did you pick it up? Outside Kiev would be my guess.'

'Odessa.' Major Nye sighed. 'I wondered about it at the time, but the chap selling it to me swore—'

'Was he Russian?'

'Greek.'

'Well, there you are. I told you. Ukrainian or Polish—they're the only ones you can trust on these little buggers. This side of the European border, anyway. They know all there is to know. They believe they have a soul and they understand it. It's a question of empathy and capacity, I always told you that.'

Nye accepted this. Only comparatively recently had he developed any kind of rapport with her. He sat down and opened his box of Sullivans. 'So if I wanted, say, one of those Astrakhan knock-offs coming out of Turkey, they wouldn't work?'

'Probably not.' She hesitated, then accepted a cigarette. 'No souls either, I'm afraid.' She was still not entirely comfortable with their new relationship. 'There are only certain machines that can develop empathy like that.'

Major Nye looked up as the security men opened the big compound gates a fraction and Jerry walked in. His goatskin coat was covered in mud and dust. His head was wrapped in an old brown-and-white turban. He had several days' growth of beard. There was a long rocket launcher over his shoulder and he was leading a big black-and-tan Bactrian camel considerably cleaner than he was. Nobody could easily identify him, certainly not by clan or even geographical location,

'It's not really a soul.' Mo reached down for the old Warlock tobacco tin he kept his wing nuts in and poured them from his fist. He enjoyed the sound they made.

'It's a group mind.' Major Nye was glad to pass along what he'd heard. 'They're all in contact, you see. The way *we're* all in contact but we're not all in sync. Ants, for instance, *are* all in sync. We're more like a mad ant colony—I mean, every individual is like a mad ant colony inside. That's as I understand old Hira's thinking. Eh? What, old boy?'

'More or less, Major.' The Brahmin hadn't really been listening to his friend. Nye's interest in what was being called *mechano-mysticism* was recent and he barely understood it all himself. He had come to the compound as a teacher but had remained to learn. 'Sometimes our minds are in better sync than others. Ants have a single motivation—to gain territory. Thrive and conquer. Different colonies have been making war for centuries and have gained less territory than the German army made on the Somme in a month.'

'Isn't that a form of insanity?' Major Nye cleaned his hands on a new rag.

'There is the Brahman, the infinite, eternal mind. But there is a place for insanity in the mind we return to Brahman so that a fraction of that eternal mind, that constant consciousness, is insane and returns that insanity back to us as dreams, nightmares, ideas and inventions, scientific theories, alchemical theories, artistic and political theories. I think a lot of scientists who follow Einstein, but not those who followed Einstein's followers, do you see?' Professor Hira was no longer as sure of himself as he had been.

The others nodded, but Mo had given up. 'I'll never get it, prof, but that's tanks for you.' Mo noticed the expression on Jerry's worn face.

'Sometimes I think I'm trapped in an Aldous Huxley novel, but with tanks instead of country houses.' Miss Brunner followed Mo's glance.

'I never did know what you had against tanks, Miss B.' Getting to his feet, Mo picked up his old rifle and walked towards Jerry.

'Nothing at all. Those little ones are sweet.'

Jerry leaned his rocket launcher against the damaged tank. 'I came along the coast and up over the downs. They've all gone. Brighton's drowning. Hastings's front is now her back. I couldn't find St Leonards's. Bexhill's wall seems to be holding.'

'So.' Mo was depressed. 'No chance of getting any spare parts for the Short, then?'

'Not on the South Coast. Maybe in Kendal. The last flying boat was tested on Windermere in 1950. She's still running between the islands. You remember Captain King.' Jerry accepted a cigarette. 'I'm famished. I could murder a pork pie.'

Miss Brunner was embarrassed. She hadn't expected him back for a few more days. She had eaten his pie for breakfast. She had been too lazy to boil her usual egg.

14. A DUEL TO THE DEATH

The prisoners cover the floor like a carpet of human despair. Many are missing eyes or limbs, some are bone thin from sickness, and most wear orange jump suits similar to what the Islamic State, the terrorist group they once belonged to, dressed its own captives in before it killed them. Upstairs, jammed into two cells with little sunlight, are more than 150 children.

—*New York Times*, October 25, 2019

A T LAST THEY were together, Jerry and company had settled in what had once been known as the Shire. There were still plenty of cottages in good condition, still thatchers to renew roofs, still custard-coloured stone to create buttresses and garden walls. Crops were plentiful. Trade was good. The physical borders, erected in the last days, had already crumbled. The gaps—once hastily filled with razor wire, willow wattles or wooden fencing— were widened and cleaned up. Those walls had been made with poorly mixed concrete. The watchtowers, built of oak and walnut by Roma craftsmen who had taken pride in their work, were reused to warn of fresh fires and floods in a still uneasy world.

Cotswoldia had been one of the first of the Sovereign States of Great Britain and, as supplies of medicines and special foodstuffs ran out, was the third to sign the Great Treaty carried across the island by the British Barbarians, mostly Londoners serving the Glorious Regathering under the Five Kings. This alliance accepted the Common Law and now included the majority of democratic republics in a decentralised world.

The new treaties ratified the almost universal Common Law. It included Europe, America, the East Asian Confederation, and Australasia. It had brought a fresh stability to Africa. The remaining countries, destroyed by typhoons, tsunamis, hurricanes, earthquakes, tornadoes, fires, and floods, barely existed. The geography and the economic and political systems of the world were irreversibly altered. National boundaries were gone. The World Council of incorruptible lawmakers appointed lawkeepers and were pledged to make the planet's resources available equally to every individual. This new order was not created from idealism but out of necessity, to maintain the health and well-being of people who had almost brought the planet to annihilation.

Communications, the means of travel, and power and healthcare were maintained through public ownership. New rail systems, airships, and roads were replacing the old-fashioned means of travel. Small, efficient hospitals were within easy reach of any individual. Zero population growth was now the only moral choice.

It wasn't a world Jerry and his friends had much use for. They created what chaos they could, only to face the tolerance and forgiveness of people who had turned them into demigods and fables. They resorted to twittering, to writing their memoirs or making movies. All in all, it was a time to lie low and hope. Things were bound to start falling apart again soon.

One weekend Jerry and Cathy took the *Agatha Christie* up to the Dales, where Miss Brunner ran her yoga and Tai Chi college. Every summer Sunday her village played cricket on the green. Professor Hira had brought his team from Oxford.

Peeling a satsuma, Jerry lazed in the garden of Elderberry House. 'It's a trap, Cathy.' He did not sound hopeful. 'Wasn't it always a trap?' Had they ever listened to him?

His sister and Miss Brunner sat arm in arm on the big swing. From the other side of the tall yew hedges came the distant sounds of the cricket match, leather on willow, cries of 'Howzat!' The garden was full of the almost overwhelming scent of roses. Bees lumbered though the heavy air. Birds and butterflies fluttered at their feeders. Sitting on the freshly cut grass, Shakey Mo Collier nostalgically stripped and cleaned the Banning he could no longer arm.

'There's not much we can do on our pensions, Mr C. Personally I'm getting a lot out of my travel pass. Let someone else do the drowning, eh? I mean you've already given your motors to the museum.'

'Buggers confiscated them.' Jerry missed his Duesenberg more than his Rolls. That car had guzzled gas in style. His panda-skin coat was now in the V&A.

'An old lady helped me cross the road a couple of days ago.' Miss Brunner was bitter. 'I couldn't shake the bitch off.'

'What did you do?' Cathy made an effort to be interested.

'Gave her a card for my yoga class. I'll set her a few positions she'll remember.' She drew a deep, unsatisfying breath. 'You can still get back at them in little ways.'

Popping an orange segment into his mouth, Jerry sank into his lounger, peering at the perfect sky. God, they were so fucking pathetic! Even Major Nye had taken up golf. Karen von Krupp represented Europe at the UW. Bishop Beesley had opened a pâtisserie in a small church somewhere near Exeter. His children were teaching Surrey *haute cuisine* in Bordeaux, having rediscovered its Edwardian taste for English cooking. He wondered why France had never created a pork pie. *Pâté de porc en croûte* just wasn't the same and their treatment of smoked haddock was barbaric.

Una Persson had heard they were visiting. 'Hello, girls! How are the kids?' She now taught rock-climbing sponsored by Theakston's Old Peculier up at Masham Tarn. She remained stylish in her long military coat, her heart-shaped face framed by her swinging pageboy. 'Hello, Jerry.' Reminiscently she stroked his long, soft hair. 'Sun's too hot. You'd better get a hat.' She kissed his nose. 'We don't want to send you home raving and throwing up *foie gras* like last time.'

Jerry sighed. Some things didn't change. Was there ever any point in resisting the concern of women?

THE END

All titles from *Union Jack, Sexton Blake Library, Boys' Friend, Ki-Gor, Whiz Comics, Dick Turpin Library, The Magnet*, and other pre-1945 story papers and pulps.